T0363660

INTRIGUE

Seek thrills. Solve crimes. Justice served.

Child In Jeopardy
Delores Fossen

Mountain Captive
Cindi Myers

MILLS & BOON

CHILD IN JEOPARDY
© 2025 by Delores Fossen
Philippine Copyright 2025
Australian Copyright 2025
New Zealand Copyright 2025

First Published 2025
First Australian Paperback Edition 2025
ISBN 978 1 038 94053 7

MOUNTAIN CAPTIVE
© 2025 by Cynthia Myers
Philippine Copyright 2025
Australian Copyright 2025
New Zealand Copyright 2025

First Published 2025
First Australian Paperback Edition 2025
ISBN 978 1 038 94053 7

MIX
Paper | Supporting
responsible forestry
FSC® C001695

Published by
Harlequin Mills & Boon
An imprint of Harlequin Enterprises (Australia) Pty Limited
(ABN 47 001 180 918), a subsidiary of HarperCollins
Publishers Australia Pty Limited
(ABN 36 009 913 517)
Level 19, 201 Elizabeth Street
SYDNEY NSW 2000 AUSTRALIA

Cover art used by arrangement with Harlequin Books S.A.. All rights reserved.

Printed and bound in Australia by McPherson's Printing Group

Child In Jeopardy

Delores Fossen

MILLS & BOON

Books by Delores Fossen

Harlequin Intrigue

Saddle Ridge Justice

The Sheriff's Baby
Protecting the Newborn
Tracking Down the Lawman's Son
Child in Jeopardy

Silver Creek Lawman: Second Generation

Targeted in Silver Creek
Maverick Detective Dad
Last Seen in Silver Creek
Marked for Revenge

The Law in Lubbock County

Sheriff in the Saddle
Maverick Justice
Lawman to the Core
Spurred to Justice

Visit the Author Profile page at millsandboon.com.au.

Delores Fossen, a *USA TODAY* bestselling author, has written over a hundred and fifty novels, with millions of copies of her books in print worldwide. She's received a Booksellers' Best Award and an RT Reviewers' Choice Best Book Award. She was also a finalist for a prestigious RITA® Award. You can contact the author through her website at www.deloresfossen.com.

CAST OF CHARACTERS

Deputy Slater McCullough—When his high school girlfriend, Stephanie, is murdered, he learns that she claimed she was his surrogate and her newborn is his. Slater's not the baby's father, but he's drawn into a dangerous investigation where he must protect not only the baby but also the woman he's spent years resisting.

Lana Walsh—She's former military and has plenty of training, but she hadn't expected to be protecting her newborn nephew and finding her sister's killer. She's also not prepared for the intense, forbidden attraction that ignites between Slater and her.

Cameron Walsh—The newborn at the center of the investigation. Whose child is he, and why did someone murder his mother?

Buck Holden—He's a person of interest in the investigation, and he seems to have a personal vendetta against Lana and Slater.

Leonard and Pamela Walsh—Stephanie and Lana's parents, who have secrets that could've led to their daughter's death.

Marsh Bray—Stephanie's wannabe boyfriend, who insists he has no idea who murdered her, but he could be lying.

Chapter One

Deputy Slater McCullough saw the baby the moment he opened his front door. Still, he blinked a couple of times to make sure his eyes weren't deceiving him. They weren't. He was looking down at a tiny newborn wrapped in a white blanket that was nestled into an infant car seat on the welcome mat of his porch.

Once he shook off the shock, Slater's head whipped up, his gaze firing around the darkness. He spotted a flare of red taillights just as a vehicle sped out of sight on his driveway that led to the road.

What the hell was going on?

Moments earlier, someone had knocked at his door, and since his house wasn't exactly on the beaten path, he'd figured it was someone in his family who'd dropped by. He hadn't taken long to get from his bedroom to the door, but obviously during that short span of time someone had left the baby and driven off.

Since Slater had put on his holster on the way to the door, he slipped his hand over the butt of his service weapon and continued to glance around, looking for any signs of danger while he also checked the baby. Sleeping. And thank God, he or she didn't appear to be harmed. There wasn't a mark or a bruise on that tiny face.

He didn't have to give a lot of thought as to why some-one would have left the child here. He was a cop, after all. A deputy in the Saddle Ridge Sheriff's Office. Abandoned babies were rare in the small ranching town, but it did oc-casionally happen, and the baby could have been brought here by someone desperate enough to leave the infant on a cop's doorstep.

Even though it was mid-October and the sun had al-ready set, it wasn't cold. Another thing he could be thank-ful for. Still, he didn't want the baby out in the night air, so he hoisted up the carrier, brought it inside and set it on his coffee table while he took out his phone. He called Sher-iff Duncan Holder, who was not only his boss but also his brother-in-law, and even though Slater knew Duncan was off shift, he answered right away.

"A problem?" Duncan immediately asked.

The question was edged with concern, probably because Slater never called just to chat. Duncan and Slater's sister, Joelle, and their infant daughter lived only a mile away, and if there was a family matter to discuss, Slater paid them a visit.

"Someone left a baby on my doorstep," Slater said. "I didn't see who. The person sped off before I could catch any details about the make of the vehicle or the license plate."

Duncan was silent for a couple of moments and then muttered some profanity. "Is the baby all right?"

"Fine as far as I can tell." But Slater did more than just a visual check of the infant's face. Sandwiching the phone between his ear and shoulder, he eased back the blanket and saw the blue pj's with little birds and clouds. He lifted the top that was no wider than his hand and saw what he'd already suspected.

"It's a newborn," Slater relayed. "The umbilical cord is

still attached, and it doesn't appear to be a home job for clamping off the cord." Which meant the baby had likely been born in a hospital, or at least with someone with medical knowledge attending the birth.

Slater heard Duncan relay the info to Joelle, and since she was also a deputy, she would no doubt start the search for missing infants along with having the night deputies combing the area for the vehicle. The CSIs would have to be called in as well to examine the baby's clothes and the carrier. And finally, Child Protective Services would have to be alerted. Thankfully, they had a foster home nearby that took in infants.

While Duncan finished giving the info to Joelle, Slater did a check of the baby's lower body. Still no signs of any kind of injury except for a bruise on the heel of the baby's right foot. Since all three of his siblings had babies, he recalled that was the location where blood was drawn for tests. So, more proof that this newborn had been born in a hospital.

"The baby's a boy," Slater added to Duncan, doing a quick check in the diaper. They'd need that gender info to compare to any missing babies, but the diaper also told Slater something else. It was dry, and since the baby didn't appear to be dehydrated, it meant he'd recently been changed.

Slater was about to relay the heel bruise and the dry diaper to Duncan when he heard a sound that stopped him cold. Something or someone had stepped onto his porch. Only then did he remember that he hadn't locked the door.

He hadn't heard the sound of a car engine nor seen any headlights through the windows, but he doubted it was a coincidence that he'd get a visitor minutes after someone had left the baby. It was possible this was the child's parent who'd already had second thoughts about what'd happened and had parked at the end of the driveway and come back for the baby.

"I might have a visitor," Slater whispered to Duncan. "I'll call you back."

Slater ended the call so he could put his phone away and free up his hands. It definitely wasn't something he wanted to happen, but it was possible this might turn into some kind of altercation. Because even if this was a remorseful parent, there was no way Slater could just hand over the child, not until he was certain the little boy would be safe.

Keeping an eye on the doorknob to see if it moved, Slater eased himself in front of the baby and waited. He didn't have to wait long.

The door opened a fraction. "Slater?" the woman asked.

She'd used his first name, not Deputy McCullough, but Slater didn't recognize the voice.

"It's me, Lana Walsh," she added.

Slater frowned and his shoulders snapped back. No way had he expected Lana to show up.

Or to have abandoned a baby on his porch.

For one thing, he hadn't seen Lana in nearly a year. Eleven months and twelve days to be exact. He knew the specific date because Lana had come to his dad's funeral. A hellish day that even now spurred the equally hellish memories of finding his father murdered.

Yeah, that wasn't going away anytime soon.

There'd been dozens of people at the funeral, but Slater had spent a good half hour talking to the sisters even though they weren't what he would call close. They once had been, though. He'd dated Lana's sister, Stephanie, when they'd been in high school, but when their parents had moved them to San Antonio, he and Stephanie had only kept in touch with the occasional text and lunch. His contact with Lana had been less frequent than that because she'd gone into the military, but he was pretty sure she was out now and was working in personal security.

"Come in," Slater muttered.

Lana stepped inside, and she spared him a glance before her attention slashed to the baby. The breath she released seemed to be one of relief, but there was no relief on her face. She locked the door behind her and went to the window as if keeping watch.

She hadn't changed much in the past eleven months and looked more like Stephanie's twin than a younger sibling. Also, while Stephanie went for glamour, Lana clearly didn't. Her dark brown hair was short and with a choppy cut. No makeup. She wasn't wearing an actual uniform, but her outfit had a military vibe to it with her dark jeans, black T-shirt and boots. It didn't seem to Slater that she'd recently had a baby. That sort of thing, though, could be hard to tell.

"Start talking," Slater insisted.

She nodded, then swallowed hard. "Is the baby yours?" Lana asked.

This night had already had some huge surprises, but that question was another one. "No." But he did do a quick mental calculation to see if that was possible.

His last relationship had lasted for over a year and had ended six months ago when the woman had taken a new job in Dallas. It'd been an amicable breakup, so Slater was still in touch with her, and if she'd been pregnant, she would have told him.

"No," he repeated with much more conviction. "Is he yours?"

Lana took another of those deep breaths. "No. Stephanie gave birth to him."

Slater automatically glanced back to see if he recognized any of Stephanie's or Lana's features. The baby had dark brown hair, but other than that, there wasn't a resemblance that stood out.

"Stephanie said she was your surrogate," Lana explained. "That she was carrying the baby for you. Did she?"

Well, hell. That was another surprise. And an out-and-out lie on Stephanie's part. Slater wanted kids someday, but he doubted he'd ever go the surrogate route.

"No," he said for the third time just as his phone rang.

The sound echoed through the room, causing the baby to stir and then whimper. Lana hurried to him, automatically rocking the carrier and murmured soothing sounds, something he'd seen his siblings do to quiet their babies. Still, Slater kept his gaze on Lana and the newborn while he looked at the phone screen.

"Duncan," he muttered.

"Don't tell anyone I'm here," Lana insisted.

Slater felt his frown deepen. "Duncan is the sheriff," he spelled out.

She nodded. "Please don't tell him or anyone else I'm here," Lana repeated. *"Please."*

Even though he didn't have nearly all the answers he wanted and didn't know why Lana had made such a request, Slater decided to take the call. "I'm chatting with my visitor now," Slater immediately relayed to the sheriff.

"Do you need backup?" Duncan asked.

"No." And he tried to figure out the best way to deal with this.

Stephanie had lied about being his surrogate. He'd need to know why. But if Stephanie had carried through with that lie for whatever reason, she might have also had Lana bring the baby to him. Of course, that prompted even more questions.

"Hold off on sending anyone out to my place for now," Slater settled for saying. He didn't want to have this talk with Lana while CPS or backup deputies were trying to arrest her or take the baby. "I'll call you back in a few minutes."

Slater hoped Lana heard the "few minutes" part because that was all the time he was giving her before he let Duncan know that she was his visitor.

"You're really not the baby's father?" she asked, and he could tell she was hoping the answer was yes.

"I'm not," Slater verified. "Now, why did your sister lie, and why do you have her baby?"

Lana pressed her lips together for a moment, but Slater still heard the sob that was threatening to tear from her throat. Tears shimmered in her eyes, but she blinked them back. After several long moments, she opened her mouth, then closed it as if rethinking what she'd been about to say.

"Seven months ago, Stephanie came to me and told me she was pregnant and that she was carrying the baby for you," she finally muttered. Lana made a visible attempt to steel herself up. "I'd just gotten out of the air force and had started working for a security company, and Stephanie wanted me to help her set up a fake identity and a secret place where she could stay while she was pregnant. A sort of safe house."

"A safe house?" he questioned. "Why? Was she in danger?"

Again, she took her time answering. "Our parents would have disowned her if they'd found out she was pregnant. At the time, they were pushing for her to marry someone within their social circle."

Ah, Slater could fill in some of the pieces now. Stephanie and Lana's parents, Leonard and Pamela Walsh, were old money, with old connections.

And the epitome of rich snobs.

Their estate near Saddle Ridge had been plenty impressive, but he'd heard the one they moved to in San Antonio was even grander. They'd "tolerated" Stephanie dating Slater in high school because his family came from money, too, but he'd known that neither Leonard nor Pamela would have even considered him worthy of anything serious with their daughter.

"If our parents disowned Stephanie, she would have lost her trust fund," Lana added. "I wrote mine off years ago, but Stephanie doesn't work, and she would have lost her income while she was pregnant."

Slater knew what "wrote mine off" meant. Lana had basically thumbed her nose at her snobby parents and had gone into the military. He had to admire her for making her own way, but that didn't give him answers to his immediate questions.

"So, Stephanie got pregnant, lied to you by saying she was my surrogate and then asked you to hide her away so she didn't have to face being penniless?" he summarized.

Lana nodded. "She didn't tell our parents about being pregnant. She insisted she was on the verge of a breakdown and told them she needed some peace and quiet for a while."

"They bought that?" Slater asked.

"No. I'm sure they didn't, but by the time Stephanie told them, I'd already set up the secret house for her outside Austin, and she went there within the hour. My parents looked for her. Hard," she emphasized. "But if they found her, neither Stephanie nor I was aware of it."

Slater took a moment to process that. It was possible the

couple had found their daughter and just monitored her. They could have learned she was pregnant and decided to wait her out. But they probably hadn't heard about the surrogate part. Because if Leonard and Pamela had thought their daughter was carrying his child, they would have come after him. Not physically, but they would have no doubt tried to make his life a living hell.

"So, who's his father?" Slater asked, tipping his head to the baby.

"I'm not sure," Lana admitted. She went back to the window and looked out again. "Stephanie and I had grown apart over the past five years or so, and I don't know who she was seeing." She swallowed hard. "When I was setting up the secret house, I ran a background check on her. On my own sister," she muttered with some self-disgust. "If she was dating someone, she didn't post anything on social media."

That wasn't like Stephanie, who went with TMI when it came to sharing. Well, when it came to sharing details that wouldn't rile her folks. So that told him that her baby's father wouldn't have met with parental approval.

"Two questions," Slater said. Now that he had the background, he wanted to move this back to the present. "Where is Stephanie, and why do you have her baby?" After that, he'd want to know what she was looking for out the window.

Lana turned and her gaze locked with his. "I have her son because I believe he's in danger. And Stephanie can't protect him because she's dead." Her voice broke and a single tear slid down her face. "Someone murdered her."

Chapter Two

Lana had to fight hard to stop herself from breaking down. She couldn't do that. She had to stay strong. Once she figured out what was going on and the baby was safe, then she could grieve for her sister.

"Murdered?" Slater repeated, automatically taking out his phone. "When and where was Stephanie killed?"

She had to clear the tightness in her throat before she could answer that. "This morning at a hospital in Austin."

That was apparently enough info for him to fire off a text to someone. No doubt to get details of the investigation. "Before you tell me how the hell Stephanie was murdered in a hospital, explain why you keep looking out the window. Is someone after you?"

"I believe so. And I don't know why. Or who," Lana quickly added. "I don't know a lot of things right now, but I need to fix that. It's why I came here. I need answers. I have to know if the baby is in danger."

Slater leveled that intense gaze on her. She'd known him most of her life, but she'd never seen him in cop mode. Before tonight, he'd always been the hot cowboy that her sister had dated in high school. The hot cowboy she'd had a secret crush on. But now, Slater was simply the person she needed to keep her nephew safe.

If he was her nephew, that is.

Lana still didn't know if this was Stephanie's biological child or if she had indeed been carrying the baby for someone else.

"Tell me what happened leading up to Stephanie's death," Slater said when he finally broke the silence.

The explanation wasn't going to be easy, and Lana knew each word would give her a slam of memories. A slam of fear, too, and that's why she took another look out the window. Thankfully, she didn't see anyone or anything suspicious.

"Like I said, Stephanie was living at the safe house I set up for her, and she was using an alias, Melody Waters," Lana started. "She called two days ago to tell me she was in labor, so I drove straight to Austin and was with her when she gave birth. Everything went well with the delivery, and I could tell Stephanie loved the baby. Since she was calling him Cameron and didn't say a word about surrogacy, I figured she'd tell me the truth."

"You doubted her surrogate story?" he was quick to ask.

"I did, right from the start," Lana admitted, "and it didn't help when she refused to tell me who'd hired her to have the baby. She didn't give me your name until..." She stopped after realizing she needed to back up and tell him something else first. "This morning, Stephanie got a call. I don't know who it was from, but I could tell it terrified her."

Lana could still see how the color had drained from her sister's face. How her hands had trembled. And the fear had burned in her eyes.

"The phone she was using was a burner, one that I'd given her when she went into hiding," Lana explained. "And to the best of my knowledge, she only used it for making her OB appointments. That's why I was surprised when someone called her on it."

"Did you hear any part of the conversation?" he wanted to know.

"No. Stephanie didn't say anything to the caller. She just listened. Then she told me to take Cameron to you, that he was your son and that she'd been your surrogate," Lana continued. She had to swallow hard before she continued. "She even gave me this."

Lana took the folded envelope from her jeans pocket, handed it to Slater and watched as he read it.

A muscle flickered in his jaw. "This first page is an Acknowledgment of Paternity, naming me as the baby's father. The second page is a surrogacy contract."

"Yes, I read them," she admitted. Her sister had used her real name and had signed both documents. Since Slater's signatures were there, too, Lana figured they had been forged. "I have to believe Stephanie had a good reason for doing that." She paused. "The last thing Stephanie said to me was for us to keep Cameron safe."

His attention whipped away from the document and to her. "Safe?" he questioned.

She nodded again. "Trust me, I grilled Stephanie about that, and she said she thought someone had found out about her having a baby. Someone who might not have his best interest at heart."

"Was she talking about your parents?" Slater asked.

"I'm not sure, but I have a hard time believing they'd hurt a baby. It's true they would be riled to the bone at Stephanie having a child, but I can't see them taking out their anger on Cameron."

Slater made a sound that could have meant anything. He certainly didn't jump to agree with her, and she recalled that years ago her parents had moved the family from Saddle Ridge because Slater's father, then Sheriff Cliff McCullough, had been investigating her parents for the disappearance of a teenage boy, Jason Denny. Lana had only been eleven at the time, but she knew Jason had been dating Stephanie and that her parents hadn't approved of the relationship.

No criminal charges had come out of the investigation, and later when Jason had resurfaced, he'd claimed someone had threatened him and that's why he'd run away. Jason refused to say who'd done the threatening, but maybe Slater's father believed her parents had been responsible.

And they might have been.

Lana didn't know the scope of her parents' dirty dealings, but she was well aware they were ruthless. It was the reason she'd cut them out of her life.

"I didn't push Stephanie nearly hard enough to tell me the truth about what was going on," Lana continued. "I thought there'd be time for that later, especially since Stephanie was insisting that I go ahead and take Cameron to you. I left the hospital and drove around for about an hour before I decided to return and talk to Stephanie. Just to make sure she was certain about handing the child over to you."

Now she had to pause again and remind herself to breathe. All the grief and fear were smothering her, and she had to look at the baby to try to steady herself. Lana had never needed an anchor to stave off panic, but she needed it now, and the baby was the ultimate reminder of what was at stake here.

"When I got back to her hospital room, there was chaos," she muttered. "I heard one of the nurses say that Stephanie had been smothered. I glanced in the room and...well, I saw her lifeless body before a nurse shooed me away and insisted I leave the area. She didn't seem to realize that I'd been with Stephanie earlier."

Lana figured she'd been in shock, because she had mindlessly walked away with Cameron cradled in her arms.

That's when she had spotted the man.

"I believe I saw Stephanie's killer," Lana spelled out. "He was peering out from one of the other rooms, and he set off every alarm in my body. I knew there was nothing I could do for Stephanie so I immediately turned around and hurried out another exit. He followed me, but once Cameron and I were in my car, I managed to lose him on the highway."

"And you came here and left the baby on my doorstep," Slater stated, clearly not approving of that.

Lana groaned. "I was worried about Cameron's safety, so I dropped him off and left only after I saw you open the door. Then I quickly drove away to make sure the man hadn't found me. If he had, I planned to lure him from the baby by having him follow me. I was never far away, and I had every intention of coming right back for him. I just didn't want him with me if I met up with that man."

"At any point did you consider calling the cops for help?" he asked, and there was a snarl in his voice now. Of course there was. The lawman in him probably didn't allow for gut feelings.

Lana needed yet another breath to finish this. "The man at the hospital was a cop."

Slater stared at her and looked ready to curse. Or to challenge that. "Name? Description?"

Lana had no trouble recalling these details since they were fixed in her mind. Just like that image of her dead sister. "About six-two. Brown hair, brown eyes, muscular build. The surname Johnson was on his uniform."

"Austin cops have their badge numbers next to their names," he pointed out.

"Yes, but I couldn't see his. He had his communication radio positioned in front of it." Probably intentional.

Well, maybe it was.

If he'd wanted to conceal his identity and murder a woman, he probably wouldn't have shown up in uniform. Not unless he was cocky or totally sure he could get away with murder.

Slater didn't get the chance to fire any more questions at her because his phone dinged, the sound shooting through the room. He silently read the text before his gaze slid back to her. She figured those intense blue eyes had unnerved plenty of suspects.

"Austin PD is investigating the suspicious death of a thirty-three year old woman, Melody Waters, aka Stephanie Walsh," he relayed to her.

So they knew who Stephanie really was. Lana wasn't sure how they would have come up with that info since Stephanie had insisted on using the alias for all of her medical appointments. It was possible, though, that Stephanie had had her real driver's license in the overnight bag she'd taken to the hospital.

"There's no officer named Johnson assigned to the case," Slater added while he continued to read. "The initial report is that next of kin has been notified."

So that's why her mom had called. A rarity for her. Lana took out her phone and showed him the two missed calls from her mother, Pamela. She hadn't left a voicemail, and Lana hadn't returned the calls yet since she'd been focused on keeping Cameron safe.

"There's no mention of you in the report," he continued, "only that Stephanie had informed the medical staff that she'd arranged for someone to take the baby to his father as per a surrogacy agreement." He lifted up the contract that had been in the envelope she'd given him. "Did you do this for her?"

"No. Not the other document, either. I didn't know she had them until she gave them to me at the hospital." Lana tipped her head to the contract. "That one might have come from an actual surrogate clinic. During that background check I mentioned that I did on Stephanie, I found out she'd visited a surrogacy clinic eight months ago. She would have been pregnant with Cameron by then, but it's possible she had a prior appointment there that I wasn't able to find."

"So Stephanie might have truly been a surrogate?" Slater muttered, glancing at the baby.

Lana had to shrug. "Maybe, but then why would Stephanie tell me you were the one who hired her?"

He didn't get a chance to speculate about that because her own phone rang, and she saw her mother's name on the screen. Slater must have seen it, too, because he said, "Are you going to answer it?"

She automatically shook her head. Her default response when it came to her parents, but she knew this had to be about Stephanie, so she stepped aside to take the call. While she did that, Slater stepped away as well, muttering something about updating the sheriff.

"Mother," Lana answered, trying to keep her voice low so she wouldn't wake the baby or disturb Slater's call.

"Your sister is dead," her mother blurted. "Murdered." A hoarse sob tore from her throat. "What do you know about it? Why didn't you stop it?"

Lana wasn't surprised by her mother's response. Even though Stephanie was the older sister, their parents had always blamed Lana for Stephanie's failures. It was yet another reason Lana had cut them from her life. But she wasn't immune to the accusation.

Why didn't you stop it?

That was a question Lana figured she'd be asking herself for the rest of her life. Over the years, she had been there for Stephanie countless times, but she hadn't been there when Stephanie needed her most. And worse, she was a cyber-security specialist at Sencor, a company that specialized in personal protection. She had bodyguard training. That hadn't been enough, though, to stop what had happened.

"Do the police know who killed her?" Lana asked.

"No," her mother snarled. "They're idiots, all of them. Your dad and I hired a team of private investigators. Not from that place where you work, either. We wanted the best."

Of course her mother had thrown in that dig, and Lana didn't even bother trying to convince her that Sencor was one of the highest-rated security companies in the state. Obviously, though, ratings didn't matter with Stephanie dead.

"The PIs will get to the bottom of it," her mother insisted, "and you're going to help them. I know you hid Stephanie from us all this time. There's no way she could have managed that on her own. I just didn't know why until the cops said Stephanie had been a surrogate. A surrogate!" her mother spat out as if it were the worst of felonies.

So her parents knew that as well.

"Did this so-called surrogate parent murder her?" her mother pressed.

"I don't think so," Lana said, but she had no idea if that was true. Slater hadn't murdered Stephanie. She was now certain of that. But that didn't mean her sister hadn't connected with her killer at the surrogacy clinic.

"You need to come home, Lana," her mother went on.

"You need to help the PIs sort all of this out so we can punish the person who killed Stephanie."

Lana waited for her mom to mention the baby. But she didn't. Certainly, if the hospital had learned Stephanie's true identity, they would have mentioned the baby as well. Maybe, though, the baby didn't mean anything to her mother, since she was dismissing Cameron as she'd dismissed the surrogacy itself.

"Did you hear me, Lana?" The venom in her mother's voice went up a notch. "Come home now. Your father is beside himself. So am I. And Marsh, too. He's ripped to pieces."

Lana knew that Marsh Bray was the man her parents had chosen for Stephanie to marry. A merger of two rich families who cared more about the business and social benefits of the union than they did their kids' happiness. That said, Marsh had always seemed on board with marrying Stephanie. The same couldn't be said for Stephanie, though. Lana didn't think her sister despised Marsh, but she definitely hadn't been eager to become his wife.

She heard Slater end the call with the sheriff, and since she wanted to know what Slater had told him, Lana quickly made her excuses to her mother. "I'll call you soon," she said, and hung up.

"Duncan will be speaking to the lead detective in charge of the investigation of Stephanie's murder, and he'll try to obtain footage from the hospital cameras," Slater said. "He'll also get us a list of all Austin cops named Johnson. It's possible, though, if this guy truly did kill Stephanie, then he was wearing a fake uniform."

Yes, that had already occurred to her, and part of Lana wished she'd confronted the man then and there. But she'd been too broken for that. Too worried about Cameron. Now that she was thinking more clearly, she realized she'd let him get away.

"My parents have hired PIs," she told him, only so he wouldn't be blindsided if one of them showed up in Saddle Ridge. "I have no idea who knows about that surrogacy contract or the Acknowledgment of Paternity, but if and when it comes to light, my parents will believe you're Cameron's father. In their eyes, that'll make you a top suspect for Stephanie's murder."

"I'm not going to keep the papers a secret," Slater was quick to say. "In fact, I'm taking you and the baby to the sheriff's office so we can both do statements that'll then be turned over to Austin PD."

She was shaking her head before he even finished. "But what about Johnson? If he knows where the baby is, he might try to come after him." If that's what the cop wanted, that is. Lana had no way of knowing if he did.

"You and the baby will be protected," Slater said with absolute confidence that Lana didn't feel, and she would have voiced plenty of disapproval about his plan if her phone hadn't dinged with a soft alarm.

Lana's heart dropped to her knees.

"It's not a text," she rattled off while she unlocked her phone screen. "It's an alert from my security system. Someone's broken into my house in San Antonio." She'd set up the security system more than a year ago, and this was the first alert she'd ever gotten.

"Will the system notify the security company or SAPD?" Slater asked, moving closer to her as she pulled up the feed from the cameras she had positioned both inside and outside the house.

"The company will be the one to notify me," she supplied just as she got a second ding from the automated monitor. Lana ignored it and adjusted the camera angle until she saw the person, the man, who was now in her living room. His back was to the camera, but there was no mistaking the cop's uniform he was wearing. He had his gun gripped in his hand.

"Johnson?" Slater asked.

"Maybe," she muttered and kept watching. The breath stalled in her throat when he turned, and she saw his face and name tag. "It's him."

"I'll text Duncan to call the Austin PD detective in charge of your sister's murder," Slater said, though she heard the doubt in his voice. Like her, Slater probably figured Johnson would be long gone before a detective showed up.

But why was Johnson there?

The drawn gun was a sign that he probably hadn't come for a friendly chat. Had he gone there to kill her? To take the baby? What the heck did he want, and had he truly been the one to kill her sister?

Lana continued to watch as the man made a quick check of the other rooms, and then he took out his phone. Lana automatically thumbed up the audio so she could hear, and after, Slater finished his text and moved back closer, no doubt so he could listen as well.

"She's not here," Johnson snarled to the person he'd called. Lana tried to shift the camera so she could see his phone screen, but the glare made it impossible for her to decipher the number. "She probably went to the deputy in Saddle Ridge." He paused, listening, and Lana wished she could hear the other side of this conversation. "All right. I'll go to Saddle Ridge, to the deputy's place now, and take care of the kid and her."

Her heart had already been racing. Her breathing, too,

and that certainly didn't help. This man was coming for Cameron and her.

Lana watched as Johnson slipped back out her front door and disappeared from view before she looked up at Slater. "We have to leave. I'll take Cameron—"

"No," he interrupted, taking out his phone again.

Again, she was ready to argue, but then Slater spelled out exactly what he intended.

"I'll have someone take him and you to the sheriff's office where you'll both be safe, but I'm staying put. When Stephanie's killer comes here, he'll be walking straight into a trap."

Chapter Three

Slater kept watch out one of the windows that would give him a good view of the road that led to his house. He wasn't sure what the heck was going on, but he was hoping he could get some answers from "Officer Johnson" when he showed up to "take care of the kid and her."

To prepare for that, Duncan had immediately arranged for a backup deputy to be with Slater and for Duncan and Deputy Sonya Grover to take Lana and the baby to the sheriff's office in town. Lana had been plenty hesitant about leaving with Duncan and Sonya, maybe because she now had a distrust of cops or because the plan seemed too risky.

There was indeed a risk, but Slater wanted to face down Johnson when Lana and Cameron weren't around to be hurt. Judging from the tone Johnson had used in that short phone conversation, he didn't have good intentions.

Slater checked the time. It'd been nearly two hours since Lana had gotten that alert about the break-in, plenty enough time for Johnson to make the drive from San Antonio to Saddle Ridge. He glanced across the room at Deputy Luca Vanetti, who was keeping watch on the other side of the house.

"No sign of him," Luca relayed, obviously noticing the glance Slater had given him.

"None here, either." And the admission made Slater want to curse along with second-guessing himself.

He hadn't officially alerted San Antonio PD about the break-in at Lana's place because if Johnson was indeed a cop, Slater hadn't wanted him to know they were onto him. Leaks could and did happen, so Slater had figured better to be safe than sorry. However, Slater had called his brother Ruston, who was an undercover detective with SAPD, and had asked Ruston to quietly monitor what was going on.

Ruston hadn't even attempted to get to Lana's house and intercept the intruder because Johnson had stayed less than a minute after telling the caller he was going "to Saddle Ridge, to the deputy's place now." In case Johnson had meant another deputy, all the cops in the sheriff's office had been put on alert, and none were alone and without backup. Since everyone was texting Duncan every fifteen minutes, Slater knew Johnson hadn't shown up at those other places, either. None of his fellow cops had been attacked or killed.

Slater felt the tightness come in his chest as the memories prowled into his head. He'd been a deputy for ten years now, and for the first nine years, he had, of course, been concerned about losing a family member or friend since two of his three siblings and his dad had been cops. But then his father had been gunned down, murdered by an unknown assailant, and the concern was much, much stronger.

It was a dark tangle of emotions, including fear and anger that he hadn't given his father justice.

He wasn't sure he could lose anyone like that again. Hell, he wasn't sure he could get through this loss at all, ever, and as long as his father's killer was out there, then Slater had failed at one of the most important things in his life. All the cop training and experience meant nothing until someone had paid for shooting his father in the chest and leaving him to die.

"You can tell me to mind my own business," Luca said, snapping Slater out of his miserable thoughts, "but is the baby yours?" It was a reasonable question since Luca, too, had gone to school with Stephanie and Lana, and he knew that Slater and Stephanie had dated.

"No," Slater assured him.

That was one of the few things Slater was certain of. He'd never had sex with Stephanie and had never visited a sperm bank or a surrogate clinic. And that meant Stephanie had lied.

"I'm guessing Stephanie was scared," Slater added. "And she knew I'd protect Lana and the baby."

Of course, that led Slater to a big question—who or what was Stephanie scared of? Her parents were a good guess, because there was that threat of losing her trust fund. But he couldn't see her folks murdering their daughter. Still, it was possible, and it was why Pamela and Leonard Walsh were on his suspect list. Not at the very top, though. At the moment Officer Johnson held that position, and Slater needed to know how this man fit into the pieces of the puzzle.

His phone vibrated with a call, and Slater saw Ruston's name on the screen. "I don't think your guy is coming to your place tonight," his brother immediately said. "I've had a monitor on the traffic cams, looking for this Officer Johnson, and there was an accident about an hour ago. Someone ran a red light, plowed into a black SUV, disabling it. The driver of the SUV ran from the scene, and he matches Johnson's description."

Slater cursed. "Do you have the camera footage?"

"I got a couple of still images from the footage. Sending them to you now," Ruston said just as Slater's phone vibrated again.

Even though they were grainy images, Slater had no trouble seeing that it was indeed Officer Johnson. The first photo was of the collision itself, and the next was of the man exiting the vehicle. The final shot was of him running away, and that meant the guy likely wasn't a real cop. If he had been, there probably wouldn't have been a reason to hurry away like that. However, staying put would have meant having to explain why he was wearing the uniform.

"I just filled Duncan in on this," Ruston went on, "and he said for Luca and you to head on to the sheriff's office so you can figure out what to do about Lana and the baby."

Slater muttered more profanity. Not because he didn't want to return to the sheriff's office and deal with the situation of Lana and the baby. He did. But he'd also wanted to catch a possible killer.

"We'll be there in ten minutes," Slater said, ending the call so that he and Luca could head into the garage where he'd parked the cruiser.

Slater also reset his security system in case Johnson finally did show up, and then did something he rarely did. He activated the security camera that was part of his doorbell. It was something he normally reserved for when he was expecting a package and there was inclement weather in the forecast.

Even though Slater suspected Johnson wouldn't be making a trip to Saddle Ridge tonight, he and Luca still kept watch. And saw nothing out of the ordinary. This was ranching country, where traffic pretty much dried up after dark, and tonight was no exception. They made it all the way to the sheriff's office without encountering another vehicle.

When Slater stepped into the building, he immediately saw Lana in Duncan's office. She was feeding the baby a bottle while she studied something on a computer screen that Duncan was showing her.

At the sound of Slater's footsteps, her head whipped up, her gaze slicing across the bullpen and reception to meet his. There was plenty of concern and wariness in her green eyes, and he so wished he could tell her the danger had passed. But it obviously hadn't. Not with Officer Johnson still out there.

Slater certainly wasn't untouched by the fear he saw on her face. He hated that she was going through this especially when there wasn't a surefire fix to the danger. Apparently, he also wasn't immune to something else.

The realization that the old attraction was still stirring between them.

Well, it was for him, anyway. The heat had been there for years, lying dormant and then igniting every time he saw her. Each time, he'd shoved the attraction firmly aside. Or rather had tried to do that, since any kind of romance between them could create more ire for her from her parents. Added to that, Slater had dated her sister, and Lana had been in the military, nowhere near Saddle Ridge.

But she was here now.

And his body obviously wanted to remind him of that.

Once again, Slater pushed aside the heat and joined them in Duncan's office while Luca went to his desk. Slater thankfully got the quick mental adjustment he needed. Because Lana was looking at images on the screen. It didn't take Slater long to realize these were photos of Austin cops with the surname of Johnson. In the top corner of the screen was the close up shot of the man running from the scene of the wrecked SUV.

"He's not a cop," Lana immediately said. "At least not one with Austin PD."

None of them seemed surprised about that, but Slater understood the sound of frustration that Duncan made. "We're running facial recognition now to try to get a match," he added.

That was a good step, but it might not be enough. "What about the hospital cameras? Maybe there's something on the footage to tell us who he is."

"Austin PD is still examining that." Duncan made another of those heavy sighs. "The cameras in the hallway had been tampered with, so there's no feed of the man going into or out of Stephanie's room. He didn't leave anything obvious behind, either, but the CSIs have gathered plenty of hairs and fibers and have sent them to the lab."

Slater figured getting anything from that was a long shot since dozens if not hundreds of people could have gone in and out of that room in the past week. Still, it was something that had to be checked.

The baby caught Slater's attention when he made a kitten-like sound after he finished the bottle. Lana set the bottle aside and moved him to her shoulder to burp him. The maneuver wasn't completely smooth, but Lana was obviously taking good care of the newborn. And under bad circumstances. Her sister was dead, and there appeared to be a killer after her.

"Why?" Slater said, voicing the question that was running through his head. Both Lana and Duncan looked at him. "Why would Stephanie's killer want to come after Lana? What's your theory?"

Both Lana and Duncan considered that for several moments, and it was Lana who spoke first. "Johnson said he would take care of me and the kid," she said. "So maybe that means someone is trying to cover up the fact that Stephanie had a child."

Slater and Duncan made quick sounds of agreement. "Who would want to do that?" Duncan asked her.

"My parents," she readily admitted. "And maybe the baby's father." Lana shifted her attention back to Slater. "Duncan's already taken a DNA sample from the baby. That might give us some answers. Fast answers," she emphasized, "since the lab will be using rapid analysis. We could have results in a matter of hours."

True, but there was no need for him to spell out that the only way they'd get a match was for the baby's father to already have his DNA in the system. That could happen if the guy had a criminal record or a job that required such info, but the vast majority of people weren't in law enforcement databases.

They all turned toward the doorway when Sonya stepped in. She was holding her laptop. "The facial recognition program came up with a hit," she said, turning the screen so they could see it. On the left was the image they'd gotten from the security camera, and on the right was the mug shot of a beefy bald man.

Lana made a soft gasp. "That's him." She repeated her words while she was making an obvious effort to rein in her emotions. Hard to do that while she was looking right at her sister's killer. "Who is he?"

"Buchanan, aka Buck, Holden," Sonya provided. Placing the laptop on the corner of Duncan's desk, she opened a file of notes that she likely planned on using to do a report. "He's thirty-nine and was arrested three years ago for stalking. He got probation."

"Stalking?" Slater questioned. "That's a huge escalation

to murder, impersonating a police officer, and breaking and entering."

Sonya nodded. "I'll do a thorough background check since there could be something else. Maybe something expunged from his record," she added. "A year ago, he and his younger brother inherited about thirty million when their parents were killed in a car accident, so unless he's blown through it, he's got plenty of money for legal fees."

"Since he's likely rich, maybe Stephanie and this Buck Holden ran in the same social circles?" Duncan suggested.

"Maybe," Lana said, but she didn't sound very convinced. "He doesn't look like Stephanie's usual type, though. She went more for the guys who were hot enough and good-looking enough to be on those calendars..." Her words trailed off when her attention slid to Slater, probably because she recalled that Stephanie had gone for him.

Slater refused to be flattered by what she'd just said. And he wanted to refuse to notice the slight flush that colored Lana's cheeks. It was better to focus on other things. No shortage of those, because he had plenty of questions flying through his head. How had he gotten involved with Stephanie? And why had he killed her if they hadn't been involved?

"I'll go through all of Stephanie's social media posts and see if there's any mention of Buck," Lana said after clearing her throat.

"I'll do the same for Buck's posts, if there are any," Sonya tacked onto that.

That would likely take some time, but there was something else that had to go at the top of their to-do list. "Lana will have to give a statement to Austin PD," Slater spelled out. "That won't be a fast in-and-out since this is a murder investigation. And they'll want her to give the statement in person. Added to that, Lana will have to get into the past eight months or so of Stephanie's life at the safe house." He looked at her. "Did you bend or break any laws to arrange that for her?"

"No," she insisted, but then she paused. "There might be some legal questions about Stephanie using an alias when she had the baby. Questions, too, about those documents I gave you."

Slater had to agree on that, but since Lana hadn't done those documents, the blame for it would be on Stephanie. And she wasn't alive to defend her actions or to be charged with any wrongdoing.

"I can take Lana to Austin," Slater went on, "but with Buck at large, it might not be the safest trip."

"You'll have backup," Duncan was quick to say, but then his attention went to the baby. He sighed. "Since we don't know who his bio-father is, Austin PD might take custody of him until it's all sorted out and then hand him over to the surviving parent."

Lana shook her head. "I don't believe Stephanie would have wanted that. She was hiding. And it's a good bet that she was doing that because she was terrified of the bio-father."

No one in the room could argue with her, and it was possible the baby's dad had been the one to murder Stephanie. Either that, or he'd hired someone like Buck to do it. No way did Slater want Cameron in clear view of a killer or his henchman.

Lana turned to him. "For now, can you just keep it to yourself that Stephanie wasn't your surrogate?" Slater groaned, but she talked right over that. "Yes, I know it's withholding evidence, but this way, we can control who has him. We won't have to hand him over."

His heart wanted to go along with that. Mercy, did it, but he couldn't. Slater tapped his badge to remind her she was talking to a cop. "That's obstruction of justice."

She huffed, closed her eyes a moment and then pled her case to Duncan. "All right, then can someone keep Cameron safe here in Saddle Ridge while I'm in Austin? Safe," she emphasized. "Because it's not just Buck we have to worry about. That call he made at my house means he's working for someone or with a partner."

"Cameron can stay at the ranch with Joelle and me," Duncan readily agreed. "We have a baby and a full-time nanny, and I can bring in a reserve deputy to help keep watch."

Slater could tell that still wasn't ideal for Lana, but then there were no ideal scenarios as long as Buck was at large and free to kill. Still, Lana knew both Duncan and Joelle, and Lana and she had even been friends in school. Added to that, Joelle was a deputy as well and had the training to protect the newborn.

"All right," Lana finally said, brushing a kiss on the top of the baby's head before she eased him back into the carrier. "Do you need a statement from me, too?" she asked Duncan.

Duncan didn't get a chance to answer, though, because of the sounds of voices. One of which was loud and insistent, and even though it'd been years since he'd heard this particular voice, Slater instantly recognized it.

Lana's mother, Pamela Walsh, and she was calling out Lana's name.

And she wasn't alone. Her husband, Leonard, was with her and so was a tall, blond, thirtysomething-year-old man. Hell. They had enough to deal with tonight without adding visitors like this to the mix.

Deputy Brandon Rooney was working at the front desk,

and he immediately got to his feet to direct the trio through the metal detectors. No alarms sounded, which meant none of them were armed.

"Lana," Pamela repeated when her attention landed on her daughter.

Lana immediately moved into the doorway of Duncan's office, and Slater thought she might be doing that so her mother didn't see the baby. Possibly because Pamela might try to take him. No way would he and Duncan let that happen, not until they had sorted out Cameron's paternity, but Pamela and her husband might try to cause a scene. Also, it was possible the blond guy with them was their lawyer.

Both Duncan and Slater moved into the doorway with Lana, positioning themselves on each side of her so they could face down what might turn out to be trouble. Luca and Brandon had moved behind the visitors while Sonya kept a watchful eye on them from her desk while she continued to work on her laptop.

Pamela and Leonard looked pretty much as they had years ago, and despite recently learning of their daughter's murder, they didn't look grief-stricken or disheveled. Just the opposite. Pamela was wearing expensive-looking brown pants and a cream sweater while Leonard was in a perfectly tailored suit. The blond guy had on khakis and a white shirt. He was the only one of the trio who appeared to be grieving or in shock.

So maybe not a lawyer, after all.

"How'd you know I was here?" Lana asked, taking the question right out of Slater's mouth.

Pamela and Leonard both froze for a moment, but then Pamela hiked up her chin. "Leonard has friends in Austin PD. They told us you were here."

This time Slater said the "hell" out loud, and he glanced

at Duncan to see if they were on the same page with this. Of course they were. There was no way a cop should have divulged that kind of information.

"I'll want the names of your friends in Austin PD," Duncan insisted, aiming a hard glare at Leonard and Pamela.

"I don't have to do that," Leonard snarled.

"All right," Duncan said, taking out his phone. "I'll make an official complaint through Austin PD Internal Affairs to open an investigation into divulging information regarding a murder investigation to a civilian. I'm sure they can get to the bottom of it and then discipline the officers involved."

Slater hadn't thought it possible, but Leonard's jaw tightened even more. "Detective David Sullivan," he said. "His father used to work for me."

Duncan put his phone away, but Slater had no doubts he'd be making a call to Austin PD to file a complaint against Detective Sullivan.

"David was doing me a favor," Leonard added, maybe hoping to minimize the trouble he'd just gotten the detective into. "He knew Pamela and I were crushed by Stephanie's murder, and we needed to find Lana, to make sure she was all right."

"I pressured them, too," the blond guy said, and then he came closer to extend his hand to Duncan and Slater. "I'm Marsh Bray. Stephanie and I were…close."

"My parents wanted Stephanie and Marsh to marry," Lana provided, earning her a sharp look from her mother.

"I'm in love with Stephanie," Marsh further explained as if not bothered by Lana's comment, "and it was my hope that Stephanie would someday agree to be my wife. That's why I gave her this time she'd asked for. That's why I waited." His voice wavered on the last word. "And now she's dead."

The grief seemed genuine. Seemed. But Slater had too much cop in him to take this at face value. Maybe Marsh hadn't been as patient as he was claiming. Maybe he'd gotten so enraged over Stephanie that he'd murdered her. But that left Slater with a huge question.

Was Marsh the baby's father?

"We need you to come home with us," Pamela said to Lana. "We need you to explain to Marsh and us exactly what happened to Stephanie." She paused. "A nurse at the hospital said Stephanie had had a baby. Is it true?"

Slater kept his attention on Marsh. The man certainly wasn't jumping to say the child was his. Just the opposite. There seemed to be some dread creeping into his expression.

"We know that Stephanie was a surrogate," her mother went on. "We hired PIs to try to find her, and we found out about her visit to a surrogacy clinic. There was a charge for it on her credit card. Why would she do that? Why would she go to a place like that to get pregnant and carry a child for someone else?"

Since the questions were aimed at Lana and not him, Slater had to figure that the surrogacy clinic hadn't given Pamela and Leonard that particular bit of info.

"I don't know," Lana muttered, and Slater knew it wasn't a lie.

Her mother groaned and squeezed her eyes shut a moment. "I'm not asking out of idle curiosity. I need to know what happened to my daughter."

"That's what we're trying to find out," Lana assured her, and she made a show of checking the time. "We need to leave so I can give a statement. That might help them find who killed Stephanie."

Slater so wished she hadn't just spelled that out to them,

since he didn't want anyone other than the cops here in the sheriff's office to know that he and Lana would be on their way to Austin.

"I'll call you after I give the statement," Lana added.

Slater hadn't thought that would be enough to make them leave, but they turned and headed toward the exit. Neither Pamela nor Leonard made a move to give their surviving daughter a hug or offer any words of comfort. That confirmed what Lana had already told Slater about being written out of her parents' lives.

"We'll need to take an alternate route to Austin," Lana said the moment their visitors were gone. "I don't trust any of them not to spill that we'll soon be on the road."

Good. He and Lana were of a like mind on this. "We can use the old highway and not the interstate."

Duncan nodded. "I'll have Luca drive with me to take the baby to the ranch, and Sonya can follow behind the two of you as backup. Brandon can man the office until I can get another deputy in here with him."

Brandon and Luca both made sounds of agreement, but Sonya stepped forward with her laptop in hand. "I found something," Sonya said, turning the screen so they could see the photo. "This was posted on Stephanie's Facebook page fifteen months ago."

Slater, Lana and Duncan all moved in to take a closer look. It was a couple's shot of Stephanie at what appeared to be a party, but Slater didn't recognize the smiling dark-haired man who had his arm draped around Stephanie's shoulder. Lana must not have, either, because she shook her head.

"Who is he?" Lana came out and asked.

"Patrick Holden, Buck's brother," Sonya provided, and

then she shifted to another open tab with a different photo of Patrick.

One for his obituary.

A quick glance at the date of death showed that he'd died only a week ago.

"Cause of death?" Duncan immediately wanted to know.

That grim look on Sonya's face told him they weren't going to like the answer. "He was murdered."

Chapter Four

Lana kept watch out the window as Slater drove on the back roads toward Austin, and she knew Slater was doing the same thing. Keeping watch. Looking for any signs of an attack.

Sonya was behind them, also in an unmarked Saddle Ridge cruiser, and she, too, was no doubt in vigilant mode. If there were any signs of trouble, she'd be able to respond.

Part of Lana wanted Buck to resurface, to come after them so they could stop him and toss him in jail. Cameron was safe, and if a showdown was coming, maybe it would be better now than later. After all, she couldn't keep Cameron in protective custody indefinitely. Even though the baby had had a horrific start to his life, he deserved a whole lot better. But better wasn't going to happen with Buck at large.

Her interview with Austin PD might help with the at-large status. Maybe there was something she could say that would pinpoint Buck's location. Then she and Slater could grab some sleep before returning to Saddle Ridge. A return that wouldn't happen tonight because of the already late hour, and it was the reason Lana had arranged for them to stay at a small house owned by Sencor, the company she worked for. She hadn't wanted to trust the security at a hotel or a short-term rental.

"Are you okay?" Slater asked.

She didn't need to know what had prompted the question. Lana had heard yet another sigh leave her mouth. She'd heard the deep, ragged breaths she'd been taking as well. She'd never had a panic attack, but, mercy, it felt as if everything was closing in on her.

"There's been no time to grieve," she settled for saying. Lana nearly left it at that, but she knew the grief was just the tip of the iceberg. "I'm worried about Cameron. Worried what else Buck will do."

Slater made a sound of agreement. Coming from most people, that would have seemed like a blasé response, but Lana could practically feel the emotions coming off him in hot waves.

"Stephanie and I weren't close," she admitted. "But she was my sister." She paused, debating if she should even voice her next comment about his father. A check of the time convinced her just to go for it. They still had thirty minutes before they arrived in Austin. "How did you deal with the grief of losing your father?"

Slater stayed quiet for so long that she was about to launch into a *forget I said that* apology. "I haven't," he muttered, and then winced as if he hadn't intended to spill that. "I'm still dealing," he amended a moment later. "Maybe I always will be. It's possible that's something that never goes away. Sorry," he tacked onto that. "I should have come up with something more, uh, supportive."

"No," she insisted. "I'd rather have the truth. I'd rather know what I'm up against."

Again, he paused. "If your experience is anything like mine, then what you're up against is what I call death plus. A natural or accidental death causes you to grieve in a thousand different ways. But murder, well, murder causes you to grieve, and hurt, and go through all the regrets and feelings that you should have done something to stop this from happening. That you should have done more."

Yes, she was already feeling some of that. Clearly, Slater was, too.

"Find someone to talk to if you can," he went on. "That might help. I did some grief therapy for a while. Just don't shut down."

The last part seemed as if it'd come from personal experience. "Is that what you did?"

"Yeah," he admitted while he continued to keep watch. "I ended a two-year relationship because it didn't feel right. Me, being happy, continuing with my life when my dad was dead. So I put everything aside but the job. Because it's the job that'll get my father justice."

"And give you some peace," she finished for him. Slater made another of those sounds of agreement.

Peace didn't seem anywhere on her radar right now, but Lana was positive that catching her sister's killer would be a start. "I keep going over every moment in the hospital," she said, hoping that saying it aloud would trigger some fresh memory that would give them that *start*. "I don't recall seeing Buck before then, but maybe he was around."

Lana stopped, muttered some profanity and then groaned. "I work for a security company, installing systems and setting up protocols to keep people safe. I couldn't do that for my own sister."

"Trust me, I get that," he said.

Of course he got it. He was a cop, and his father was dead. "I believe it was Buck who called Stephanie this morning." Heavens, had it really been less than twenty-four hours? In some ways, it seemed an eternity.

"Austin PD will have her phone," Slater reminded her. "They might be able to figure out if it was Buck."

She knew the odds of that were slim, but, yes, the cops would try. Still, she figured Buck wouldn't have been careless enough to use a phone that could be traced back to him.

"The hospital cameras were tampered with," she explained. "And it's no easy feat breaking into my house. I keep all the doors and windows double-locked. I have to assume that Buck or his accomplice has the skill set to do those sort of things."

"Yes, but he didn't disable your security system," Slater pointed out in a tone to let her know he was giving that some thought. "Why not? I mean, if he was able to tamper with the hospital cameras, why not do that at your place?"

Lana immediately thought of a possibility. "My system isn't easy to disable." But then she had to shake her head. "The same should have been true of the hospital cameras."

"True, and that could mean Buck didn't care if you knew he'd broken in. Maybe he thought if you were there, he could just overpower you before anyone could respond to the security alarm."

The thought of that sent a shiver down her spine. Because Buck could have possibly done just that.

Slater reached over and gave her hand a gentle squeeze. "We'll catch him. Something might turn up in his background check that'll tell us just what his skill sets are when it comes to tampering with equipment." He eased his hand back and gave her another quick glance. "Or it could be someone you know. Someone who would have known how to access your house."

He sounded very much like a cop right now, and she was thankful for it. Focusing on the investigation was the only thing taking the edge off her nerves.

"I don't have a boyfriend or anyone like that I'd trust with my security codes," she stated.

Slater glanced at her, maybe a reaction to the no-boyfriend admission, but despite everything going on, she felt the blasted attraction again. Lana blamed it on the emotional cocktails swirling around in her body. Slater was like a safe harbor right now, and that had likely amped up the heat.

Or at least that's what she was telling herself.

This wasn't the time or the place to get into the fact that she'd always wanted him. And that he'd always been off-limits because of Stephanie. Now he was off-limits because it was obvious Slater wasn't in the right frame of mind to deal with attraction and such.

"How about your parents?" he asked.

She opened her mouth to say they wouldn't have broken in, but Lana had no idea if that was true. "They might have hired someone to break in if they thought Stephanie was there. But I can't see them hiring, or even knowing, someone like Buck."

"Maybe," Slater muttered, not sounding at all convinced of that. "Consider this. Your parents find out Stephanie's dead and they know she visited a surrogacy clinic. They must believe the baby was born from that surrogacy and isn't their grandchild because they didn't even ask to see him."

No, they hadn't. At the time, Lana had been thankful for that because she hadn't wanted the risk of them trying to take the baby. But they hadn't even asked if he was all right.

"I think I know what might be playing into this," she said. "Might," Lana emphasized. "My father's planning on running for the state senate next year. A murdered daughter will generate press, but it'll be the sympathetic kind. Some people, though, are opposed to surrogacy, and it could be my parents would rather keep that hush-hush."

"Your dad would be that worried about negative press?" Slater asked, but then quickly waved that off. "Yeah, he would be. So, how exactly would he handle things if he finds out there was no surrogacy and that Stephanie has perhaps been in hiding all this time?"

"He wouldn't handle it well," she was quick to admit. "Neither would my mother. Or Marsh, for that matter. The plan is for Stephanie to marry Marsh in that whole tra-ditional wedding deal that'll flash across society pages all over the state. It would considerably sour the image if Stephanie had just given birth to another man's baby. Right now, the surrogacy story likely suits the three of them just fine."

But not Lana. Because she was certain the surrogacy was a lie. A lie that had led to her sister's murder.

Lana was still considering that when a sound cut through the cruiser. She instantly got a jolt of adrenaline before she realized it was her phone. Austin PD came up on the dash screen, and because she figured Slater would want to hear this conversation, she took the call on speaker.

"I'm Detective Lisa Thayer," the caller said after Lana had identified herself and informed the caller they were on speaker. "I'm sorry to have to do this, but I'll need to reschedule your interview. The ME is finished with an au-topsy, and I need to get a briefing from him."

"My sister's body?" Lana asked.

The detective paused. "Yes," she finally said. "And I'm sorry, but I can't allow you there for that," she was quick to add.

Lana wasn't sure she could have handled that anyway, but she was hoping the autopsy could confirm how Stephanie had died and who had killed her. She thought the "who" was Buck, but unless he'd left some form of trace evidence or DNA, then it would be hard to pin the murder on him. Just because Lana had seen him near Stephanie's hospital room, it didn't prove he'd been the one to kill her.

"Any chance you can come into the station tomorrow at ten?" Detective Thayer asked.

Lana glanced at Slater and got the nod. "Yes, ten is fine."

"Good. I'm guessing you're probably already on your way here to Austin," the detective commented. Neither Slater nor she answered. They didn't know this cop, and while she was likely trustworthy, there was no need to announce their location. "I just wanted to know if you needed an officer to accompany you to wherever you'll be spending the night."

"No," Lana assured her. "We have backup with us."

"Good," Thayer concluded. "FYI, I just sent the background check report on Buck Holden to the Saddle Ridge sheriff. I haven't had a chance to read it myself, but I will before the interview tomorrow morning. I'll see you then," she tacked onto that, and ended the call.

Since they weren't going to the police station, Slater headed toward the safe house. She didn't need to put in the address since she'd memorized the route. Best not to put that kind of info in the GPS in case someone managed to hack it.

"I'll let Sonya know what's going on," Slater said, taking out his phone to call the deputy. "How good is the security at this place where we're staying?"

"Good," Lana verified.

"Enough so that Sonya can peel off and go home once we're inside? She could come back tomorrow to escort us to the interview."

Lana thought of the security measures she'd personally put in place on this particular house. "Nothing is hack-proof," she admitted, "but it's as safe as it can possibly be. We should be fine with Sonya returning home." She hoped so, anyway. The sad truth, though, was if Buck was planning on attacking them, he would do that with or without Sonya being present.

Slater nodded and made the call to Sonya while he continued the drive to the house. It wasn't a showy place, of course. A simple two-story stucco tucked into a cookie-cutter neighborhood. The lots were large, and the fences were high. This wasn't a community where residents had block parties or stopped by to chat. It was the reason the house had been chosen. Most residents were couples who were at work all day and not around to see the comings and goings of others.

Slater finished talking with Sonya and then called Duncan to fill him in and request a copy of the report on Buck the detective had sent him. He'd just gotten the assurance from Duncan that it would be emailed to him as Slater pulled into the driveway of the house.

She used her phone to open the garage and immediately closed it behind them once they were inside. She also did a sweep of the place to see if any cameras and sensors had been triggered. They hadn't been, but that wouldn't stop her from doing a room-to-room search.

Slater was obviously in agreement with her about that because they went in together. And they both drew their guns. They stopped for a moment, listening for any sounds that someone was there. Nothing. Then he tipped his head to the left to indicate he'd start the search there. Lana went to the right and into the dining and kitchen area.

Since the house wasn't huge, it didn't take them long

to go through the rooms there, and they went up the stairs together where she knew there were three bedrooms and two baths. She didn't release the breath she'd been holding until they cleared each one and saw no signs of a security breach or break-in.

Slater texted Sonya to let her know all was well, and they made their way back to the bedroom that had been converted to an office and security command post. Once again, she used her phone to bring the monitors to life. Six of them mounted on the wall and each of them showing the feed from a different security camera.

"There are internal cameras and monitors," she explained, "and if they're triggered, then that'll show up on the screens." Lana motioned toward the door and windows. "This can become a panic room if necessary. The bathroom's through there." She tipped her head to the door. "And there's even a supply of food and water. Backup communications, too."

He made a sound of approval but then shook his head. "No way did you set all of this up since Stephanie's murder," he stated.

"No. It's been here for about six months. It's used to hide spouses of domestic abuse, victims of stalkers, that sort of thing. I set up something similar for Stephanie since I could tell she was scared." She stopped. Had to. And Lana took a moment just to level out her breathing. "I just wish I'd pushed her harder to find out what had terrified her. If I had—"

Slater cut off the rest of that by pulling her into his arms. "You can't do this to yourself, because I'm sure you did everything possible to keep her safe."

"I didn't arrange for a bodyguard at the hospital," she was quick to point out.

"Because you didn't know the threat was there. Stephanie probably didn't, either, or she would have asked for more protection. She certainly had no trouble asking you to hide her away while she was pregnant."

Lana knew that was true, but it still didn't ease this guilt that felt like a deadweight on her shoulders.

They stood there for several long moments, and Lana became aware of their body-to-body contact. Nothing sexual. Well, nothing meant to be sexual, anyway. Slater had given her a hug of comfort, that was all, but being pressed against him reminded her body of the attraction. Since that attraction could be a deadly distraction, she stepped away, ready to explain that nothing could happen between them. She didn't get a chance to do that, though, because his phone rang.

"It's Joelle," he relayed, giving her an instant jolt of panic. Lana prayed nothing had happened to the baby.

"Is Cameron all right?" Lana asked the moment Slater took the call on speaker.

"He's fine," Joelle was quick to assure her. "I know it's hard, but try not to worry about him. He's getting plenty of TLC."

"Thank you," Lana muttered, knowing that she would indeed still worry. However, she also owed Joelle and Duncan a huge thanks for taking care of the baby. No way had she wanted to bring him all the way to Austin.

"Are you settled in somewhere so we can talk?" Joelle asked a moment later. "I've just started reading through the report on Buck and something jumped out at me."

"We haven't had a chance to read it yet," Slater explained, booting up the laptop that was on the desk. "What jumped out at you?" he asked as he started to log in to his account.

"The cops are investigating Buck for his brother's and

his parents' deaths. In fact, he's their prime suspect, but they don't have any evidence to charge him." Joelle paused, and it sounded as if she was muttering what she was reading. "Wow, listen to this. Their late parents' will was worded so that any grandchild would inherit a hefty share of the estate, and Buck might have been willing to eliminate not only his own brother but his brother's offspring."

Lana's stomach twisted, and her heart began to pound. This was why Buck had killed Stephanie. Well, maybe. Why had he waited until after she gave birth to get rid of any competition for family money? Maybe because he hadn't been able to find Stephanie?

"Any other motive for Buck to kill other than the money he inherited?" Slater asked. He accessed the report, the pages loading on the screen.

Joelle paused again, and Lana figured she was skimming the report. "There's a history of what I guess you could call sibling rivalry. Buck and Patrick were involved in a fistfight when Patrick was in college. It landed them both in jail. Temporarily, anyway, until their parents bailed them out."

"Please tell me DNA samples were collected," Slater said.

"They were, since the fight led to a serious injury of a bystander. Buck was initially charged with that, but the charges were pleaded way down. I'm guessing it was because of pressure or influence from the parents. Anyway, I just read a couple of witness statements that said Buck always seemed to have it in for his brother. I'm guessing because he didn't want to share the family estate with him."

That brought Lana back to a big concern. "Patrick's only been dead a week so if Stephanine and he were involved, he could be Cameron's father. If Buck sees Cameron as a threat to his family inheritance, then the baby will be a target."

"Yes," Joelle agreed. "That's why I'm hoping there'll be something in this report that'll help the Austin cops find him. His face is being plastered on the media as a person of interest so that might…" Her words trailed off. "Oh, God," she said on a gasp.

"What's wrong?" Slater demanded, but he seemed to stop skimming the report, too. He froze, and Lana hurried to the laptop to see what had caused the reaction. She saw it the moment Joelle spelled it out.

"Oh, God," Joelle repeated. "Austin PD thinks Buck might have been the one who killed our father."

Chapter Five

Slater kept watch of the security monitors, fought off the fatigue and rehashed everything he'd uncovered since Joelle's bombshell.

Buck might have been the one who killed our father.

Since Buck hadn't been on Slater's radar before tonight, Slater hadn't latched onto the theory. But that had changed after he and Lana had spent the last two hours going through any and all background on Buck.

They hadn't found any direct proof, but the connection was indeed there, and Slater could now see why Austin PD had flagged it as part of their investigation into Buck's involvement in the deaths of his brother and parents. It was yet another circumstantial piece that when put with the other pieces could point to murder.

"I should have seen this sooner," he muttered, scrubbing his hand over his face to keep himself alert and awake.

"How?" Lana questioned. "It wasn't even your father's case."

True, but after poring over every one of his dad's investigations, he should have widened the net to other cases. If so, he might have found the details about Alicia Monroe, a nineteen-year-old woman who'd disappeared from Weston, a small town near Saddle Ridge. There'd been enough blood at the scene of Alicia's small apartment to declare her dead, but they'd never found her body. Alicia's mother, Maryanne, had been old high school friends with Slater's parents and had asked his dad, then sheriff, to look into the matter.

And his father had.

Slater had managed to find notes about it in an old file that his dad had marked personal. In those notes, his dad had listed several scenarios and suspects for Alicia's death. It'd been a lengthy list since Alicia had apparently been considered a party girl and had a huge circle of friends.

Including Buck.

There'd been nothing concrete about Buck in his dad's notes or in the investigation that the Weston PD had conducted, but Buck had been a person of interest since he'd had a relationship with Alicia. And a volatile temper even back then. Several people had verified that the breakup with Buck hadn't been amicable, but there were no specifics about such things as stalking or violence. Buck had been just nineteen at the time, and with the lack of evidence, he'd been questioned and released. That wasn't the end of the story, though.

Slater stared at the notes now. Observations made by his father that had started nearly twenty years earlier and had continued until right before his death. Even though Alicia's death was considered a cold case, his dad had continued to dig into it, had continued to ask questions, had still considered it an active if unofficial investigation. That maybe meant he'd continued to ruffle some feathers as well.

Had Buck found out about the investigation and murdered Slater's dad to silence him once and for all?

Maybe.

There was one note in particular that troubled him. The

month before his father's murder, he'd jotted down a comment that he wanted to reinterview the persons of interest, and he'd listed some of Alicia's friends, including Buck. If his father had actually talked with any of them, there was no indication of it in the file notes. Or maybe he'd died before he could add them.

The bottom line was his father could have spoken to Buck, spooked him, and that could have prompted Buck to murder him.

"Do you remember when Alicia disappeared?" Lana asked, drawing his attention back to her. Not that it'd strayed far since she was literally sitting shoulder to shoulder with him.

"I do." He'd been sixteen at the time, and even though it'd happened one town over, it'd caused some panic among the townsfolk who'd speculated there might be a killer on the loose. "You?"

She nodded. "Stephanie knew Alicia, and she talked a lot about the murder."

Slater turned toward her before he realized that shoulder to shoulder could quickly turn into mouth to mouth. He eased back his chair a little and waited for her to continue.

"After Alicia disappeared," Lana went on, "Stephanie confessed to me that she'd sneaked out of the house when she'd been grounded and had gone with a friend to a party at Alicia's. Apparently, Alicia's parents were out of town so there was no adult supervision."

That rang an instant bell with Slater. "Yeah, I remember Stephanie calling me and asking me to take her to a party. She didn't tell me where, only that it was at a friend of a friend's. I couldn't go, so I guess she went with someone else."

"Does that bother you?" Lana came out and asked. "That Stephanie saw other guys when you two were dating?"

"No." And he didn't have to think hard about that response. "Stephanie wasn't exactly the 'settle down with one guy' type. And we were teenagers. We had enough on-again, off-again times that I dated other girls during the offs."

He studied Lana's face and saw what he always saw simmering there. The heat. The old attraction they'd never acted on because of Stephanie. Lana looked as if she wanted to say something about that, but then she glanced away, visibly regrouping and getting them back on the subject of the investigation.

"From what I can recall, the party happened about a week before Alicia disappeared," Lana went on. "I remember because it was Stephanie's sixteenth birthday, and she was grounded. I think that's why she went. So she'd have a celebration of sorts. But then she got there and said there was a lot of drinking and some drugs, and when some fights broke out, she and her friend left."

Slater considered that. "Was Alicia involved in the fights?"

"Not that Stephanie said."

Still, it was something to consider, and Slater made a mental note to try to find out from anyone who'd attended. "Was Buck at the party?" he wanted to know.

He saw the regret in her eyes a split second before she shook her head. "I don't recall Stephanie mentioning him."

That would have been a long shot, and Slater was sorry he'd brought this up. It was no doubt a reminder that Stephanie was dead and couldn't be questioned about the party.

"I'm guessing Stephanie didn't mention the party to the Weston cops?" Slater asked.

Another shake of her head. "Not a chance. She'd sneaked

out of the house when she was grounded and was probably with someone our parents wouldn't have approved of. She would have been in serious trouble."

He considered that a moment. "Serious trouble," he repeated. "Was there anything like physical abuse from your parents?"

It twisted at him that Lana didn't immediately deny it. Instead, she dragged in a long breath. "My mother slapped Stephanie and me a couple of times when we broke the rules. She didn't want a whisper of gossip about our behavior, so when the gossip happened, she often flew off the handle."

Slater wasn't surprised that this was the first time he was hearing of this. He'd always suspected that Lana's parents weren't the sort to air any dirty laundry and would make sure their daughters did the same.

And he wondered if that played into what had happened to Stephanie.

It was hard for him to believe one of them had murdered their own daughter, but it was something he had to consider. After all, Stephanie would have no doubt broken plenty of their rules by having the baby.

Lana tapped something on his father's notes. It was the date Alicia's disappearance had been categorized as a murder. "We moved to San Antonio shortly after this," she said.

He'd known that, but he hadn't connected the move to anything involving Alicia. And maybe it wasn't. It was yet another thread, though, that needed to be checked.

"Do you recall your parents ever talking about Alicia?" he asked.

She paused and then went with another headshake. "They rarely discussed anyone who wasn't in their social circles. You were the exception," she added. "You must know they didn't approve of you dating Stephanie."

"Yeah, I knew, and I think that was part of the appeal for your sister. Being with me was breaking the rules."

Lana didn't argue with that. But she did yawn, a reminder that it was already past midnight. She quickly tried to cover the yawn and look back at the notes, but he knew it was time to call it a night.

"Let's try to get some sleep," he suggested, glancing at the monitors and then at the sofa. "I can sleep in here and keep an eye on the security cameras. I'm guessing they'll make some kind of sound if someone comes near the place?"

Lana nodded and held up her phone. "It'll beep, and the system will alert me, too, on the app." She motioned toward the adjoining bath. "There are toiletries and even some clothes in there. Not sure any of them will fit you, but my boss tries to keep a wide range of sizes stocked in case he has to move someone here with just the clothes on their back."

Slater had showered and changed into clean clothes right before Lana had left the baby on his doorstep so he figured he'd be okay, especially since they'd be heading back to Saddle Ridge as soon as her interview was finished.

Lana's phone dinged with a text, and she frowned when she glanced at the screen.

"One of your parents?" Slater asked.

She shook her head. "It's Taylor Galway, someone who used to be friends with Stephanie, but I know they had some kind of falling-out. Taylor wants to know if it's true, if Stephanie is really dead. I suspect now that word of her death is out, I'll be getting more calls and texts," she added in a mutter.

"That might not be a bad thing," Slater said. "Did Stephanie have contact with these friends while she was hiding out?"

Lana's first instinct was to say no, that Stephanie had been too scared for that, but she simply didn't know. "Maybe."

That would have been his guess, too, and if Stephanie had spoken to anyone, she might have doled out some info that could help with the investigation. Lana clearly picked up on that, too, because she fired off a response to Taylor.

It's true, Lana texted as Slater looked over her shoulder. She waited a few moments but got no response back from the woman. "I really don't think Stephanie had contact with Taylor, though, because the couple of times the woman's name recently came up, Stephanie didn't have anything kind to say about her. Just the opposite."

"Do you know why?" he asked. It wasn't an idle question. Sometimes, bad blood led to bad stuff happening.

"I'm not sure. I recall Stephanie calling her a backstabber, and she added some choice words of profanity to that." She paused a moment. "It's possible their falling-out was over Marsh."

"Marsh?" Slater certainly hadn't expected that.

Lana nodded. "Our parents were pressuring Stephanie to marry Marsh, but I know that Marsh was once involved with Taylor, so maybe Taylor wasn't over him. Or maybe she just didn't want Stephanie hooking up with her ex."

Ironic since it appeared that Stephanie hadn't wanted Marsh. At least she hadn't wanted to marry him, anyway. It was possible, though, she would have changed her mind about that had she lived.

Even though Lana yawned for the third time, she went to the window and looked out. Despite this being a residential neighborhood, the city lights were right there, only a few blocks away, and there were even more lights beyond that. In the distance, there were the sounds of traffic and even the howl of a police siren. He wasn't sure how people slept with that kind of noise going on, but he'd have to give it a try. He needed at least a little sleep to stand a chance of having a clear head.

"A fish out of water," he muttered. That's what he felt like right now.

The corner of Lana's mouth lifted. "I felt that way after we moved from Saddle Ridge. Stephanie was in her element in the city, but I never was."

That was a reminder of the things he and Lana had in common, and if there hadn't been a two-year age difference between them, Slater figured he would have dated Lana in high school, not Stephanie.

Maybe sensing that the moment was turning too personal, Lana turned from the window. "I'll be in the room right across from here."

She started in that direction, only to stop when Slater's phone rang. "Is it Joelle?" she immediately asked, and he knew the concern in her voice was because she was afraid something had happened to the baby.

He shook his head. "It's Duncan."

Lana didn't relax one bit, so Slater quickly answered the call and put it on speaker. "Lana's in the room with me," he informed Duncan just in case he needed to soften any bad news he might have. "Is the baby all right?"

"He's fine," Duncan assured him. "And there's been no sign of any kind of trouble here. What about there?"

"Nothing," he said, and then waited for Duncan to get into why he'd called. Thankfully, he didn't have to wait long.

"Two things. I just got back two reports. The first is for Stephanie's cell phone records. The person who called her in the hospital used a blocked number. No way to trace it."

That surprised exactly no one. Of course a killer planning a murder wouldn't have left something that could be linked back to him. But it did make Slater wonder why the person had called Stephanie. Or maybe the call wasn't from the killer at all but from someone else.

"The other report I got back was from the Rapid DNA test," Duncan added a moment later. Slater heard him drag in a long breath. "Cameron's father isn't Patrick. It's Buck."

Chapter Six

With Slater right by her side and Detective Lisa Thayer across the table, Lana sat in the interview room of Austin PD and read through the now-typed statement she'd just given about her sister's murder. It was all there. All spelled out.

Details that twisted and ate away at her like acid.

In hindsight, she could see so much potential for an outcome like this. Stephanie's secrecy. The fear she'd seen in her sister's eyes. Lana hadn't gotten to the source of that fear, hadn't managed to fix it in time, and now Stephanie had paid the ultimate price.

"Buck," Lana muttered under her breath when her gaze landed on his name in the statement. She was well aware she'd spoken it like profanity, and it wasn't the first time. It was something she'd been doing most of the night and now into the morning.

She couldn't wrap her mind around Stephanie hooking up with a man like Buck, especially since according to those photos on social media, she had been involved with Buck's brother, Patrick. Knowing Cameron's bio-father didn't lessen Lana's love for her nephew, not one bit, but she knew it made their situation even more complicated.

If Patrick had been the dad, he could have petitioned for custody of Cameron. Had Patrick not been murdered, that is. But Buck was very much alive. And possibly a killer. Lana didn't want someone like that to try to stake a claim on the baby.

"There's still no sign of him," Detective Thayer remarked after checking her phone. "Buck," she added, though no clarification was needed.

Lana wondered where he was. Wondered if he was trying to figure out how to get to Cameron or her. She doubted the man would just run and hide, and part of her hoped he didn't. She didn't want to have to look over her shoulder for years, waiting for Buck to attack.

"You've got enough to arrest him if you find him," Slater said. Not a question. He was no doubt just looking for verification.

Thayer nodded. "We've got the security camera footage from the break-in at Lana's. The footage, too, of his hit-and-run. That'll be enough to hold him while we build a case for murder."

Murder.

There it was. Another word all spelled out, and even though it wasn't fresh info, just hearing it brought back the avalanche of emotions. Lana had spent half the night crying for a sister she wasn't even sure she loved. That had brought on yet another mother lode of guilt, not loving her only sibling. But there'd been so many times when Stephanie just hadn't been likable.

That lack of love didn't extend to Cameron, though. Just the opposite. Lana had loved him from the moment she'd laid eyes on him. And now she had a fierce instinct to protect him from the scum who was his biological father.

Did Buck know that he was Cameron's father?

Maybe.

That could be the reason he'd gone after Stephanie, but

it was just as likely he would want to eliminate Stephanie and Cameron regardless if he or his brother was the father. Because any baby born to either of them would be a threat to the inheritance.

Thayer's phone dinged with another text, and her face seemed to relax a little. "Your parents and Marsh Bray are coming in at one today for interviews. Their lawyers had been stonewalling that, but I guess they gave in." The detective looked at Slater. "If you're interested, I can let you observe the interviews."

"I'm very interested. Thanks," Slater added.

The detective sighed a little when she turned to Lana. "I'm afraid I can't extend that offer to you. Slater's a cop with a vested interest in the outcome of this investigation, but I can't let civilians observe."

"I understand," Lana said, and she did. She wanted this all done by the book so that Buck wouldn't be able to shake off some of the charges on a technicality. She wanted him to serve the maximum time possible.

Thayer checked her watch. "It'll be at least four hours before the interviews," she said. "You're welcome to wait in the lounge, or you can come back. I can have a police escort follow you to wherever you want to go."

"We have a deputy from Saddle Ridge waiting outside," Slater explained, standing when Thayer did.

As planned, Sonya had returned to Austin to escort them to police headquarters for the statement, and she'd be following them when they drove back to Saddle Ridge.

"Any chance during the interviews you can bring up Alicia Monroe and any possible connection to my father's murder?" Slater asked Thayer.

The detective certainly didn't jump to agree to that. Nor did she ask who Alicia was. That was because she'd already mentioned that she had gone through all the case notes on Buck and had seen that Buck had once been involved with the murdered teenager.

"You can't think that Leonard and Pamela Walsh know anything about that particular murder," Thayer finally said. "Do you?"

Slater shrugged. "Stephanie was at a party at Alicia's house, and Stephanie clearly knew Buck, so maybe her folks did, too." He stopped, shook his head. "Yeah, it's a long shot, but I'd like to know if they, well, have any details we don't already know about. It's possible when you bring up Alicia's name, they might recall Stephanie mentioning Buck or her."

Lana considered what he'd just said and had a theory. "When Stephanie and I were teenagers, our parents made a habit of hiring PIs to keep an eye on us. They didn't want us getting into any trouble that would cause bad publicity. So they might have known about Stephanie going to that party." She paused. "They might have known about Buck and Alicia, too."

"If they did, why wouldn't they have volunteered that sooner?" Thayer came out and asked.

Lana didn't have to think about this. "Again, bad publicity. They might have hoped to keep my sister's pregnancy under wraps, but when she was murdered, they would want to do any possible damage control."

"Not lying to the police, though, right?" Thayer questioned.

Lana had no choice but to just spell this out. "Lying is second nature to them. And right now, their focus isn't on losing a daughter but rather keeping a lid on unsavory details that might come out. They won't be happy to learn that a thug like Buck fathered Stephanie's child."

Thayer stayed quiet a moment. "So, maybe I can use that. They don't know he's the father, right?"

"They didn't learn it from us," Lana assured her.

"Good. Then I can mention it and see how they react. That'd be a good lead-in to bringing up Alicia and that party."

Lana wished she could see her parents' reaction to that. And Marsh's. She wondered if Marsh would see Stephanie's pregnancy as a betrayal. If so, that would give him motive for murder.

"I'll let you know everything that happens in the interview," Slater told Lana as they made their way out of the interview room.

Lana had had no doubts about that and murmured a thanks while she considered something else. "Once they know about Buck being Cameron's father, my parents might feel obligated to try to get custody of him. I mean, how would it look in the press if they didn't?"

It sickened her to think of handing over that precious baby to people like her parents. Thankfully, there'd be no way Buck could try to assert his parental rights. Not with his criminal record and the charges about to be leveled against him. Buck wouldn't be a threat to custody. However, her parents might put up a good fight if they thought it would benefit them.

After they made their way down to the bottom floor, Slater texted Sonya to let her know they would soon be coming out of the building. That would mean another uneasy walk through the large visitors' parking lot.

She and Slater retrieved their weapons from the security checkpoint at the front of the building and stepped outside, immediately glancing around for any signs of a threat. There were some uniformed cops going in and out of the sprawling headquarters complex. Some civilians, too. The place was a beehive of activity, which didn't settle Lana's nerves one bit.

As they threaded their way through the sea of parked cars, Lana's phone vibrated, a reminder that she'd silenced it during the interview, and she frowned when she saw her mother's name on the screen. She didn't answer, not wanting to deal with either of her parents right now, but her mother immediately texted her.

Did you see the headlines? her mother asked. Someone is spreading lies about Stephanie.

Groaning, she showed the message to Slater just as he got his own text from Detective Thayer. The media's picked up the story about Stephanie's murder.

Great. It had to be bad press for the cop to give them a heads-up. Lana figured she'd need to glance through the article on the way back to the safe house. Not now, though. She didn't want the distraction.

That thought had no sooner crossed her mind when Lana sensed the motion to her right. She snapped in that direction, her gaze automatically scanning for any sign of threat. She didn't see any, but every nerve in her body was yelling for her to take notice. That danger was near.

And every nerve in her body was right.

Before she could even see exactly what the threat was, the man jumped out from behind the back of a large SUV, and Lana caught just a glimpse of the weapon before he jammed it against her chest. She felt the jolt of the stun gun go through her. Felt it rob her of all of the sensations in her body except for the pain. She could feel the pain. Every bit of it. And it literally brought her to her knees.

The feeling in her legs vanished, and she was suddenly boneless. Unable to move. Lana had no choice but to drop down on the concrete. Hard. So hard that it seemed to send a jolt through her.

Beside her, she heard the frantic footsteps, the spewed profanity, all mixed with the sickening thud of flesh slamming into flesh. But she couldn't tell what was going on.

Oh, God. Was this Buck, and was he now going after Slater since he'd neutralized her? And she was neutralized. There was no question about that. Lana couldn't reach for her gun. She couldn't do anything to save Slater and herself.

It took every ounce of her energy, but Lana finally managed to roll onto her back so she could look up at the nightmare that was playing out in front of her. Slater hadn't managed to draw his weapon, and he was in a hand-to-hand fight with a hulking brute. It was Buck all right, and he was even bigger and bulkier then he had seemed in his photos. He towered over Slater and outweighed him by at least fifty pounds. She could only watch as Buck slammed one of his huge fists toward Slater's face.

Slater managed to turn just in time so the fist was a glancing blow rather than a full-on punch, but that deflection didn't stop Buck. He merely tried again, and when that one missed, he grabbed hold of Slater's shoulder to drag him closer.

Around them, Lana could hear the shouts, and she prayed help was coming. Buck's face was etched with rage, and she had no doubt if he got the chance, he would beat Slater to death.

Lana tried to kick out, hoping she could make contact with Buck's leg so she could off-balance him, but the impact only seemed to anger him further. He looked down at her, cursing her.

"You're a dead woman," he snarled.

The threat cost him, because Slater took advantage

of Buck's distraction and drew his gun. Buck acted fast, though, latching onto Lana's hair and dragging her up in front of him as a human shield. He pressed his back against the SUV.

"I'll snap her neck," Buck growled, the raging heat and anger in every word. "I'll kill her where she stands."

"No, you won't," Slater said. In contrast, his voice was all ice. As was his expression. "Because then you'll have no cover. Look around you, Buck. Look at what you're up against."

Lana couldn't fully turn her head, but from her peripheral vision, she could see several cops. All had their weapons drawn and aimed at Buck. She felt Buck's breath quicken and could feel his heart slamming against her back. Lana also felt something else. The movement of Buck's arm. When she felt the cold barrel of a gun jam against her head, she realized he, too, was armed.

"Yeah, but she'll still be dead," Buck taunted. "Tell your badge friends to back off, and she lives."

Lana figured there was little to no chance of that. She suspected Buck wanted to use her to get to Cameron, and once she'd served her purpose, he'd kill her just as easily as he had Stephanie.

But she wouldn't help him get to Cameron.

No way.

She'd die here before she let that happen.

"I think you badges call this a standoff," Buck grumbled. "None of you has a clean shot. Can't risk shooting me without putting bullets in her and any other unlucky person in the parking lot."

Lana knew all of that was true. But she also knew that Slater wouldn't just let Buck drag her away from here.

"So here's my suggestion," Buck went on. "Lana and

me get in this SUV, and I drive off. I dump her a couple of blocks over—"

"No," Slater said, his fierce gaze locked on Buck. "You'll let her go now and will surrender to Austin PD."

Buck made a snarky yeah-right. "And I guess you'll say I'll live happily ever after."

"No," Slater repeated. "You'll be arrested and tried. But the alternative is dying right here, right now. At least with a trial you stand a chance of walking away a free man."

He did. But Lana tried not to think of that as a possibility. She wanted this monster to pay for what he had done, for what he was continuing to do.

Lana tried to keep her breathing steady and tested some of her muscles. Slowly, the movement was starting to return. Not enough for her to have full control over her body, but she could maybe do something. Lana did more testing, trying to loosen the muscles in her neck while she tried not to panic over Buck's tightening grip around her throat.

She made direct eye contact with Slater, trying to let him know that she was about to attempt something. Something he likely wouldn't approve of, since it would be dangerous. But anything she did at this point could turn out to be fatal. It was the same if she did nothing at all.

Yelling to give herself a jolt of adrenaline, Lana rammed the back of her head into Buck's face. She put as much force behind it as she could manage, and when he howled in pain, she rammed her elbow into his gut. That wasn't nearly as effective as the headbutt, but it was enough to cause him to loosen his grip on her. The second he did, Lana dropped to the ground.

The sound of the shot immediately blasted through the air.

For a horrifying moment, she had no idea who'd been

shot, and she was terrified that Buck had managed to shoot Slater. She looked up, trying to pick through the blaring morning light, and she saw Slater. Standing and with his gun still aimed.

Buck collapsed next to her.

She saw the blood spreading on the front of his shirt, but that didn't stop Buck from reaching for her. He was going to try to pull her back into that human shield position. But Slater put a stop to that. He took hold of her arm and dragged her away from Buck, and in the same motion, he kicked away Buck's gun.

Three other cops, including Sonya, moved in, all of them continuing to keep their guns trained on Buck. He didn't move, though. Didn't try to grab her again or attempt to fight back. Not that he could have. Lana was pretty sure he was bleeding out.

Slater hoisted her up, moving her behind him and anchoring her between him and a car. Good thing, too, since Lana didn't have the feeling back in many parts of her body and she wasn't sure she could stand on her own.

"Ambulance is on the way," someone shouted. Several of the Austin cops moved in and one began to check the wound on Buck's chest. "Is this the guy wanted for murder?"

Slater muttered, "Yes," but continued to stare at Buck. "Did you kill Stephanie?" he asked.

Buck laughed. Or rather attempted one, anyway. It sounded more like a throaty gurgle. "No comment," he managed.

So, even now, he wasn't going to confess to relieve his conscience. Maybe because he thought he was going to live. Lana seriously doubted that, though, and obviously so did the cop tending to his wound. He was adding pressure to try to slow the bleeding, but it wasn't working.

"Did you kill Sheriff Cliff McCullough?" Slater tried again.

Buck didn't snarl out a verbal response, but he stared at Slater for a long time. In the distance, Lana could hear the wails of an ambulance.

"Did you kill him?" Slater repeated, speaking now through clenched teeth.

"I'm not gonna give you that," Buck muttered, his voice growing weaker while the rage still flared in his dying eyes. "Here's what I'll give Lana and you. The truth. I'm not working by my lonesome. I've got a helper. A cold-blooded one. And Lana and you are going to die."

Chapter Seven

Slater fought the adrenaline crash with another cup of strong black coffee. Even though it was his third cup, he could still feel the fatigue all the way to his bones. Judging from the exhausted look on Lana's face, she was dealing with the same thing.

That and the flashbacks.

Yeah, those had already started, and Slater figured they wouldn't be letting up anytime soon. Buck had come darn close to killing both of them, and that wasn't something they'd just be able to shut out.

Lana stood at the window of the break room in Austin PD headquarters, drinking her own cup of coffee and staring out at the crime scene that was now being processed in the parking lot below. Buck's body had already been moved, and there was a final canvass going on for any evidence Buck might have left behind.

Slater had had to surrender his gun, of course. That was standard procedure, though he was certain none of the cops here thought he'd overreacted. Deadly force had been necessary, period, and if Slater hadn't shot and killed Buck, then Lana might be dead. There were plenty of witnesses and even surveillance footage to back that up.

He and Lana had already given their statements of the

incident. Technically, they were free to go, but Lana hadn't jumped at the chance to go back to the safe house only to return so that Slater could observe Marsh and her parents' interviews.

And Slater couldn't blame her.

Buck's words were no doubt repeating like gunfire in her head. *Lana and you are going to die.* The thing was they just didn't know if the threat was real or if it'd been one last shot by a dying man. Buck had indeed spoken to someone on the phone when he'd broken into Lana's house, so he hadn't been working alone. However, that didn't mean the accomplice would continue to do his bidding now that he was dead.

It was somewhat of a miracle that Lana hadn't been seriously injured, but Slater had still insisted she be examined by the EMTs. Thankfully, they hadn't found any damage from her being hit with the stun gun.

"Are you okay?" Lana asked, turning from the window and fixing her gaze on him.

Slater knew it wasn't a simple question. Nor did he have a simple answer. Only three hours earlier, he'd killed a man. A man who'd seemed hell-bent on murdering Lana. But Buck had been more than their attacker. He'd been a suspect in the murders of Stephanie and Slater's father. Maybe Buck had ended both their lives.

And maybe he hadn't.

"Now I know how people feel who've had loved ones disappear," she muttered. "No real answers. Only speculation."

Yeah, he understood that. Of course, a disappearance wasn't necessarily a murder. Murder was final. But without the answers as to the who and the why, he and Lana wouldn't have that elusive closure. Mercy, he needed that, and he was certain Lana did, too. It was the only way they were going to be able to look past the now and move on to the future.

At the thought of "future," the baby came to mind, and he knew Cameron was weighing heavily on Lana right now. It was obvious she loved the baby and was worried about him. That's why it was critical for them to find out the identity of Buck's accomplice.

Slater had plenty of wheels in motion for that. Both his fellow cops and Austin PD were digging through Buck's phone records and financials, looking for anything that could give them a lead. Slater wanted to dive right in to that research, too, and he would just as soon as they got these interviews out of the way. Maybe Marsh or Lana's parents would spill something that would help.

The door to the break room opened, and both Slater and Lana automatically reached for guns that weren't there. Lana, too, had had to surrender her gun since personal firearms weren't allowed in the headquarters.

Their reaction, though, wasn't necessary since it wasn't a threat. It was Detective Thayer, and judging from her troubled expression, something else had gone wrong. Lana must have picked up on it as well.

"Is the baby all right?" Lana asked, the frantic edge in her voice.

"As far as I know," Thayer said. "I haven't gotten any alerts or anything."

That verbal assurance didn't appease Lana, and Slater saw her fire off a text to Joelle. Something Lana had already done several times since Buck's death. His sister's response was equally fast and told Lana that all was well.

"I'm not here about the baby," Thayer went on once Lana looked up from her phone. "I wanted to let you know that someone leaked to the press." She walked closer to them, bringing up some images on her phone.

Slater steeled himself up to see pictures of Buck's body. Or maybe even Slater shooting the man. It was so easy these days for people to post such things on social media. If the photos were "compelling" enough, then media would pick them up, too.

Both he and Lana leaned in to take a look, and he heard the soft sound of surprise that Lana made when she realized what she was looking at. Not Buck. But rather Stephanie. And these weren't death photos but rather of Stephanie clearly in party mode.

In the first shot, Stephanie was wearing just her underwear and was dancing. Since she had a cocktail glass in her hand, she had likely been drinking. The second one was of another party with Stephanie making out with some guy. Neither shot was flattering. Ditto for the third. It'd been taken from behind, and a grinning, inebriated Stephanie was looking over her shoulder just as she was about to dive into a pool.

"Who posted these?" Lana wanted to know.

"We're not sure, but they were on Stephanie's Facebook page," Thayer explained. "Stephanie obviously hadn't used the page in a while, but she had it set to public, which means anyone could have tagged her so they'd wind up there."

"You can trace the person who posted these?" Slater asked.

Thayer shrugged. "The photos were published from a new account, one without an actual profile name, only numbers, but we'll try to find who's responsible." She paused. "And the pictures were also put on every one of Stephanie's friends' pages."

Lana dragged in a long breath. "Could Buck have done this?"

"No," Thayer was quick to say. "These showed up an hour ago, and they hadn't been scheduled in advance. Maybe it's some kind of smear campaign from his accomplice, but that doesn't feel right."

Slater made a sound of agreement. "An accomplice wouldn't want to draw this kind of attention." That got nods from both Lana and the detective.

"So why do it?" Lana asked. "Stephanie's dead. She…" She trailed off and muttered some profanity under her breath. "This could be meant to get back at my parents." Lana stopped again and groaned. "Or someone who wants to make people believe Stephanie was irresponsible and deserved to die."

That could be a large pool of people. Stephanie had likely made some enemies, and Slater had no doubts that her parents had, too.

"Anyway, I thought you should know about this before the interviews," Thayer said, checking the time. "The Walshes and Marsh Bray will be here soon, and any info about Stephanie's potential enemies might come out in their statements. If they haven't seen the photos already, I'm sure they soon will."

No doubt, and maybe that would set one of them off enough that they'd reveal something they'd rather keep secret.

"I'll come back and get you when the interviews are ready to start," Thayer told Slater right before she walked out.

Since Lana looked unsteady on her feet, Slater went to her and took a huge risk. By pulling her into his arms. Hugs, even one of comfort, could still spur the heat between them.

And it did this time, too, but they obviously had way too much on their plates to think about acting on it.

He hoped.

Sighing, Lana dropped her head on his shoulder. "I want to ask my boss to use some of the Sencor resources to help us. Traffic cam footage, deep background checks, informal interviews with anyone who was near the hospital when Stephanie was murdered. Anything that'll link to Stephanie, Buck or anyone he might have been working with."

Slater had already considered this angle. "I can't agree to anything illegal," he spelled out.

"It wouldn't be. But they've got the manpower to interview anyone who crossed paths with Stephanie and Buck. Somebody must know what happened and why Stephanie went into hiding when she realized she was pregnant with Buck's child. Unless the blowup between them was totally in private, then there might be something to find."

That was a long way to go back, eight months or so, but Slater could see the reasoning for that to be the starting point. With Stephanie in hiding, Buck might have been digging to find her location, and if so, there could be traces of that. Traces that then might link back to his partner.

"All right," Slater said.

The moment the agreement was out of his mouth, Lana eased away from him so she could compose a text, no doubt to get the ball rolling on the search. When he heard the swooshing sound of the text being sent, he expected Lana to move back to the window. Or anywhere else in the room that wasn't so close to him.

She didn't.

Lana came right back into his arms, and he heard the whisper of a soft sob that she managed to choke down. She was grieving. Scared, too, and Slater wished he could do something to help. The only thing he could manage, though, was to stand there and hold her.

The moments slid by, and he wasn't sure exactly how much time passed before she moved again. This time, she looked at him. Their gazes locked. Held. Her breath met his. Slater saw the grief. But the heat was there as well, and it didn't seem to matter that neither of them wanted to feel like this. Not now, anyway. That didn't stop it. Didn't stop Lana from moving in and doing the unthinkable.

She pressed her mouth to his.

It wasn't a hard, hungry kiss born of need. Not solely, anyway. The need was there, but this seemed to be so much more. Slater tried to give her exactly that—more—without pushing this too far. He simply kissed her.

Of course, there was nothing *simply* about it since this was Lana. The heat rose as the pressure of her mouth went up a whole bunch of notches. That wasn't all, either. With the new level of the kiss came the maneuvering of their bodies, and that didn't stop until they were pressed against each other. Until this felt like a whole lot more than just a kiss.

Thankfully, they both seemed to regain their common sense at the same moment because they stepped away from each other. Slater was sure he looked as if someone had sucker punched him, because he was gulping in breaths as if this had been a making-out marathon. Lana wasn't faring much better. She looked shocked and maybe appalled that she had done such a thing.

"Don't say you're sorry," he insisted when she opened her mouth. "No need. You can blame it on the grief and the fact that we were nearly killed today. You can blame it on whatever you need it to be."

She stared at him a long time and shook her head. "I try

not to lie to myself," she murmured. "So I'll blame it on this pull I've had to you for...too long," she added in a whisper.

Slater had known the heat was there, but he might have questioned that "too long" part if the door hadn't opened. Even though he and Lana were no longer standing close to each other, they still moved farther apart, and the guilt was probably flashing like a proverbial neon sign on their faces.

Detective Thayer stuck her head inside the partially opened door, and she seemed to hesitate for a second or two before her gaze went to Lana. "Your parents and Marsh are here. But they've asked to speak to you before the interviews. I told them I'd check. You can say no," Thayer tacked onto that.

Lana didn't just say no or anything else, but then she nodded. "I want to see how they react to Buck coming after me."

Slater wanted to see that reaction, too. Heck, he wanted to see them respond to a lot of things, including if they had any part in their daughter's murder. Of course, neither of them would likely just admit to that, but they might say something off the record.

Thayer waited as if checking to see if Lana was certain, and then she murmured, "I'll bring them here to the break room."

Lana pulled back her shoulders and ran her hand through her hair, obviously trying to make herself look as steady as possible. She was pulling it off, too. For the most part, anyway, but Slater dreaded that Lana was about to have to face the emotional wringer her parents would no doubt put her through.

It didn't take long before the door opened again, and the detective ushered in Leonard and Pamela. Marsh was right behind them. None of them rushed to Lana, but Leonard gave Thayer a dismissive glance before insisting, "We'll speak to our daughter alone."

"No, you won't," Lana said before Slater or Thayer got the chance. "Slater and the detective are staying put."

Oh, that did not please Leonard, and Slater saw the anger tighten every muscle in the man's face. "Fine," Leonard spat out. "We only wanted to make sure you were okay. I understand from news reports that you were attacked in the parking lot."

Lana nodded. And didn't add anything else.

Pamela huffed and aimed a glare at Thayer. "Obviously, you've failed at your job if a thug can go after my only surviving daughter right under your nose." Tears sprang to her eyes, and Slater wondered if they were genuine.

"Lana wasn't under police protection when she was attacked," Thayer said, the annoyance coating her voice. "And my team and I are not only investigating the attack but your other daughter's murder."

"But you let that thug get to her," Leonard said. His voice cracked. "A thug who must have raped Stephanie since he fathered her baby."

Thayer fired a quick glance at Lana and Slater to see if they'd spilled. Both shook their heads, indicating they hadn't.

"What makes you think Stephanie had Buck's baby?" Slater came out and asked.

Judging from the way his face went tight again, Leonard was sorry he'd admitted knowing that. Slater made a mental note to check and see if anyone in Austin PD was continuing to feed Leonard information.

"That horrible man was the father of Stephanie's baby?" Pamela asked, and the woman seemed genuinely shocked.

She turned her wide eyes toward Marsh as if checking to see if he knew.

Marsh shook his head. "Did he rape Stephanie?" he immediately wanted to know. But he didn't wait for an answer. He groaned and closed his eyes for a moment. "Did he?" he repeated, posing the question first to Leonard and then to Lana.

"I don't know," Lana admitted.

"It would explain so much," Marsh went on. "There was no reason for Stephanie to go into hiding the way she did unless she was scared of Buck."

Slater had to admit that rang true with him. But it might have only been a part of it. "And maybe she didn't want to face you and her parents."

Another flash of anger crossed Leonard's face, but Pamela and Marsh didn't have the same reaction. Marsh groaned, stepped away and pressed his forehead against the wall. Pamela went to him, patting his back.

"I don't know why Stephanie wouldn't have gone to the police," Pamela murmured. "Instead, she went to Lana, and now she's dead. Lana could have been killed, too," Pamela quickly tacked onto that, but the arrow had already found its mark. Some of the color had drained from Lana's face, and she was no doubt going through another round of guilt over her sister's murder.

"Did Buck confess to killing Stephanie?" Marsh asked when he turned back around to face them.

Slater had to shake his head. "He said no comment." Slater debated if he should say more and then decided to go for it. "He claimed he had an accomplice."

That got the expected reactions from the three visitors. Shock, followed by concern. Leonard's concern, though, quickly morphed into what seemed to be his default reaction. Anger.

"You should call in the Texas Rangers," Leonard snarled, snapping toward Lana. "And I can arrange for private security for you—"

"I can arrange my own security," Lana interrupted.

Leonard made a show of rolling his eyes. "Clearly, that's worked out well for you. How close did you come to dying today, Lana?"

"Close," Lana admitted, and she didn't wither under her father's intense glare. "But I'm not handing over my safety to you."

"What the hell does that mean?" Leonard demanded.

Again, Lana didn't verbally respond. She just stared at her father, waiting. It was a good ploy, and Leonard lost the waiting game because he muttered more profanity.

"I don't know what it is you think I've done, but you're wrong," Leonard grumbled.

"If you've got the resources to find out the identity of the man who fathered Stephanie's baby, then I figure you know a whole lot more," Lana spelled out. "Enough that you could have maybe stopped Buck from killing Stephanie."

"No." Leonard's denial was fast and loud. It took him a couple of seconds to rein in his temper. A temper so fierce that it made Slater believe this was a man who was capable of murder. Or at least capable of getting someone to commit murder for him.

But why would Leonard want Stephanie dead?

Was he so consumed with his image and reputation that he thought she was better off dead? If so, then he could have joined forces with Buck, who had his own strong motive for wanting Stephanie eliminated. But then, that left the baby. Slater didn't want to think Leonard or even Buck capable of harming a child. And maybe that hadn't been the plan. The baby could have simply been given to someone who had no idea of his paternity. That would mean, though, eliminating anyone who might spill the secret down the road.

Such as Lana.

Yes, the theory of Leonard and Buck teaming up might work, but the teaming could have been done with Marsh and Buck. Or Buck and Pamela. Slater silently groaned. Because the accomplice could be someone else, and maybe the trio in this room were indeed innocent.

"Did any of you know Buck?" Slater came out and asked.

Marsh was the first to respond. "I didn't know him, but after I saw a picture of him, I think he might have been at parties that Stephanie and I attended. He seemed familiar."

"But you never spoke to him or vice versa?" Slater pressed.

Marsh shook his head. "And I don't recall Stephanie showing any interest in him."

"Of course she wouldn't," Leonard snapped. "The man was scum. Stephanie wouldn't have given him the time of day."

Maybe. But there was that whole bad-boy, forbidden-attraction thing, and while Slater wasn't certain if that would have appealed to Stephanie, he couldn't rule out that the sex between them hadn't been consensual.

"What about the two of you?" Slater continued, glancing at both Pamela and Leonard. "Did either of you know Buck?"

"No," Pamela said, and Leonard repeated that, but it seemed to Slater there wasn't a whole lot of conviction in the man's answer.

"You're sure?" Lana challenged. "Because as we speak, there are people combing through old social media and articles. If there's any connection between Buck and the three of you, they'll find it."

"They won't find anything," Leonard snapped, and his glare had returned. But Slater thought he saw plenty of nerves beneath that steely stare.

"If I've crossed paths with Buck, I don't recall," Pamela muttered. "And I think I would have."

So, she'd given herself an out. Maybe a genuine one, but Slater didn't intend to trust any of them. His cop's instincts told him that they knew more than they were admitting.

"Like I said, I think I saw Buck at parties," Marsh spoke up. "It's possible, too, that he was an acquaintance of my ex. I seem to recall Taylor mentioning Patrick, and that means she likely knew Buck, too."

"Taylor?" Slater questioned, recalling the text Lana had gotten from a woman by that name.

Marsh nodded. "Taylor Galway," he provided.

Leonard muttered the woman's name like profanity. "She should be arrested for stalking and harassing both Stephanie and Marsh."

That got Slater's attention, and he also remembered Lana mentioning that Stephanie and Taylor had been friends but had a falling-out. "Stalking?" he prompted, aiming that at Marsh.

Marsh's sigh was long and heavy as if he was tired of rehashing this particular subject. "I ended my relationship with Taylor two years ago when I started seeing Stephanie. It was never serious between Taylor and me," he was quick to add. "Stephanie was always my one true love." His voice trailed off, and he blinked back tears.

"I assume Taylor didn't take the breakup well?" Slater asked.

"She didn't," Leonard snarled. "Like I said, she stalked

and harassed Stephanie and Marsh. Always trying to tear them apart. I wouldn't be surprised if Taylor was the reason Stephanie went into hiding."

Slater considered that a moment. Maybe it had played into it, but his money was still on the pregnancy and Buck. "Did you report any of Taylor's behavior to the police?" But he already knew the answer.

"No," Leonard said, confirming Slater's thoughts. The man wouldn't have wanted that publicity. "Marsh kept a file with dates and stuff in case...well, in case things escalated," Leonard explained.

"I'll want to see that file," Thayer was quick to interject.

Marsh nodded. "I'll send it to you." He swallowed hard. "I saw the photos of Stephanie that someone posted. I think Taylor might have done that."

"Any proof?" Thayer asked.

"No, but it's something Taylor would do. She hated Stephanie," he added in a murmur. "Taylor hired a PI to look for Stephanie when she disappeared."

"What?" Lana blurted. "Why would she do that?"

Slater had the same question. If Taylor hated Stephanie so much, she'd want her gone, not found.

Marsh gave another of those weary sighs. "Because Taylor said until I had a clean break with Stephanie that I could never move on. She wanted Stephanie to tell me to my face that it was over between us."

Slater decided they were painting a picture of a deeply troubled woman. One who might not be emotionally stable.

Marsh took out his phone. "Yesterday, shortly before I learned that Stephanie had died, I got a text from Taylor," he said, scrolling through his messages. "It was about Stephanie."

"A text about Stephanie?" Lana said. "And you're just now telling us?"

"I just now remembered," Marsh muttered. "Once I heard Stephanie was dead, I forgot all about it. All I could think of was the woman I loved had been murdered."

Marsh's hands were trembling now. So was his voice. The cynical cop in Slater wondered though if it was all an act. Marsh continued to scroll until he found the one he was clearly looking for, and he held up the screen so Slater and Lana could read it. According to the contact, it was indeed from Taylor.

I found Stephanie, Taylor had texted. Now, this can all finally be over.

Chapter Eight

Despite the sickening worry and dread, Lana smiled when she saw Cameron on the FaceTime call to Joelle. The baby was sleeping, and everything about his precious little face looked so peaceful. Lana was thankful for that. She didn't want him to sense any of the fear.

But the fear was there.

For Lana, it was bone deep. And it wouldn't be going away until they had answers about Buck's accomplice, who might or might not be Taylor. At the moment, they just didn't know, but Lana was hoping they could soon remedy that since Detective Thayer had already called the woman. Taylor hadn't answered, but Thayer had left a terse voicemail for Taylor to contact her right away.

Maybe Taylor would do that and admit to any part she'd played in Stephanie's death. While Lana was hoping, she added that maybe Thayer was getting yet more details in the interviews with Marsh and Lana's parents. Slater might pick up on something, too, since he was observing them.

Lana had elected to wait in the break room for those interviews to finish and had been trying to get some work done using her phone, but she'd finally admitted her focus was practically nil and had made the call to Joelle.

Thankfully, Joelle had understood how important it was

for Lana to see the baby and had quietly slipped into the makeshift nursery. The sight of Cameron had given Lana some peace of mind. So had seeing the nanny in the room with the baby. Ditto for Joelle wearing a shoulder holster and gun. Joelle was an experienced deputy and would protect not only her own baby but Cameron, too, if there was a threat.

"You haven't seen anyone suspicious?" Lana verified after Joelle had slipped out of the nursery and back into the hall.

"No." Joelle smiled, but there was a steely resolve in her cop's eyes. "And if I did, there are armed ranch hands here to back me up. Also, Luca's downstairs. He'll be here until Duncan gets home."

Lana already knew all the security precautions, but it was good to hear them repeated.

"How are things going there?" Joelle asked.

Lana's mind was whirling with everything they'd learned, and it was hard for her to sort out what Slater had already told Duncan in an update call right before he'd left to observe the interviews.

"I suspect my parents know a lot more than they're saying about Stephanie and Buck," Lana admitted.

Joelle's quick sound of agreement told Lana that the deputy had come to the same conclusion. "Your father won't make it easy for the cops to investigate any wrongdoing."

"He won't. He did speak to Slater and me without his lawyers, but he had two with him when he went in for the official interview with Detective Thayer. I suspect they'll keep him and my mother from saying something they'd rather keep to themselves."

And it riled Lana to the core that they would do that instead of leaving no stone unturned to get justice for their murdered daughter. Yes, Buck was dead, but there was no absolute proof that he'd actually killed Stephanie. It was possible his accomplice had done that.

Lana mentally stopped and shook her head.

She couldn't see Marsh or her parents sneaking into Stephanie's hospital room to kill her. But maybe one of them did. Or perhaps it'd been Taylor. That's why it was so important to speak to the woman, but Lana reminded herself that what Marsh had said about Taylor might not even be true. He could be throwing Taylor under a bus to cover up his own guilt. Still, she did recall Stephanie saying that she and Taylor were no longer friends.

The break room door opened, and thankfully this time Lana didn't reach for her gun. A sign that hopefully her nerves were settling just a little. Her nerves settled even more when she saw Slater.

"Joelle, call me if anything…well, if there's anything," Lana told the woman before they ended the call.

"Is everything okay at the ranch?" Slater asked, tipping his head to her phone.

Lana nodded. "I just wanted to see Cameron, so I Face-Timed with your sister." She went closer, studying his face to see if there were signs that he was about to deliver some devastating news.

But Slater shook his head. "Nothing new came out in the interviews. Your dad admitted on the record that he knew Buck had fathered Stephanie's child, but he said he got the info from an anonymous call made to one of the PIs he keeps on retainer."

Lana wanted to roll her eyes. "The PI could have hacked into police records to get it, or my father could have another mole here in Austin PD." Either, or both, was possible, and it was a reminder for Lana not to trust someone just because they were a cop.

Slater took hold of her hand and gave it a gentle squeeze. "Your mother broke down during her interview. The tears seemed real enough."

That didn't surprise Lana. "Stephanie was my mother's golden child. Well, more golden than me, anyway. She knew she stood no chance of pushing me into an arranged marriage, but I believe she thought she could pressure Stephanie into it."

"Pressure?" Slater questioned.

"Stephanie's been arrested twice. Once for DUI and another for possession of a small amount of narcotics. Both times, our parents got her out of it. No parole, no community service. The charges just went away. Stephanie never came out and said it, but I think she was worried they'd hold that over her and use it to keep her in line." She paused. "Obviously, that didn't work."

Slater stayed quiet a moment. "Maybe it did. Have you considered that Stephanie being in hiding was exactly what your parents wanted? No, that doesn't mean they wanted her dead," he was quick to add. "It could mean that they'd hoped to sweep the pregnancy under the rug and have her return to marry Marsh."

Lana thought back through her conversations with Stephanie, and while her sister had never admitted to something like that, it could definitely be true. And that meant she had possibly been used as a dupe in all of this.

Slater's grip tightened on her hand, and he eased her to him. No kiss this time. He just held her while she tried to process another disturbing possibility in this investigation.

"Do you want me to go ahead and call Sonya so we can start the drive back to Saddle Ridge?" he asked.

Her first instinct was to say yes because she desperately wanted to see the baby. But Lana held back on that response and spelled out her concern. "Be honest. If I'm near Cameron, will that put him in more danger?"

Slater pulled back from her and met her gaze. "I don't know. If we go with the theory of Buck wanting to eliminate any competition for his family estate, then there shouldn't be a threat to Cameron and you since Buck's dead."

True. But the threat still felt very real. "No other relatives who might take up claim to the money?"

"No. I checked on that while I was in observation for the interviews. With Patrick and Buck both deceased, the inheritance would go to their heirs. Right now, that's only Cameron, and there isn't anyone on record who could challenge that claim."

Lana didn't want a penny of that estate for Cameron, but she also knew it might not be her decision to make. "What about heirs who might come forward? A secret baby maybe?"

"It's possible," he admitted, "but I can't see Buck working with someone who could inherit something he wanted to keep all for himself."

"No," she agreed. "So, maybe not a threat for the money but possibly Buck left orders with his accomplice. Orders to kill me because I helped hide Stephanie from him."

"Maybe." He paused, repeated that and then groaned softly. "But this feels bigger than that. Buck could have killed you on the spot, but he didn't. He stunned you instead and was obviously going to try to escape with you."

"He could have just wanted a human shield," Lana muttered, blinking back the flashbacks. "The plan could have been to kill me as soon as he was out of harm's way."

If so, that bolstered her revenge theory, that Buck wanted

her to pay for helping Stephanie. But would he have been so obsessed with payback that he wanted to strike out at her from beyond the grave?

Or was this about something else?

Something that involved her parents and maybe Marsh, too? If so, she and Slater could dig into that in Saddle Ridge.

"Call Sonya," Lana said just as her phone rang, and the moment she saw the caller, she answered it on speaker. "Taylor," she greeted, but she didn't manage to say more because Taylor spoke right over her.

"Why does an Austin cop want to talk to me?" Taylor demanded. "She left a voicemail telling me to contact her. What does she want?"

Lana ignored the woman and went with a question of her own. "Where are you, Taylor?"

Taylor's huff was plenty loud. "Why does an Austin cop want to talk to me?" she repeated, enunciating each word as if talking to a child.

Lana debated how to go with this, but then Slater gave her a nod. "The cops want to talk to you about Stephanie's death."

"Of course," she said in the same tone as an annoyance but not anything big. "Well, they'll waste my time and theirs because I don't know anything about it. She's dead, period." Taylor paused. "She is dead, right? That wasn't all some kind of stupid hoax, was it?"

"Stephanie's dead," Lana verified, speaking around the sudden lump in her throat. Even though she and Stephanie weren't best pals, it still hurt to hear Taylor's callous attitude toward her sister.

"Good," Taylor declared, but then she must have realized who she was talking to. "I'm sorry for your loss and all, but you know I'd be lying if I said I wish Stephanie was alive."

"Yes," Lana softly agreed, and then went with another question. "Why did you hate Stephanie so much?"

A burst of air left Taylor's mouth, not quite laughter but close. "Oh, let me count the ways. I was seeing Marsh when Stephanie horned in on our relationship. She got your parents and Marsh's to persuade him to dump me so Stephanie and he could go through with what would have basically been a business merger marriage."

Lana thought back to something Marsh had said. "Marsh called Stephanie the love of his life."

That brought on a string of raw profanity from Taylor, and she ended it with, "No way in hell. He just said that to keep your precious daddy on his side. Marsh has political aspirations, too, and Leonard Walsh is his ticket. That's all."

Lana wasn't sure she'd ever heard Marsh mention anything about politics, but it was possible he was brownnosing her father to keep in his good graces. But Marsh's feelings for Stephanie had seemed genuine. *Seemed.*

"Now that Stephanie's out of the way, Marsh will come back to me," Taylor went on. "And I can play nice with your father, too, because that's how much I want Marsh."

"Did you want Marsh enough to kill Stephanie?" Lana blurted before she could stop herself.

Taylor made an outraged gasp. "No. Of course not. That man on the news killed her. The same man who tried to murder you."

It didn't surprise Lana that the attack had already hit the media, and she wondered just how much detail was already out there. "So you didn't have any part in Stephanie's murder? Because that's what the cops want to question you about."

"No part whatsoever," Taylor insisted. "And I'll tell the detective that, too. There's no crime in hating a man-stealing ex-friend." She paused. "I've heard some rumors. Did Stephanie have Marsh's baby?"

Slater pressed his finger to his mouth in a *keep quiet about that* gesture. Lana hadn't planned on spilling it, anyway. "Why would you care if the child is Marsh's?" Lana argued.

"Because a baby would give him a tie to Stephanie. I don't want any ties." Her tone was now one of a pouty child. "I want him to see her for what she was. A cheater who didn't care one bit about him. If Stephanie gave birth to his baby, then he might never get over her."

Lana couldn't be sure, but it sounded as if Taylor choked back a sob. She doubted the sadness, or whatever emotion she'd heard, had anything to do with Stephanie, though.

"You should talk to Detective Thayer about this," Lana finally said. Not that Thayer would answer the question of the baby's paternity, but the conversation might end up being productive for the investigation.

"I don't want to talk to her," Taylor whined. "In fact, I'm not going to talk to any cops. They'll have to arrest me first, and then I'll use my lawyers to bury them."

That was a threat with no teeth because Thayer had cause to interview Taylor. The woman's hatred for Stephanie was plenty motive to work with Buck to commit murder.

Taylor ended the call, but before Lana could even put her phone away, it rang again, and she saw yet another familiar name.

"It's Julia Munson," Lana told Slater. "Someone I work with at Sencor." She answered it and said, "Julia, I'm putting you on speaker. Deputy Slater McCullough is here with me."

"Hello, Deputy McCullough," Julia greeted, and she launched right into the reason for the call. "We found something that probably won't be a news flash to you, but it confirms something. We interviewed visitors at the hospital where Stephanie died, and a new father, Asa Burkhart, was recording the maternity ward where his daughter had just been born. I'm sending you the footage now."

Moments later, Lana's phone dinged again, and she automatically held her breath. Julia had said this wouldn't be a surprise, so Lana already had an idea of what Slater and she were about to see. Still, it felt as if someone had clamped a vise around her lungs.

The recording loaded, and there were a couple of seconds of the new father panning his phone around while providing a few verbal details like the name of the hospital, the room number and the obstetrician. When the camera shifted toward the other end of the hall, Lana saw the man.

Buck.

He was in a small alcove with the vending machines, and he peered out. Just seeing him gave Lana another slam of the flashbacks of him stunning and grabbing her in the parking lot. But those slams were a drop in the bucket compared to what she felt as she watched him move out of vending and across the hall. He disappeared into Stephanie's room.

Lana nearly shouted to alert someone to stop him. But the avalanche of dread came when she realized it was too late for that. Buck had already murdered her sister and now he, too, was dead.

That was all of the footage, the blur of motion as Buck went into Stephanie's room. The new father had obviously finished recording since there was no footage of Buck coming out.

"The hospital security cameras were tampered with," Julia explained, "but they were working again by the time you came back to the hospital with the baby. There's about a half-hour lapse between Buck entering the room and your arrival."

A half hour when Lana hadn't known that her sister had been murdered. "Yes," Lana said. "I was driving around, deciding what to do. Stephanie had wanted me to take the baby to Slater, but I decided to go back and talk to her, to make sure she was certain this was the right thing to do. I didn't see Buck when I left the first time, but I believe I saw him after I came back."

"You probably did," Julia provided. "We got footage from a dash camera of a taxi that shows Buck outside the hospital thirty-two minutes after he went into Stephanie's room. That would have given you time to drive around and return."

So he had lingered around. Maybe because he'd been trying to find Stephanie's baby. It sickened Lana to think about what could have happened when she saw Buck outside her sister's room, how close he had been to Cameron.

"Was anyone with Buck?" Slater asked.

"No," Julia answered, "but we're checking for other dashcams and private security equipment to try to track his movements. There are traffic cams around there, but it's my guess he avoided those since Austin PD hasn't been able to find any footage of him."

That was Lana's guess, too. Clearly, Buck had been concerned about being recorded, and that's why he, or maybe his accomplice, had tampered with the hospital security cameras.

"There's more," Julia added a moment later, and Lana could tell from her coworker's tone that this was not going to be good news. "I'm guessing you're both familiar with a woman named Taylor Galway?"

Lana certainly hadn't expected Julia to bring her up. "Yes. In fact, she called me right before you did."

"Did she admit to hiring a computer hacker?" Julia asked.

"No," Slater and Lana answered in unison.

"I thought not. It's not something you'd admit to a cop," Julia added. "Anyway, last night Taylor hired BoBo."

Lana groaned and looked up at Slater to provide an explanation. "BoBo is a well-known hacker with no loyalty whatsoever. His favorite scam is to have a client pay him well for info and then to turn around and find out how he can get even more money by informing someone of the hacking."

"Bingo," Julia agreed. "And about an hour ago, BoBo, aka Robbie Jansky, called here asking to speak to you. He said you'd be very interested in some information he came by. I told him you were tied up with some personal stuff and agreed to the thousand bucks he was asking for."

"I'll pay you back," Lana was quick to say.

"I knew you would, and I also figured it'd be worth the price. BoBo usually has something good. And, Deputy McCullough, I know all of this must be setting your cop's teeth on edge, but please understand, we don't use any of the hacked info in court cases. We use it as more of a jumping-off point to find our own data and sources to corroborate what he gave us."

Julia had been right about Slater's teeth being on edge. There was definitely some disapproval on his face, but that didn't stop him from pressing Julia for what she'd learned. "And did this hacker give you something good this time?"

"He did." Julia stopped, sighed. "Well, you might consider it more of a hornet's nest, but here goes. BoBo hacked into Leonard's emails and learned that Lana's father not only knew Stephanie was pregnant, but he also knew her location at least for the last three months she was alive. There's a flurry of emails about it between him and one of his PIs."

Lana wanted to curse, and it meant her father had out-and-out lied to her. Of course, she suspected that wasn't the first time he'd done something like that.

"The PI had Stephanie and Lana under surveillance," Julia went on. "And Buck, too."

"Buck?" Slater repeated.

"Buck," Julia verified. "The emails don't come out and say that Leonard knew Buck had gotten Stephanie pregnant, but Leonard instructed his PI to keep close tabs on the man to make sure he didn't go sniffing around Stephanie again."

"And did he keep close tabs on Buck?" Lana wanted to know. Because if he had, her father might have known that Buck planned to kill Stephanie.

"He did. There's another flurry of reports about that and even some surveillance-type photos of Buck shopping and eating out."

"Please tell me Buck was with someone in those photos," Lana said. "Someone who could have been his accomplice."

"Nothing, but again, this is a jumping-off point. Using the hacked PI reports, we now have some locations where we know Buck was. You know how this works, Lana. We'll go to those locations and talk to people. Look for more security footage. We'll create a digital map of where he was and who he might have encountered."

Yes, Lana did know this was how it worked. The info from BoBo was essentially tips from a criminal informant, and none of it could be used to make an arrest. However, if the accomplice did turn up on camera or through eyewitness accounts, then the cops could get the pieces to put the person behind bars.

Lana hoped.

She had to believe there'd be justice for her sister and a safe future for Cameron. That she wouldn't have to spend the rest of her life looking over her shoulder for a killer.

"Now, to the hornet's nest," Julia added a moment later.

Lana shook her head. "I thought that was my father knowing about Stephanie and Buck."

"No, there's more. I just don't know if it's related to Stephanie or if it means anything at all, but the way it's worded makes me think there's something your dad's trying to cover up."

"What?" Lana managed to say.

Julia cleared her throat. "Does the name Alicia mean anything to either of you?"

Lana felt as if someone had punched her, and she figured from the way Slater's jaw tightened, he felt the same way. "Alicia Monroe," he provided. "My father was investigating her murder when he was killed. And we recently learned that Buck was a person of interest in Alicia's death."

"Yes, I pieced that together when I did a search for the name. The email didn't mention her surname, by the way," Julia tacked onto that. She stopped, muttered an apology. "Let me start from the beginning. In one of Leonard's emails to his PI, the PI expressed some concern about Stephanie being a loose cannon. His exact words," she emphasized.

"Did my father say why?" Lana asked.

"The timing fits for him finding out she was pregnant so maybe that's it. But it was also around the time your dad first mentioned Buck and that he needed to be monitored. Again, Leonard's exact word. And now here's the hornet's nest. Leonard adds, and I quote, *I don't want another Alicia on my hands.*"

"Oh, God," Lana heard herself mutter.

She looked up at Slater to see his reaction. Every muscle in his face had turned to iron. And Lana knew this was indeed a hornet's nest.

Lana cursed. Had her own dad played some part in murdering Slater's father?

Chapter Nine

Slater sat in the living room of the safe house and continued to scour the reports that were pouring in. Reports from Duncan, Luca, Julia and Detective Thayer. Nothing was as nerve-rattling as Julia's earlier news.

I don't want another Alicia on my hands.

Still, Slater was hoping he'd find something to either link Leonard to Alicia's and his dad's murders or be able to clear him as a suspect. After all, everything was circumstantial. Even that remark about Alicia. Leonard could have possibly just been worried about Buck murdering someone else, and in this case, that someone else would be Stephanie.

But there was a problem with that theory.

How had Leonard even known about Buck's connection to Alicia? Slater had only recently learned of it himself. And if Leonard had indeed suspected that Buck murdered Alicia, why hadn't he given that info to the cops?

That was one of at least a dozen questions for which Slater didn't have an answer, and it was the reason he was glad Lana and he had decided to delay the trip back to Saddle Ridge so they could immerse themselves here in the investigation. Exactly what they'd been doing for the past three hours.

Getting to the safe house, though, hadn't exactly been

a piece of cake. Within minutes of leaving the police station with Sonya as backup, they realized they were being followed. Slater had called in the plates to Thayer, who'd quickly informed him that the vehicle belonged to a PI agency that Leonard frequently employed.

Since Slater hadn't wanted the PI or Leonard to know the location of the safe house, that'd meant trying to lose it. Not easy in Austin traffic. So Slater had called in the big guns. He'd had Thayer send out a patrol cop to pull over the vehicle. The moment that'd happened, Slater and Sonya had sped away.

Thankfully, that'd been the only drama of the afternoon, and now Lana sat across from him, working on her laptop and probably digging through the same reports he was. He was hoping a second pair of eyes would catch something he might miss. Hoping, too, that they'd get that one vital piece of info that would blow this case wide open.

Slater hated that the hornet's nest revelations had come from a hacker. As a cop, he wanted to find this BoBo and arrest him. But as the son of a murdered man, he was grateful for what they might be able to use to build a case against Leonard. So far, though, they didn't have nearly enough for that.

Because he was a cop, Slater had had a fierce debate with himself when it came to telling Detective Thayer about the hacked emails. No way could she use any part of them in her investigation, but it hadn't felt right to keep them from her. And Lana had agreed. Even though it might ultimately cast a negative light on Sencor for dealing with hackers like BoBo, Thayer needed to have the big picture.

Thayer, of course, hadn't exactly thanked him for spilling details that would essentially muddy the investigative waters and might lead to nothing. Still, Slater figured it wouldn't hurt to have a third person, Thayer, looking at this new information with the hopes of verifying it. So far, though, verification simply hadn't happened.

"Ted Bennington," Slater said, hoping that by saying it aloud, it would jog something. Lana immediately looked up from her laptop, her attention zooming straight to him. "He's worked for your father for over twenty-five years." And he was the PI in the hacked emails. "Do you know him?"

"I've met him a couple of times when he came to visit my dad. He seemed all business, and he certainly never said anything about his actual job."

That made sense. Leonard wouldn't keep a blabbermouth on the payroll. "Bennington would have worked for him when Alicia was murdered, and we know that Stephanie went to a party at Alicia's. So, if it weren't for those three last words in the email, I would dismiss what Leonard said as some cautionary tale of him not wanting Stephanie to end up dead like Alicia."

Lana nodded. Then sighed. "But those three last words are there. *On my hands*," she recited. "That sounds a lot more personal than a cautionary tale."

It did, and that's why Slater was piecing together other theories. "Bennington or another PI could have seen or heard something that would ID Buck as Alicia's killer. I'm having a hard time figuring out why they wouldn't have taken that info to the cops, but maybe what they saw or overheard involved Stephanie. Not as a killer," he was quick to add.

She nodded again, and her forehead bunched up as she gave that some thought. "But maybe the PI heard or saw something that would in turn incriminate Stephanie. My dad would have definitely tried to cover that up, and in doing so, he might have covered up Buck's guilt. That could work." She paused. "But then why would Buck go after your father?"

Slater shrugged. "Maybe my dad was asking the wrong questions, and Buck got spooked."

"And maybe my father got spooked, too," Lana added. She set her laptop aside and leaned forward. "Just speculation here, but whatever the PI or my father learned about Alicia could make him some kind of accessory after the fact. That's some serious jail time."

"Yeah, it would be." And that led Slater to another point. "Alicia's body was never found, so maybe that's where Leonard comes in. Maybe he or his PI helped Buck dispose of the body in some way." He stopped and scrubbed his hand over his face. "But again, his reason for doing that would be to protect Stephanie."

Lana made a sound of agreement. "Stephanie never once mentioned anything about Alicia's murder, and I think she would have let something slip if she had witnessed it."

Slater made his own sound of agreement. "But what if Buck convinced Leonard that Stephanie had been involved in some way? That would spur Leonard to do a cover-up."

"It would, and it would also explain why my father wanted to monitor Buck. Maybe he wanted to make sure Buck didn't get too close to Stephanie." She stopped. "Of course, all the monitoring didn't stop Buck from killing her."

Slater heard the pain in Lana's voice. Saw it on her face, too, and he set his own laptop aside to go to her. Yes, it wasn't exactly a safe move, not with them being alone, but he hated to see her suffer like this. However, Slater had barely reached Lana before his phone rang, and when he saw Detective Thayer's name on the screen, he knew it was a call he needed to take.

"You're on speaker," Slater said when he answered. And he hoped she was calling with good news.

"I just interviewed Taylor Galway," the detective said.

Surprised, Slater shook his head. "I guess she changed her mind about coming in."

"Well, she brought three lawyers with her and spent most of the interview saying no comment, but she came in without any additional prodding."

"Did Taylor admit to posting those pictures of Stephanie?" Lana asked.

Thayer groaned softly. "That was one of the no comments. Ditto for hiring a hacker. About the only thing she did admit to was that she hated Stephanie and that she had an alibi for the time of Stephanie's murder. It's an airtight alibi, by the way. She was front and center at some charity fashion show."

"As an accomplice, she wouldn't need an alibi," Slater muttered.

"No, she wouldn't, but she might have thought it best if she wasn't anywhere near the hospital at the time of the murder. And she wasn't. The fashion show was on the other side of the city." Thayer paused a moment. "I didn't get Buck's phone records until after Taylor left so I'll have to get the woman back in here to question her about it."

Slater latched right onto that. So did Lana. They both moved closer to the phone. "Buck called Taylor?"

"Twice," Thayer verified. "But don't get your hopes up. It wasn't recent. The techs had to go back six years to find it. Hardly a smoking gun unless they'd been planning murder all this time."

No. Those calls were likely about something else. Probably a party or something.

"Any calls about a murder would have likely been done

on burner phones," Slater muttered. "What about the phone Buck had on him when he died?"

"A burner, but he hadn't used it to call anyone yet. There weren't any in his house, either, but there were two crushed ones in his garbage. The techs will see if they can recover anything from those. Other than the phones, there was no evidence in his house as to what he'd been planning."

So Buck had been thorough. Slater had hoped he wouldn't be. "Have the techs been able to access any of Buck's emails?"

"Not a one," Thayer said. "Everything on his laptop was encrypted, and so far, they haven't been able to get past it. They'll keep trying," she tacked onto that, maybe just trying to give them a glimmer of hope. "What about the two of you?" Thayer asked. "Have you found anything?"

"No," Slater said, and Lana echoed the same. It was Lana, though, who continued.

"If the hacked emails do point to my father as being Buck's accomplice, my father will never admit to it. In fact, we won't even get to ask the question because his lawyers will block it," Lana spelled out. "So I'm thinking of calling my mother to see if she knows anything."

"You think she'll admit it if she does know something?" Thayer asked. "Because I didn't get the impression she'd go against your father."

"She won't," Lana was quick to say. "But I think she's grieving for Stephanie, and that makes her vulnerable." Lana stopped, cringed. "I know that sounds callous—"

"It doesn't," Slater interrupted. "You need answers about your sister's death, and your mother might be able to provide them. And, no, I'm not saying Pamela had anything to do with killing her own daughter, but she's got eyes and ears, and she might have heard or seen something that'll help us ID Buck's accomplice."

"Yes," Thayer quickly added. "All of that. I have no idea if this accomplice is dangerous and will come after the two of you. Or heaven forbid, the baby. But I know I'll feel a whole lot better once we have this person. Call your mother," she insisted. "And let me know what she says."

Lana assured Thayer that she would, and Slater ended the call just as Lana took out her own phone. However, she didn't press her mother's number. She sat there a moment as if trying to gather her thoughts. He didn't blame her. This could turn out to be a critical conversation.

"If I tell her you're listening, then my mother will almost certainly be more careful about what she says," Lana said. "But I want you to hear every word. You might pick up on something I miss."

He nodded, though he knew what this meant. If the call was on speaker and Pamela spilled something incriminating, then her lawyers could argue that the admission had been obtained illegally. But she could only do that if she knew Slater was listening.

Slater cursed because he knew what he was about to do. He was going to bend the hell out of the law with the goal of finding a killer's accomplice. No way would he have done it if the threat to life had been over, but it wasn't. Lana and possibly the baby could still be in the line of fire.

He nodded. "Put the call on speaker," he instructed. "I won't say anything to let her know I'm listening."

She nodded as well, and she finally pressed her mother's number. Thankfully, they didn't have to wait long because Pamela answered on the first ring.

"Lana," her mother said, the word rushing out with her heavy breath. "Are you all right?"

Since this was more concern than the woman had previously shown, Slater was surprised. Clearly, so was Lana.

"I'm safe," Lana replied, her response obviously cautious.

"Good." Her mother let out another heavy breath and repeated it. "I was worried because you refused the bodyguards your father wanted you to have."

"Yes, and we got rid of the PI he had following us," Lana was quick to point out.

"Your father and I are both worried about you," her mother said as if that excused everything. "We don't want you involved in something that could be dangerous. Deputy McCullough can't protect you the way we can."

Lana looked at him and managed a weary smile. Despite everything that was going on, Slater latched right onto that smile, savoring it and committing it to memory. He and Lana hadn't had many quiet, warm moments, but that was one of them.

It didn't last.

"Are you there?" Pamela demanded. "Did you hear what I said?"

"I heard," Lana assured her. "Where is Dad now?"

"In his office. He's so upset," she added in a mutter, and she lowered her voice to a whisper. "Some man called him and said he'd been hired to hack into his emails. He tried to blackmail your father."

BoBo had obviously struck again. The hacker was attempting to get paid three times for his crime.

"Blackmail," Lana repeated. "What is he going to do about it?"

"I'm not sure," Pamela was quick to say. "He's with some of the lawyers and the PIs now."

But not the cops. Nope. Slater was betting Leonard wouldn't be reporting this to the police, and he made a mental note to tell Julia that she should warn BoBo that he could be in danger for poking a rattlesnake like Leonard.

"What emails did this man hack?" Lana pressed.

"I have no idea, but they must have been important because your father hit the roof. I'm sure he'll find the hacker and make him pay."

Yeah. Slater definitely needed to give Julia a heads-up.

"Mom, I'm calling to let you know that a video has surfaced," Lana continued. "It proves Buck murdered Stephanie."

Pamela gasped. "Oh, God. So it's true. He really did kill her."

"It's true," Lana verified, and then paused. "There's been a lot of security camera footage collected of Buck, and one of Dad's PIs was following him. Did you know that?"

"No." Pamela sounded adamant about that, too. "Why…" But that trailed off. "Because he was worried about Stephanie. Rightfully so." She cried out a hoarse sob. "I wish the PI would have been able to stop Buck. I wish someone could have, and then Stephanie would still be alive."

"Yes," Lana muttered, and it seemed to Slater that she was affected by her mother's grief.

"Alive," Pamela repeated a moment later, "and she would have done the right thing."

Lana pulled back her shoulders. "The right thing?"

"Stephanie would have married Marsh." Again, Pamela was adamant. "I'm sure of it."

That caused Lana's sympathy for her mother to vanish. "I think Stephanie's priority would have been her son." She looked as if she wanted to add a *maybe* to that, and he understood why. After all, Stephanie had had Lana bring the baby to him, so maybe she'd never had any intention of raising the child.

"I think you're wrong," Pamela argued. "Stephanie showed no interest in being a mother."

"That might be, but she had a baby," Lana argued right back. "Your grandson."

"That child is not my grandson," Pamela spat out.

Lana's eyes went cold and flat. "So you won't be challenging me for custody of him?"

"Of course not..." She stopped again. "Wait, are you saying you intend to raise that baby?"

"My nephew," Lana said. "Yes. I love him and I'll raise him. I think that's what Stephanie would want me to do."

"Stephanie would have wanted to put her past behind her and marry Marsh. Marsh is a very forgiving man, practically a saint, but I don't believe even he would want to raise Stephanie's mistake. Unless...has Marsh said something to you about that? Is he willing to raise the child with you?"

Lana cursed, and it wasn't under her breath. It was plenty loud enough for her mother to hear. Pamela scolded her, but Lana talked right over her. "Stephanie did the paperwork to declare Slater as the baby's father, so if I raise Cameron with anyone, it'll be him."

"With that cop?" Pamela said like the profanity Lana had just used. The woman geared up for what would no doubt be a tirade, but Lana ended the call.

"Sorry for bringing you into that," Lana muttered. "I don't expect you to be a father to Cameron."

She was giving him an out, but Slater didn't jump on it. At the moment, he wasn't sure what his future would be with Lana and the baby, but he sure as hell didn't want to be excluded.

Sighing, he moved onto the sofa with her, but before he doled out any TLC to repair the damage her mother had just done, he tapped her phone. "Let Julia know to warn BoBo."

She nodded so fast that calling Julia must have already been on her to-do list. Lana sent the text, and then every last drop of energy seemed to drain right out of her. Or so he thought. But then Lana did something that he was certain shocked both of them.

She kissed him.

Her mouth landed on his, not particularly hard, but this wasn't just a peck of reassurance, either. It was a full-blown kiss that she quickly deepened.

The taste of her roared through him and fired up everything inside him. Much too hot, much too fast. This was the kind of kiss that lovers shared. A foreplay moment right before landing in bed. And while his body was suddenly all up for that, Slater figured it wasn't a good idea. Not at the moment, anyway.

Lana only took her mouth from his when she was forced to breathe, and she gulped in some air. "I'm not going to say I'm sorry," she insisted. "I'm not going to regret this." She stopped, though, and squeezed her eyes shut a moment. "All right, maybe I regret it some. It feels as if I'm using you to help me get through the grief."

Slater wanted to nip this in the bud. "Were you attracted to me before Stephanie died?" he asked.

She blinked, nodded. "Yes."

"Then the heat is real, period, and there's no rule against kissing someone you're attracted to because it feels good. Or because it makes you feel as if you're not in this alone. Because you're not."

Lana stared at him a long time, and the corner of her mouth lifted as if she might manage a smile. The sound of her phone ringing put an automatic stop to that, though. She muttered something about it probably being her mother and looked at the screen, only to shake her head.

"It's Taylor," she said, and Lana's sigh told Slater that she really didn't have the desire to deal with the woman, but that didn't stop her from answering the call on speaker.

"I want you to meet me, and I don't want you to bring a lot of cops with you." Taylor said in lieu of a greeting. "Just Deputy McCullough and you. Hear that? Just the two of you. I can't make it today, but I'll be at True Blue Coffeeshop tomorrow morning at nine."

"And why would I want to go there?" she asked. "Why do you want to see me?"

Taylor huffed. "You'll want to do it because it's important." She added a duh.

"If it's that important, why not just tell me over the phone?" Lana demanded.

"Because I know something you don't, that's why." The woman's tone was beyond mere snark. "Be there tomorrow if you want to know the name of the person who teamed up with Buck to murder your sister."

Chapter Ten

Lana made the mistake of taking in a deep breath just as Slater walked into the living room after finishing his shower. He smelled amazing, not just of soap, but his own unique scent that lingered just beneath.

His hair was damp, and he ran a hand through it, all that was needed to make it look as if it'd been tousled and fallen in the perfect way to frame his face. A face that apparently had the ability to arouse her with a mere glance.

If they hadn't been neck-deep in an investigation, she might have gone the reckless route and kissed him again. But she instinctively knew that a kiss wouldn't just stay a kiss. The heat had escalated too much for that. The next time their mouths met, they'd likely end up in bed. That's why she'd kept her distance from him the night before and now this morning. And she'd been faring fairly well until she'd seen this hot, damp cowboy version of the man who seemed to have nailed down more than his share of hotness.

Lana cleared her throat and drank some coffee while she glanced out at the Austin skyline. She certainly hadn't expected to spend another night at the safe house, but that's what she and Slater had ended up doing. All to accommodate Taylor, who wouldn't budge on giving them the info unless it was in person. Of course, it had occurred to them that this could all be a ruse to draw her and Slater out, but after a long debate, they had decided to go for it.

With serious precautions.

Even though Taylor had insisted they not bring any cops, that wasn't going to happen. Detective Thayer and some of her fellow officers had already scoped out the coffee shop, and while they would be keeping watch in a building across the street, one of the cops would be undercover as a waitress. After all, if Taylor truly did know something about an accomplice and had withheld that, the woman could be charged with obstruction of justice.

Taylor would no doubt curse and protest if an arrest happened, but Lana didn't care. The only thing she wanted was the name of the person responsible so he or she could be arrested. Then, she and Slater could return to Saddle Ridge, and…well, she didn't know what would happen next, but "next" couldn't even begin until she was certain Cameron would be safe.

"How's the baby this morning?" he asked, tipping his head to her phone she was still holding. Slater also knew that while he was showering, she'd phoned his sister.

"He was awake and so alert," Lana said, well aware that she sounded like a gushing new mother. But Cameron had indeed been alert, and even though she'd read that a newborn's eyes couldn't focus well, it had seemed the baby was looking right at her.

"You'll be back with him soon," Slater assured her.

"Yes, hopefully soon and with no killer after us." She waved that off, though, when he started toward her, no doubt to dole out some TLC. "It's okay. I don't have much faith that Taylor can actually give us a name, but I'm hoping whatever she tells us will lead to something."

Slater made a sound of agreement and sank down on

the sofa next to her, bringing his scent and that amazing face even closer to her. "If Taylor is the accomplice, then the danger could be over even if there isn't enough to arrest her. Everything in her background points to her being an obsessed ex-girlfriend. She has no history of any kind of violence and no criminal record."

That was all true. Marsh hadn't even gotten a restraining order against Taylor when she'd basically stalked him. And not once had she attacked Marsh. Well, nothing official anyway, and Marsh certainly hadn't mentioned it.

"You're saying that without Buck to do her bidding Taylor won't try to kill us," she stated.

Slater nodded. "I can't say the same, though, about what she might do to Marsh, and I hope he's taking precautions. Taylor won't be happy if he doesn't reunite with her now that Stephanie is out of the picture."

Again, that was true, and while it would be awful if Taylor hurt or killed him, Lana had her own concerns without taking him on.

Slater's phone dinged with a text, and Lana immediately guessed who it was. And she was right.

"Sonya's waiting for us out front," Slater said as he read the message.

That meant it was time for them to leave for the True Blue Coffeeshop. Time to step out the door and pray that all their security measures were enough to keep them alive.

Since the plan was for Slater and her to return to Saddle Ridge right after the meeting, they grabbed their things, and Lana locked up on their way out. They got in the cruiser in the garage, checking their surroundings as Slater backed out.

Lana glanced at Sonya, who was also making some glances around, but she thankfully didn't see any alarm on the deputy's face. Didn't see anything or anyone suspicious, either.

Both she and Slater had already mapped out the safest route to the coffee shop, so they didn't go the most direct way since it would have meant long stops at traffic lights. Stops where someone could have taken shots at them. Instead, they went the side streets that were not only less busy but also meant fewer stops.

When they arrived at the True Blue, Slater went past the shop and as planned parked in a lot just around the corner. Of course, anyone looking for them would easily spot the cruiser, but they hadn't wanted to use a lot where someone would have had time to plant explosives or such.

They parked, and after getting the green light from Thayer, she and Slater went inside while Sonya waited in her cruiser. The deputy would be able to swoop in quickly if something went wrong and get Slater and Lana out of there fast.

Still keeping watch, they stepped in to the expected strong scents of coffee and sugary pastries. True to its name, the decor was of varying shades of blue, and despite it being crowded, Lana noticed Taylor right away. She was at one of the back booths, away from the storefront windows. That was by design as well, since it was where the undercover cop had seated her.

Taylor was drinking something white and foamy from a cobalt mug while reading something on her phone and didn't seem to immediately spot them. When Slater and Lana slid into the seat across from her, she finally looked up.

"I thought you might chicken out and not come," Taylor grumbled. "You'll be glad you didn't."

Lana hoped she was right, and she wondered if Taylor

knew what kind of risk she was taking. Especially if she was about to spill anything about the hacker she'd hired. Thayer wouldn't arrest Taylor on the spot for that, but Lana had no doubts that the woman would eventually be charged. For now, though, the plan was to see if Taylor actually had any info helpful to the investigation.

Slater waved off a waitress who came over to ask if they wanted anything, and he pinned his stare to Taylor. "Tell us why we'll be glad about deciding to come here."

Taylor had a long sip of her drink first, and when she lifted her gaze, Lana saw the red in her eyes. Maybe from crying. But Lana figured she'd shed no tears for Stephanie. This had to be about something or someone else.

"Who's Buck's accomplice?" Slater came out and asked.

Annoyance flashed through Taylor's eyes. "I'll get to that, but there are some other things you need to know. Marsh and I are over. Yesterday, when I went to his place to try to comfort him, he basically told me to get lost. The SOB didn't even want to see me." She clamped her teeth over her bottom lip for a moment. "After all the waiting around I did for him, he wanted nothing to do with me."

That didn't surprise Lana, and judging from the sound Slater made, it didn't surprise him, either. Marsh was all about Stephanie. Well, he seemingly was anyway, and if he'd planned on getting back with Taylor, he likely would have done it after Stephanie disappeared. Did that mean that Taylor was about to try to get some revenge by naming Marsh as the accomplice?

"So, this means I don't care what happens to the SOB," Taylor went on. "And I'm done protecting him."

That got Lana's and Slater's attention. "You protected Marsh?" Slater questioned. "How?"

"By not telling the cops that Marsh knew where Stephanie was hiding out. He knew," Taylor insisted, shifting her gaze to Lana. "Marsh found out just a week before Stephanie was killed. And I think your father knew that Marsh had found out. He might have even been the one to tell Marsh."

Again, Lana wasn't surprised since she now knew that her father had indeed learned Stephanie's location. It was something he probably would have passed along to Marsh in the hopes that it would spur Stephanie and Marsh to reconcile.

"Did Marsh go see Stephanie when she was here in Austin?" Lana asked.

"Probably," Taylor spat out. "Of course, he never admitted that to me, and I don't have any actual proof that he saw her. But Marsh was a sad, sick puppy when it came to Stephanie, and he was too blind to see that Stephanie didn't even want him. I blame your father for that, too. He made Marsh believe the only woman for him was your precious sister."

Lana blamed her father for that as well. But then, he'd done a lot of things that she disapproved of.

"How did you learn that Marsh knew where Stephanie was?" Slater pressed when the woman fell silent.

Taylor's attention went back to her drink. "I had a PI keep track of him. I did it for his own good," she was quick to add. "Because I needed to know if he was about to make a huge mistake by trying to see Stephanie. Like I said, I was protecting him."

"Yet Stephanie is the one who ended up dead," Slater threw out there.

Taylor's gaze slashed back to him again. "Marsh didn't kill her. He's not Buck's accomplice."

"Do you believe that because you're still in love with Marsh?" Lana wanted to know.

"I believe it because it's true," Taylor snarled. "I didn't

ask you to come here so I could get you to arrest my ex-
lover. I want your father arrested."

Lana waited, but Taylor didn't add more. She certainly
didn't add any proof, and then it occurred to Lana what
might be going on here. Taylor clearly blamed Leonard for
orchestrating the relationship between Marsh and Stephanie, and Taylor wanted him to pay for that.

"Are you saying that Leonard is Buck's accomplice?"
Slater demanded.

Taylor gave a firm nod. And that was it. Nothing more.

Slater huffed. "If you have proof that Leonard is the accomplice, then you should have told Detective Thayer."

"I'm not telling her anything," Taylor snapped. "She
questioned me like I was a common criminal, and I won't
be treated like that."

"So instead you're telling us, knowing we'll report it to
Thayer," Slater summarized. On a heavy sigh, he leaned
back in his seat. "There's just one problem with that. No
cop will arrest Leonard Walsh just because of what you've
said. They need proof."

Taylor gave him an indignant look. "I have proof," she
said, picking up her phone from the table. "I remembered
this picture I took, but it took me a while to find it because
I've put my photos in several different online storages over
the years. It's all the proof you'll need that Leonard and
Buck are best buds."

Lana held her breath and waited while Taylor tapped
her screen and showed them the photo. It appeared to have
been taken at a party, not a recent one, either, and it was of
her father and Buck. Her father was smiling and had his
arm slung around a very youthful, fresh-faced Buck. There
were no traces of the thug that Buck had become in recent

years. In this shot, he looked like the other preppy-dressed partiers milling in the background.

One of those preppy partiers was Marsh. Lana had no trouble recognizing him, either. He was standing back from Buck and Leonard, but he didn't seem to have his attention on them.

"When was this taken?" Slater asked.

"According to the date in the storage cloud, it was nearly twenty years ago," Taylor answered. "That would have been my first year of college. I think Leonard was there because Marsh's family hosted it."

So that's why Marsh was there. Perhaps Lana's mother had been, too.

Slater made an odd sound, a sort of grunt that came deep from within his chest, and Lana turned to see what'd caused it. She doubted his reaction was because of this old picture of her father and Buck, which in no way proved they were best buds or had ever conspired to commit murder.

Slater took the phone, causing Taylor to snarl out a protest, but he ignored it and enlarged the photo. Not the portion with her father and Buck. But of the person next to them. And that's when Lana saw it.

Or rather Lana saw *her.*

Alicia Monroe.

Sweet heaven. It was the young woman who'd been murdered nearly twenty years ago. The woman whose murder Slater's father had been investigating. Slater clearly saw her, too, and he muttered some profanity under his breath.

"Buck was a person of interest in Alicia's murder," Slater said. "And here they are."

Yes, they were in the same photo, which was proof that Buck did indeed know her. But in this picture, there was an odd sort of dynamic going on. Marsh was looking at Alicia. Lana could see that now. And Alicia wasn't looking at either Buck or Marsh. No. Alicia and Leonard were staring at each other, and in that frozen snapshot of time, Lana could practically see the attraction sizzling between them.

Lana gasped. Oh, mercy. Had her father and Alicia been lovers?

Chapter Eleven

While Slater read through the latest report from Detective Thayer, he kept an eye on Lana. The worry was still etched on her face, but she was definitely more relaxed as she sat in the rocking chair and fed Cameron his bottle. Slater thought he was more relaxed as well now that they were back in Saddle Ridge.

But being home didn't mean they were safe.

He'd hoped Taylor would be able to give them proof of Buck's accomplice so the person could be arrested and any potential threat neutralized. That hadn't happened, though. The woman hadn't provided them with any proof that Leonard and Buck were coconspirators. Heck, she hadn't even given them proof that Leonard had been involved with Alicia.

It had certainly looked that way, though, to Slater.

And that created a boatload of questions and concerns. Had Leonard and Alicia had an affair? Maybe. Julia at Sencor was digging into that. But even if the pair had been lovers, it didn't mean Leonard or even Buck for that matter had been responsible for Alicia's death.

Still, the photo was pretty damning since Leonard was a married man, and at the time of that lustful look, he'd been nearly forty, and Alicia had been just eighteen. Any relationship between them would have been a scandal, but it wasn't anything Leonard could be arrested for.

Or even questioned about.

He and Lana had discussed that on the entire drive back to Saddle Ridge, and they'd agreed that if they confronted her father about it, he'd dismiss it as a simple party photo. Which it very well might be. That's why Julia and Lana were looking for more, and Slater was certain Lana would get back to the search when she'd finished feeding the baby.

He was thankful Cameron had needed a bottle. Thankful, too, that Lana had been the one to give it to him, and to burp him. Even with all the uncertainty surrounding this investigation, Lana needed this moment or two of downtime.

The other thing they needed was a long-term plan. For now, staying at his family's ranch was a good temporary solution. Here, in this makeshift nursery where Cameron had plenty of protection. Here, in the two guest rooms he and Lana were using where none of their suspects could come just waltzing up and try to finish what Buck had started.

But *here* wasn't home for Lana.

Soon, she'd want to find somewhere more permanent to live with Cameron. Slater was just hoping she'd hold off on that until Buck's accomplice had been arrested.

Lana was still holding Cameron against her shoulder when her phone dinged with a text. "It's Julia," she relayed to him, keeping her voice at a whisper. She glanced through whatever Julia had sent, sighed and got up to ease Cameron back into his crib. The baby didn't even stir and stayed fast asleep. "She just emailed me a report with some pictures."

Slater went to her, and they moved to the other side of the room where they'd set up a small office area, and she opened her laptop to access the email and two attached photos. Not of her father and Alicia but rather of Buck and

Stephanie at a party. These weren't from twenty years ago, either, and looked fairly recent.

"This was taken last year," Lana provided, reading through the report in the email. "Julia found them on social media." She paused to read some more. "Julia also interviewed four people who were at that party, and two of them verified that Stephanie and Buck had come together. Another, Cassandra Milburn, has agreed to talk to me about Stephanie."

Julia had provided the woman's number with instructions for Lana to call Cassandra first chance she got. Lana immediately did that, putting the call on speaker when it was answered.

"Lana?" the woman greeted. "Julia said you'd be calling me, and that Deputy Slater McCullough would be with you and that he'd want to talk to me, too."

"Yes," Lana verified. "You're on speaker, and Deputy Mc-Cullough is listening." She paused. "I don't believe we've met."

"We haven't. Stephanie told me about you, though, so when Julia brought up your name, I knew who you were."

"You were friends with Stephanie?" Lana asked.

"Friendly," Cassandra corrected. "We traveled in the same social circles and have similar backgrounds. My mother was an assistant attorney general for the state. Old money and a mile-wide snobbery streak," she added in a tone to indicate that had been a thorn in her side.

Yes, that was a similar background, and Slater was hoping that meant Stephanie had confided in this woman.

"How honest do you want me to be about your sister?" Cassandra came out and asked.

"Honest," Lana insisted.

"Good. Because I didn't want to paint a rosy picture when Stephanie was going through a tough time."

Lana sighed again. "A tough time with Buck?"

"No. With your parents. They were pressuring her to marry Marsh, and she was rebelling in her own way, and one of those ways was to hook up with Buck. I don't need to tell you that he was a bad boy to the core. Not the redeemable kind, either. I always thought Buck was dangerous, and when Stephanie got involved with him, I tried to warn her that she was playing with fire."

"Why did you think Buck was dangerous?" Slater asked, hoping this would dovetail with Alicia's murder as well.

"Because I dated him when I was sixteen," she admitted without hesitation. "He was an exciting adrenaline junkie who knew how to have fun. His mood could also change in a heartbeat." Cassandra's voice wavered on that last word.

"Was he ever violent with you?" Slater pressed.

"No, but after we had an argument, I thought the potential was there for violence. He scared me, Deputy Mc-Cullough, and that's why I ended things with him. He didn't take that well, and I didn't know how to handle him because I was a teenager, and he'd been my first boyfriend," Cassandra added. "After the breakup, he stalked me for a while until my mother intervened and put a stop to it. She never told me what she said to him, but Buck quit bothering me."

So, Buck didn't handle rejection well. At least he hadn't back then. Maybe that's what had happened with Alicia? Maybe he'd lost his temper and killed her, and Alicia hadn't had Cassandra's powerful mother to intercede.

"Was Buck ever violent with my sister?" Lana asked.

"I don't think so. They had a hot and fast affair, and like I said, I believe Stephanie was rebelling against your parents. And then she got pregnant," Cassandra tacked onto that.

Lana jumped right in with another question. "You knew she was pregnant?"

"Yes, I'm a doctor, and Stephanie came to me after she'd done a home pregnancy test. I can't get into the specifics of what we discussed since doctor-patient confidentiality continues even after death, but I will say that Stephanie was worried about how your parents would react."

Lana and he both stayed quiet a moment, processing that. "But she wasn't worried about Buck?"

Cassandra wasn't so quick to answer. "I thought you might ask that, and I've been trying to figure out what to say. Judging from the stories on the news, Buck murdered her? Is that right?"

"Yes," Lana confirmed.

Again, Cassandra took her time to respond. "I will say that whenever I met with Stephanie, she didn't claim to be scared of any person in particular. She was just adamant that I not tell anyone she was pregnant."

Slater considered that a moment. Since Cassandra had already warned Stephanie about Buck being dangerous, it seemed reasonable that Stephanie would have voiced any concerns she had about the father of her baby. Maybe, though, those concerns had surfaced later.

"I'm really sorry about Stephanie," Cassandra added a moment later. "Could you please tell me what will happen to her child?"

"He'll be taken care of," Lana was quick to say. "I have an online appointment with a lawyer tomorrow and will be petitioning for custody."

"Good, I'm glad," Cassandra said. "I have to go, but if you have any questions you think I might be able to answer, feel free to call me."

"I will," Lana assured her, and ended the call.

They sat there in silence for several moments, and Slater decided to spell out what they'd just learned. "Buck probably didn't sexually assault Stephanie."

Lana made a sound of agreement. "And she likely went into hiding, initially anyway, because of our parents and not because of Buck. That doesn't mean, though, that Buck didn't threaten her afterward."

Slater was fast to agree with that as well. "If Stephanie had trusted Buck, she wouldn't have done the Acknowledgment of Paternity, naming me as the baby's father."

Lana's gaze came to his and held. "You could challenge me for custody because of that. Stephanie obviously wanted you to raise her son."

"Because she knew I'd protect Cameron from Buck. Or from your parents. Or from anyone else for that matter who might be a threat to him," Slater reminded her. "And, no, I still have no intentions of challenging you for custody."

Lana didn't seem surprised by that, only reassured. Good. She had enough to deal with without worrying about Cameron's future.

"Thank you," she muttered, and she glanced at her laptop as if ready to go back to work.

But she didn't.

She stood, went to him, leaned down and kissed him. Slater hadn't seen it coming so he hadn't had time to steel himself for the heat. It hit him full blast and dissolved the reins he had on this need for her. With no reins, he moved right into the kiss as well, letting her taste and the feel of her mouth take him to another time, another place. Where there was no investigation, no threat. Where anything was possible.

He started to stand so he could pull her to him, but Lana placed her palm on his chest, indicating he should remain seated. Instead, she was the one who initiated the body-to-body contact by moving onto his lap. Her breasts landed against his chest, and her hip pressed against the zipper of his jeans.

Slater immediately felt the heat skyrocket. So did the need. Then again, the need was always there when it came to Lana, but with her mouth on his, it drilled the point home.

Everything inside him pointed to her. To this edgy heat that she had created inside him. To all these intense feelings he had for her. And there were so many feelings. Too many to sort out, and even if he had wanted to do that right now, he couldn't. No way could he think straight when she was kissing him like this.

She slid her hand around the back of his neck, bringing him even closer to her. Deepening the kiss. And giving the heat another jolt that it in no way needed. This wasn't just a kiss. This wasn't just foreplay. This was many steps beyond that, and it was those steps that could lead them straight to bed if they weren't careful.

Slater's body was all for them landing in bed, but his brain knew there would be consequences. Consequences that he did not want for Lana. When the timing was better, when it was right, he wanted only pleasure for her. Now, though, there would be guilt and doubt, and so many other things that he didn't want her to feel.

Even after mapping out all the reasons why he should stop, Slater didn't do that. He took more of the kiss. Took more of Lana. Until the need had turned into a fiery ache that was demanding to be sated.

"Just a little more," she murmured when he started to ease back from her.

The more was, well, a lot, but Slater just sank right into the kiss and let her take what she needed. Somewhere along the way, he lost sight of why they should even stop, and he found himself taking hold of her and pulling her closer. And closer. Until he'd turned Lana so she was now straddling him.

This definitely wasn't going to cool them down, but it gave him a good glimpse of what it would be like for them to have full-blown sex. It'd be amazing, that was for certain.

Amazing, with really bad timing.

He latched onto that thought again, but it wasn't helping him fight this battle he was having with himself. Slater couldn't figure out how to make himself stop. Thankfully, though, Lana seemed to figure it out. He eased back, gulping in air, and she looked at him.

"I'm not sorry," she said just as Slater said, "Don't you dare apologize."

The corner of her mouth quivered, and she smiled. It was an incredible thing to see, and it eased some of the ache in his body. Not the need, though. Nope. It was there to stay. But it felt so good to see her smile.

"You've been a fantasy of mine for a long time now," she admitted.

He was flattered. And aroused all over again. Slater hoped, though, that she wasn't about to qualify that with something he didn't want to hear. Something along the lines that it would never work between them. Thankfully, she didn't go that route. She just kept it at that, which kept the door open to them fulfilling a fantasy or two when things weren't so uncertain.

"Work," she said as if trying to convince herself to move.

But she didn't move one inch. Lana stayed on his lap and continued to stare at him until that need took on a whole new urgency. Slater was a hundred percent certain he would have acted on that urgency had Lana's phone not started ringing. Both of them muttered some profanity at the interruption and then checked the crib to make sure the sound hadn't woken up the baby. It hadn't. Cameron stayed asleep.

Lana took out her phone and muttered more profanity when she saw the name on the screen. So did Slater, because it was Pamela. While Lana's mother wasn't the last person he wanted to speak to, she was close to it. Apparently, Lana felt the same way because she groaned softly when she moved off his lap and onto the chair next to him.

"Lana," her mother said the moment she answered, and Slater immediately heard the distress in the woman's voice. It seemed as if she'd spoken her daughter's name on a sob.

"What's wrong?" Lana asked, clearly picking up on her mother's tone.

"That man who tried to blackmail your father just called me," Pamela blurted, her words running together.

"BoBo," Slater muttered on a groan, but he kept his voice low enough so that Pamela wouldn't hear him. He figured Pamela might hang up if she knew he was listening.

"What did he want?" Lana pressed.

"He wanted money." Pamela made another of those sobbing sounds. "He claimed to have emails from your father and one of his private investigators. Emails that prove your father knew where Stephanie was the whole time she was pregnant."

So, Austin PD hadn't managed to arrest BoBo yet if he was calling Pamela. Or maybe the guy was already out on bail and looking for yet another way to cash in on the hacking job that Taylor had paid him to do. It was also possible that BoBo hadn't managed to get a cent from Leonard so he'd then gone after Pamela.

"Is it true?" Pamela pleaded. "Did your father know where Stephanie was when she was pregnant?"

Lana groaned again. "What did Dad have to say about it?"

"He's not here, and he's not answering his phone. Marsh doesn't know where he is, either. I'm sure your father's avoiding me because he doesn't want to answer my questions."

"Is he aware you know about the emails?" Lana asked.

"I think so. When he didn't answer his phone, I sent him a text to let him know the blackmailer had called me, and I asked him how I should handle it. Then the blackmailer told me about those emails so I tried to call your father again. I left him a scathing voicemail," she added, and broke down into what sounded like a full-fledged crying jag.

Slater figured the woman had to be plenty upset, but considering she'd been married to Leonard for nearly four decades, she must have known he was capable of keeping a secret like this. Yet she seemed stunned and heartbroken. Either it was an act or Leonard had truly done a stellar job at hiding the truth.

And maybe not just this truth, either.

He thought of that photo, of the way Alicia had been looking at Leonard. Then he recalled Cassandra's warning about Buck being dangerous. It was possible that Leonard had known about Buck's dangerous streak, too, and that the streak had gone all the way back to Alicia. That left Slater with a huge question.

Had Leonard known that Buck murdered Alicia?

If so, Leonard might have been hell-bent on keeping Buck away from Stephanie. It could have been why he'd had both Buck and Stephanie under surveillance of his PIs.

"Your father knew where Stephanie was," Pamela went on, "and he didn't tell me. He let me worry all that time. And I was worried sick," she ranted. "I needed to see my daughter. He knew that, and still he didn't tell me."

"I'm not trying to excuse what Dad did," Lana tried to explain, "but Stephanie wouldn't have wanted to see you or Dad. She didn't want to see anyone, including me. Maybe because she was scared of Buck or maybe because she didn't want to face you while she was pregnant."

Her mother didn't answer right away, but she continued to cry. "There's more," she said. "Lana, there's more."

Lana's gaze fired to his, and Slater saw plenty of fresh concern there. Slater was sure he was showing some concern, too, because he didn't like the sound of that.

"What?" Lana asked when her mother didn't add anything to that.

"After that horrible blackmailer called me, I phoned Taylor."

"Why?" Lana was quick to demand.

"Because I heard your father mention her. Something about her being the reason this man was trying to blackmail him. I didn't know what Taylor had done, but I figured she'd be able to give me answers."

"And did she?" Lana prompted after her mother broke into a fresh sob. This one was even louder than the other one.

"Taylor gave me…something. Something I don't want to believe," Pamela wailed. "Lana, I think I need to leave. I think I should go to a safe house, a place like the one you set up for Stephanie."

Now there was alarm on Lana's face. "Did Taylor threaten you? Are you scared of her?"

"No." And that was all Pamela said for several long moments. "I'm not scared of Taylor. I'm scared of your father."

Lana groaned and scrubbed her hand over her face. "Why? What happened? What did Taylor tell you to make you afraid of him?"

"She said…" Another sob stopped Pamela. "Taylor said that it was your father who killed Stephanie and that it wasn't the first time he'd killed someone." Both her voice and her breath broke. "Taylor said he killed Slater's father, too."

Chapter Twelve

Part of Lana just wanted to stay shut inside the ranch house with Cameron and Slater. She wanted to hold on to this peace that settled over her whenever she was with the two of them. But the peace was merely a facade, and she didn't stand a chance of it being real until she had all the answers about her sister's murder.

And Slater's father's.

One look at Slater, and Lana could see there'd be no peace for him, either. For nearly a year he'd been driven to find the person who'd ended his father's life, and now he might finally know.

Might.

"My mother could be wrong," Lana spelled out. Not for the first time, either. She'd been saying variations of that for the past hour since her mother's bombshell call.

Slater finished reading through the latest text he'd gotten from Duncan and nodded. Yes, he was well aware that anything to do with her mother could end up being a wild-goose chase, but now that the allegation had been made, it needed to be investigated. They had to know if Leonard was truly the person behind Sheriff McCullough's, Stephanie's and maybe even Alicia's murders.

Of course, they couldn't just go charging in and demanding answers from her father. Nor could they simply send in the cops, because Leonard would just stonewall with his lawyers. No, this had to be done with some finesse, and Lana had known from the moment she'd ended the call with her mother that as Leonard's daughter, she was their best bet at learning the truth.

Slater hadn't immediately agreed to that, of course. He wanted her safe, but safe wasn't going to get them those answers.

"Your mother just arrived at the secure location," Slater relayed after firing off a text response to Duncan. "It's Ruston's apartment in San Antonio, and he's the one who escorted Pamela there. He doesn't actually live there anymore now that he's married and has a baby. He commutes from Saddle Ridge, but he kept the place in case he had to pull some all-nighters on an investigation."

"Good," Lana said. "Thank you for arranging that."

The accommodations probably wouldn't be up to her mother's usual high standards, but Ruston was a cop at SAPD, and that meant his apartment would have decent security. Not that Lana expected her mother to be in actual danger and in need of such measures, but still, precautions needed to be taken in case everything Pamela had said was true. If her husband was indeed a killer, then he might also go after a wife who'd revealed what could be his deadly secrets.

"The next step is for us to decide, well, the next step," Slater continued a moment later.

Yes, they'd discussed this, too, but Slater hadn't yet approved the plan that Lana had suggested.

"There's no proof of my father doing anything, nothing to arrest him on," she reminded him. "And there's the part about him stonewalling any and all cops who could question him about what my mother claims. But I believe he will talk to me, especially if I frame it as a visit to tell him about some concerns about my conversation with Mom. He'll want to know what I have to say."

She hoped. But her father could be unpredictable, and he might very well try to shut down any and all conversations.

"I could just call him and ask for a meeting," Lana went on, knowing she hadn't yet convinced Slater this was the way to approach this. "Of course, you'd go with me. Maybe Sonya, too, though it'd probably be best if she waited outside as backup."

Backup that Lana prayed wouldn't be needed. She didn't believe she and Slater would be walking into an actual ambush. She couldn't imagine her father arranging something like that at his home.

The muscles in Slater's jaw seemed to be at war with each other. "You really think your father is a killer?" he came out and asked.

It was something she'd been rolling around in her mind, and Lana still didn't know. "I'm not sure. I think he could be capable of murder," she admitted.

Slater's sound of agreement let her know that he felt the same way.

"As you know, he's ruthless, and I could maybe see him killing to cover up a crime." She had to try to ease the lump in her throat to get out the rest. "But for Stephanie, that feels different. It would have been premeditated. And for what? Because she'd defied him by getting pregnant with Buck's baby? That just doesn't make sense."

He made another sound of agreement. "Maybe your father had another motive for wanting her dead. For instance, maybe Stephanie was planning on blackmailing him about

something. Or she could have been planning some bad publicity campaign to smear him."

Slater stopped, shook his head. "That doesn't seem like
a strong enough motive, either," he amended. "Your father seems the sort to fight fire with fire. If Stephanie had
threatened him in some way, he could have run his own
smear campaign against her. He certainly would have had
plenty of ammunition for that."

"True," Lana muttered. "And that brings us back to Buck.
He had motive to kill Stephanie, and maybe my father isn't
his accomplice. Taylor could be. Now, she's someone with
motive to want Stephanie dead."

Of course, if Taylor was the accomplice, then that meant
Leonard could be innocent. Well, of this particular crime,
anyway. That didn't mean he hadn't had some part in killing Slater's father.

She took out her phone, lifting it for Slater to see. "Should
I call him and arrange a meeting?" she asked.

Slater sighed. Then nodded.

Lana didn't waste any time in case Slater changed his
mind. She pressed her father's number and was somewhat
surprised when he answered on the first ring.

"Where's your mother?" her father demanded.

"I'm not sure," Lana lied. No way did she want to spill
over the phone anything her mother had said. She wanted
to see her father's face, to try to gauge if he was lying or
withholding something. "What happened?"

Her father cursed. "I have no idea, but she's not here
at the estate. I came home because one of the housekeepers called me and said your mother left with a packed bag
about an hour ago."

That would have been when her mother had driven to
meet Ruston, and it didn't surprise Lana that one of the

"housekeepers" had alerted her father. Leonard no doubt had many employees to keep an eye on things.

"Mom called me," Lana informed him, "and I want to talk to you about some of the things she said."

"What did she say?" he demanded.

"I'll tell you when I see you," Lana insisted right back. "You said you were at the estate?"

"I am, but I want to know what your mother told you," he snapped.

"Slater and I'll be there in about thirty minutes," Lana said, and she ended the call, but not before hearing her father snarl out Slater's name.

Of course, Leonard tried to call her right back, but Lana declined the call as she went to the crib to kiss Cameron. The baby was asleep, and the moment she and Slater stepped out of the room, the nanny came out from the nursery across the hall and took the baby monitor that Lana handed her. They'd already talked to Joelle, Duncan and the nanny about this possible plan so everything was in place for them to leave immediately for the estate.

Including Sonya.

The deputy saw them coming down the stairs and stood to go with them outside to the cruiser. Slater, Sonya and Lana were already armed, all three wearing shoulder holsters. Lana had put a jacket over hers, but Sonya and Slater had kept theirs visible. She also knew the deputies were carrying backup weapons.

Slater had a quick word with Joelle and Luca, who'd be doing guard duty while they were gone. Which hopefully wouldn't be long. In an ideal scenario, her father would confess to, well, everything, and Slater could have him arrested. The threat to Cameron could be over and done within an hour.

Lana doubted, though, this would be an ideal scenario.

Her father likely wouldn't admit to anything, but in his shock over hearing what his wife had said, he might spill something they could use to build a case against him. And if he was innocent, then it would be time to take a harder look at Taylor. Or even Marsh for that matter, since it was possible that he'd been so jealous and outraged about Stephanie being pregnant that he'd snapped and had her killed.

As they'd done on previous trips both here in Saddle Ridge and in Austin, they kept watch, looking for any threats. Unlike those other trips, Sonya was driving in the cruiser with them so she could provide immediate backup if they were attacked along the route. But there were no signs of anyone suspicious, just the usual late-afternoon rancher and farmer type of traffic that would normally be on the road that led to the interstate.

Lana couldn't shut off her thoughts, and as each mile took them closer to the estate, she realized it'd been over five years since she'd been to her parents' home. For a good reason. They'd both made it obvious they hadn't approved of her lifestyle despite her military service giving her father some good press for a daughter "serving her country." Maybe that had been the difference between Stephanie and her. They'd both rebelled, but her rebellion had been tolerable compared to her sister's.

"You can still change your mind about this," Slater said, reaching across the seat to give her hand a gentle squeeze.

She looked at him, and for some reason the skin-to-skin contact made her think of that scalding kiss they'd shared. A kiss that probably would have led to a big *where is this going?* discussion if her mother hadn't called. At the time, Lana hadn't been happy about the interruption, but in hindsight, it was a good thing. The personal discussions would have to wait. As would more kisses.

And she hoped her body understood that.

At the moment, it only seemed to want to spur her to dole out another kiss.

"I won't change my mind," Lana answered. "We need to do this."

Slater didn't dispute that, but she figured he'd rather be doing this chat alone with her father. Or maybe with Sonya as backup and with Lana tucked away safely at his family's ranch. It was tempting for her to want the same thing, but there was no way she would let Slater face down her father without her.

As expected, the drive took only a half hour since it was on the outskirts of San Antonio and not directly in the city. Sonya followed the GPS to the massive wrought iron gates that fronted the twenty-acre estate. Every acre and every building on the grounds had been designed to impress. That included the sprawling three-story house that sat at the end of a tree-lined private road.

The gates were already open, letting Lana know that despite her not returning her father's call, he wasn't going to deny them entry. Then again, it was possible he kept them open these days since this wasn't a high-crime area.

Sonya pulled to a stop behind a shiny silver Jag that was already parked in the circular drive, and after taking a couple of deep breaths, Lana looked at Slater, and when he gave her a go-ahead nod, they got out. Like the rest of the house, the porch was massive and spanned all the way across the front of the house. Again, it was meant to impress with the nearly dozen steps leading up to it.

They went to the double doors to ring the bell. The doors opened, though, before she could do that, and she met her father's steely, narrowed gaze head-on. Yeah, he was not happy.

Her father was dressed in one of his pricey suits, a pale gray one that was nearly the same color as the expertly placed threads of "salt" in his salt-and-pepper hair. She doubted he'd groomed himself for their visit, either. This was his norm.

"This visit wasn't necessary," he grumbled. "You could have told me this over the phone."

Lana opened her mouth to argue that, but then she spotted the woman standing in the foyer behind her father. Taylor.

"What's she doing here?" Lana asked.

"I came to warn him about Marsh," Taylor spoke up before Leonard could answer.

Her father huffed, and while he didn't roll his eyes, it was a close enough gesture to let Lana know he wasn't happy about Taylor's visit. Or maybe he was objecting to her accusations. As far as Lana knew, Marsh was still the golden boy.

"Marsh is up to something," Taylor went on. "I just know it."

They stepped into the foyer, and Taylor came closer, moving to her father's side. Really close to his side. So that their arms were touching. It was a little thing, but it seemed…big. And Lana immediately wondered if something was going on with these two.

Were they having an affair?

But she rethought that. Until Marsh had ended things with Taylor only the day before, Taylor had seemed completely obsessed with the man. Still, that didn't mean Taylor hadn't had a relationship on the side.

Her father turned to Taylor, and again, it seemed to Lana

that something passed between them. Something too intimate for this to be a visit for Taylor to gripe about Marsh.

"Taylor, I need to speak to Lana and Slater," Leonard said, clearly not inviting Taylor to be part of that conversation. No surprise there, since it would be a chat about things his wife had claimed.

"But I haven't finished telling you my suspicions about Marsh," Taylor protested, sounding like a pouty brat. "You need to hear them, Leonard. You need to understand that Marsh could be a dangerous man."

"I want to hear what you have to say," he assured her, "but I have to talk to Lana and Slater first."

Her father's words didn't match his expression. Leonard seemed to be ready to get rid of Taylor. However, he didn't spew out one of his usual tirades that he likely would have to most people. That could be yet more proof they were having an affair.

"I'll wait for you then," Taylor insisted, not heading for the door but into the formal living room that was just to their right. The moment the woman flounced in, a housekeeper came in to offer her a drink.

Sighing, her father gave Taylor one last glance and then motioned for Lana and Slater to follow him. He headed in the direction of his office, and along the way, Lana saw a man in a suit who was no doubt one of Leonard's assistants or lawyers. Maybe even a PI. She didn't know his name and was thankful when her father didn't invite him into the massive office with them.

"Where's your mother?" Leonard demanded the moment they were behind closed doors.

"Someplace safe," Lana settled for saying.

Her father cursed. "Did you convince her that she wouldn't be safe here, right here in her own home?"

"No," Slater and Lana said in unison. It was Lana who continued. "Mom said she was afraid and she wanted to go where she wouldn't be at risk."

Leonard stared at her as if she'd just told him the most unbelievable lie he'd ever heard. "What exactly did she say?" he demanded, and now he wasn't just glaring, he'd also clenched his teeth so tight that Lana was surprised he could even speak.

Lana glanced at Slater, and while they'd already discussed what to say, she wanted to make sure he hadn't changed his mind about being so direct. His nod indicated he hadn't.

"Mom believes you might have had some part in Stephanie's murder—"

"What?" her father howled before Lana got a chance to finish.

"Were you Buck's accomplice?" Slater came out and asked.

If looks could kill, her father would have ended Slater's life right then, right there. "No," he said, his voice a low, dangerous growl. "Of course not. I wouldn't kill my own daughter."

"Not even if she was about to cause you a publicity nightmare?" Lana pushed.

Leonard turned that icy look on her. "No," he repeated. "Not even then, and I sure as hell wouldn't have worked with a hothead like Buck. I think the only reason Stephanie got involved with him was because she was trying to get back at me for pushing her to marry Marsh."

That was exactly what Lana had thought he would say. She certainly hadn't expected him to accept any blame. So that's why she went ahead and hit him with the next accusation.

"Mom also thought you might have had something to do with Alicia Monroe's death," Lana said. "And before you deny knowing who that is, I personally saw a photo of Alicia and you at a party."

Her father had already opened his mouth, no doubt to interrupt her again with verbal fire, but that caused him to go silent for a couple of moments. "What the hell are you talking about?" But he didn't give her a chance to respond. "You think because I was at a party with some woman who ended up dead, that I could have killed her?"

Lana shrugged. "Mom seems to think that's possible."

He tried to speak, but apparently the muscles in his throat didn't immediately cooperate. He gutted out some profanity, groaned and went to his desk to drop down in his chair.

"Your mother actually believes that?" he questioned with his face now buried in his hands. "She truly thinks I could have murdered Stephanie and that woman."

"My father, too," Slater added.

Lana expected that to ignite a fresh flash of temper in her father. It didn't. He groaned again and kept his hand on his face for what seemed an eternity. When he finally looked at them again, it wasn't anger she saw. But rather hurt.

Hurt that he could be faking, she reminded herself.

"Well, it's obvious someone has brainwashed your mother," he finally muttered. "I'm guessing you're not going to own up to it being you? Or you?" he asked, shifting his gaze to Slater.

"It was neither Lana nor me," Slater said, and now he was the one who paused. Maybe because he didn't intend to point the finger at Taylor. "Pamela called Lana out of the blue and asked for protection because she was afraid of your involvement in these murders." Slater stopped again. "Did you kill them?"

"No." He squeezed his eyes shut a moment and repeated

it. "I had nothing to do with murdering my daughter, Alicia or your father."

"Then why would your wife think that?" Slater pressed.

"I have no idea," Leonard was quick to say. "Maybe she's trying to get back at me for something she thinks I did."

"It must be a pretty bad *something* for her to accuse you of murder," Lana pointed out. "An affair, maybe? Or maybe lying to her about knowing exactly where Stephanie was when she was so worried about her?"

Her father didn't deny either of those things, and judging from the way his jaw set again, Lana thought he might order her and Slater out of his office. He didn't get a chance to do that, though, because two other things happened.

Slater's phone dinged with a text. When he showed Lana the screen, she saw that the message was from Sonya, and the deputy was giving them a heads-up that Marsh had just arrived and gone into the house. Moments later, she heard Taylor shout something.

Leonard gave a weary sigh when Taylor's shouting got even louder, and he stood and went to the door. He'd barely had time to open it when Taylor barged in.

"You aren't going to believe why Marsh is here," Taylor blurted.

"I asked her if she was responsible for Stephanie being murdered," Marsh quickly volunteered. "Because someone left this on my car."

Marsh held up a grainy picture of what appeared to be Taylor and Buck. If Lana wasn't mistaken, they seemed to be at the same coffee shop where Taylor had met with her and Slater.

"It's a fake," Taylor insisted. "I wouldn't kill your precious Stephanie," she snarled with Oh, so much venom in her voice.

Marsh looked at her, and it didn't take long for his stare to become a glare. "I don't believe you," he stated. "You disgust me."

Taylor whirled toward Leonard as if she expected him to defend her. He didn't. That only fueled the woman's anger, and she aimed all of it at Marsh.

"You disgust me," Taylor fired right back at him. "And I'll make you pay, Marsh. Just wait and see. You'll pay for what you just said."

And with that, the woman stormed out.

Chapter Thirteen

Slater listened to Taylor shouting profanities and threats all the way out of the house. Moments later, Sonya texted him to let him know that Taylor had gotten in her Jag and driven off. Slater was betting, though, that she wouldn't stay gone. There was something going on between her and Leonard, and Taylor would no doubt return once she'd burned off some of her anger.

"I'm sorry," Marsh muttered, directing the apology to Leonard. "I didn't know Taylor would be here, but when I saw her car, I thought she might be…well, I didn't know if she was trying to make you believe I was the one who killed Stephanie. I didn't," he emphasized, glancing at all three of them.

"But you believe Taylor did team up with Buck," Slater said, taking the photo from Marsh to get a better look.

Slater studied the image, but it was hard to tell if it had indeed been photoshopped. Even if it was the real deal, though, it didn't prove Taylor's guilt. After all, the woman had already admitted that she knew Buck.

"I don't know for certain," Marsh said. "But something's going on with her." He groaned, shook his head. "She wanted us to get back together, and when I told her no, that it was never going to happen, she just seemed to lose it."

Slater glanced at Leonard to see how he was reacting to that. Not well. He was scowling and looked to be on the verge of muttering something. He didn't. When he noticed Slater staring at him, he shut down and on went his poker face. If the man was having an affair with Taylor, though, he probably wasn't pleased about Taylor trying to reconcile with Marsh.

Well, maybe he wasn't.

It was possible that if an affair was truly going on between him and Taylor, it was only about sex.

"You can keep the photo," Marsh told Slater. "In case you want to send it to the crime lab. I took a picture of it," he added, lifting his phone.

Slater nodded, but while it probably wouldn't give them any new information, he would indeed send it to the lab since it possibly contained fingerprints of the person who'd left it. If those prints belonged to Leonard, then it could add to the circumstantial evidence against him.

Marsh said his goodbyes to Leonard and headed out, but when he opened the office door, Slater didn't see the guy in the suit who'd been there earlier, and he wondered if this "assistant" had stepped out to make sure Taylor had truly left.

"Where's your mother?" Leonard asked Lana the moment Marsh was gone.

Lana sighed. "I'm not going to tell you that."

And just like that, Leonard's fierce anger returned. "She won't answer my calls, and I have to talk to her. I need to find out why she's telling these lies about me before the lies get out of hand."

In other words, before the press picked up on them. But Slater had no intention of helping the man defuse that kind of bad press. Apparently, neither did Lana.

"No," she said, and there was no indication in her tone that she would change her mind.

Her father must have realized that, too, because he cursed again. "Get out," Leonard told them. "Both of you. Now."

Slater looked at her and nodded. They weren't going to get a confession or anything else from her father. The man had dug in his heels and had already taken out his phone, no doubt to get started on finding his wife. Slater had to make sure that didn't happen. At the moment, Pamela didn't have a guard with her, but that could be arranged.

He and Lana threaded their way through the massive house to the front door and out onto the porch. Still no sign of the guy in the suit, but Slater immediately noticed the black Mercedes that hadn't been there when they'd arrived.

Sonya stepped out of the cruiser and looked at them from over the top of the vehicle. "It's Marsh's," she said, tipping her head toward the thick gardens on the right side of the house. "He muttered something about going for a walk."

Slater immediately got an uneasy feeling about that. If Marsh had needed to cool off, why do it here? Why not just go back to his own place?

Some movement from the corner of his eye caught his attention, and Slater saw something else he didn't like. Taylor's car. It was parked up by the gate—which was also on the right side of the property. He couldn't tell, though, if she was still inside.

"She drove off but then came back," Sonya explained as Slater and Lana started down the steps.

Maybe waiting for all of them to leave so she could go in and try to mend fences with Leonard. But again, that made Slater uneasy.

"Did she get out?" Slater wanted to know. If she'd seen

Marsh walking, Taylor might have wanted to continue her argument with the man.

"It's possible," Sonya admitted. "The passenger side of her car is hidden by the gate post."

It was, and Taylor could have slipped out that way if she hadn't wanted Sonya or anyone else to see her.

"Get in the cruiser," he told Lana.

But he was already too late.

The shot blasted through the air, tearing into the wood column right next to where Lana was standing. She dropped onto the limestone steps. So did Slater, and he immediately tried to pinpoint where the shot had come from. If he wasn't mistaken, it had come from the area where Marsh had gone for his "walk."

Slater drew his gun and lifted his head. No sign of the shooter, but thankfully Sonya had taken cover back in the cruiser. That was where Slater wanted Lana to be right now, but there were eight porch steps between them and the driveway and another ten feet of space after that. Not especially far, but they'd be easy targets if they stood still.

Another shot came right at them, and the shooter had obviously adjusted his aim because this one smacked into the step just above Lana's head. Lana was clearly the target here, and the shooter had too good an aim. He had to get her out of the line of fire and fast.

Cursing, Slater caught on to Lana and rolled with her to the side. More shots came. One right behind the other, each tearing up the stone and sending shards flying. Slater prayed none of them hit Lana.

They finally reached the side of the steps, and they dropped down into the shrubs. The bushes definitely wouldn't stop any bullets, but at least this way, the shooter might not be able to see them.

"Stay down and let's move," Slater instructed. He wanted them away from the spot near the porch where the shooter had last seen them.

Lana had drawn her gun, too, and she kept it gripped in her hand as she maneuvered onto her belly. Her breath was gusting now, and she was probably getting hit with the mother lode of adrenaline. She had to be terrified, but she got moving, crawling away from the porch.

The shooting didn't stop, and even though Slater hadn't actually counted the number of bullets fired, he figured the shooter either had more than one weapon or had reloaded. In other words, he or she had come prepared for this.

But who was it?

Who was trying to kill Lana?

It was possibly Marsh, who hadn't actually gone for that walk after all but rather had positioned himself for this attack. But it could also be the guy in the suit who worked for Leonard. If so, Leonard would have been the one to order Lana's murder. Maybe just as he'd ordered Stephanie's.

However, Slater's money was on Taylor.

He had no idea if she'd had firearms training, but that wouldn't be hard to get. And with her temper, she could want to get back at Lana—especially if Taylor was Buck's accomplice.

I'm not working by my lonesome. I've got a helper. A cold-blooded one. And Lana and you are going to die.

Those had been Buck's dying words, and while Slater had hoped it was all a lie, it was possible this was the plan Buck had set in motion before Slater's bullet had killed him.

There was a flurry of more shots, and Slater moved so he could send his own bullet in the direction of the shooter. He double-tapped the trigger, hoping he'd get lucky and take out this person. There was no yelp of pain, though, no thud to indicate a bullet hitting flesh.

And the gunfire continued.

But Slater heard something else. The sound of a car engine, and it was moving closer to him and Lana. Hell, he hoped the shooter hadn't managed to get into a vehicle and was now planning on ramming into them. The alarm he saw in Lana's eyes let him know she was thinking the same thing.

His phone dinged with a text, and when Slater managed to get it out of his pocket, he saw Sonya's name on the screen. And her message eased some of the knotted muscles in Slater's gut.

"Sonya's moving the cruiser between us and the shots," he relayed.

It was a welcome ploy, but it wasn't without risk to Sonya. The cruiser was bullet-resistant, but that didn't mean gunshots couldn't get through. If the shooter was determined enough, he or she could now try to kill Sonya.

More shots came, and Slater could hear them now slamming into the cruiser. He could see the cruiser, too, through the tiny gaps in the row of thick shrubs. Sonya wasn't just maneuvering so the cruiser would be a shield. Slater thought Sonya was trying to get into position so he and Lana could be able to crawl into the cruiser through the passenger-side door.

In the distance, Slater heard a welcome sound. Sirens. Maybe Leonard had called the cops, but he was betting Sonya had been the one to do that. Even if Leonard's assistant wasn't the one firing those shots, Lana's father probably would have preferred to handle this himself and not deal with the publicity that was certain to follow.

At the thought of Leonard, Slater glanced back at the

porch steps. He couldn't actually see the front door from his position, but he didn't think it was open. He hadn't expected it to be, but where was Lana's father right now? Was he cowering inside, or was he waiting for his assistant to finish the job he'd started?

Sonya continued to draw fire as she backed the cruiser into place, and the moment she was dead even with him and Lana, she must have leaned across the seat because the back door of the cruiser opened.

There wasn't an easy way to get inside it since it meant them squeezing through the shrubs that scratched and tore at them. Still, it was better than staying put where they could be shot and killed if the shooter changed positions.

The wail of the sirens got even closer, and Slater gave Lana a final push through the shrubs so she could scramble into the back seat. He was right after her, and he slammed the door shut behind them.

"Get down," Slater told Sonya. "It's too dangerous to try to drive out of here."

Sonya made a quick sound of agreement and dropped down. Good thing, too, because the next shot finally weakened the side window and put a fist-sized hole through it.

Slater climbed on top of Lana, his front against her back so he could try to protect her. He knew she wouldn't thank him for the move. She wouldn't want him risking his life for hers, but Slater stayed put.

And waited.

He also lifted his head enough to try to see if the shooter was coming for them. One last-ditch effort to kill them before the cops arrived. But he didn't see anyone. Nor did he hear anything other than the sirens.

The shots had stopped.

Slater cursed, because that probably meant the shooter

was trying to get away, but he intended to have Leonard, Taylor, Marsh and the assistant all tested for gunshot residue. If one of them had fired all these shots, then the test might prove it.

"Two SAPD cruisers," Slater relayed to Sonya and Lana.

"I called them," Sonya said, and he heard her make a call, no doubt to fill the responding officers in on the situation.

The cops in the cruisers didn't drive toward the house. They stayed at the gate, maybe waiting until Sonya had given them a picture of what had happened. And what could possibly happen if the shooter started firing again.

"Unknown number of people inside the house," Sonya said, responding to a question she'd been asked. "But, yes, the owner, Leonard Walsh, is here. Or rather he was. And, no, I don't have eyes on him." Sonya paused. "What?" she blurted. "You're sure?"

That got Slater's attention, and the alarm shot through him when Sonya looked at him. He could tell from her expression that something was wrong.

"It's Taylor," Sonya said. "She's in her car. And she's dead."

LANA SAT IN the interview room at SAPD headquarters and read through the statement she'd just given Detective Josh O'Malley about the shooting. Slater's brother, Ruston, was there, standing with his back against the wall, but he hadn't participated in the interview because it could have been construed as a conflict of interest.

Because of where the shooting had taken place, everything was being done by the book. Her father had a lot of political pull, and it was obvious no one here wanted that pull used against them. But even her father couldn't stop himself from being interviewed.

And interrogated.

From what Slater and Ruston had said, Leonard had been treated just as anyone else in his position would have been. As a possible suspect or at least someone who might have key information. A woman had been murdered; the shooter had attempted to kill Lana and two cops.

That wasn't going to be swept under the rug.

"This is accurate," Lana said after reading the statement that she then signed. She figured Slater was doing something similar in the interview room across the hall. Now that they'd gotten the formality of the interview out of the way, she needed to see him. She needed to make sure he was truly okay.

They'd both been examined by EMTs, and their cuts and scrapes from the shrubs had been treated. Ditto for Sonya, who'd gotten nicked by some of the glass when it'd been shot out in the cruiser. But Lana knew none of their injuries were serious, which meant they'd gotten lucky.

Unlike Taylor.

As Lana, Slater and Sonya had been driven away from the estate in one of a patrol cars, she had gotten a glimpse of Taylor. The woman had been slumped against the steering wheel of her Jag, and she had a gunshot wound to the head. It hadn't looked self-inflicted to Lana, and she would be surprised if it had been, because Taylor didn't seem the type to take her own life.

"Can I get you some water or something to eat?" Detective O'Malley asked Lana as they stood.

She shook her head. Lana figured she should be hungry since she hadn't eaten since lunch, but there was no way she wanted to try to eat. Not with her stomach still churning.

When O'Malley walked out, Ruston went to her, and maybe because she looked ready to collapse, he put his arm around her and led her out of the room. Thankfully,

Slater was right there, waiting, and Lana went to him, slipping right into his welcoming embrace. He brushed a kiss on her forehead, and while it was such a simple gesture, it took away some of the ice that had seemingly seeped all the way to her bones.

Mercy, it was wrong to need Slater like this, but Lana couldn't seem to stop herself. Maybe it was a combination of the intense attraction, the memories of that kiss, grief over her sister's murder and the spent adrenaline from coming so close to dying. If that was it, then it was a potent blend that made her want to hold on to him and never let go.

"Did everything go okay in there?" Slater asked his brother.

Ruston nodded but didn't get a chance to add anything before his phone rang. "I need to take this," he said, stepping away from them.

Lana eased back enough so she could look up at Slater. "What updates do you have?" Because she knew he'd been communicating with both Duncan and Detective Thayer in Austin. Communicating with the cops here, too, since so many of them knew him through his brother.

"Taylor was murdered," Slater said after he drew in a long breath. "The shot that killed her came from the window on the passenger side of her car."

Lana considered that for a moment, thinking of the placement of trees and shrubs by the gate. It was possible her killer had been able to make that shot without Taylor even seeing him.

But who had killed her?

"They tested my gun," Slater went on, "and the shot didn't come from me."

She hadn't thought for a second that it had. Slater had fired into the trees, not in the direction of the gate.

"Did Taylor have a gun with her?" Lana wanted to know. "Could she have been the one who fired shots at us?" Though the logistics of that would be hard unless Taylor had shot at them and hurried back to her car, only to be killed there.

He shook his head. "No gun and no GSR on her. The CSIs will compare the bullet that killed her to any others the shooter might have left behind."

"So, the theory is one gunman," she concluded. "And Taylor could have been killed either at the beginning of the attack on us or at the end."

"Either," he confirmed. "And since the attack only lasted a couple of minutes, the ME probably won't be able to pinpoint the exact time of the kill shot."

A couple of minutes. It had felt like a lifetime or two with them pinned down and bullets flying.

"Marsh is up the hall giving his statement," Slater went on. "But I heard him tell the detective that he heard the shots and hid so he wouldn't be hit. He thought Taylor was shooting at him."

That seemed reasonable since Taylor had threatened him. Well, it was reasonable unless Marsh was lying and had been the shooter.

"There wasn't any GSR on Marsh," Slater let her know before she had to ask. "Of course, he could have worn gloves and disposed of them somewhere on the grounds. The CSIs will look for that," he added.

Good. But twenty acres was a lot to search, and Marsh could have hidden them in plenty of places. Places he was well aware of, since he was a frequent visitor to the estate.

"Your father is still in interview, too," Slater went on. "He waited until his lawyers were here before he agreed to give his statement."

"Did they test him for GSR?" Lana immediately wanted to know.

Slater's mouth tightened. "Not yet. His lawyers are fighting it, claiming that Leonard is a victim, not the perpetrator."

Lana huffed. "That could mean he's guilty." But she had to mentally wave that off. Her father was arrogant enough to believe he was above such measures of the law, and even if he was innocent, he likely would have refused any test.

"I'm hoping his lawyers won't be able to stall forever," Slater muttered, but there was enough doubt in his eyes to let her know that it could indeed be the outcome.

"What about my father's assistant and the housekeepers?" Lana asked. "Is it possible one of them was the shooter?"

"They're all being questioned, all being tested for GSR," he assured her. "The estate does have security cameras, but your father said they weren't on at the time, that he normally only has them on at night. Is that true?"

Lana had to shrug. "I know there are cameras, but he never gave anyone access to the control panel for the security system." She paused. "You think it's a coincidence that the cameras weren't on during the shooting."

"Maybe." Slater groaned softly. "I don't like coincidences, but maybe this is one."

"True," she admitted. "It doesn't feel right that my father would orchestrate an attack at the estate. If he wanted to send someone after us, he could have done that on our drive back to Saddle Ridge."

That wasn't exactly a comforting thought, but it's how she would have done it had she been a killer.

"Has my father said who he believes fired those shots?" Lana asked.

"He thinks it was Taylor and that she then killed herself." Slater took another of those long breaths. "I suppose it's possible if there was a second gunman who shot her and then took her weapon. He or she would have also had to wipe the GSR from her hands." He shook his head. "I'm not sure there was enough time for a gunman to do that in between the shots being fired at us. Unless..."

"Unless there were two people involved in this." She stopped, groaned. It was too much to think of having multiple killers after them.

"The CSIs are going through Taylor's house as we speak," Slater went on. "Ruston's been getting regular updates and texting them to me. They're already found two burners that were used to call Buck, and they're focusing on finding other communications she might have had with him."

"Burners," Lana muttered, and she let the meaning of that sink in. The phones could be proof that Taylor was Buck's accomplice. After all, if she simply wanted to talk to the man, she could have used her regular phone. "It was stupid of Taylor to leave those lying around."

"Stupid or she was set up," Slater said, spelling out exactly what Lana was thinking.

"It would tie up everything in a neat little bow if Taylor was the accomplice. She's dead and can't say otherwise." And that led Lana to another thought. "If Buck's real accomplice thinks he's out of potential hot water, maybe he won't come after us again. Maybe the attacks will stop."

"Yes," he murmured as if considering that. "No more attacks, but also maybe no answers about Alicia's and my father's murders. You might not ever be sure, too, of who worked with Buck to kill Stephanie."

Again, that was all true, and while Lana desperately wanted the attacks to be over and done, she needed the truth, too. And she was certain Slater felt the same. Neither of them would just let this drop, and soon, Buck's real accomplice would understand that and would no doubt once again try to kill them.

"We can go back to Saddle Ridge and regroup," Slater said, once again answering her unspoken question. "We can look for proof of someone entering Taylor's house to set her up."

Yes, that would be a good place to start, especially since she figured they wouldn't be getting any immediate answers from her father.

She turned to the sound of the approaching footsteps and saw Ruston making his way back toward them. He was still sporting the scowl that'd appeared on his face when he'd left to take a phone call.

"What's wrong?" Slater immediately wanted to know.

"This," Ruston said, holding up his phone so they could see the screen.

The image was clear enough, but Lana had to shake her head. "That's my mother."

"It is," Ruston verified. "I gave your mother the codes to my security system in case she had to step out for some reason and told her to keep the system on when she was there so that I'd get an alert if someone tried to break in."

That was a good precaution, one that Lana herself had suggested. That would prevent Ruston from having to personally check on her mother while he was at work.

"Your mother apparently did step out," Ruston went on, "and I just got a call from my security company because she didn't get the code punched back in time to prevent it from being triggered."

Lana shook her head. "Why would my mother leave your apartment?"

"That's something I think you'll want to ask her." Ruston motioned toward the time stamp of his mother's return, and she saw that it was about fifteen minutes ago. Then Ruston shifted to another photo of her mother. "I had the security company go back through the feed, and this is a photo of Pamela leaving."

Once again, he tapped the time stamp.

And Lana immediately realized why he was scowling. Because her mother had left the apartment over an hour before the shooting at the estate. That wasn't all. The security camera had caught Pamela's purse at just the right angle for Lana to see something else.

The gun that her mother was carrying.

Chapter Fourteen

Slater knew this had already been a hellishly long day, but it apparently wasn't over yet. After finishing with the San Antonio cops about the shooting, they'd returned to the ranch in Saddle Ridge, and even though Lana looked ready to drop after getting Cameron down for the night, she still had one more thing on her to-do list.

She had to call her mother.

Lana needed answers as to where the woman had been during the shooting. Answers that she'd then pass along to Duncan, Ruston, Thayer and any other cop involved in the investigation. Well, if there was anything new to pass along. For Duncan, that would be easy since he and Joelle were just down the hall in the main suite. Slater could update the others with short texts.

Sighing, Lana sat on the foot of the guest bed, the baby monitor right next to her, when she made the call to Pamela. It wasn't the first attempt since they'd seen that photo of her mother leaving the apartment with a gun in her purse. Lana had tried to call her immediately afterward, but the woman hadn't answered. Definitely not something Slater and Lana had wanted.

However, Pamela had texted back within the hour to check and make sure Lana was all right and to let her know that the San Antonio police had asked her to come in for an interview about the shooting. Pamela didn't offer any details of that interview and had messaged that she would be able to speak to Lana later.

Well, it was later, and Slater sincerely hoped the woman responded. If not, he was going to have to call Ruston again and see what he could find out. Slater wasn't surprised that the cops would want to speak to Pamela, since the shooting had happened on the estate where she lived.

And because of the recent rift she'd had with her husband.

Yeah, the cops would definitely want to question her about that, since it could play into motive. If she was the shooter, that is. Slater had no idea if Pamela was actually capable of that, but it was possible, especially if there had been an affair going on between Taylor and Leonard.

Since Lana put the call on speaker, Slater heard the three rings and silently cursed, figuring this was about to go to voicemail. It didn't, though. Pamela finally answered.

"Lana, are you sure you're all right?" Pamela immediately asked.

"Slater and I are fine. He's here with me, and I have the call on speaker so he can listen." Lana's tone stayed cool. "I'm sure you've heard, though, that Taylor is dead."

"Yes. It's all such a mess. The detective who questioned me wouldn't say what had happened so I called Marsh, and he filled me in."

Marsh, not Leonard, and that meant there was still a rift between husband and wife.

"Did you see the person who shot at you?" Pamela added.

Lana paused, maybe to see how her mother would respond to the silence, but Pamela kept quiet as well. "No," Lana finally said.

"I'm so sorry." Pamela sounded genuine about that, and it made Slater wish he could see the woman's face so he could try to detect a lie. "Do you think it was Taylor?"

Lana sighed again, and instead of answering her mother's question, she went with one of her own. "Why'd you leave the apartment earlier today?"

"I told you. I went to the interview with the detective at SAPD."

"Not then, Mother. Before that. Before the shooting. You left the safe place you had us arrange for you, and you had a gun with you."

Again, Pamela went silent for several moments. "I didn't want to tell you about that, but I met with a private investigator." Another pause, even longer than the others. "I asked the person to dig up any dirt on your father. And I'm sure there's plenty of that to find."

Slater couldn't argue with that, but the timing seemed way off. "You were worried about your safety," Slater pointed out. "So why not just talk with the PI over the phone?"

"I did speak to her briefly, but I wanted to meet with her in person to make sure our conversation wouldn't be recorded. Leonard has a lot of important people in his pocket, and I didn't know if this particular PI was one of them. It's Julia Munson from Sensor. She works with Lana."

He and Lana exchanged glances, and Lana immediately fired off a text to Julia. No doubt to confirm there had indeed been a meeting.

"What do you expect Julia to find on Leonard?" Slater asked Pamela.

"Anything I can use. I plan on divorcing him," Pamela added, and her voice wavered. "And I'll need any and all ammunition. Before I left the estate, I copied some files from Leonard's computer, and I wanted Julia to see if there was something in them."

Slater huffed. "If you copied the files without permission, then you probably won't be able to use anything incriminating."

"That's what Julia told me, but I asked her to look, anyway." Another pause. "I want proof that he was having sex with Taylor. Taylor!" she repeated, and there was a jab of fury in her tone. "I've turned a blind eye to that sort of thing for years, but I'm fed up with it. Taylor flaunted the affair by telling her friends all about it. Leonard should have known the gossip would get back to me."

Slater wondered if Pamela had just spelled out her motive for the shooting. She could have fired the shots at him and Lana as a diversion with the actual target being Taylor.

"Did the detective who questioned you take your gun?" Slater asked.

"No. I didn't have it with me when I went to the police station. I took it to the PI's office because, well, as you said, I was scared. I didn't know if Leonard was going to use one of his goons to try to silence me."

And there was Leonard's motive all spelled out. Again, Taylor could have been the target to stop her from gossiping about their affair. It sickened Slater to think Lana could have been killed in what would have been just collateral damage to Leonard. Or to Pamela. Then again, the same could apply to Marsh.

As far as Slater was concerned, all three were still suspects, and that's why he sent his own text. This one to Ruston to remind him they needed to get Pamela's gun.

"Anyway, since I decided I could trust Julia," Pamela went on, "I asked her to put an entire team together to go through those files and find anything they could. Not just about his affair with Taylor but with others. I know there were others," she added in a mutter.

Slater thought of the photo Taylor had shown Lana and him. "Did he have an affair with Alicia?" Slater came out and asked.

"I honestly don't know," Pamela said, and all the anger seemed to have seeped from her. There was a weariness in her voice now. "I didn't suspect it at the time, but I asked Julia to go back as far as she could. If he carried on with Alicia, there might be some proof of it."

Maybe, and Slater figured it was practically impossible to keep something like that a total secret. Maybe Julia would be able to find something, and if so, there'd be the link from Alicia to the murder of Slater's father.

"I'd like to stay here at the apartment awhile longer," Pamela continued. "Maybe just a day or two, but I plan on getting my own place. Julia said she could set that up for me, too. Where will you go that's safe, Lana?" she tacked onto that.

"Cameron and I will be fine where we are," Lana assured her.

Lana obviously didn't give her mother her location, and Pamela didn't ask. The woman probably suspected, though, that Lana, the baby and he were somewhere in Saddle Ridge.

"Have a good night," Pamela said, ending the call.

Before Lana could even put her phone away, she got a text. "It's Julia," she relayed. "She confirmed my mother came in to see her today."

"Does the timing work to give her an alibi for not being near the estate during the shooting?" he asked.

She shook her head. "Not really. According to Julia, she had a long conversation with my mother over the phone, but their visit only lasted a couple of minutes, long enough for my mother to give Julia the files and to pay the retainer."

Pamela definitely hadn't mentioned that, and if she'd told the detective the truth during the questioning, the San Antonio cops would be looking for any proof that Pamela was in the vicinity of the shooting.

As if Ruston had read his mind, Slater got a text as well, and he was glad to see his brother's response. He figured it'd please Lana, too, so he read it aloud. "'Detective O'Malley and I are going to the apartment now to take Pamela's gun. It'll be sent for immediate testing.'"

Good. That way, they'd know not only if it'd been recently fired but if it was the weapon that'd been used to kill Taylor.

Lana sat there, staring at her phone as if trying to process, well, everything. They'd gotten so much information over the past two days and had been attacked twice. And even after all that, they still didn't know if Taylor had actually been Buck's accomplice or if she'd been set up. Heck, they didn't even know if the accomplice had anything to do with the attacks. They weren't exactly at square one in the investigation, but it felt like it.

The sound Lana made was of pure frustration, and Slater went to her. It wasn't a smart move, but he sat down next to her and put his arm around her.

"You believe what your mother said?" Slater asked.

"I don't know. I want to believe her, but that's not the same thing."

No, it wasn't, and he was glad she understood that. Glad that she could try to look at all of this with some objectivity. He rethought that, though, when she looked at him, and he saw no trace of that objectivity in her eyes. It was a mix of weariness, fatigue and…resignation.

Slater understood all three of those emotions. Because he was feeling them himself. The first two, the weariness and fatigue, were because of the attacks and the investigation. But the third, that was all about this intensity between them on a personal level. The attraction.

The need.

Yeah, it was all that and more, and even though it would have been easy to blame it on the sense of urgency and immediacy caused by the danger, it was more than that. Maybe it always had been but they'd managed to keep a leash on it.

The leash was gone now.

Slater could see that, too, in Lana's eyes as she stood, dropped both the baby monitor and her phone onto the bed and went to him. Before she even made it to him, they were reaching for each other.

Their mouths immediately met, and this was no gentle, soothing kiss. This was all about the need. All about that urgency. And there was no leash in sight that could contain this. Even more, Slater didn't want to contain it, and it was obvious that Lana felt the same way.

He couldn't say which of them deepened the kiss. It seemed to happen at the exact second, and with that same intensity, that was swirling around them. Her taste roared through him, but there was no time to savor it. No. The need was too strong for that. The savoring would have to happen later. This was all about sating that need that just wouldn't stop.

Her arms went around him, and he slid his around her waist, pulling them body to body. Until they were pressed against each other. Of course, that only amplified everything, especially since the hungry kiss continued.

Somehow with Lana still in his arms, Slater made it to the door to close it and lock it so they would have some privacy to finish this. With the baby just next door, there was always the possibility of an interruption if Cameron woke up, and if he did, they would hear him on the baby monitor. For now, though, they just focused on this, on being together.

The kissing somehow managed to become even more fierce, and that urged on some touching. He slid his hand over her bottom, cupping her, and pressing her against his erection. Lana did her share of touching, too, and ran her hands over his back, her fingers digging into him.

It didn't take long for them to start grappling to get out of their clothes. This had to happen much faster than either of them wanted, but they went with the breakneck pace. Slater caught on to her top, pulling it off over her head and tossing it aside so he could kiss her breasts. In the back of his mind, he knew he would like to savor this part of her even more, but this was going to be a situation where foreplay happened afterward.

Lana rid him of his shirt, too, but first she had to remove his shoulder holster. No easy feat, and Slater had to stop the kissing and touching for a couple of seconds while he helped her with that. Finally, though, they both had their shirts off, and to complete the skin-to-skin contact, he eased off her bra.

Despite the need demanding release, Slater took a moment to kiss her neck. And then her stomach. Of course, that only fueled the heat even more until Lana was pulling him toward the bed. Her back landed on the soft mattress, and he landed on top of her. He hadn't thought it possible, but the heat went up even more, and the battle began to get out of the rest of their clothes.

He wanted her naked, now, and obviously Lana had the same idea. Slater had to move off her so she could undo his belt. Again, not easy since their hands were frantic now, so he helped her with that as well and was thankful that getting her out of her jeans was a much simpler process. He slid them off her. Her panties, too. And soon he had his hands and mouth on a naked Lana.

She was beautiful, of course. Everything he'd expected and more. More because she moved with him as if they'd been born to be in sync with each other.

"Condom," he managed to mutter, and Slater took the one from his wallet before Lana tossed his jeans and boxers onto the floor. He was pretty sure they landed somewhere near Lana's jeans and panties.

"Now," she insisted.

And that's exactly what he gave her once he had on the condom. Slater pushed into her, feeling the slam of intense pleasure that nearly robbed him of his breath. He apparently didn't need breath to finish this, though, because Lana lifted her hips, starting the thrusts inside her.

The pleasure built. And built. Until Slater could feel the freight train of pressure roaring through him. He silently cursed that he couldn't hang on to the pleasure, but Lana couldn't hold on, either. Her climax rippled through her, clamping on to him and forcing him to let go.

Slater gathered her into his arms and gave in to the heat. He gave in to Lana.

LANA LAY ON the guest bed and waited for Slater to come out of the adjoining bathroom. Thankfully, her body was still buzzing from pleasure so she hadn't delved into any thoughts or regrets. She simply let herself stay slack while she kept her gaze pinned to the baby monitor.

Cameron was still asleep. For how long, Lana didn't know. Apparently, some newborns defied the cliché of sleeping like a baby, and Lana had learned in her very short time with him that sleep could last as little as an hour or stretch to three or four. That meant she had to be ready to get up and give him a bottle, which was the reason she'd put back on her clothes after Slater had gone in for the pit stop in the bathroom.

The nanny and Joelle had both offered to take the night shift for her so she could get some sleep, but Lana had declined. She needed to get used to Cameron's unpredictable routine, which was her new normal. Or rather it would be her normal once the investigation was finished.

Whenever that would be.

Lana shoved that aside, too, and concentrated on hanging on to her buzz. Slater helped with that by coming out of the bathroom. Unlike her, he was naked, and he certainly made an amazing picture walking toward her. His lanky body had just the right amount of muscles. His face, the right amount of character to prevent him from being an outright pretty boy.

He was smiling a little when he came to her, leaned down and kissed her. That helped rebuild the buzz, too, and the kiss turned so hot she nearly asked if he had a second condom.

"I don't want either of us to overthink this," she said instead.

That widened his smile. "Good." He ran his gaze over her body. "I seem a little underdressed."

She sat up, took his hand and looked him over as well. "It suits me." And she sighed. "You're...hot," she settled for saying.

Now he chuckled and moved in to give her one of his scorcher kisses when her phone rang. Both of them groaned, but they knew they couldn't just ignore it. Lana especially knew that was true when she saw the name on the screen.

"It's Julia," she relayed, automatically checking the time. It was just after 9:00 p.m., past the usual time for a friendly chat, so Lana answered it right away in case there was an emergency of some kind. "Is something wrong?" she asked, putting the call on speaker.

Julia certainly didn't jump to reassure her that all was well. "Yes. I'm obviously working late, and I found something in one of the files your mother wanted me to look at."

Since there were plenty of things a thorough PI like Julia could have found, Lana didn't speculate. She just waited for Julia to continue. Slater must have realized the potential for truly bad news because he started getting dressed.

"In one of the files, there were some copies of email conversations between your father and Buck. I intend to send them to a tech to make sure they're real and that the file is actually as old as it seems to be." Julia paused. "The emails appear to go back nearly twenty years."

Twenty years. Lana immediately made a connection with that since it'd been when Alicia was murdered. Judging from the intense look Slater got in his eyes, he'd made the connection, too.

"The emails by themselves aren't confessions," Julia went on. "The wording seems to be intentionally vague. Here, I'll just read you one, and you can see what I mean. This is from Buck. 'I moved her to where you said, and nobody saw me. There was too much mess to clean up so I left it.'"

Everything inside Lana went still. Yes, she could see why the email would have alarmed Julia. "And the date on them?"

Julia sighed. "The night of Alicia Monroe's murder."

Of course it was. "What was my father's response?"

"'Make sure no one finds her. Ever. If they do, you'll go

down for this.'" Again, she paused. "It sounds as if Buck
and Leonard were in on this together. Sounds," Julia emphasized. "That's why I want to have the techs look at it. It's
possible someone planted this on your father's computer.
Someone like BoBo."

That was true, but it was equally possible the emails
were real.

"Why would Buck and Leonard have a conversation
like this via email rather than texts or calls?" Slater asked.

Lana silently cursed herself for not having already considered that. It might be an indication these were indeed
faked.

"I have no idea, unless they didn't want there to be any
phone records. Burners were around then, but maybe one
of them didn't have a burner. Still, if it's secrecy you're
going for, then why keep the emails?"

Unfortunately, Lana could think of a reason. "Insurance," Slater and she said together. So obviously he'd considered this as well.

"This way, if Buck rats him out, Leonard has proof that
Buck was involved. Maybe even the actual killer."

That was true, but Lana's stomach twisted. Because
maybe Buck was just the cleanup man and her father had
been the one to kill Alicia. Lana was still considering that
when her phone dinged with an incoming call.

"My mother is calling," Lana relayed to Julia. "Does she
know about what you've found?"

"No, I wanted to tell you first, but your mom copied the
files before she gave them to me, and she said she planned
to go through them. So maybe she found the emails as
well."

Yes, and if she did, her mother would be frantic.

"Go ahead and take her call," Julia encouraged, "and

if you have any questions, you can phone me back. In the meantime, I'll send these emails to one of our techs."

She ended the call with Julia so she could talk with her mother. The moment she heard her mom's voice, Lana knew that something was indeed wrong.

"Lana," her mother blurted. "Oh, God, Lana. Something horrible happened."

"What?" Lana asked through the muscles that had tightened in her throat.

"It's all there in the files from your father's computer." She broke into a loud sob. "It's all there."

"What's there?" Lana insisted.

Her mother didn't answer for a long time. "God, Lana. Your father murdered Alicia, and I believe I know where her body is buried."

Chapter Fifteen

Slater felt as if all the air had been sucked out of the room. Out of his body. And he had no doubts Lana was battling the same thing right now.

The shock and sickening dread of what Pamela had just said.

Your father murdered Alicia, and I believe I know where her body is buried.

Slater had to shove aside the emotion of that accusation and remind himself to think like a cop. And that meant questioning things well beyond the surface level.

"Pamela, what did you find to make you think that?" Slater demanded once he was able to speak.

"Some old emails from the files I took from Leonard's computer." Pamela was still crying, but her words were rushed, as if she couldn't say them fast enough. "I saw the date on them. It was when Alicia was murdered, and then I remembered something else. One of our vehicles had to be towed then. I don't know why I recalled it, but it just flashed in my head when I read those emails."

"Slow down, Mother," Lana instructed. "What does a possible car malfunction have to do with Alicia's murder and the emails?"

"Everything," Pamela insisted, and she repeated the

word several times before she finally continued. "I got a call from a tow truck company that night, and the person told me they had pulled the car out of a bog but there was some damage to the front end, and they wanted to know if they should go ahead and take it to the garage where the estate vehicles were normally taken for servicing and such."

Slater mentally worked his way through that. This was obviously a towing service that Leonard was accustomed to using if they knew where to take the damaged vehicle.

"A bog?" Lana questioned.

"Yes, I think they said it'd gotten stuck in the mud."

"Was Leonard driving the car?" Slater pressed, and again, he reminded himself that this could all mean nothing.

"I'm not sure. I don't think so. He was supposed to be at a fundraiser that night. I didn't go because I had one of my migraines, but normally, Leonard would have a driver take us to and from such things."

"Do you recall the name of the fundraiser or where it was held?" Slater wanted to know.

"I'm sorry, I don't, but you could probably check the date since it was the night Alicia was killed. I'm not sure, though, if people would actually remember Leonard being there or not. It's been so long."

Yes, it had been. Twenty years was a long time to try to confirm an alibi, but it was possible that someone had taken or posted photos of the event.

"I'm not sure why they called me instead of your father," Pamela went on several moments later, "and I didn't think of asking them. I just wrote down the info, including the location of the pickup and the time." She sobbed again. "It was at that old abandoned rodeo arena. The one out on Carston Road."

Slater knew the one. It'd been an active site for small

rodeos when he was a kid, but it had shut down about twenty-five years ago. Which meant it would have indeed been abandoned and empty when Alicia had died. As far as Slater knew, the owners had just left the place to rot away. It was a good place to bury a body.

"I think Buck or Leonard took Alicia there," Pamela spelled out. "And I think a clue to where she's buried is in one of the emails. Buck told Leonard that he'd 'moved her to where you said,' and Leonard answered, 'Make sure no one finds her. Ever.'"

That was exactly what Julia had already relayed to them. "That doesn't give you a specific location for a grave," Slater pointed out. "Leonard or Buck probably wouldn't have allowed the tow truck to come that close if a body had been buried there."

"I agree, and that's why I kept digging through the files." Pamela paused a heartbeat. "I found another email. This one came the following day, and in it, Buck said, and I quote, 'I put her with the horses.'"

Slater glanced at Lana to see if she had a clue as to what that meant, but she shook her head. "Did he mean one of the stalls inside the old arena?"

"I don't think so," Pamela was quick to say. "I found an article on the internet about some horses being buried on the west side of the arena. Apparently, the owner created a sort of cemetery there."

That jogged his memory, and Slater recalled hearing about the burials. He quickly used his phone to do a search, and while there weren't many articles on the old arena that had once been called Rodeo Park, he did find one that mentioned the graves. Apparently, the owner had used the boggy area to bury some of the horses that had been champions.

"At the time of Alicia's death," Pamela went on, "the rodeo arena would have been closed for five years. No visitors to find a fresh grave. And there's this other thing I found. Buck's grandparents had a ranch less than five miles from the arena. I'm betting he visited there when he was a kid."

Slater was betting the same thing, and while there was still no concrete proof that's where Alicia was buried, or that Buck and Leonard had been the ones to kill her, the circumstantial evidence was starting to come together.

Alicia and Leonard had been having an affair, and something could have happened between them. An argument that'd turned violent. Or maybe some kind of jealous altercation involving Buck, Leonard and Alicia that had led to her death. Unless Leonard confessed about that, they might never know exactly what'd happened, but if there was indeed a body at Rodeo Park, then that added some physical proof to the circumstantial.

Slater's attention went back to Pamela when she made another of those raw sobbing sounds. "And this means Buck and Leonard could have murdered Slater's father," she ground out. "They could have done it to silence him. Maybe Sheriff McCullough was getting too close to uncovering the truth."

Hearing that said aloud felt like another punch to Slater's gut, though his mind had already gone in that direction. And it was a direction he had to take.

"I'll start arranging for a CSI team to go out to Rodeo Park and check for any signs of Alicia's grave," he said, somehow managing to keep his voice level. Inside, though, was a whole different story. He was battling an emotional hurricane that was ripping right through him.

"You'll let me know if they find anything," Pamela muttered, and then she quickly added, "I have to go." And she broke down crying.

"Mom?" Lana tried, but the woman had already ended the call.

Lana turned to him, and even though he wanted to get started with that call to Duncan and the CSIs, Slater took a moment to try to settle some of the panic and dread he saw on Lana's face.

He pulled her into his arms and brushed a kiss on her forehead. "One step at a time," he murmured. "It could take hours or even days for Duncan to get a warrant to search the grounds. It's in his jurisdiction," Slater added. "So we won't have to deal with the San Antonio cops."

At least they wouldn't unless there was a body buried there. Then it would mean Leonard's arrest. Or at least the man being brought in for questioning. After that, a body would have to be sent to the medical examiner and maybe even a forensic scientist for evaluation. This was going to be a long, grueling ordeal, and at the tail end of it would be yet another new level of investigation into his father's murder.

After a couple of moments, Lana finally eased back and looked up at him. "Slater, I'm so sorry."

It took him a moment to realize why she was apologizing. Hell. No way did he want her to take a drop of blame for anything her father might have done. So he kissed her again. This time on the mouth. He hoped it settled some of her nerves because that's what it did for him, and then he stepped away from her to go up the hall to talk to Duncan. It would no doubt be a long conversation, followed by getting all the cogs moving for the warrant and the CSIs. In other words, it was going to be a very long night.

"I'll have Duncan come in here so we can talk," Slater

suggested. Of course, Joelle would likely want to be involved with that, too.

He left Lana while he went down the hall and lightly tapped on the door of the main bedroom. Slater immediately heard the footsteps, and a moment later both his sister and Duncan answered the door.

"What happened?" his sister wanted to know. Like Duncan, she wasn't dressed for bed, but Slater spotted two laptops and a baby monitor in the small seating area of the room.

"We need to talk," Slater said, motioning for them to follow him. "There have been some developments."

That was all he got a chance to say before Lana rushed out into the hall. She, too, had the baby monitor in one hand and her phone in the other.

"There's a problem," Lana blurted. "My mom just called and said she was going to Rodeo Park."

Hell. Not this.

"I tried to talk her out of it," Lana quickly added. "But she won't listen. Slater, she's already on her way there to look for Alicia's grave."

LANA CURSED UNDER her breath when she tried again to call her mother, and like the other four times, her mother didn't answer. The calls went straight to voicemail. Lana had left three other messages for her mother not to go anywhere near the Rodeo Park, but she didn't even bother to leave a fourth.

Her mother was no doubt on her way to what could be a burial site.

If Pamela did find something, then the evidence could be destroyed. But that wasn't even her biggest concern at the moment. It was Leonard. What would he do if he found out where his wife was going? As much as Lana hated to consider it, she had to.

Her father might try to murder her mother.

It didn't matter that Lana wasn't close to either of them. Heck, she didn't even like them. But she didn't want another person to die.

Obviously, Duncan and Slater felt the same way because they were hurriedly assembling a plan. A plan that was being amended as they spoke. At the first suggestion, Duncan and Slater said they'd be going alone, but Lana had nixed that. If anyone could convince her mother to back off, it'd be her. It had taken Lana some time to convince Slater of that, but he'd finally relented.

"Luca, Sonya and Joelle will stay here with the babies," Slater spelled out while he, Duncan and Lana strapped on their weapons.

Lana was thankful for the extra security since she didn't want Buck's accomplice to take advantage of their absence to try to kidnap Cameron.

"And, Duncan, you and I will take precautions in case this turns out to be something different from what it seems," Slater added to her.

She was quick to agree. Because she, too, had already considered several disturbing possibilities. Maybe her mother was the accomplice and this was to draw them out. Or the accomplice could be using her mother to set all of this up. The emails could be fake, designed to draw them all out to a secluded location where they could be attacked.

And that led right back to her father.

Or Marsh.

No way was Lana going to cross him off the list of suspects. After all, Marsh had been around when Alicia was murdered, too, and he could have murdered her alone or teamed up with Buck.

"Stay safe," Joelle muttered when they started for the door and the cruiser that was waiting for them outside. She kissed her husband and gave her brother and Lana hugs. "Stay safe," she repeated.

"We will," Duncan promised, and they stepped out of the house and into the night.

There was a chill in the air, and the drop in temps had caused a wispy gray fog to hover just over the yard and driveway. Lana hadn't needed anything else to rev up the tension inside her, but the spookiness only added to it.

"Try your mother again," Duncan instructed once they were on the road with Duncan behind the wheel and her and Slater in the back.

Lana did, but like the other times, it went straight to voicemail. This time, though, Lana did leave another message.

"Don't look for the grave, Mother. Sheriff Holder, Slater and I are on the way. Stay put."

Whether her mother would obey was anyone's guess, but Lana was hoping this spooky atmosphere and the night would at least give Pamela cause to stop and rethink what she was doing.

"Have you been to Rodeo Park before?" Slater asked her.

Lana shook her head. "I've only driven past it."

But she knew it wasn't far. Only about five miles away. Still, it would be a very long drive since they had to stay vigilant for any attacks along the way.

"My dad used to take me and my siblings there," Slater muttered, keeping watch out the window. "It used to be a fairly open field, but last time I saw it a couple of years ago, the nearby woods had practically taken it over. Unless your mother's dressed for a hike, she probably won't have gotten far."

Good. Better yet, maybe Pamela had already changed her mind and already turned back toward the apartment.

Duncan threaded the cruiser around the deep curves of the country road, and when they reached the turnoff, the road narrowed even more. Obviously, there wasn't a beaten track because what was left of the asphalt was pocked with potholes and even some weeds sticking up through massive cracks.

Thankfully, it didn't take long for a building to come into sight. Well, what was left of the building, anyway. Lana could see glimpses of what had once been a rodeo arena, but portions of the massive roof had collapsed. Slater had been right, too, about the woods reclaiming the place. The wild shrubs now littered what was once a parking lot, and the massive tree limbs were like a canopy that was doing an effective job of shutting out the sliver of moonlight.

Lana sighed when she saw something else. Her mother's car. It was parked in one of the few spots on the concrete where the weeds and shrubs hadn't spread. The headlights were on, and the driver's-side door was open.

But there was no sign of her mother.

"Keep watch," Slater reminded her when Lana automatically hurried to get out and find her mom.

He was right. This could still be some kind of trap, but if her father and Marsh had come here, they'd parked out of sight. Unfortunately, that would be plenty doable because of the trees. It was possible her father had even sent a henchman to silence her mother, and if so, it could already be too...

Lana cut off that thought. She couldn't think of another murder right now. She had to focus on getting her mother safely out of there so she didn't contaminate a scene that needed to be examined.

Duncan stepped from the cruiser and put his hand over his gun. "Mrs. Walsh?" he called out.

Her mother didn't answer, and the grounds were almost totally silence. There wasn't even any buzzing of mosquitoes. Worse, the fog seemed to be getting even thicker and was swirling around their legs.

Duncan called out to her mother again, and when there was no response this second time, Lana got out of the cruiser as well. She stayed behind the cover of the door, knowing it wouldn't do much good if someone tried to shoot her in the head. Still, she looked around and saw no one ready to gun them down.

"Mom?" Lana tried.

And there was an instant reaction. Sort of a muffled sound of relief, and several seconds later, her mother came out from behind one of the trees. Lana felt both relief and anger that her mother had come here.

Pamela wasn't near the crumbling arena building but rather on what Lana thought was the west side of the property where the horse cemetery would be. Her mother was holding a flashlight that she had pointed toward the ground.

"I didn't know who drove up," her mother said, not coming closer. She stayed put, her body partially hidden behind the massive oak. "I wanted to make sure it wasn't your father or Marsh."

Lana could understand that, but it didn't ease her anger. "You shouldn't be here," she warned her.

"I have to find out the truth," Pamela insisted.

"No, you don't," Duncan said, sounding very much like

the lawman in charge. "We'll have a warrant soon, and then a CSI team."

Her mother frantically shook her head. "It might be too late. If Leonard knows we're onto him, he could do something to destroy the scene. He could set a fire or something."

A fire would definitely do some damage, but it likely wouldn't obliterate a body in the ground.

"Come back to your car, Mrs. Walsh," Duncan ordered.

Again, her mother didn't respond. Not with words, anyway. But Pamela turned and started running.

Both Slater and Duncan cursed, and the three of them went after her. Thankfully, her mother wasn't hard to follow because she kept on her flashlight, and Lana could see it bobbing through the dark and fog as her mother ran. Not for long, though. Her mother stopped.

Then screamed.

The sound ripped through the night and caused her, Slater and Duncan to speed up. Lana tried to tamp down any worst-case scenarios. And failed. There were just too many dangerous possibilities, ranging from a killer to wildlife about to attack.

By the time they made it to Pamela, she turned. Her eyes were wide, and her mouth was open as if preparing for another scream.

"There," her mother said, and she aimed a trembling hand at something on the ground in front of her.

Steeling herself for what she might see, Lana moved closer. And closer. Until the fog cleared for a second or two so she could see the headstones for what she presumed were the horses' graves. Then she saw something else.

Something that sent her heart to her knees.

Because there was another grave, an unmarked one, and it wasn't covered, either. It was now a gaping hole.

Duncan fanned his flashlight into the hole and groaned. Lana soon saw why. At the bottom of the hole were the bleached white bones of what had once been a body.

Chapter Sixteen

Slater cursed when he caught glimpses of the body through the breaks in the fog. Or rather what was left of the body, anyway. Not all the bones seemed to be there, but there were enough of them for him to know it was human remains.

The skull was evidence of that.

The cop part of him warned him not to jump to any conclusions. That this might not be Alicia Monroe. But with the emails and the tow truck that'd picked up a vehicle here, it was hard for him not to look at those bones and see the young woman that Alicia had once been.

Duncan was muttering some profanity, too, and he fanned his flashlight around the grave, no doubt looking for any footprints that didn't belong to any of them. Slater didn't immediately see any, but the weeds and grass likely would have prevented deep impressions into the ground.

"It's true," Pamela sobbed. "It's all true." She buried her face against Lana's shoulder when Lana pulled the woman into her arms. "Leonard killed Alicia and buried her here."

Maybe, but no matter who this was, the scene had to be preserved. Of course, it had already been compromised. And recently. Slater looked at the mounds of dirt around the sides of the grave, and he was pretty sure someone had attempted to dig it up.

But why?

To remove the body?

If so, the person had failed because the body was still there. Maybe the digging had been step one, and the person was coming back to finish the exhumation. Again, though, he had to ask himself why. The immediate answer that came to mind was that Buck had realized the location was about to be compromised and had dug it up, only to die before he could finish the job.

Was that it?

Slater continued to mull that over and was about to escort Lana and Pamela back to the cruiser so that he and Duncan could start the necessary phone calls needed in a situation like this. But Slater stopped when the glint of something caught his eye. Duncan stopped, too, fixing the flashlight onto the upper torso of the skeleton.

And Slater saw it then.

A silver heart pendant on a thick chain.

"What is it?" Pamela asked, trying to get a look at what had caught their attention.

Lana must have thought they'd seen something ghoulish, because she gathered her mother into her arms and started leading her away from the grave. Slater was all for that. In fact, he wanted Lana back in the cruiser where she'd be safer, but first he used his phone to take some photos of the skeleton and that necklace.

A necklace he thought he remembered seeing before.

But where?

"Let's go with them," Duncan instructed, taking out his phone. "We still need that warrant, because anything we find here might not be admissible without it."

True, and it could mean a killer could walk. No way did

they want that to happen. Not when they had perhaps finally found Alicia's body.

While they kept watch around them and started back
toward the parking lot, Duncan made a phone call to the
county district attorney so he could give a push on that
warrant. The fog had gotten even thicker now. Even if they
managed that warrant in the next couple of hours, the CSI
team might not be able to start right away because of visibility. Still, they had to try, and they might be able to set up
enough fans and blowers to keep away the fog while they
at least set up something to secure the grave and remains.

"Will you arrest Leonard for murder?" Pamela asked.
It took Slater a moment to realize she was directing the
question at him.

"I'm not sure what will happen," he answered honestly
as Lana helped her mother into the back seat of the cruiser.
Duncan got behind the wheel, and Slater took shotgun.

"He'll be arrested," Pamela concluded, breaking into
another sob. "He must have killed Taylor. And Stephanie.
I know it was Buck who smothered her, but Leonard would
have been part of that, too."

Yeah, he would have been if Leonard was actually Buck's
accomplice. It meant Leonard had also been responsible for
the attacks on him and Lana.

Hell.

If Leonard had truly done all of this, then Slater would
make sure the man paid and paid hard.

Lana kept her arm around her mother, but she pinned
her gaze to Slater. "What did you see in the grave?" she
mouthed.

Slater went through the photos he'd taken and enlarged
the one that showed the heart pendant. Lana studied it,

frowned and shook her head. "It looks familiar," she said, again mouthing the words.

He nodded an agreement and tried to force himself to think. And then Slater recalled the party photo of Alicia, Leonard, Buck and Marsh that Taylor had shown them. After Taylor's murder, the phone she'd had with her had been taken into evidence, and Slater was hoping that photo was still on the phone and that Taylor hadn't moved it back to the storage cloud the woman had mentioned.

Slater called the lab and said a quick thanks when someone actually answered. Better yet, it was a tech, Mark Gonzales, who Slater knew well.

"I need a favor," Slater said to Mark after they'd exchanged greetings. "I need you to check the photos on Taylor Galway's phone. I'm looking for a picture taken twenty years ago at a party. Leonard Walsh is in the shot. So is Buck Holden," he added, knowing that Mark would likely recognize those two faces.

Slater was hoping that Pamela wouldn't be listening to the conversation, but when he glanced back at Lana and her, he realized Pamela was now staring at him.

"Taylor sent me a picture of Leonard and Buck at a party," Pamela muttered, and she began to fish her phone from her pocket.

"Got it," Mark said just as Pamela started scrolling through her own photos. "I'm texting it to you now."

Slater's phone dinged, and the picture loaded. Yeah, it was the one all right, and he immediately saw what he'd been pretty sure he remembered.

The heart pendant.

Alicia was wearing it.

Hell. Slater doubted that was a coincidence, and it was

yet another piece of evidence pointing to it being Alicia's body in the grave.

"Thanks," Slater told Mark, and he ended the call. Since Duncan had finished talking to the DA, Slater passed him his phone so he, too, could take a look.

"Here it is," Pamela said, lifting up her own phone for them to see.

It was the same photo all right. The one that had convinced Slater that Alicia and Leonard had been having an affair. It was also the one where Marsh had seemed to be mooning over Alicia. And where Buck and Leonard had appeared to be very friendly.

"Why did you want to see it?" Pamela asked, but she didn't wait for an answer. She turned the photo back toward her, and her gaze combed over it. Anger flashed in her eyes. Raw, vicious anger that she quickly shut down. "Leonard was sleeping with her, and then he killed her."

"Why would he have done that?" Duncan came out and asked.

Pamela lifted her shoulder in a shrug and kept her attention on the photo. "Maybe because Alicia tried to blackmail him or something. He opened himself up to blackmail when he got in bed with her." She stopped and gasped. "The necklace," she muttered.

Slater and Duncan exchanged surprised glances. "What necklace?" Lana asked, taking the phone from her mother so she could see.

"That one. The heart," Pamela blurted, but then she made another of those sobbing sounds. "It's the same one. I'm sure of it."

Lana took hold of Pamela's arms and turned her mother to face her. "What do you mean?"

"I mean, your father bought that necklace. Or one just

like it. I found it in a little gift bag in his car—" Pamela stopped when her voice broke. "He said it was a birthday gift for someone who worked in his office. I thought he was lying, but I never thought…" She stopped again and began to cry while sucking in loud, jerky breaths.

Slater looked at Lana. There was no anger in her eyes. Just a deep sadness that seemed to go all the way to her heart. She had to be thinking that she'd lived under the roof of a killer. One who'd killed his lover and had her buried here.

"Oh, God. I'm going to be sick," Pamela blurted, and before Lana could even reach for her, she bolted from the cruiser.

Pamela ran toward the arena, catching on to a thick log post that had once framed the entry. She lowered her head, and Slater heard the retching.

On a sigh, Lana got out, no doubt so she could go to her mother and try to offer her some comfort. Slater and Duncan got out as well, and even though Pamela's life seemed to be falling apart right now, they kept watch around them.

Lana took slow steps toward Pamela and was still a good twenty feet away when Pamela's body lurched. It was as if she'd either dived forward or had been yanked by someone.

Pamela screamed. A blood-curdling sound that echoed through the arena. And then the woman disappeared into the darkness.

FOR A MOMENT, Lana stood there frozen in shock over what she'd just seen and heard, but she quickly shook it off and bolted toward the arena. Or rather that's what she tried to do when Slater darted in front of her.

"You could be gunned down if you go in there," Slater

said, using the warning as they continued to move with Duncan right next to them.

Slater was right, of course. It looked as if someone had grabbed hold of her mother, and if so, that person could be Buck's accomplice. And this could be a setup to draw them out of the relative safety of the cruiser and into a building where they'd be easier prey.

Lana considered calling out to her mother, but she decided against it. She'd heard her mother's scream well enough, and if Pamela was capable of doing that again, she likely would have.

Which meant she could be gagged. Or hurt.

Or worse.

Lana didn't want to consider the worst. Couldn't. She had to stay focused on whatever danger they were about to face inside.

Duncan and Slater were clearly ready for the danger. In the sprint toward the arena, they had both stayed low while drawing their guns. Lana did the same, and when they reached the building, none of them rushed in. They stood there for a moment and just listened.

Lana thought she heard some footsteps, but the sound that stood out the most was the creaking of the roof. She prayed it wasn't about to collapse on them.

Slater stepped into the darkness first, and he moved even lower, practically to a squatting position, no doubt so he wouldn't be an easy target. Duncan moved in behind Lana, shielding her, she realized. She didn't want or expect him to take that kind of risk, but Duncan would likely consider it his duty to the badge.

A few seconds passed before Slater moved even deeper into the arena. Lana and Duncan were right behind him, and now that her eyes had had time to adjust to the darkness, she was able to better see the place. It wasn't a closed-in space but rather had walls that went up about six feet, allowing for the night breeze to rush through. It felt cold and damp, and the entire place smelled of mold and things she'd rather not smell. There was a sense of death here.

The dirt-filled center area, where once the performances and competitions had taken place, was huge. The weeds had made it into this part of the arena, too, but they weren't nearly as thick as they were in the parking lot and on the grounds.

The roof had indeed collapsed on one side, but a good portion of it was still intact. As were the bleachers that stretched out most of the length of the competition area. To the right were the stalls. Again, a large space where the horses and bulls would have been contained.

Lana didn't see her mother in any of those spots.

So where had the person taken her? There had to be exits, and it occurred to Lana that might be the plan. To drag her mother in here, only to hurry out to a waiting vehicle so she could be taken elsewhere.

But why?

Was it because the accomplice wanted to silence her? Maybe. If so, then her father or Marsh could be here.

Or it could be *something else*.

As much as Lana hated to consider that something else, she knew she had to. If Pamela had been the one to work with Buck, then it was possible the only threat she, Slater and Duncan were about to face would come from her mother.

Following Slater's direction and pace and while keeping their footsteps soft, they moved even deeper into the building. Lana focused on keeping watch on the stalls and the bleachers where there were plenty of spots for someone to hide.

Slater stopped, motioned toward the floor, and Lana saw the scuff marks in the dust and dirt on the ground. And there were more of them in the direction of the stalls. They started toward them, but the sound stopped them cold.

It was a moan.

Lana couldn't tell if her mother had made it or if the sound was one of pain, and again, she had to fight her instincts to bolt toward it. A good thing, too.

Because there was another sound.

A gunshot.

It rang out. A loud blast that tore through the air and sent them to the ground. A second one quickly followed. Then another. Lana couldn't tell where the bullets were landing, but she prayed they hadn't hit any of them. Or her mother. Of course, it could be her mother firing those shots.

Lana knew that her mother had firearms training and had even competed in target shooting competitions when she was younger. But that moan had come from the stalls, and the gunfire seemed to be coming from the bleachers.

Oh, God. Did they have two attackers?

Any of their suspects could have hired a henchman. However, there was another sickening possibility that the two of them had teamed up.

But why?

Was this about covering up Alicia's murder? Taylor's? Lana didn't know, but she hoped she soon had the answer so the danger could finally end.

There was another shot, and this time Lana had no trouble figuring out where it had hit. It slammed into the log post right next to Slater. Once again, they had to drop down and wait out the next flurry of gunfire.

Slater looked back at her, their gazes locking for a couple of seconds, and Lana saw the storm of emotions and worry in his eyes that was no doubt in hers as well. She didn't want any of them to die, but it could happen. It was obvious the shooter wanted them dead.

After what seemed an eternity, the gunshots stopped, and the silence that followed allowed Lana to hear another moan. Again, it'd come from the stalls, and Slater began to inch his way there. He stayed close to the partial wall, and with Duncan and Lana right behind them, they were only a few feet away from the stalls and those moans when another shot rang out.

This one smacked into the ground, so close to Slater that Lana saw the dust that the bullet had kicked up land on his arm. Cursing, Slater moved back, but Lana reached for him, pulling him away from the stall. Just as another shot came. And another.

"The shots are coming from there," Duncan said, tipping his head to the top of the bleachers on the far side of the arena.

Lana pivoted in that direction, automatically taking aim, but she didn't see anyone. The shooter had likely dropped down into the footwell space below the seats.

The anger roared through her, and she cursed this person who wanted them dead. And why? Because the shooter didn't want to have to pay for crimes that he or she had committed? Well, she wanted this snake to pay, and somehow she would figure out a way to make that happen.

"I'll shoot into the bleachers," Duncan said, keeping his voice at a whisper since any and every sound seemed to echo in the arena. "The two of you go to the stall and find out who's moaning. Be careful," he added. "It could be a trap."

Yes, it could be, because the person in the stall might be lying in wait for them and possibly didn't even need help.

Slater stayed in front of her as they began to move, and behind them, Duncan started shooting. Lana could hear the bullets slamming into the metal seats of the bleachers, and she prayed his gunfire was pinning down the shooter so he or she couldn't get off more shots.

It seemed to work.

No bullets came at her and Slater as they hurried toward the stalls. There were at least a dozen of them, and it was hard to pinpoint exactly where they'd heard those moans.

Slater kicked open the first stall gate and then immediately moved back in case there was an attacker inside. But it was empty.

Behind them, Duncan continued to fire, pausing only long enough to reload, and she and Slater went to the next stall. The gate to this one had already fallen off so they had no trouble seeing that no one was inside it.

They moved on to the next stall with the same results. Empty. And Lana began to wonder if the person who'd moaned was no longer there. Was this part of the ruse to kill them? Maybe. But she and Slater kept moving. Kept checking, and they made it to another stall. Slater kicked in the gate, darted to the side.

And Lana heard the moan.

Neither she nor Slater rushed in. They stayed put a couple of seconds before Slater peered into the stall, and because Lana was pressed right against his back, she felt his muscles tighten even more than they already were.

She looked over his shoulder to see what had caused that reaction. And Lana saw the person lying on the ground. Not Pamela.

But her father.

Chapter Seventeen

Slater definitely hadn't expected to find Leonard in the stall, and a whole bunch of questions immediately began to fly through his head.

Why the hell was Lana's father here? What did he want? And where was Pamela? She certainly wasn't in the stall with her husband, so had she been taken?

Or was she the person firing those shots?

Slater figured any and all of those possibilities could be true, but for now he focused on Leonard.

And the gun that the man had gripped in his hand.

Leonard didn't aim the gun at them. In fact, he stayed against the wall, his body sort of slumped to the side. Slater didn't want to take a chance, though, that Leonard might turn that gun on them, so he reached in and snatched it away. All without Leonard putting up a fight.

The man moaned again and shook his head. "Who's shooting?" he asked, his words slurred.

There was indeed some gunfire going on, and it was all coming from Duncan. Either he'd managed to pin down the shooter, or else the shooter had given up the fight and was escaping.

"Leonard's in here," Slater relayed to Duncan, figuring that wouldn't be info that Duncan was expecting.

"I'll check him for more weapons," Lana insisted, moving into the stall so she could frisk her father.

Again, her father put up no resistance whatsoever, and when Slater used the flashlight on his phone to aim it at the man, he saw Leonard's slack face and unfocused gaze. It was possible he'd been injured, but there wasn't any blood. However, the sleeve of his shirt had been shoved up, and there appeared to be a puncture mark on his arm. Not from a weapon but possibly from a needle.

"How did you get here, Leonard?" Slater asked while he continued to keep watch around them. He didn't want someone hiding in another stall to attack him and Lana while they were occupied with her father.

Leonard shook his head and ran his tongue over his bottom lip. "Here?" he questioned.

Yeah, he'd been drugged all right, but Slater figured that didn't mean the man hadn't committed murder. He could have done this to himself so he'd look innocent. After all, they'd just found the body of a woman he'd likely had some part in murdering.

Outside the stall, Duncan's shots trailed off some, and he was probably testing to see if the shooter would start up again. Hopefully not. Even though he and Lana were in the stall, it wouldn't give them much protection from bullets coming at them. And Duncan was practically out in the open where he, too, could be gunned down.

"Lana," Leonard murmured, clearly trying to focus his eyes on his daughter. "What happened?"

"You tell me," she countered. "You can explain how you got here and why your former lover, Alicia Monroe, is buried in a grave just a stone's throw away."

There was rage in her voice, and Slater couldn't blame her

one bit. He was feeling plenty of that himself. Not just for Alicia but for the danger that had nearly cost Lana her life.

"Buried?" Leonard repeated, shaking his head, but then he stopped. Just stopped. And any trace of color drained from his face. "Alicia." He said the name as a low moan that ended in a groan.

"Yes, Alicia," Lana snapped. "You murdered her and—"

"No," her father argued, and while that response was still slurred, he seemed adamant about it. "I didn't kill her."

"Then who did?" Lana snapped.

Leonard shook his head again. "Buck, I think. I think he did it. Because he was jealous. He was seeing her, too."

Lana grounded out some raw profanity. "And why didn't you report that to the cops?"

"No proof." Leonard repeated that a couple of times, and while he sounded somewhat convincing, Slater wasn't ready to buy it.

Not with so many unanswered questions.

There were those emails in the files that Pamela had taken from Leonard's computer. Or rather had supposedly taken. Slater had to concede it was possible that was a setup to frame Leonard for a murder he'd had no part in committing.

"It's me," Slater heard Duncan say, and a few seconds later, he slipped into the stall behind him and Lana. "There's no movement in the bleachers, no sign of the shooter. Or Pamela. I've called for backup."

Good. Because Slater wanted all the help they could get, and he knew this was far from over. They had to find Pamela. And the person who'd fired those shots. They could be one and the same, but they had to know.

"What the hell happened to him?" Duncan asked, tipping his head to Leonard while he continued to keep watch on the bleachers and the arena.

"To be determined. But I think he was drugged." Slater motioned to the puncture mark on his arm.

"Self-inflicted?" Duncan immediately wanted to know.

"Again, to be determined," Slater repeated.

"Drugged," Leonard muttered, and he, too, looked down at his arm. "Yes. Someone drugged me."

"Who did that?" Lana demanded, and she clearly wasn't ready to dole out any TLC. If it turned out her father was innocent, there'd be time for that later. For now, they had to take every precaution.

And that included treating Leonard like the killer he very well could be.

"I, uh, don't know," Leonard said, his eyelids fluttering down.

Lana huffed. "How did you get here? What's the last thing you remember?"

Leonard didn't give her the fast responses that she clearly wanted. "Don't know," he said, but then his eyes popped open again. "I was at the estate. I had a drink. Then I woke up here." He stopped, groaned. "Alicia's dead?"

Duncan huffed, too, and took out his phone. "I'll request an ambulance." He hadn't managed to press in the number, though, when there was a shout.

"Help," someone yelled, and it was a voice that Slater instantly recognized.

Pamela.

"It came from the bleachers," Duncan said, and both Lana and Slater pivoted in that direction.

Slater couldn't see Pamela, but he had no trouble hearing a second shout for help. Either the woman was in trouble or else this was part of the ploy to kill them.

"I'll go look for her," Duncan said.

"You're not going out there without backup," Slater insisted.

Then he had a fierce mental debate with himself. No way would he leave Lana here alone in case her father's drugging was all an act. Leonard didn't have any other weapons on him, but he could have a henchman waiting nearby to kill Lana.

Slater took out the pair of plastic cuffs he always carried with him, and he slapped them on Leonard. "If he's got a phone on him, take it," he instructed Lana.

"He didn't have one," she answered.

Good. Slater didn't want Leonard to have a way to contact anyone. "If he's not the killer," Slater spelled out, "then the real killer put him here. He or she could have just murdered Leonard but didn't so maybe he's a patsy, meant to be set up for whatever else is supposed to happen here. But in case Leonard's faking being drugged, I don't want him to be able to communicate with any thug who's helping him."

That's why Slater tore off the sleeve of his shirt and used it as a gag on Leonard's mouth. Again, if the man was innocent he could dole out an apology later, but the restraints and the gag just might stop Leonard from issuing an order to kill.

"Help me," Pamela shouted again, and it seemed to Slater as if the woman was on the move. Maybe running.

Slater didn't intend to take anything happening at face value, and when he, Duncan and Lana moved out of the stall, he did so with one thought. When they got to Pamela, she, too, would be treated as a killer until proven otherwise.

He glanced at Lana, and there were so many things Slater wanted to say to her. But now wasn't the time. Later, though, he needed to tell her just how much she meant to him. For now, he settled for a warning that he hoped she would obey.

"Stay behind me and keep your head down," he insisted.

A fierce look went through her eyes. "You stay alive. Hear me? Stay alive," she repeated.

"You do the same," Slater fired back before brushing a quick kiss on her mouth. Very quick. Since this wasn't the time for that, either.

With Slater going first, then Lana and Duncan, they scurried out of the stall and toward the bleachers. Not directly toward them, though. They raced toward the wall. Slater wanted a look beneath the bleachers to see if he could spot Pamela and anyone else. He only hoped the seats were stable enough and didn't come crashing down on top of them.

The three of them stopped when they reached the bleachers and listened. Slater cursed the silence and the darkness. He couldn't see anything, but he especially listened for any footsteps behind them. He didn't want anyone sneaking up on them or trying to get into the stall with Leonard.

"Keep an eye on the stall with your father," Slater whispered to her.

Lana nodded and shifted her position so she could do that as they inched farther beneath the bleachers. That's when he spotted the flashlight lying on the ground. He couldn't be certain, but it appeared to be the one that Pamela had been using.

Slater turned it on, and the powerful light illuminated a good portion of the space under the seats. Still no sounds or signs of anyone, though, and just when Slater had started to believe that maybe someone had escaped with Pamela, he heard something.

Movement out in the arena.

They all pivoted in that direction, and in the darkness, Slater shifted the flashlight toward the woman. Pamela. She was running across the massive stretch of dirt that made up the arena floor.

And her hands were tied in front of her.

"Help," she shouted.

Slater moved so he could get a better look at her and check to see if she was armed. After all, her hands might not be tied at all. Pamela shouted out a call for help again and kept running.

He, Duncan and Lana moved out from the bleachers, and Pamela must have seen them because she started running toward them. She didn't get far, though, because the gunshot stopped her.

It slammed into the ground right in front of her, causing her to skitter to a stop.

And the shot hadn't come from Pamela, either. It'd come from the bleachers. Slater turned the flashlight in the direction of the shooter and cursed.

Marsh was standing there.

LANA HAD KNOWN Marsh most of her life, but she'd never seen him with a gun. Nor had she ever seen that expression on his face.

The expression of a killer.

She caught just a glimpse of him before he ducked down out of sight. Marsh hadn't been smiling or gloating as Buck had done. No, Marsh's stare had been pure ice, and the shadows created by the flashlight had made him look like the monster that he was. In that moment, Lana realized Marsh was a cold-blooded murderer.

Slater must have realized that, too, because he pulled

Lana back, and while he kept both his gun and flashlight aimed at Marsh, he and Duncan kept cover of the bleachers.

"Stay put, Pamela," Marsh ordered when her mother started to struggle to get to her feet.

Marsh was peeking over one of the bleacher seats, his head barely visible. He didn't fire another shot. So, what was he waiting for? Maybe he had hired thugs on the way to help him. But she, Duncan and Slater had their own help in the form of backup that she hoped would be there soon.

"Marsh grabbed me and dragged me in here," Pamela sobbed. "He punched me, but I got away."

Despite the troubles that she and her mother had had, Lana was sorry that had happened to her. But Pamela was alive, and that was more than she could say for Alicia, Stephanie and Taylor.

But had Marsh been responsible for their murders? Lana wanted to shout that question, but she knew it could turn out to be a distraction that Duncan and Slater didn't need. Their goal right now was probably to get her mother out of harm's way and to make sure they weren't attacked.

At the thought of that, Lana turned to make sure her father was still in the stall. He was. They hadn't shut the door, and she could see him cuffed, gagged and sitting on the floor. She couldn't be sure, but she thought maybe he had slipped back into unconsciousness.

In the distance, Lana heard a welcome sound. Sirens. And she hoped it would prompt Marsh to surrender.

It didn't.

She heard the footsteps on the bleachers and braced herself for an attack. It didn't come. There was a thud as if someone had dropped to the ground. Several seconds later, the footsteps resumed and got a whole lot faster.

Marsh was running away.

Lana saw the split-second debate Duncan and Slater had about what to do. No way could they just leave her parents here, since Marsh could circle back and kill them. And they couldn't wait for backup, either, because Marsh could be long gone by then.

"Slater and I can go after him," Lana said.

She hoped it sounded much stronger than a mere suggestion. Because it was the best option. Duncan and Slater wouldn't want to leave her there while they went in pursuit, and whoever did go after Marsh would need backup. Duncan must have decided the same thing because he nodded.

"Go," Duncan ordered.

She and Slater took off running with Slater automatically moving in front of her again. Thankfully, they could still hear the sound of running footsteps, but they were on the other side of the arena so that's where they headed.

The fog was still slithering around the ground, so Lana couldn't actually see where their feet were landing, and she hoped they didn't trip over something. Hoped, too, that this wasn't a trap, but she had to accept that's exactly what it was.

They stayed low and kept moving, keeping watch around them in case Marsh had planted thugs out here to attack them. They ran, following the sound of those footsteps, and just ahead, Lana spotted Marsh. Thankfully, the trees weren't so thick here so there was light from the moon they could use to track his movements.

He was heading for the road.

And the car that was parked there.

They wouldn't have been able to see the vehicle when they arrived since Marsh had parked it in a bend just away from the arena. He'd no doubt done that on purpose. But why?

Why was he even here?

Marsh hadn't killed her parents even though he'd had plenty of chances, especially if he'd been the one who'd drugged her father and put him in that stall. And, yes, Marsh had fired shots at them, but most hadn't come close to hitting them. He could have just gunned them down, or rather tried to do that, when they'd arrived or when they'd been at the grave.

Lana didn't have the answer to any of those things, but she hoped she got the chance to catch and question Marsh.

Ahead of them, Marsh made a beeline for his car, but Lana kicked up the speed to close the distance between them. When they were only a few feet away, Slater bolted forward, diving at Marsh and tackling him. They landed hard on the asphalt.

Lana moved into a position so she could take aim at Marsh, but the man surprised her when he didn't fight. He looked up at her. Still no smile or gloating, but there was… something. She wasn't sure what, but that look chilled her to the bone.

Behind them, an explosion ripped through the arena.

The noise wasn't exactly deafening, but it had definitely been some kind of blast, and Lana's first thought was a horrible one. Had Duncan and her parents been killed? Oh, my God. Were they dead?

She gasped, instinctively pivoting toward the arena. So did Slater. And that's when Marsh made his move. Marsh rammed his elbow into Slater's jaw, knocking Slater off him. In the same motion, Marsh got to his feet and pointed his gun at them.

Lana could barely think, but she relied on her training. She brought up her own gun so she could fire. But Marsh managed to do that first. He pulled the trigger just as Slater caught hold of the man's legs and yanked him down. Marsh's shot went wild, slamming into a nearby tree.

The sounds of sirens got closer. So did the thuds of flesh punching flesh with the blows that Slater and Marsh were landing on each other. Both men still had their guns, and she knew it would be too easy for Marsh to try to put a bullet in Slater.

Still keeping watch for any help Marsh might have brought with him, Lana maneuvered around the fight, looking for any way she could put an end to it. She couldn't shoot. She couldn't risk hitting Slater. So she went old-school, and when Marsh pulled back his left hand to deliver another punch to Slater, Lana kicked Marsh in the head.

Marsh howled in pain and twisted his body to look back at her. It was the only opening Slater needed because he latched onto Marsh and put him in a choke hold. Marsh continued to fight, but Lana helped with that, too. She stomped down as hard as she could on his foot and then kicked the gun from his hand. It went flying and landed behind her.

But Marsh still wasn't finished with the fight. He clamped on to Slater's arm with his teeth and was flinging his head back and forth like a rabid dog. Lana delivered more kicks, this time to Marsh's kneecaps, and yelling in pain, the man dropped to the ground with Slater keeping his arm around Marsh's neck.

"I don't have any cuffs," Slater said, his breath gusting. The adrenaline was no doubt firing on all cylinders inside him, and he shot a glance in the direction of the arena.

The building was still in one piece, but Lana had no idea how much damage had been done. Or if Duncan and her parents had made it out alive.

"Backup will be here soon," she muttered to Slater and to herself for the reassurance they'd soon have help.

She was volleying glances at Slater, Marsh and their surroundings when there was another blast, the one much louder than the first. Lana could only watch in horror as she heard the sharp groan of the roof before it collapsed onto the arena.

Chapter Eighteen

Slater's heart slammed against his chest, and he had to fight his instincts to let go of Marsh and run toward the arena. Duncan and Lana's parents could be trying to claw their way out of the wreckage.

But he couldn't leave Lana alone with a killer.

And he had no doubts, none, that Marsh was exactly that.

Lana's hands were shaking and she'd gone ashen when she reached for Marsh's belt. It took Slater a couple of seconds to figure out what she was doing. She yanked the leather belt from the man's khakis and used it to make cuffs to restrain Marsh's hands behind his back. She didn't stop there. Lana took Slater's belt and did the same to Marsh's feet, hooking one belt through the other to essentially truss him up.

Slater snatched up Marsh's gun so the man wouldn't be able to somehow crawl his way to it, and he and Lana took off running toward the collapsed building. He was sure they were praying along the way. Slater certainly was, and he hoped that Duncan had somehow managed to get Pamela and Leonard out before the second blast.

The blue lights from the two approaching cruisers slashed through the darkness, and the moment the they stopped, Deputies David Morales and Ronnie Bishop bolted out of one of them. Luca and Deputy Brandon Rooney came out of the other.

"Arrest him and read him his rights," Slater instructed Luca, motioning toward Marsh, and he and Lana kept running with David and Ronnie right behind them.

Some of the muscles in Slater's chest unclenched when he saw that one of his prayers had been answered. Duncan was making his way toward them. His face and clothes were covered with dirt and dust, but he didn't seem injured.

Also thankfully, Duncan wasn't alone. Pamela's hands were no longer tied, and she was hobbling alongside her husband, who no longer seemed as drugged as he had earlier. Pamela bolted ahead of them and practically fell into Lana's arms.

"You made it out," Slater said, and there was a whole lot of relief in his voice and his entire body.

Duncan nodded. "We were by the stalls with Leonard for the first blast and were already outside for the second one." He looked in Marsh's direction. "Did he confess to setting the explosions?"

"Not yet, but he tried to escape. Then he tried to kill Lana and me."

Hearing his own words drilled home just how close they'd come to dying, and when Pamela let go of Lana, Slater pulled Lana into his arms. He didn't care who was watching. He just needed to hold her for a moment.

Like him, she was still plenty unsteady, and this would no doubt give them both hellish memories for the rest of their lives, but like Duncan, Leonard and Pamela, they were alive. They could deal with the rest later. He let go of Lana and turned back to her mother.

"Marsh was going to kill us," Pamela muttered. "He was going to kill us all."

Slater thought she might start crying, but she didn't. A fiery streak of temper crossed the woman's face, and Pamela bolted toward Marsh when she saw him. She hurled a string of vicious profanity at the man and tried to kick him before Luca held her back.

"You should be dead," Marsh snarled, aiming his own profanity at the woman. "You should have died in the blast. Hell, I wish I'd killed you a long time ago. You and your despicable SOB of a husband."

Judging from the way Lana, Pamela and Leonard stared at Marsh, they hadn't known his true feelings. Marsh had obviously kept his venom for them close to the chest.

Or maybe those feelings were a recent development.

Slater decided to test that theory.

"Did you want to punish Leonard for keeping Stephanie's whereabouts from you?" Slater asked.

"Yes," Marsh snapped while two of the other deputies began to untruss Marsh so they could cuff him. "I was worried sick about Stephanie. I couldn't think of anything but her and what she might be going through. And Leonard knew where she was and didn't tell me. So did she." He aimed a stone cold glare at Pamela.

Pamela frantically shook her head. "How? I didn't know."

"You should have known," Marsh yelled. "You should have been a better mother to Stephanie and she wouldn't have run off like that and hidden. And Lana was the one to hide her," he added in a snarl. "You kept the woman I love from me." Now he was the one who broke down and cried.

And Slater thought he knew how this had all played out, but he needed to hear it from Marsh. "Tell me what happened," Slater ordered. "Start with your part in Alicia's death. Because you wouldn't have known to come here had you not had some part in it."

It took a while for Marsh to gain enough composure to speak. "Buck is to blame for that."

"Buck?" Slater questioned. "He's the one who killed Alicia?"

"No," Marsh muttered, repeating that denial several times. He made a heavy sigh. "Alicia and I had just started seeing each other, and I went to her place and Buck was there." He swallowed hard. "Things got out of hand, and Alicia shoved me, told me to get out. I shoved her back, and she fell. She hit her head." His voice trailed off to a whisper, and Slater thought Marsh might be caught up in those memories of that horrible night. "There was blood. So much blood."

"What happened then?" Slater asked.

"Alicia was dead. And I didn't know what to do. I was in shock and couldn't even make myself move. Buck said he could take care of things but that I would owe him. I agreed. I would have agreed to anything just to make it all go away."

"You're a killer," Pamela blurted. "All this time I was pushing Stephanie to marry you, and you were a killer."

Marsh didn't deny it and didn't try to add any sugarcoating. Good. Slater didn't want to hear any lame excuses for the hell he'd caused.

"You and Buck emailed after he'd disposed of Alicia's body," Slater threw out there. "And after you learned Leonard had known where Stephanie was, you planted the emails on his computer."

Marsh didn't deny that, either. Couldn't. Because the truth was there, all over his face.

"And you made sure I found them," Pamela murmured. She turned to Leonard. "I'm so sorry. I thought you were the one who murdered Alicia."

Leonard was still obviously dazed, but he pulled his wife into his arms, and he surprised Slater by murmuring, "It's all going to be okay."

No, it wasn't. Not for Marsh, anyway, and since the man was clearly in a confessing mood, Slater pressed harder. He wanted the truth all out there, and then Marsh could be hauled away to jail.

"Alicia's murder might not have been premeditated, but you knew Buck was going to murder Stephanie and that you were going to kill Taylor," Slater pointed out.

"I didn't know Buck was going to kill Stephanie," Marsh yelled just as the deputies got him out of the belts and cuffed his hands. They pulled him to his feet so he was now eye level with Slater. "If I'd known, I would have stopped him. I would have killed him."

"You knew Stephanie was pregnant with his baby?" Lana asked.

"He told me, but I didn't believe him. I thought the baby was mine." Marsh shook his head. "But then I realized if it had been, Stephanie wouldn't be in hiding. She was scared of Buck, and Buck was a monster."

"He was your partner," Slater reminded him. "You were his accomplice."

"Not because I wanted to be." Marsh groaned. "It all got so messed up. He killed Stephanie and then said if I didn't help him cover it up, he'd give the cops a recording he made of the night Alicia died. Buck blackmailed me while I was sick with grief over losing Stephanie. This is all his fault."

The wimp was trying to deflect the blame, but Slater knew there was enough blame for both Buck and Marsh. "It wasn't Buck's fault that you killed Taylor. Buck was already dead by then. Why did you kill her? Because she was getting too close to the truth?"

"She got to the truth," Marsh clarified. "Taylor had worked it all out. She didn't have proof yet, but she would have kept digging until she found it. She wanted to hurt me for telling her to get lost." He paused. "In hindsight, I should have led her on and let her think she stood a chance of being with me, but I couldn't stand the sight of her. Not after all those things she said about Stephanie."

Yeah, hindsight might have saved Taylor long enough for them to figure out Marsh was the accomplice, but Taylor might not have been willing to play along with that.

"You were willing to kill Sheriff Holder, Lana and me to get back at Leonard," Slater stated. "Why didn't you just kill Leonard when you drugged him and brought him here?"

More anger fired through Marsh. "Because I wanted you all to pay for Stephanie dying. You should have figured everything out sooner, and then you would have come gunning for me. You were all supposed to get trapped in the first explosion, and the second one should have killed you all."

"How did you even know how to build explosives?" That question came from Duncan, who was motioning for the EMTs to move in to examine Leonard.

"Buck did them. All of this was his backup plan to cover his own butt if the cops pinned Stephanie's murder on him. He thought he was going to get away with that since he'd jammed the security cameras."

It sickened Slater to think Buck might have indeed gotten away with it if Lana hadn't seen him. Then again, if she hadn't, then Buck might not have come after her.

Marsh likely would have, though.

The rage was too strong for Marsh just to have dropped this. He wanted revenge for all those who'd kept Stephanie from him. And it didn't matter that Stephanie had been the one who'd initiated the hiding.

"I must have messed up the timing of the explosives," Marsh snarled. "Buck didn't leave good enough instructions. The first wasn't supposed to do much damage but give me time to get away once I had all of you in the arena. Then, the second one was supposed to go off within seconds so you'd all be punished for what you did."

Marsh stopped his tirade to launch into another one. All aimed at Leonard when the EMTs started taking the man toward the ambulance. Pamela was trailing along right behind them, and while she might never forgive her husband for his affairs, she certainly didn't appear to be ready to leave him, either.

"Who dug up Alicia's body?" Slater asked, trying to get Marsh back on track so he could get as much information from him as possible.

Especially since Slater had a huge question he needed answering.

"Buck did," Marsh muttered as if weren't important. "That was part of his backup plan, too. To use Alicia's body to blackmail Leonard so he'd help him. I figured I'd piggyback on that and use it to lure Pamela and Lana here. And you," he added, and now there was the tone of importance.

Marsh smiled at him. A sickening smile that slammed Slater with anger. Because Slater knew what was coming next.

"I shot your father because he wouldn't butt his nose out of the investigation into Alicia's death." Marsh said the words slowly, punctuating them with that smile that was straight from hell.

There it was. The answer Slater had needed. And it cut him to the bone. His father had been gunned down for doing his job.

Slater felt a hand on his arm and realized it was Lana.

He hadn't even noticed her moving closer to him. Hadn't noticed anything. Except the smiling monster standing in front of him. He'd always heard the expression "seeing red," but Slater hadn't known it was real. But the red came. Wave after wave of rage that was closing in on him.

"Kill me, Deputy McCullough," Marsh taunted. "You know you want to. That way, you get your so-called justice, and I don't have to spend the rest of my life in a cage."

Slater wanted that justice. Wanted it more than his next breath.

Or so he thought.

Then he felt Lana's grip tighten on his arm, and she gently turned Slater to face her. "Marsh will be punished every day he's in jail," she said. "No trust fund. No pampered lifestyle. He'll be with other killers who'll make him sorry he was ever born. He'll have to spend every moment looking over his shoulder, waiting to be attacked by monsters worse than he can ever imagine. Every moment will be his own personal hell that he can't escape."

The cockiness and taunting drained from Marsh's face. Slater could thank Lana for painting that vivid picture of what the man's future would be. Yes, Slater would get plenty satisfaction from killing Marsh right here, right now. But this way, Marsh would pay for the rest of his miserable life.

Slater gave Marsh one last look, and while the grief didn't vanish, some of the tightness did in his chest. Tightness he'd been carrying for a year since his father's murder.

"Thank you," Slater managed to say, and he leaned in and kissed her. Again, it wasn't the best timing, but he needed it.

He needed her.

"I'm in love with you," Slater heard himself say.

Even though he'd surprised himself with the words, it

didn't seem to surprise anyone else around them. Duncan muttered, "About time," and the other deputies voiced agreement.

Marsh cursed them, but Slater tuned him out as Duncan and the deputies led him away to one of the cruisers. He and Lana stayed put, and she smiled when she stared up at him.

"About time," she repeated, leaning in to brush a kiss on his mouth. "I've been half in love with you for a long time. Now it's the real deal, fully in love. Are you okay with that?"

"Better than okay," he assured her.

It wasn't exactly a prime spot for the kind of deep kiss they gave each other. After all, this was a crime scene, and the blasted fog was getting thicker. Along with the stench of the explosion, there was nothing romantic about it.

But it was still perfect.

Because of Lana. Because of the man he was when he was with her.

"Let's tie up any loose ends with Marsh," he suggested. "Then let's go to the ranch, give Cameron some cuddles and then find a bed so I can get you naked."

"The perfect plan," she quickly agreed, glancing at her parents. "And I'll say a quick word to them, too. All is not well there, but I don't want anything I feel for them interfering with what I feel for you."

Good. Slater wanted the same thing.

"You make me a better man," he told her. "You soothe me. You fire me up. You give me exactly what I need. I'm in love with you," Slater repeated, and thought he'd be saying that a whole lot more, not just tonight but for a long time. "And I want Cameron and you in my life forever."

Lana smiled. "Good, because I love you, too, and forever works for me."

   She kissed him with that amazing smile. Kissed him and
helped heal all those dark places that'd been inside him.
   Yeah, forever would work just fine.

* * * * *

Mountain Captive
Cindi Myers

MILLS & BOON

Books by Cindi Myers

Harlequin Intrigue

Eagle Mountain: Criminal History

Mile High Mystery
Colorado Kidnapping
Twin Jeopardy
Mountain Captive

Eagle Mountain: Critical Response

Deception at Dixon Pass
Pursuit at Panther Point
Killer on Kestrel Trail
Secrets of Silverpeak Mine

Eagle Mountain Search and Rescue

Eagle Mountain Cliffhanger
Canyon Kidnapping
Mountain Terror
Close Call in Colorado

Visit the Author Profile page at
millsandboon.com.au.

Cindi Myers is the author of more than seventy-five novels. When she's not plotting new romance storylines, she enjoys skiing, gardening, cooking, crafting and daydreaming. A lover of small-town life, she lives with her husband and two spoiled dogs in the Colorado mountains.

CAST OF CHARACTERS

Dr. Rand Martin—Army veteran and trauma surgeon Rand Martin joins search and rescue to become more involved in his new community.

Chris Mercer—Search and rescue volunteer Chris Mercer has a reputation for being dedicated, artistically talented and standoffish. But the arrival of a new group of campers in the area reveals the dark secrets of Chris's past.

Edmund Harrison—The charismatic leader of a group called the Vine, Harrison goes by the title of "the Exalted" and claimed Chris as his own when she was only nine. He has come to Eagle Mountain to claim her.

Jedediah—The Exalted's right-hand man makes sure everyone follows their leader's commands, and he's determined to bring Chris back into the fold.

Serena Rogers—Born into the Vine, ten-year-old Serena, now an orphan, has been selected as the Exalted's next young bride.

Harley—The Rhodesian ridgeback is Chris's protector and best friend.

Chapter One

Rand Martin had built his reputation on noticing details—the tiny nick in an artery that was the source of life-threatening blood loss; the almost microscopic bit of shrapnel that might lead to a deadly infection; the panic in a wounded man's eyes that could send his vitals out of control; the tremor in a fellow surgeon's hand that meant he wasn't fit to operate. As a trauma surgeon—first in the military, then in civilian life—Rand noticed the little things others overlooked. It made him a better doctor, and it equipped him to deal with the people in his life.

But sometimes that focus on the small picture got in the way of his big-picture job. Today, his first call as medical adviser for Eagle Mountain Search and Rescue, he was supposed to be focusing on the sixty-something man sprawled on the side of a high mountain trail. But Rand's attention kept shifting to the woman who knelt beside the man. Her blue-and-yellow vest identified her as a member of the search and rescue team, but her turquoise hair and full sleeve of colorful tattoos set her apart from the other volunteers. That, and the wariness that radiated off her as she surveyed the crowd that was fast gathering around her and her patient on the popular hiking trail.

"Everyone move back and give us some space," Rand

ordered, and, like the men and women he had commanded in his mobile surgical unit in Kabul, the crowd obeyed and fell back.

SAR Captain Danny Irwin rose from where he had been crouched on the patient's other side and greeted Rand. "Thanks for coming out," he said.

"Are you the doctor?" Another woman, blond hair in a ponytail that streamed down her back, rushed forward.

"Dr. Rand Martin." He didn't offer his hand, already pulling on latex gloves, ready to examine his patient. The blue-haired woman had risen also, and was edging to one side of the trail. As if she was trying to blend in with the crowd—a notion Rand found curious. Nothing about this woman would allow her to blend in. Even without the wildly colored hair and the ink down her arm, she was too striking to ever be invisible.

"My dad has a heart condition," the blonde said. "I tried to tell him he shouldn't be hiking at this altitude, but he wouldn't listen, and now this has happened."

"Margo, please!" This, from the man on the ground. He had propped himself up on his elbows and was frowning at the woman, presumably his daughter. "I hurt my leg. It has nothing to do with my heart."

"You don't know that," she said. "Maybe you fell because you were lightheaded or had an irregular heartbeat. If you weren't so stubborn—"

A balding man close to the woman's age moved up and put his hands on the woman's shoulders. "Let's wait and see what the doctor has to say," he said, and led Margo a few feet away.

Rand crouched beside the man. He was pale, sweating and breathing hard. Not that unusual, considering the bone sticking out of his lower leg. He was probably in a lot of pain from that compound fracture, and despite his protestation that nothing was wrong with his heart, the pain and shock could aggravate an existing cardiac condition. "What happened?" Rand asked.

"We were coming down the trail and Buddy fell." This, from another woman, with short gray curls. She sat a few feet away, flanked by two boys—early- or preteens, Rand guessed. The boys were staring at the man on the ground, freckles standing out against their pale skin.

"I stepped on a rock, and it rolled," Buddy offered. "I heard a snap." He grimaced. "Hurts like the devil."

"We'll get you something for the pain." Rand saw that someone—Danny or the blue-haired woman—had already started an intravenous line. "Do you have a medical history?" he asked Danny.

The SAR captain—an RN in his day job—handed over a small clipboard. Buddy was apparently sixty-seven, on a couple of common cardiac drugs. No history of medication allergies, though Rand questioned him again to be absolutely sure. Then he checked the clipboard once more. "Mr. Morrison, we're going to give you some morphine for the pain. It should take effect within a few minutes. Then we're going to splint your leg, pack it in ice to keep the swelling down, and get you down the mountain and to the hospital for X-rays and treatment."

"But his heart!" Margo, who'd shoved away from the balding man—her husband, perhaps—rushed forward again.

"Are you experiencing any chest pain?" Rand asked, even as he pulled out a stethoscope. "Palpitations?"

"No." Buddy glanced toward his daughter and lowered

his voice, his tone confiding. "I had a quadruple bypass nine months ago. I completed cardiac rehab, and I'm just fine. Despite what my daughter would have you believe, I'm not an idiot. My doctor thought this vacation was a fine idea. I'm under no activity restrictions."

"Your doctor probably has no idea you would decide to hike six miles at ten thousand feet," Margo said.

Rand slid the stethoscope beneath Buddy Morrison's T-shirt and listened to the strong, if somewhat rapid, heartbeat. He studied the man's pupils, which were fine. Some of the color was returning to his cheeks. Rand moved to check the pulse in his leg below the break.

"Chris, come hold this," Danny called over to the young blue-haired woman after he had hooked the man's IV line to a bag of saline. She held it, elevated, while he injected the morphine into the line. Rand watched her while trying to appear not to. Up close, she had fine lines at the corners of her eyes, which were a chocolatey brown, fringed with heavily mascaraed lashes. She had a round face, with a slight point to her chin and a Cupid's bow mouth with a slightly fuller lower lip. It was a strikingly beautiful face, with a mouth he would have liked to kiss.

He pushed the inappropriate thought away and focused on working with Danny to straighten the man's leg. Buddy groaned as the broken tip of the bone slid back under the skin, and the gray-haired woman let out a small cry as well. Margo took a step toward them. "What are you doing?" she asked. "You're hurting him!"

"He'll feel a lot better when the bones of the leg are in line and stabilized," Rand said, and began to fit the inflatable splint around the man's leg. Once air was added, the splint would form a tight, formfitting wrap that would make for a much more comfortable trip down the mountain on the litter.

The splint in place, Rand stood and stepped back. "You can take it from here," he told Danny, and watched as half a dozen more volunteers swarmed in to assemble a wheeled litter, transferred Buddy onto it, and secured him, complete with a crash helmet, ice packs around his leg and warm blankets over the rest of his body.

While they worked, another female volunteer explained to Buddy's family what would happen next. In addition to the family and the search and rescue volunteers, a crowd of maybe a dozen people clogged the trail, so each new hiker who descended the route was forced to join the bottleneck and wait. The onlookers talked among themselves, and more than a few snapped photographs.

Danny moved to Rand's side. "It's a little different from assessing a patient at the hospital ER," Danny said.

"Different from the battlefield too," Rand said. There was no scent of mortar rounds and burning structures here, and no overpowering disinfectant scent of a hospital setting. Only sunshine and a warm breeze with the vanilla-tinged scent of ponderosa pine.

"Thanks for coming out," Danny said again.

"You could have handled it fine without me," Rand said. He had heard enough from people around town to know Eagle Mountain SAR was considered one of the top wilderness-response teams in the state.

"The family calmed down a lot when I assured them we had a 'real doctor' on the way to take care of their father," Danny said. He glanced over to where Margo and her mother were huddled with the balding man and the two boys, their anxious faces focused on the process of loading

Buddy into the litter. "But I won't call you except in cases of emergency, if that's what you want."

"No. I want you to treat me like any other volunteer," Rand said.

"You mean, go through the training, attend the meetings, stuff like that?"

"Yes. That's exactly what I mean. I like being outdoors, and I need to get out of the office and the operating room. I'm in good physical shape, so I think I could be an asset to the team, beyond my medical knowledge."

"That's terrific," Danny said. "We'd be happy to have you. If you have time, come back to headquarters with us, and I'll introduce you around. Or come to the next regular meeting. Most of the volunteers will be there. I'll give you a training schedule and a bunch of paperwork to sign."

"Sounds good." Rand turned back to the crowd around the litter as it began to move forward. He searched among the dozen or so volunteers for the woman with the blue hair but didn't see her. Then he spotted her to one side. She stood in the shadow of a pine, staring up the trail.

He followed her gaze, trying to determine what had caught her attention. Then he spotted the man—midforties, a dirty yellow ball cap covering his hair and hiding his eyes. But he was definitely focused on the woman, his posture rigid.

Rand looked back toward the blue-haired woman, but she was gone. She wasn't by the tree. She wasn't with the volunteers or in the crowd of onlookers that was now making its way down the trail.

"Is something wrong?" Danny asked.

"The volunteer who was with Mr. Morrison when I arrived," he said. "With the blue hair."

"Chris. Chris Mercer."

"Has she been a volunteer long?"

"Off and on for four years. Her work has taken her away a couple of times—she's an artist. But she always comes back to the group." Danny looked around. "I don't see her now."

"She was just here," Rand said. "I was wondering where she went."

"There's no telling with Chris. She's a little unconventional but a good volunteer. She told me she was hiking about a mile down the trail when the call went out, so she was first on the scene," Danny said. "She's supposed to stick around for report back at the station. Maybe she's already headed back there."

"Looks like she left something behind," Rand said. He made his way to the spot where she had been standing and picked up a blue day pack, the nylon outer shell faded and scuffed. He unzipped the outer pocket and took out a business card. "'Chris Mercer, Aspen Leaf Gallery,'" he read.

"That's Chris's," Danny said. He held out his hand. "I'll put it in the lost and found bin at headquarters."

"That's okay. I'll take it to her." Rand slipped one strap of the pack over his shoulder.

"Suit yourself," Danny said. He and Rand fell into step behind the group wheeling the litter. Morrison's family was hiking ahead, though the daughter, Margo, kept looking back to check on their progress. Every twenty minutes or so, the volunteers switched positions, supporting the litter and guiding it down the trail or walking alongside it with the IV bag suspended. They continually checked on Mr. Morrison, asking him how he was doing, assessing his condition, staying alert for any change that might indicate something they had missed. Something going wrong.

Rand felt the tension in his own body, even as he reminded himself that this was a simple accident—a fall that had resulted in a fracture, free of the kinds of complications that had plagued his patients on the battlefield, and the motor vehicle collision and gunshot victims he often met in the emergency room where he now worked.

Heavy footfalls on the trail behind them made Rand turn, in time to see the man in the dirty yellow ball cap barreling toward them. The man brushed against Rand as he hurried by, head down, boots raising small puffs of dirt with each forceful step. "Hey!" Rand called out, prepared to tell the man to be more careful. But the guy broke into a run and soon disappeared down the trail.

"Guess he had somewhere he needed to be," Danny said.

"Guess so," Rand said, but the hair on the back of his neck rose as he remembered the expression on Chris's face as she had stared at the man.

She hadn't merely been curious or even afraid of the man.

She had been terrified.

Chapter Two

Chris prowled the bedroom of her apartment above the art gallery, throwing random items into the suitcase on her bed, her mother's voice on the phone trying, but failing, to soothe her jangled nerves. "I'm sure the man was only looking at you because you're so striking," April Mercer said.

Chris stepped over her dog, Harley, who raised his head and looked at her with brown eyes full of concern. The Rhodesian ridgeback mix had picked up on her mood as soon as she entered the apartment, and he refused to be more than a few inches away from her. "I don't think so," Chris told her mother. "He looked familiar. Do you remember that guy who used to stand at the back of the room, glaring at everyone during Sunday-night meetings? Jedediah?" Chris grabbed a handful of socks and stuffed them into the side of the suitcase. A shudder went through her as she remembered the man on the trail.

"Oh, honey, I'm sure it wasn't him," April said. "It's been so long. I'm sure all of those people have forgotten about you by now."

"Do you really believe that, Mom?"

Her mother's silence was all the answer she needed. Jedediah and the others hadn't forgotten about Chris. That hadn't been her name back them, but that wouldn't matter to them.

"Would you really remember what he looked like after all these years?" April asked finally.

It wasn't the man's features that had been so familiar to her, but the look in his eyes. So full of hate. "He sure acted as if he recognized me."

"How could he?" April asked. "You changed your hair and had that nose job. And you were twelve years old. You were a child when he saw you last."

"I know." She swallowed down the rising panic and forced herself to stop and breathe deeply. "I just... The way he looked at me."

Harley stood and leaned against her. She bent and rubbed behind the dog's ears, finding solace in his solid presence.

"He's just a creep," April said. "There are plenty of them out there. If you really think he's a threat, tell the sheriff. Didn't you tell me he's a decent guy?"

"Yes. I mean, I've only interacted with Sheriff Walker on search and rescue missions, but he has a good reputation." Still, how would he react if she told him someone she had last seen when she was twelve had been glaring at her? And did she really want to reveal that whole sordid story to anyone here?

"You know you're always welcome to stay with me for a while if it makes you feel better," April said.

"I know." But Chris had already hidden out at her mom's place three times in the past two years. And at least one of those times had been a false alarm. She had heard the talk from other search and rescue members about how often she was out of town. Everyone seemed understanding, but that was probably because they thought her work as an artist was taking her away for weeks or months at a time. "I'm tired of running away," she said.

"Oh, honey."

The tenderness in April's voice might have broken a weaker woman. But Chris had had years to develop a hard shell around her emotions. "I was just wondering if you had heard anything about Jedediah. If you knew if he had a reason to be in this area."

"No," April said. "I try to keep tabs on people, but I have to rely on the few friendly contacts I still have, and they're understandably reluctant to reveal too much. But Colorado and Jedediah have never come up in our conversations."

Chris nodded, even though she knew her mother couldn't see her. "Okay, that's good. I guess."

"I'm sorry this happened to upset you," her mother said. "But I don't think it has anything to do with what happened all those years ago."

"You're right." Chris let go of the dog and turned to stare at the suitcase, into which she had apparently packed a dozen T-shirts and eight pairs of socks but no underwear or pants. "I'll just…keep my eyes open, and if I see anyone suspicious or threatening, I'll tell the sheriff."

"That sounds like a good plan," April said. "But know you can come stay with me anytime."

A knock on the door set her heart racing. Was it Jedediah? Had he managed to find her? "I have to go now, Mom."

"I love you," April said.

Harley was already moving toward the door. He hadn't barked or even growled, but the ridge of hair along his spine stood at attention.

"I love you too," Chris whispered. She slid the phone into

her pocket and tiptoed toward the door, careful not to make a sound. Holding her breath, she peered through the peephole with Harley pressed against her side, his body taut.

Chris exhaled in a rush as she recognized the man on the other side. She unfastened the security chain and dead bolt and eased the door open a scant two inches. "Hello?"

"Chris Mercer?" The doctor who was now working with search and rescue asked. She couldn't remember his name, but she wasn't likely to forget his face anytime soon. Blue eyes, curly dark hair, cleft chin—he had definitely made her look twice when she had first seen him.

"What do you want?" she asked.

He held up her day pack. "You left this behind on the trail. I thought you'd want it back."

"How did you find me?" She didn't like the idea that a stranger—no matter how good looking or well intentioned— could walk right up to her front door.

"There's a card for the gallery downstairs in the outside pocket of the pack," he said. "I asked and the woman at the register told me you were upstairs."

Chris frowned. She would have to have a talk with Jasmine. "Thanks." She opened the door wider and reached for the pack. Thoughtless of her to have left it, but that showed how shaken up she had been.

Harley shoved forward and stuck his head out the door. He glared at the doctor, a low rumble vibrating the air.

The doctor took a step back. "Hello, there," he addressed the dog.

"That's Harley. He won't hurt you." Not unless she told him to. The dog was trained to protect, though most of the time he was a genuine sweetheart. "Just hand me the pack."

The doctor—why couldn't she remember his name?—held it out of reach. "Are you okay?" he asked.

"I'm fine. Can I have my pack, please?"

He handed it over. "You left the trail in a hurry," he said. "We didn't get a chance to meet. I'm Rand Martin."

"Thanks for returning my pack, Rand." She tried to close the door, but he caught the frame and held it.

Harley's growl intensified, his body rigid. Rand glanced down at him but held his ground. "First, I want to make sure you're okay," he said. "You looked really upset back there on the trail. You still look upset."

"I'm fine."

"Who was the man watching you?"

Her breath caught. "You saw him too?"

"Yes."

"Do you know him?" she asked.

"Why don't I come in, and we'll talk about it?"

Just then, Jasmine, a petite woman with short red hair and white-rimmed glasses, appeared at the top of the stairs at the end of the hall. "Is everything okay, Chris?" she asked. Her gaze shifted to Rand, then back to Chris, eyes bright with curiosity.

"Everything is fine." Chris signaled for Harley to stand down and opened the door a little wider. "Come on in," she said to Rand. At least if he turned out to be a threat, Jasmine would be able to identify him. Not that there was anything particularly threatening about the doctor. He was older than Chris—early forties, maybe—but he was fit and strong. He exuded calm, and he struck her as someone who would be good to have on her side should Jedediah, or whoever that man had been, decide to show up.

He moved into her apartment, and she shut the door behind him. Harley stayed between them, silent but wary. Rand stopped in front of a painting beside the front door, an eight-by-ten canvas depicting a young girl crouched beside a pool in a mountain stream. A face was reflected in the water—a much older woman meant to represent the girl in her later years. "One of yours?" Rand asked.

"Yes." She dropped the pack onto the floor beside the sofa. "Do you know the man who was watching me there on the trail?"

He shook his head. "No. But you looked like you recognized him."

"I thought I did, but I was wrong."

"Then why were you afraid?"

"I wasn't afraid." The lie came easily. She was practiced at hiding that part of herself.

"You were terrified." He spoke with such certainty, as if he knew her and her innermost thoughts. But he wasn't saying the words to use her emotions against her as a weapon. If anything, his expression telegraphed understanding. As if he, too, had felt terror before and knew its paralyzing power.

She turned away from him. "I'm a single woman," she said. "I don't appreciate when a man I don't know takes such an intense interest in me." Would Rand take the hint that he, himself, should leave her alone?

"For what it's worth, I looked for him on the way down the trail, but I didn't see him again." He looked around her place. "I take it he didn't follow you here?"

She shook her head. She had made sure she was alone before she risked coming here. "Thanks for returning my pack," she said. "I really have things to do now." Unpack her suitcase, for one. Maybe do a little research online and try to find out what happened to Jedediah. Could she dredge up his last name from memory? Had she ever known it?

"Would you have dinner with me?"

The question startled her so much her mouth dropped open. She stared. Rand stared back, his lips tipped up at one corner, blue eyes full of amusement. Was he laughing at her? "What did you say?" she asked.

"Would you have dinner with me?"

"No." Absolutely not.

"Why not?"

"I don't date."

"Why not?"

"I just… I'm not interested in a relationship."

"Neither am I," he said.

"Why not?" She hadn't meant to say the words out loud, but seriously, the man was gorgeous. A doctor. He appeared to have a decent personality.

"I'm a trauma surgeon. I have a terrible schedule. I can't even get a dog, my hours are so unpredictable. Any woman in my life invariably ends up feeling neglected and resenting me."

"Then why ask me out? I don't do one-night stands either."

That little barb didn't faze him. "Everyone can use a friend," he said gently.

She hugged her arms across her chest. "You don't want to be friends with me."

"Why not?"

"I come with a lot of baggage."

He laughed. A loud, hearty guffaw. The sound elicited a sharp rebuke from Harley.

"It's okay," Rand said to the dog. He crouched and offered his hand for the dog to sniff. Harley approached cautiously, then allowed Rand to pet his sleek side.

Chris glared at him. "What's so funny?"

"Show me a person over twenty who doesn't have baggage, and I'll show you someone not worth knowing," he said. "Come on. Have a burger and a beer with me."

The offer tempted her, if only for the chance to have an evening outside her own head. She took a step back. "No. I think you need to leave now."

She expected him to argue, to turn charming or pleading. Instead, he only stood and took a card from his wallet and offered it to her.

She stared at it but didn't take it. He laid it on the table beside the sofa. "That's my number, if you need anything." He shrugged. "In case that guy shows up, for instance."

"What are you going to do if he does?"

"I could probably persuade him to leave you alone."

From anyone else, the words might have come across as a brag. From Rand, they rang true. He wasn't an overly big man, but he had a wiry strength, and the attitude of someone who wouldn't back down from a fight. "Thanks," she said. "But I'll be fine."

He nodded and left, letting himself out and shutting the door softly behind him. She locked up, then leaned against the paneled surface of the door. If Rand could find her so easily, Jedediah could too. The thought ought to have renewed the terror she'd felt earlier, but instead, the idea annoyed her. She had told her mother the truth when she said she was tired of running away. Jedediah had been powerful and threatening when she had known him before, capable of hurting her. But she wasn't a child anymore. And she knew the truth behind the lies he and others had told. She didn't have to keep running. She could stay and resist.

This time, she might even win.

Chapter Three

The parking lot at Eagle Mountain Search and Rescue head-quarters was full by the time Rand pulled in Thursday evening. He had just had time to grab a quick shower and a sandwich before leaving for this first training meeting. His adrenaline was still revved when he stepped into the cavernous garage-like space and studied the group arranged in an assortment of chairs and old furniture angled toward the front of the room.

He spotted a few faces familiar to him from the previous Saturday's rescue, but found himself searching for Chris. He spotted her in a far corner, at one end of a sofa, her dog, Harley, at her feet. He took the empty seat beside her. "Hello," he said.

She eyed him coolly. "Hey."

Harley approached and Rand petted the dog. He wanted the animal to trust him, even if his mistress didn't. "How are you?" he asked.

"Fine."

She wasn't exactly unfriendly, just…guarded. Which only made him want to break through her reserve more. "I saw some of your paintings at a restaurant in town," he said. "I really like your work."

"They're all for sale."

"I might buy one. I've always enjoyed landscapes, and yours are beautiful—but they're also complex." He glanced at her arm and the artwork there. She wore a sleeveless blouse, revealing a tapestry of colorful flowers and birds from shoulder to wrist on the arm closest to him. Columbines, bluebells, foxglove, a bluebird, and a gold finch. The scene reminded him of one of her paintings. And yes, there, just above her elbow, half-hidden between a dragonfly and a sunflower, a woman peered out with large dark eyes, hiding and watchful. "Mysterious."

"Hmmm. Not that I don't like it when people say nice things about my work, but it's not going to convince me to go out with you."

"Can't blame a man for trying." He smiled.

She looked away.

"Let's get started, everybody." Danny spoke from the front of the room, and the chatter died down. "I'll start by introducing our newest team member. Some of you already know Dr. Rand Martin, who assisted with our rescue of the injured hiker on Saturday. In addition to serving as our medical adviser, Rand has decided to join as a full-fledged volunteer."

Scattered applause from the gathered volunteers. Rand nodded. Danny continued, "Just so you know, Rand's a rookie, but he has a lot of experience. He served with a mobile surgical unit in Afghanistan and is the new director of emergency services at St. Joseph's Hospital in Junction."

More applause, and a few shouts of "Welcome!"

"You can introduce yourselves at the break," Danny said. "Now, let's get down to business." He consulted the clipboard in his hand and read off a list of upcoming training opportunities, certification deadlines and local news. "The sheriff asked me to remind everyone that the annual Back-country Base Camp rally is August 1 through 4. There's also a scout group from Denver planning a wilderness-skills camp up on Dakota Ridge starting August 5. Both of those groups could mean more calls for us."

"A bunch of kids playing with fire and knives?" a big man near the back of the room said. "What could go wrong?"

Danny smiled and waited for the chuckles to die down. "I'm going to turn it over to Tony now for our training unit on wilderness searches. For some of you this will be a re-view, but pay attention, because we have some new pro-tocols based on the latest research. And for you newbies, know that you could be called to put this into practice any day now. We have a lot of wilderness we're responsible for, and it's easy for people to get lost out there."

Rand pulled out a notebook and pen and settled in as a tall, thin man, his blond hair and goatee threaded with sil-ver, moved to the front of the room. Chris passed Rand a sheaf of handouts. "Pretty much everything is on these," she said.

"Thanks."

He pretended to study the first sheet of the handout, but he was really focused on her. She was more relaxed than she had been Saturday, but she still had the hyperawareness he recognized from his time in Afghanistan. In a war zone, chaos could break out at any second, even in the middle of dinner or when you were trying to sleep after a hard battle. Soldiers lived on high alert, and being in constant fight-or-flight mode took its toll physically and psychologically.

But Chris wasn't in a war zone. So why so tense?

The room darkened and Tony began his presentation.

Rand forced himself to concentrate on the lesson. Apparently, people who became lost tended to behave in established patterns depending on their age, gender and history. "Knowing these patterns doesn't guarantee we'll locate them," Tony said. "But it helps us establish a search plan and can increase the odds of finding them."

Rand underlined phrases on the handout and wrote notes in the margin. And here he had thought his training would consist of learning to tie knots and reviewing how to administer first aid. He was so absorbed in the material he had to shake himself out of a kind of trance when the lights went up again. He checked his watch and was surprised to find over an hour had passed.

"We'll break for ten minutes, then finish up this unit," Tony said.

Chairs slid back and the hum of conversation rose. Rand turned to address Chris, but she was already out of her chair and moving across the room. Danny waylaid her, and the two fell into earnest conversation. Curious, Rand worked his way toward them but was stopped by other volunteers who wanted to introduce themselves. He made small talk, all the while working his way over to Chris and Danny, who stood in the hallway outside the restrooms.

Rand positioned himself in front of a bulletin board around the corner from them and listened. "I'm sorry," Chris said. "I know I shouldn't have disappeared like that, but it was an emergency. I got a call from my mom. She's okay now, but I thought at first I was going to have to rush to her."

"I'm sorry to hear that," Danny said. "I've been in that position myself. But next time, let someone know. Send a text or something."

"I will. I promise."

"Are you sure that's all that's going on?" Danny asked.

"Of course." Rand thought he recognized a forced cheerfulness in her voice. He moved over to get a better look, and Chris collided with him as she came around the corner.

"Sorry," he said, steadying her with one hand but immediately releasing her. She was skittish as a wild colt, and he didn't want to upset her.

She stared up at him, eyes wide, then moved away. Rand watched her cross the room, half believing she would leave altogether. Instead, she stopped by a table of refreshments and began filling a plate.

She didn't return to her seat until Tony had resumed the lesson. She slid onto the sofa beside him just as the lights went down, as if she had timed her arrival to avoid further conversation.

When the evening ended, Rand started after her but was halted by a trio of men, including the big guy who had made the remark about the scouts. They introduced themselves as Eldon Ramsey, Ryan Welch and Caleb Garrison. "Have you done any climbing?" the big guy, Eldon, asked.

"Only a little," Rand asked.

"It's a skill that comes in handy on a lot of the rescues we're called out on," Ryan said. "You'll have training opportunities, but any time you want to get in some practice on your own, give us a shout."

"We're climbing in Caspar Canyon most weekends during the season," Caleb said. "Come on out and join us anytime."

"Thanks," Rand said. "I'll do that."

The instructor for the evening, Tony Meisner, introduced himself next, along with Sheri Stevens, Jake and Hannah

Gwynn, Grace Wilcox, and several others whose names Rand couldn't remember. Everyone was friendly and offered to help him in any way they could. By the time the building emptied out, Rand had accepted that he wasn't going to talk to Chris tonight. She would have left long ago.

Except, apparently, she hadn't. He spotted her and Harley walking across the parking lot and headed after her while trying to appear as if he wasn't in a hurry. She glanced over her shoulder at his approach but said nothing. The stiffness in her shoulders told him she was a few breaths from telling him to get lost. No sense wasting the opportunity with small talk. "Have you seen any more of the man who was watching you Saturday?" he asked.

She slowed her steps. "No. I must have been mistaken. He was looking at something else."

She didn't believe that, he thought.

"Mind if I walk you to your car?" he asked.

She shrugged. "Suit yourself."

Seconds later, they arrived at a dusty blue Subaru. She stopped and turned to him. Before she could say anything, he took a step back. "I'm not trying to be a creep or harass you," he said. "If you don't want to go out with me, that's your call. But I saw that guy on the trail Saturday and how you reacted to his attention. If you need help or you just want to talk to someone, I'm here. That's all I want you to know."

Some of the stiffness went out of her posture, and she looked at him with less suspicion. "Thanks," she said. "But it's not really anything you need to worry about." She clicked her key fob. The car beeped and flashed its lights, and she opened the rear driver's-side door. "In you go, Harley."

The dog started to jump into the car, then stopped and backed out, something in his mouth. "What has he got?" Rand leaned in for a closer look.

Chris took the object from the dog, and all the color left her face. She collapsed against the side of the car, eyes wide.

Rand took the item from her. It was a bird—a hummingbird, made of folded emerald green paper. "Is this origami?" he asked.

She nodded, the look on her face frantic now.

Still holding the paper bird, he reached for her. "Chris," he said.

But she turned away, clutching her stomach, and vomited on the gravel beside the car.

He pulled her close, half-afraid she would collapse. She leaned heavily against him, shudders running through her. "Tell me why you're so upset," he said.

"I can't."

Seventeen Years Ago

Ten-year-old Chris was seated at a folding table in a cold, drafty room, a stack of colored paper in front of her—pink, blue, red, orange, purple, green. Pretty colors, but looking at them didn't make Chris happy. No one called her Chris then. They knew her as Elita. She willed away tears as she painstakingly folded and smoothed the paper to make a hummingbird like the model in front of her. "You need five thousand of them," the woman across from her—Helen—said. "You will make some every day. And when you are done, it will be time."

Tears slipped past her tight-closed lids and made a hot

path down her cheeks. She tried to wipe them away, hoping Helen hadn't seen. "What if I can't make five thousand of them?" she asked. It seemed an impossibly large number.

"You will. You have a couple of years. It will take that long until you're ready for the duties ahead of you."

Chris shuddered. She didn't want to think about those "duties." Not that she had a terribly clear idea what those might include, but she had heard whispers...

She made a wrong fold, and the paper creased, the hummingbird crumpling in her hand. Helen took the mangled paper from her. "Start with a fresh sheet. Pay attention, and take your time."

"Maybe I can't do it because I'm not the right person," Chris said. "Maybe I'm not worthy."

Helen smiled. "You are the right person. You have been chosen."

Choose someone else! Chris wanted to shout. But she only bit her lip as another tear betrayed her.

Helen frowned. "You should be happy you have been singled out for such an honor. You shouldn't be so ungrateful."

"I'm... I'm not," she lied, and bit the inside of her cheek. Anything to stem the tears. She couldn't let Helen see what her true feelings were. Even at her young age, she knew that was dangerous.

"Chris." Rand snapped his fingers in front of her face. "What's going on? Why are you so afraid?"

"I have to go." She pushed him aside and slid into the car. Harley bolted in after her, climbing over Chris and settling in the passenger seat. Rand was talking to her, but she couldn't hear him over the buzzing panic in her head. She drove away, gripping the steering wheel so tightly her fingers ached. She checked her mirrors every few seconds, but no one appeared to be following her.

When she was in her parking space in the alley behind the gallery, she made sure the doors of her car were locked, then laid her head on the steering wheel and closed her eyes, her whole body trembling. She never had made the five thousand hummingbirds. She had believed getting away had ended her ordeal.

But someone had pushed that bird through the gap in her car window. When she had parked at search and rescue headquarters, she thought the lot was safe enough for her to leave the rear windows down just a few inches to keep the interior cool. Jedediah, or someone else, had taken advantage of that, letting her know she could never truly escape. They were telling her it was time to fulfill what they thought was her destiny. The one thing she was determined never to do.

Chapter Four

Early Saturday morning, Rand drove home from Junction. He had been called in after midnight to tend to a young man who had suffered multiple injuries as a result of wrapping his car around a tree along a curvy road—fractured sternum, broken ribs and collarbone, a fractured arm, and multiple bruises and cuts. Rand had spent hours wiring the man's bones back together. Weariness set in when he was halfway home, so he did what he always did to try to stay awake: he opened a window to let in fresh air and thought about something other than himself and his fatigue.

He had stayed away from Chris since Thursday night, even though the desire to know what was going on with her gnawed at him, a low-level ache. If she wanted his help, she would ask. To keep pressing himself on her could be seen as harassment. He wanted to be her friend, not someone else she was afraid of.

He thought of the origami hummingbird. Not exactly a threatening item, yet Chris had been physically ill at the sight of it. He had a bad feeling about that moment, but maybe he was putting too much of himself and his own history into it. Maybe the hummingbird had been a kind of sick joke that only had meaning to her, not a real threat.

But could anyone be so upset by a joke that they would throw up?

His phone vibrated, and seconds later the video screen on his dash showed he had an incoming text. He pressed the button to hear the message, and the car's mechanical female voice recited, "Wildfire on national forest land south end of County Road 3. All search and rescue volunteers needed to evacuate campers in the area."

Rand increased his speed and headed toward search and rescue headquarters. He parked and joined the crowd of volunteers just inside. He spotted Chris right away, her blue hair standing out in the sea of blondes and brunettes. "Hello," she said when he approached. No animosity. No particular warmth either.

"What should I do to help?" he asked.

She shoved a lidded plastic bin into his hands. "Put these first aid supplies in the Beast." She indicated a boxy orange Jeep with oversize tires and a red cross on the back door. "And do whatever Danny or whoever he appoints as incident commander tells you."

He joined a line of volunteers passing gear to the vehicles, then followed Ryan and Caleb to a Toyota truck. He, Caleb and Carrie Andrews squeezed into the back seat. Ryan drove, and Eldon took the passenger seat. They followed the Beast to the highway, then turned onto a county road that grew progressively narrower and bumpier as they climbed in elevation.

"Check out the smoke," Eldon said, and pointed at the windshield to a black plume rising in the distance.

"People who don't live here don't understand how dangerous these dry conditions are," Ryan said. "One spark from a campfire or a discarded cigarette can set a blaze that destroys hundreds of thousands of acres."

Ahead of them, the orange Jeep slowed, then pulled over to the side and stopped. Ryan pulled his truck in behind it and rolled down the window. The headlights of a vehicle moved toward them. Tony stepped out from the driver's side of the Jeep and flagged down the vehicle. Rand leaned his head out the open back window to hear the conversation. A second car idled behind the first. The driver of the first—a man perhaps in his fifties, his brown hair heavily streaked with white—spoke clearly enough for Rand to hear.

"Are you with the campers who are back here?" Danny asked.

"I don't know about that," the man said.

"Were you camped in the national forest?" Danny tried again.

"Yes. We saw the smoke getting heavier and decided to leave."

"How many are with you?" Danny glanced toward the other vehicle.

"There are six of us here."

"Only six?" Danny asked.

"More'll be along soon," the man said. "They're packing up camp."

"How many people?" Danny's tone signaled that he was quickly losing patience with the man's casual attitude.

"Maybe a dozen."

"Men? Women? Children?"

"What business is that of yours?" the driver asked.

"Whoever is back there needs to get out now," Danny said. "They don't have time to pack. The winds are pushing the fire this way. We're here to help with the evacuation."

"They're just a few miles back," the man said. "You won't have any trouble finding them." He shifted the car into gear and lurched forward, the other vehicle close on his bumper. As they passed, Rand got a glimpse through tinted glass of two adults in the first vehicle and four in the second. All men, he thought.

Tony climbed back into the Beast, and the caravan of volunteers set out again, driving a little faster now, their sense of urgency heightened by the thickening smoke. "Do we know anything about these campers?" Rand asked after a moment. "Who they are or where they're from?"

"Danny said he got a call from the sheriff that one of the spotters in a plane flying over the fire saw a group of tents in a clearing and called it in," Caleb said. "Cell phone coverage is spotty to nonexistent back in here, so they might not have realized the fire had even started."

"No missing all this smoke," Eldon said. "Anyone with any sense would know to get out of Dodge by now."

The Jeep stopped again, this time in the middle of the road. Ryan halted the truck, too, and everyone piled out. Smoke stung Rand's eyes, and the scent of burning wood hung heavy in the air. "There's active flames ahead," Tony said. "We can't go any further or we risk getting trapped. We need to turn around."

"What about the other campers?" Carrie asked. "The driver of the car said there were others."

Danny glanced over his shoulder. Smoke obscured the road ahead, though occasional orange flares illuminated burning trees. "We don't know who or how many are in there," he said. "We can't put our own lives at risk. That doesn't help anyone."

Rand wanted to volunteer to go ahead on foot to scout

the situation. But then what? He could end up injured or trapped, and the other volunteers might feel obligated to go in after him. But he hated this feeling of helplessness and defeat.

"Hello? Help! Oh, please help!"

They turned toward the sound as a woman stumbled down the road toward them. She was almost bent double beneath what Rand thought at first was a large pack but turned out to be a child wrapped in a sleeping bag, clinging to her back. As they rushed toward her, other figures emerged from the smoke—more women, half a dozen children and a single man, all carrying supplies and bundles of clothing, bedding, and who knew what else.

The lone man brought up the rear of the group. He had a blanket roll on his back and a large wooden box in his arms. "The truck broke down, and we had to walk," he said, his words cut short by a fit of coughing.

Rand stared at the collection of women and children— some with soot on their faces, holes from sparks burned in their clothing—and thought of the men in the two cars. They had left women and children to *walk* out of a fire?

He flinched at a crack like a gunshot, then realized it was a tree not thirty yards away, bursting into flame. "We have to get out of here," Danny said. He took the nearest woman's arm. "Into the vehicles. Drop whatever you're carrying and get in. You'll have to sit on laps, on the floorboards—wherever you can fit."

Another woman spoke up. "That isn't necessary." She seemed a little taller than the others, but maybe it was only that she stood straighter and looked them in the eye when she spoke. "We will carry our possessions and walk out."

"You can't walk fast enough to stay ahead of the fire," Danny said.

"We have divine protection."

The words snapped Rand's patience. "Get in the trucks now!" he shouted. He picked up the closest child and shoved them into the back seat of the truck.

Caleb and Ryan reached for other children. Eldon picked up a woman and deposited her in the front passenger seat. Others began relieving the stranded campers of their burdens and leading them to the vehicles. They seemed to come out of their trance then. The man and several of the women and older children crowded into the back of the truck.

"What about our things?" one of the women wailed.

"We don't have room for them," Tony said.

She began to cry. Others were already weeping, children screaming.

"Is there anyone else?" Danny asked. He had to raise his voice above the din . "Any stragglers we should wait for?"

"No." The man shook his head. "No one."

Rand hoped the man was telling the truth. The flames were near enough he could feel the heat now, smoke so heavy he could no longer make out the road, the roar of the fire so loud they had to shout to be heard. A hot wind swirled around them, sparks stinging bare skin and smoldering on clothing. They didn't have time to search for anyone who might have been left behind.

Somehow, they managed to turn the vehicles and head back down the road, forced by poor visibility to creep along yet driving as fast as they dared in order to escape the flames. Everyone was coughing now, everyone's eyes streaming tears.

They slowed to steer around a burning tree that had

fallen on the side of the road, and the weight in the back of the truck shifted. The wailing rose in pitch, and Rand looked back to see that the man had jumped from the truck and was running down the road, back in the direction they had come. He had his hand on the door, about to open it, when Caleb gripped his arm. "Let him go. We have to save the rest."

Rand forced his body to relax and nodded. Even if he had wanted, he couldn't have exited the vehicle. He was held down by a child on each thigh, a boy and a girl, who were about nine or ten. They sat stiffly and wouldn't meet his gaze, hands clenched in front of them, eyes downcast. Obviously, they were terrified. Traumatized. Maybe that explained why they weren't acting like any children he had ever met.

After what felt like the longest ride of his life but was probably only half an hour, they arrived at the staging area on the picnic grounds at the turnoff for the county road. Paramedics, the sheriff and his deputies, and other volunteers surrounded the Beast and the truck, someone taking charge of each of the campers as they emerged. "We found them trying to walk out of the fire," Danny explained to the sheriff.

Sheriff Travis Walker was a tall man in his midthirties, with dark hair and eyes, a sharply pressed khaki uniform, and a grim expression on his face. "Any idea what a bunch of women and children were doing camping back in there with no transportation?" he asked.

"There was a man with them," Ryan said. "He bailed out of the truck and ran back in the direction of the camp not long after we set out."

"There were six other men, in two vehicles," Tony said.

"We passed them on the way out. They told us they had left the others—" he nodded at the women and children "—to pack up the camp and follow."

The sheriff's frown deepened. "We'll question them later, find out what's going on."

"I think they might belong to some kind of cult," Rand said.

Everyone turned to stare at him. "What makes you say that?" Travis asked.

"One of the women told us they weren't worried about the fire because they were under 'divine protection.' That, and the fact that a group of able-bodied men, probably the leaders, left a bunch of women and children to fend for themselves, and the women aren't questioning—at least not out loud—their right to do so. Blind obedience that goes against all common sense is one hallmark of a cult."

Thankfully, the sheriff didn't ask how Rand knew this. "We'll question them and find out as much as we can," he said.

"How do you know that? About cults?"

Rand tensed at the familiar voice and turned to look at Chris.

"My sister was in a cult," he said. "I learned a lot about them when we were trying to persuade her to leave."

"Did she leave?" Chris stared at him, lips parted, leaning toward him as if something important depended on his answer.

He shook his head. "No. She never did."

Her expression softened, and she put her hand on his arm. A familiar tightness rose in his throat, but he forced himself not to turn away. He didn't see pity in Chris's eyes, but some other emotion, one he couldn't quite read.

And then she whirled away from him, propelled by a hand on her shoulder. The driver of the car they had met in the burning forest stood with two other men, all crowded around Chris.

Rand moved in behind her, but the men ignored him. All three were middle-aged, from the fortysomething blond Rand had seen on the trail a week ago to the slightly older driver of the car, to a shorter, red-faced man with a round, boyish face but iron gray hair who stood between them. "Hello, Elita," the driver said.

"My name isn't Elita," Chris said. But her voice trembled.

"Your time has come," the blond said.

"I don't know what you're talking about." She tried to turn away, but the blond grabbed her.

Rand took the man's wrist and squeezed, hard, his thumb digging in between the fine bones in a way that was guaranteed to hurt. The man released her but turned on Rand. "This is no business of yours," he said.

"Don't touch her again," Rand said. He kept his voice low, but anyone would know he meant business. He was dimly aware that a crowd had gathered, among them the sheriff and one of his deputies.

The blond turned back to Chris. "You can't deny your destiny," he said. He glanced at those around them and raised his voice so that it carried to everyone. "We will start the wedding preparations today."

Chapter Five

Sheriff Walker stepped forward. "What is your name?" he asked the driver.

The blond spoke first. "This doesn't concern you, Sheriff," he said.

Travis's expression didn't change. "The three of you need to come to the sheriff's department and provide statements about the fire and how it started."

"We don't know how it started," the round-faced man said. "That has nothing to do with us."

"I also want to know why the three of you left a group of women and children to make their way out of the area on foot," Travis said.

The blond man moved closer. He was taller than the others, not large, but imposing. "We left a man in charge of the women and children," he said. "Joshua was bringing them in the truck." He looked around. "Where is Joshua?"

"The man who was with the women and children ran back into the woods," Rand said.

The blond shifted his attention to Rand. "Who are you?" It wasn't a question as much as a demand.

"I'm one of the volunteers who helped save those women and children you abandoned," Rand said.

The man glared at him but addressed the sheriff. "You

need to talk to Joshua. I can't help you." He turned away, and the others started to follow him.

"Before you leave, I need your names and contact information," the sheriff said.

The blond man nodded to the round-faced man. He pulled a small case from his pocket and handed the sheriff a business card. "That's the name of our attorney," he said. "You can contact him."

The three walked away. Travis pocketed the card and glanced over as his brother, Sergeant Gage Walker, joined the group. "The car is registered to something called the Vine, LLC," he said.

Travis turned to Chris. She had remained silent since the men had approached, pale and still. "What do you know about this?" he asked.

She swallowed hard. "The blond man is named Jedediah," she said. "I don't know his last name. He works for a man named Edmund Harrison, though most people know him as the Exalted. He leads the Vine. I don't know the other two, but they're probably part of the Exalted's inner circle— the ones charged with keeping order within the group."

"What is the Vine?" Gage asked. "Some kind of vineyard or something?"

Chris shook her head. "The Vine is, well, I guess you'd say it's a cult. A kind of religion, but not exactly. Edmund Harrison is the leader, the Exalted."

"What's your connection to the group?" Travis asked.

She stared at the ground. "My mother and father were members—a long time ago. My father died, and after that…" She paused. Rand could sense her struggling to control her emotions. Her shoulders drew inward, and she clenched her hands tightly. But after a long moment, she lifted her head. "My mother broke with the group when I was twelve. I haven't seen or heard from them since."

She was lying. Rand was sure of it. She had seen Jedediah on the trail last Saturday and had recognized him. And he had recognized her.

"What was all that about a wedding?" Ryan asked. "And why did he call you by that other name—Lisa or something?"

"Elita." She blew out a breath. "It's a long story."

"I'd like you to come to my office and tell me about it," Travis said. "If it turns out they were responsible for that fire, or the death of anyone in it, I need to know as much about them as possible."

"I'll come with you," Rand said.

Chris turned to him, and he braced himself for her to tell him to back off, that this was none of his business. "You don't have to do this alone," he said softly. Whatever was behind this, the encounter had clearly shaken her. He wanted to be there to lend her strength. To take away a little of her fear.

She nodded. "All right."

"We can go now," Travis said. "I want to get your statement before Jedidiah and the others have a chance to get too far away."

"They won't go far," Chris said. "Not until they have me. I'm the reason they're here."

Eighteen years ago

"WE'VE COME TODAY to reveal that Elita has been selected for an amazing honor."

Elita had been trying to teach herself to knit by following the illustrations in a library book when the two women and one man had knocked on the door of the travel trailer where she and her mother and father lived, on the edge of an apple grove owned by the Vine. The trailer was old—hot in the summer and cold in the winter, and when it rained, the roof over Elita's bunk bed leaked—but they had lived here since Elita was five years old, and she was nine now.

She hadn't been called *Elita* when they'd first moved here. She had been Christine Elizabeth back then. But one day, not long after they had arrived, her father had announced they were all taking new names. Her new name was Elita. "It means 'the chosen one,'" he told her. "The Exalted himself named you. It's a very special honor."

She thought it was strange to suddenly have a new name, but she knew better than to argue, and over time, she got used to being Elita instead of Christine.

The woman who spoke, Helen, was older than Elita's mom. She had long brown hair almost to her waist, the strands glinting with silver, and pale blue eyes. She oversaw the Sunday school Elita attended, and whenever she smiled at Elita, the little girl felt warm and happy.

The other woman, Sarai, was older and sour-faced. She taught the younger children and carried a switch when she walked between the rows of students, and didn't hesitate to pop them on the back of the hand if they gave a wrong answer to her questions. Elita didn't like her, and she avoided looking at her now.

But the man—Jedediah—was the one who really frightened her. The way he watched everyone, especially the girls, made her feel sick to her stomach. He was supposed to be one of the holiest among them, serving as the Exalted's right hand. But to her, he seemed evil.

Elita's mother—whom everyone called Lana now, though she had been born Amy—came and stood behind Elita, resting both hands on her shoulders. "This is a surprise," she said. "Why would Elita be singled out for an honor?"

"She has found favor with the Exalted," Helen said. She smiled at Elita, but this time the little girl didn't feel warm or happy. She felt cold and scared. Like Jedediah, the Exalted frightened her. Not because he was mean or creepy, but because everyone acted afraid of him, and there were a lot of rules about how to behave around him. Not just anyone could speak to the Exalted. And her mother had told her once that the best way to behave around the Exalted was to pretend to be invisible. Elita hadn't understood what she meant. People couldn't be invisible.

Mom's hands tightened on her shoulders. "What is this great honor?" she asked.

"The Exalted has chosen Elita to be his bride." Helen said the words with a breathless awe, her cheeks flushed and eyes alight.

Elita's mother gasped. "She's only nine years old."

"It isn't to happen right away," Helen said. "There will be years for her to prepare. But when she has reached maturity, there will be a grand wedding."

Her father moved in to stand beside them. He patted Elita's shoulder and smiled when she looked up at him. "This is indeed an honor," he said. "Thank the Exalted for us."

"But the Exalted is already married," Elita said. She had seen his wife, Miracle, seated beside him at the ceremonies. And they had children—four of them, all blond like Miracle.

"Yes." Helen turned to Elita, no longer smiling. "The Exalted has chosen you as his second wife."

Her mother's fingers were digging into Elita's shoulders now. "That is indeed a great honor," she said carefully. "But Elita is so young. Surely there are other, more suitable women..."

"He has chosen Elita," Jedediah said, his voice overly loud in the small space. Harsh. "How dare you question his choice."

"I meant no disrespect," Mom said, and bowed her head. But Elita could feel her trembling.

"Of course she doesn't," her father said. "And it's good that Elita has been chosen now. She will have years to learn all she will need to know for such an honored position."

"Of course," Helen said. She smiled at Elita once more. "We have much to do to prepare you for your future role."

"What does she need to do?" Mom asked.

"I will instruct her myself," Helen said. "I will teach her all she needs to know to be a fitting bride for our Exalted leader." She took a step back. "I'm sure you are both in awe. I will leave you to ponder your good fortune."

She and Sarai turned and left, but Jedediah stayed behind. He fixed them with a hard gaze. "Don't think you're going to get out of this," he said. "Remember what happened to Elim."

As soon as the door closed behind him, Elita's mother sank to her knees. Elita sat beside her. "Mom, what's wrong?" she asked.

Her mother pulled her close and stroked her hair. "I won't let anyone hurt you," she whispered.

"They're not going to hurt her," her father said. "This is a great honor."

"She's a child," her mother said, her expression fierce. "And if she does decide to marry one day, she should be free to make her own choice. The idea of her being married off to some old man who already has one wife—it's positively medieval."

"The Old Testament kings all had many wives," her father said.

"The Exalted is not an Old Testament king. And I can't believe you're going along with this."

Her father's expression sagged, and he looked away. "I don't see that we have any choice," he said. "No one goes against the Exalted's decrees."

"When we came here, it was because the Vine offered a better way of life—one full of cooperation and peace and contributing positive things to the world. No one ever said anything about marrying off children."

"She's not going to marry him right away," her father said. "The wedding will be years away, and anything could happen before then."

"We could leave," her mother said.

"We can't leave." He leaned closer and lowered his voice, as if Elita wasn't sitting right there between them. "You heard what Jedediah said—about Elim."

"Who's Elim?" Elita asked.

"Just…someone who used to belong to the Vine," her mother said.

"What happened to him?" Elita asked.

"He went away," her father said. "But we aren't going anywhere." He sounded almost angry. Elita leaned against her mom, trying to make herself smaller.

"We're going to take care of Elita," her mother said. "We're going to do whatever it takes to look after her." Her mother sounded angry, too, and Elita felt like crying. Whatever was going on was Jedediah's fault. And maybe the Exalted's fault too. Though she would never say that out loud. Everyone—even kids like her—knew that you didn't say anything bad about the Exalted. She didn't know what would happen to her if she did, but she was pretty sure it would be terrible.

"MY PARENTS JOINED the Vine when I was five." Chris was calmer now, seated next to Rand in an interview room at the sheriff's department, several hours after the confrontation in the woods. Travis and Gage Walker sat across from them—looking as relaxed as two uniformed lawmen could, she thought. She ran a hand through her bright blue hair. "They met some members at the ice-cream shop they owned in town and liked what they had to say and ended up selling everything and moving into a mobile home on some land the Vine owned. Or maybe the group was squatting on the land. I don't really know. Anyway, things were fine until the year I turned nine."

When she didn't continue, Travis prodded her. "What happened when you were nine?"

"One of the women who was close to the Exalted, came to my parents and told them that the Exalted had decided that I would be his second wife."

"When you were *nine*?" Rand didn't try to hide his shock.

She nodded. "The wedding wasn't going to take place until I was older. My dad told me it wouldn't happen until I was all grown up, and by then I would be looking forward to it. He went along with the idea that I'd been chosen for a great honor, but my mom didn't feel that way. I remember they argued about it."

The old sadness returned as she remembered the tense

atmosphere in her family in the days after the announcement. "I had to take classes from a woman named Helen. Things like etiquette, and I had to memorize a lot of the Exalted's sayings. They were like proverbs, I guess. And I had to learn to sew and cook and read poetry. I was just a kid, and I thought a lot of it was dumb and boring, yet it didn't really feel dangerous or anything. But my mom really didn't like me taking the classes. My dad thought they wouldn't hurt anything, so they fought about that too." She sighed. "Things went along like that until I turned twelve. Then Jedediah and Helen showed up one evening and announced that the wedding would take place in a couple of weeks."

"When you were twelve," Rand clarified.

"Yes." She swallowed, recalling the details of that day. Details these people didn't need to hear. No one spoke, waiting. She could feel their eyes on her, especially Rand's. It was as if everyone in the room was holding their breath in anticipation of her next words. "My father died the day after that announcement was made. My mother said he tried to convince the Exalted that I was too young. The official story was that Dad died from eating poisonous mushrooms, but my mom and I always believed he was killed for getting in the way of something the Exalted wanted."

She studied her hands on the table, fingers laced together, reliving those awful days.

"You think someone in the group murdered your father?" Travis asked.

"Yes. But we don't have any proof, and my mom was too afraid to say anything. A few days later, she and I ran away."

"No one came after you?" Gage asked.

"They came looking for us," Chris said. "We knew they would. For years, we kept bags packed, and we would move every time we saw anyone we recognized from the Vine. Then, for a long time, we didn't see anyone. I thought we had gotten away." She glanced at Rand. "Until I saw Jedediah on the trail that day. I knew he recognized me, and it would be only a matter of time."

"He can't force you to marry someone," Travis said.

"The law may say he can't, but the Vine makes their own laws," she said.

"Have you found out anything more about these people?" Rand asked the sheriff. "Do they have any kind of criminal record?"

"We contacted the lawyer on the business card we were given," Travis said. "He declined to identify any of the principals in the Vine, LLC. We'll run a check on Edmund Harrison."

"Can you charge them in connection with the fire?" Rand asked.

"The fire appears to have started from a lightning strike. We haven't located the man you and others saw running away, back toward camp. No one else was harmed. Right now they haven't broken any laws."

"No one within the group will give evidence against them," Chris said. "They're either true believers who can't imagine the Exalted would ever do anything wrong or they're too afraid to speak out. And Harrison and those closest to him are careful."

"Have they made any specific threats to you?" Travis asked.

She shook her head. "Nothing more than what you heard, and that was more of a statement than a threat."

"That they would begin the wedding preparations today," Rand said. "But they can't force you to marry someone against your will."

"They believe they can." She hugged her arms across the chest. "They might try to kidnap me or drug me or threaten me. I don't know. I don't want to find out."

"If they do threaten you or try to force you to come with them, contact me." Travis handed her a business card. "Until then, there's not a lot we can do."

"I understand." She shoved back her chair. "If that's all, I'd like to go home now."

WHEN SHE STOOD, Rand rose also and followed her out. On the sidewalk, she turned to face him. "Thanks for the moral support, but I'm fine," she said. "I've dealt with these people most of my life. I know how to take care of myself."

"What are you going to do?" he asked.

"That's none of your business." She turned and started walking away.

She was right, but he followed her anyway. "Don't let them frighten you away."

"You don't know anything about it," she said, and kept walking.

"I know that you were strong enough to get away from them once," he said. "They may not like it, but it gives you the upper hand. You could expose them for what they really are and maybe save others."

"I just want them to leave me alone."

"I want that too. But I want more. I want to stop them from ruining other lives."

She halted alongside her Subaru, keys in hand. He

stopped, too, five feet away, giving her space but hoping she would listen. "Why do you even care?" she asked.

"Because I like you. And I don't want you to leave when we've just met."

She shook her head and opened the driver's-side door of the car. "Sorry to disappoint you," she said.

"And because I didn't do enough to help my sister."

She stilled, holding her position for a long, breathless moment, until at last she lifted her head and met his gaze. "You mean, you couldn't persuade her to leave," she said. "But that was her decision to make, if she was an adult."

"I should have dragged her away from them when I had the chance," he said. "I'll never get over that regret, but I can help others now."

"You can't make someone leave that lifestyle unless they want to," she said.

"I should have at least tried." His face was flushed, his breathing ragged. "We tried for two years to persuade her to leave, but she wouldn't. And then we found out she had committed suicide." He could say the words now without the stabbing pain they had once caused, but the hurt would never completely go away.

"I'm sorry," she said, her previous anger replaced by softness.

"So am I. And I'm sorry there was nothing we could do to stop that cult from ensnaring others. But I'll do anything I can to help you stop the Vine."

"What do you think we could do?"

"I don't know. But if they're really going to stay around here until you go with them, that gives us a little time to find out what else they've been up to. And if they do come after you, we'll stop them."

"I'm not sure they can be stopped," she said. "They have a lot of money, and that gives them power."

"Does that give them power over you?"

She didn't hesitate in her reply. "No."

"And they don't have any power over me." He moved closer until he was standing right in front of her. "Together, maybe we can find a way to stop them from hurting anyone else."

"All right." She slid into the car. "I need time to think. And to talk to my mom. She might know or remember something that can help us."

"Call me," he said.

She nodded and started the engine.

He stepped back and watched her leave, his stomach in knots. It was easy to make bold declarations about stopping these people, but all the talk in the world hadn't saved his sister.

Chapter Six

Chris gripped her phone tightly and paced her small living room as she told her mother about that morning's encounter with the Exalted's followers. "They walked right up and said all that about planning a wedding—in front of my friends and the sheriff and everyone. Now I know they all think I'm a freak."

Harley sat up on his bed by the sofa and watched her, forehead wrinkled in what seemed to Chris to be an expression of worry.

"It doesn't matter what they think of you," April said. "You can't let the Vine get you in their clutches again."

"I know that, Mom. And I'm being careful."

"Now that they've found you, they won't give up until they have you back," April said. "You need to leave."

Leaving had been Chris's first thought too. But Rand's plea wasn't the only thing that had stopped her from packing up and fleeing. "I have a good life here," she said. "I'm tired of running."

"Then come stay with me for a while. Just until they give up and leave town."

"And risk leading them to you? No." Her mother had worked hard to get away from the Vine. She had changed her name, her job, and her appearance, and kept a low pro-

file in a small town in Ohio. Chris stopped at the window
that looked down into the alley below. Her car was parked
there, next to a large trash bin. Otherwise, the alley was
empty. "I talked to the local sheriff today," she said. "I told
him about Dad."

"He'll never find evidence that he was murdered," her
mother said. "The Vine would make sure of that."

"I know we buried Dad in the woods," Chris said. "But
I don't remember much about it."

"There was a funeral. The Exalted gave the eulogy,
which was supposed to be a great honor. I don't remember
anything he said."

"That didn't strike you as odd—that no law enforcement
was called, or a local coroner, or anything?"

"No. We didn't involve outsiders. Our motto was that
we took care of our own. Now I can see how that allowed
the group to get away with horrible things, but at the time
it seemed perfectly normal."

"There's a doctor here. He works with search and rescue, and he was there when Jedediah and two other men
confronted me. Rand—the doctor—said if I stay, he'll help
me fight the Vine."

"He doesn't know anything about them. He's probably
just trying to impress you."

"He said his sister belonged to a cult. She committed suicide. He wants to keep them from hurting anyone else." She
could still feel the impact of Rand's confession. He hadn't
dismissed the idea that strangers would try to force her
to marry or that she might be in danger from a harmless-
looking back-to-nature group. He knew the power groups
like the Vine could wield.

"Do you trust him?" April asked.

Chris didn't trust anyone. It had never felt safe to do so. "I believe he's sincere," she said. That wasn't the same as trust, exactly, but it was more than she could say about many of the people she'd met.

"Then let him help you. But don't depend on him."

"I know, Mom. The only person I can depend on is myself." How often had she repeated those words over the years? But they didn't make her feel stronger—only more alone.

"And me," April said. "You know I'll help you any way I can."

Harley stood and whined. Chris glanced at the dog. "I need to go now, Mom. I'll keep you posted on what happens here."

"I'll meet you anywhere, anytime you need me," April said. "I love you."

"I love you, too, Mom." She ended the call. Harley paced, the hair on the back of his neck and along his spine standing up. He let out a low growl and trotted over to the door.

Chris was on her way to the door when she heard footsteps in the hallway. Heart pounding, she checked the peephole. Jedediah's grim features glared back at her. Then he pounded on the door.

"Go away!" she said.

"We need to talk."

"I have nothing to say to you."

"The Exalted wants to see you."

"I don't have anything to say to him either. Go away."

"I'm here to take you to him."

"I'm calling the sheriff right now," she said, and pulled her phone from her pocket. She hit the nine and the one, then watched as Jedediah turned and left.

She sank to her knees and wrapped her arms around Harley, who still trembled with agitation. When she felt a little calmer, she focused on her phone once more. She didn't call 911. Instead, she selected the number she had programmed into the phone only that afternoon.

"Chris? Is everything okay?" Rand sounded a little out of breath. She tried to picture him, perhaps in doctor's scrubs. Or would he be at home?

"Jedediah was just here," she said.

"Did you call the sheriff?"

"I told him I would, so he left. I just… I wanted someone to know." Someone who might understand.

"I'm at the hospital in Junction. Is there someone else you can call to stay with you?"

"No, I'm okay. I have Harley. He let me know Jedediah was here before he even got to the door."

"What happened?" Rand asked. "What did he say to you?"

"He told me the Exalted wants to see me. I told him I didn't have anything to say to him, and then I said I was going to call the sheriff. He left. It's almost funny, really, that he thought I would meekly come with him. As if I was still nine years old."

"If he comes back, don't waste time talking to him," Rand said. "Dial 911 right away."

"I will. I won't keep you any longer. I'll see you at the training tonight."

"I'll pick you up, and we can go together," he said.

She started to protest, then imagined parking in that alley in the dark. It would be so easy for Jedediah and others to grab her. "All right," she said. "Thanks."

She ended the call and stood. Harley followed her to

the desk in the corner, where Chris opened her laptop. She would write down everything she knew about the Vine and do some research online to learn whatever she could. Some people said knowledge was power. She would need every advantage to defeat someone like the Exalted, who was so accustomed to getting his own way.

RAND CHANGED OUT of his scrubs and made a quick stop at his house before he drove to pick up Chris. He removed his Sig Sauer M17 from the safe, loaded it and slipped it into his pocket. He didn't trust the members of the Vine not to come after Chris again, and he wanted to be prepared.

He parked in the alley next to Chris's Subaru and waited a moment after he shut off the engine, searching the darkness outside the circle of light cast by the single bulb over the door leading to the stairs to Chris's apartment. Nothing moved within those shadows, so he pulled out his phone and texted Chris. On my way up.

She met him at the door, her dog by her side. Harley eyed him warily but made no sound as Rand said hello, then offered the back of his hand for a sniff. "Good dog," Chris praised, rubbing behind the ridgeback's ear. "I'm ready to go," she said, and picked up her keys.

He waited while she locked her door, then preceded her down the steps, pausing to check the alley before he stepped out in it. He was a little surprised at how easily he slipped back into this mode of being on patrol, as if he was back in Afghanistan, where something as simple as walking to the latrine could make you a target.

Chris said nothing as she stood close behind him, then hurried after him to his car, head down. Harley followed, and hopped into the back seat of Rand's SUV. "I couldn't leave him," she said of the dog. "I'm too afraid Jedediah or someone else might try to hurt him."

"No problem," Rand said. "I like dogs."

She remained silent all the way to search and rescue headquarters. The brightness of the room and the hum of conversation was jarring after the tension in his car, but he felt her relax as she sank into the end of the sofa and took out a notebook and pen. He sat beside her and did the same but couldn't shed his wariness as easily.

"Hey, Chris, how are you doing?"

"Everything okay, Chris?"

"Hey, Chris. You good?"

One by one, the gathered volunteers made a point to stop by and say hello. Those who hadn't been at the call-out for the fire would have heard about Chris's encounter with the members of the Vine. None of them asked any questions, though Rand read the curiosity in their eyes.

Chris accepted the attention calmly. "I'm good, thanks," she told anyone who inquired.

An elfin young woman with a cloud of dark curls approached. "Hey, Chris, how are you doing?" she asked. "I've been meaning to tell you how much I love your hair. And your tattoos." She glanced at her own bare arms. "I've been thinking of getting a tattoo myself, but my mom would probably have a heart attack if I did, and my three brothers would lose their minds." She grinned, deep dimples forming on either side of her mouth. "Which is kind of why I want to do it."

"Bethany, this is Rand," Chris said.

"Hey, Rand." Bethany offered her hand. "I'm glad you joined the group. For one thing, it means I'm no longer the newest rookie." She bent and patted Harley. "I miss my dog," she said. "But when I moved here my parents wouldn't let me take Charlie with me. I think they thought if they said that, I wouldn't leave, but they were wrong about that."

"Where are you from?" Rand asked, as much to spare Chris from the steady stream of chatter as out of genuine curiosity.

"Waterbury, Vermont. I'm one of four and the only girl. To say that my parents and brothers are overprotective is an understatement. I practically had an armed guard with me everywhere I went. Living here, by myself, is a whole new experience."

Sheri Stevens took her place at the front of the room. "I better get to my seat," Bethany said. "I just wanted to say hi. Maybe we can get together for coffee or a drink sometime."

Before Chris could answer, she was gone.

"She's certainly friendly," Rand said.

"She's a little overwhelming," Chris said.

"All right, everyone. Let's focus on this evening's topic of wilderness first aid," Sheri began. "This will be a review for some of you, but it's a requirement, and standard practices do get updated from time to time, so pay attention."

Rand figured he could have taught the class, given his experiences in a field hospital, though he hoped a local search and rescue group would never have to deal with treating people who had been hit by improvised explosives or sniper fire. His mind drifted to his fellow volunteers. He didn't know most of them very well, but he was impressed that they would give so much time and attention to helping others, most of whom were probably strangers passing through the area, on vacation or on their way to somewhere else.

After an hour, they took a break. Ryan and Caleb joined

him and Chris at the refreshment table. "We think that group that escaped the fire is camping out at Davis Draw," Ryan said. He picked up a peanut butter cookie and bit into it.

"Where is Davis Draw?" Chris asked. She didn't look alarmed.

"It's off a forest service road at the end of County Road 14," Caleb said. "It's not as nice as the area where they were—less trees, mostly desert scrub. And they'll have to haul water."

"How did you find this out?" Chris asked. She stirred sugar into a cup of coffee.

"We drove out there and saw a bunch of trailers and big tents," Ryan said. "Some guys asked what we were doing, and we told them we were looking for a place to camp. They said they had the whole area. We asked what they were doing, and they said it was a religious retreat."

Chris nodded but said nothing.

"I guess it's good to know where they are," Rand said.

"There's a two-week limit on camping in the area," Caleb said.

"I don't know how well that's enforced," Ryan added.

Chris shrugged. "They can do whatever they like," she said. "I really don't care."

"Time to get back to work," Sheri called, and they moved back to their places.

Chris leaned toward Rand again. "There may be a two-week camping limit, but they aren't going to leave until they have me," she said.

"They will if we persuade them that they're wasting their time," he said.

She pressed her lips together and shook her head, but

she said nothing else as the lights dimmed and Sheri resumed her lecture.

At evening's end, they stayed to rearrange chairs and clean up. Danny found Rand carting the coffee urn into the tiny galley. "Did I tell you that one of your jobs as medical adviser is to help update our treatment protocols?"

"Sure, I can do that." Rand set the urn on the counter. "Any particular protocols?"

Danny made a face. "It's been a while since any of them were reviewed. Could you meet one day next week to go over them?"

"I'm off on Tuesday. Would that work?"

"That would be great." He glanced over his shoulder, then turned back, his voice lower. "I saw you sticking pretty close to Chris. Is she okay?"

"I'm fine." She moved in behind them with a handful of paper plates. She shoved the plates into the trash and faced Danny. "If you want to know how I'm doing, ask me."

"Sorry." He held up both hands. "But if you need anything—anything at all—you can call on any member of the team. We're not just about saving tourists, you know."

Her expression softened. "Thanks. That means a lot."

They exited the building and started across the parking lot, only to be hailed by Bethany. "I work at Peak Jeep Tours," she said. "Stop by if you're ever in the neighborhood. I'd really like to know you better."

"Um, sure." Chris hurried away, and Rand sped up to keep pace with her.

"Why is she so interested in me?" Chris asked when he caught up with her.

"I think she's just friendly."

"I'm not used to other people focusing on me—or caring so much," Chris said when she and Rand were in his car, headed back toward her apartment. "It feels a little uncomfortable."

"*Uncomfortable* but not *bad*, right?"

"Yeah."

"Can I ask you a personal question?"

"You can ask. That doesn't mean I'll answer."

"Fair enough. The blue hair and the tattoos—is that a fashion choice or another way of disguising yourself?"

She didn't say anything for so long he thought he might have offended her. But he had learned early in his medical career about the value of giving people plenty of time to answer hard questions. "A little of both, I think," she said. "My mother dyed my hair the day we escaped the camp, and I kept changing it over the years so I would look unfamiliar to anyone who knew me before. As for the tattoos—" she held out her arm "—we were taught that religious offerings were supposed to be perfect. Unblemished. I think in the back of my head I thought the Exalted would view a tattoo as an imperfection. That's why I got the first one, but after that, I liked it. It was another artistic expression." She shifted in the seat. "Why do you ask?"

"Just curious. They seem to suit you."

He pulled up to the door at the back of her building this time and met her beneath the light, waiting while she unlocked the outside entrance. They mounted the stairs side by side. She glanced down at his hand tensed at his side, as if reaching for something. "Are you carrying a gun?" she asked.

"Yes." He pulled up his shirt enough to show a holstered pistol. "I was in the military for years. I got used to walking around armed."

She nodded and they continued to her door. Once there, she turned to face him. "Look, I appreciate your concern. I really do. But these people are unpredictable. They seem nice and normal, until they aren't."

"I know that already. Remember, I've dealt with a cult before. They reel people in by appearing perfectly sensible and smarter than everyone else."

"Right. It's just…if something goes wrong, don't blame yourself, okay? You're not responsible for me. I'm not your sister."

Her expression was so earnest, her dark eyes so full of concern. As if she was more worried about him than about herself. His gaze shifted to her lips, full and slightly parted. "I don't feel about you like I do my sister." The words emerged more gruffly than he had planned. Then he yielded to temptation and kissed her.

For a fraction of a breath, she became a statue once his lips were on hers, unmoving. Not breathing. Then she pressed one hand to his chest, fingers slightly curled, seeking purchase. She arched into him, returning the kiss. He cupped his hand to her cheek, her skin hot, as if blushing at his touch. With a breathy moan, her lips parted, and she pressed against him, fitted to him, supple and strong. He wrapped both arms around her, cradling her to him yet holding back, his feelings so intense he feared crushing her.

She broke the kiss and stared up at him, a dazed expression in her eyes. "You'd better go," she whispered.

He wanted to argue but didn't. Instead, he reluctantly released his hold and waited while she unlocked her door and disappeared inside. He heard the dead bolt engage, then turned and moved away, down the stairs and into the darkness. So much of him was still there on that landing, wrapped up in that unexpected kiss.

He didn't see the person who came up behind him, only felt his presence and started to turn; then something hard crashed into his head, driving him to his knees. "Chris!" he tried to shout, but the word came out as a murmur as darkness swallowed him.

Chapter Seven

Chris sank onto the sofa, head back, eyes closed. That kiss! She hadn't even realized she was interested in Rand that way—that climb-his-body, take-me-now, where-have-you-been-all-my-life, passion-turned-up-to-ten kind of way—and then she was. When had she ever been kissed like that? Never. She had *never* been kissed like that. She didn't let men get that close. But Rand had vaulted right over her defenses and ambushed her with that kiss.

And she had willingly surrendered. Except it hadn't felt like losing—it felt like winning a grand prize. The rush of victory was overwhelming. It had been all she could do to pull herself together enough to send him away. At least she had that much of a sense of self-preservation left. After years of caution, she wasn't going to leap off that cliff just yet.

Harley climbed up onto the sofa beside her and began licking her cheek. She opened her eyes and hugged the dog. "I'm okay," she said. "Everything's okay."

Whomp!

The sound jolted her upright. Harley barked loudly, the ridge of hair along his back at attention. Something heavy had hit her door. It came again, an impact that made the door rattle in its frame. Heart pounding painfully, she jumped up, scrambling to free her phone from her pocket. A third impact shook the door, and Harley's barking became more frantic.

She stabbed at the phone as she moved toward the back door. "Nine-one-one. What is your emergency?"

"Someone is breaking into my apartment." She reached the kitchen just as the glass in the door's small window shattered inward. "Please hurry!"

"What is your location, ma'am?"

Chris rattled off her address as she grabbed the chef's knife from the magnet by the stove. She looked around for anything else she could use as a weapon. The frying pan? A rolling pin? Then she spotted the fire extinguisher and pulled it from its bracket on the wall. "Come on, Harley," she called, and headed toward the bedroom. She heard the back door give way as she dove into the closet and shut the door behind her and the dog. They would find her soon enough, but she hoped she would be able to hold them off until help arrived.

RAND GROANED AND tried to sit, but a wave of dizziness dragged him down again. He was aware of noises—someone shouting, pounding footsteps. Then hands grabbed him roughly. He fought back, punching out, and tried to shout, but no words emerged. He tried to open his eyes yet saw nothing but blackness.

"Hey, it's okay. You're all right now. You're safe. Lie still." The voice was firm but reassuring. Strong hands urged him to lie back, and he surrendered to the pull of gravity. A bright light shone on his face, and he squinted against it. A man he didn't know peered down at him. "Who are you?" Rand managed to force out.

"I'm Lee. I'm a paramedic with Rayford County Emergency Services. Looks like you hit your head pretty hard. Can you tell me what happened?"

Rand closed his eyes again, trying to remember. "Someone jumped me," he said.

"Lie still, okay? You're still bleeding a little. Do you know who hit you?"

He was starting to think more clearly, and the memory of what had happened before he was hit came flooding back. "Chris!" He tried to sit up again, though the EMTs held him down. "Is Chris all right? I have to go to her."

"Is Chris the person who called for an ambulance?" Lee asked someone out of Rand's field of vision. He was still holding Rand down. Rand lay back, gathering strength for another attempt to rise.

"No. Someone named Susan, in the apartment across the alley," a female voice answered. "She said she heard a shout and looked out the window to see someone fall to the ground and someone else run away. She called 911, and they dispatched us." A woman with strawberry blond hair and freckles leaned over Rand. "A sheriff's deputy is on the way. I hear the siren now."

Rand heard it too—a high-pitched wailing that grew louder and louder. He sat up again. This time no one stopped him. The woman probed at the back of his head while Lee unwrapped a blood pressure cuff from around Rand's left arm.

"Your vitals are good," Lee said. "How are you feeling?"

The dizziness and nausea had subsided. His head throbbed, but he could live with that. "I'm better," he said. "I have to check on Chris. The person who hit me could have got to her."

Lee's forehead wrinkled. "This Chris person was with you when you were attacked?"

"No. She lives upstairs, over the art gallery. I was just leaving her apartment. Whoever hit me must have been waiting in the alley."

"If she's upstairs, she should be all—" A loud crash interrupted him. He turned to look toward the sound behind him, and Rand staggered to his feet.

"Sir, you need to be still—"

Rand ignored the words and started for the building. He was certain now that his attacker had been waiting to disable him so he could go after Chris. But he had taken only a few steps when a sheriff's department SUV turned into the alley. The wail of the siren bounced off the buildings, and Rand instinctively put his hands to his ears. "Freeze, with your hands where I can see them!" a voice from the SUV ordered.

Rand did as he was asked and squinted in the glare of the spotlight centered on him. Then the light cut off, and a man stepped out from the car. "Rand, what are you doing here?"

Jake Gwynn moved toward Rand, converging on him at the same time the two EMTs caught up with him. "You need to check on Chris," Rand said. "I had just left her apartment when someone attacked me, but I think their real target was her."

"Chris called 911 and said someone was breaking into her apartment." Jake looked at the outer door. "Gage is on his way."

"We don't have time to wait," Rand said. "I'll back you up."

Jake's gaze shifted to Rand's head. "You're bleeding."

"I'll be fine. We don't have time to loo—"

A woman's scream overhead launched him toward the door, with Jake right behind him. But the door was locked. Jake pounded on it. "Open up! Sheriff's department!" he shouted.

But the only reply was scuffling noises overhead and another loud crash. "Is there a back way in?" Jake asked.

"I don't know," Rand said. He tried to remember anything about Chris's apartment, but he hadn't been paying attention, and he hadn't been past the living room. "Maybe a fire escape?"

"Stay here. I'm going around back."

As soon as Jake was gone, Rand turned his attention back to the door. It was a heavy metal door; he doubted he could bash it in. He couldn't pick the lock either. Could he ram it with his car?

A second siren's wail filled the air. "That must be Gage," Lee said.

Rand moved to the middle of the alley and stared up at what he thought was Chris's window. "Chris!" he shouted. But no answer came.

A second black-and-white SUV entered the alley, and Sergeant Gage Walker stepped out almost before it had come to a complete stop. "What's going on?" he asked.

"Chris is upstairs," Rand said. "She called 911, saying someone was breaking into her apartment. I had just left her, and someone must have been waiting for me. They attacked me and knocked me out. I came to when the paramedics arrived."

"Dispatch sent us over in response to a call from a neighbor about a man being attacked in the alley," Lee said.

Gage pulled out his phone. "I'll call the building owner and see if we can get a key."

Rand shook his head and started around the corner of the building. Jake met him at the corner. "Where are you going?" he asked, his hands on Rand's shoulders.

"I'm going up the fire escape," Rand said. "I'm not waiting for a key."

"The stairs aren't down," Jake said. "No one's been up there."

"Or they've been up there and pulled the stairs up after them," Rand said. He pushed past Jake and headed toward the fire escape. As Jake had said, the bottom of the stairs was ten feet overhead, out of his reach.

Rand pulled out his phone and dialed Chris's number. It rang five times before going to voicemail. "I can't take your call right now…" He ended the call and shoved the phone back into his pocket. By this time, Jake had caught up with him. "She's not answering," Rand said. "I know something's wrong."

Gage called to them from the corner of the building. "The landlord is on the way," he said. "She said she'll be here in five minutes."

Rand looked up at the fire escape again. If he parked his SUV beneath it, he could climb on top and maybe reach the bottom of the ladder from there. He pulled his keys from his pocket. "Where are you going?" Jake asked.

"To help Chris." Waiting was only buying more time for her to end up hurt. Or worse.

CHRIS HEARD THE SIREN, growing louder by the second until the wailing was directly below. Then the sound shut off. Help was almost here. She just had to hang on a little longer.

The intruder was in the house now, footsteps lumbering as they—because it sounded like more than one person—

searched the apartment. Something heavy, a piece of furniture, fell to the floor with a crash. "We know you're in here, Elita!" a man—Jedediah?—called out.

Harley growled, a low and menacing rumble. Chris buried her fingers in the thick ruff at his neck. "Quiet!" she hissed. They needed to remain hidden until the deputies arrived. What was taking them so long?

The footsteps entered the bedroom. Chris's heart hammered. She let go of the dog and gripped the knife in her right hand, then thought better of that and slid it into her pocket. She hefted the fire extinguisher and looped her finger into the metal ring on the handle.

Crash! A scream escaped her as something hit the closet door, causing it to bow inward. Harley lunged at the door, barking furiously. Chris braced against the back wall of the closet and stood, shoving clothes aside and balancing the fire extinguisher on one thigh. Her pulse sounded so loud in her ear she could scarcely hear anything else, though the dog's barking echoed in the small space.

The door burst open, splinters flying. Chris pulled the ring from the handle of the fire extinguisher, aimed the hose and squeezed the trigger. She hit her intruder right in the face. When the second man shoved the first out of the way and lunged for her, she got him, too, white powder billowing up and coating his glasses and hair and filling his mouth when he opened it to shout.

When the extinguisher was empty, Chris swung it like a club. She hit the second man hard on the shoulder. When he staggered back, the first man rushed forward, and she thrust the bottom of the extinguisher into his forehead, connecting with a sickening *thwack*—like a hammer hitting a watermelon. The first man grabbed on to the door of the closet but remained standing, only to be driven farther back by Harley, who rushed forward, teeth bared.

"Freeze! Sheriff's department!" came a shout from the front room.

The first man turned; then the second grabbed his shoulder. "We better get out of here," he said. They raced from the room. Chris dropped the fire extinguisher and sank to her knees, arms wrapped around Harley, who was still barking and lunging.

That was how Jake Gwynn found her. She had to calm the dog before he could approach, but once she had convinced Harley that everything was okay, Jake helped her to the end of the bed, where she sat and contemplated the closet's shattered door and the carpeting coated with white powder.

"There were two men," she said. "They broke in, and I hid in the closet with Harley. They ran when they heard you coming."

"Gage went after them," Jake said. "Do you know who they are?"

"Oh, I'm sure they were members of the Vine," she said. "They're the only ones who would want to hurt me. One of them might have been Jedediah."

"Did you get a good look at them?" Jake asked. "Could you identify them?"

She shook her head. "By the time I saw them, they were covered in the powder from the fire extinguisher." She closed her eyes, replaying those few split seconds. "And I think their faces were covered. They wore ski masks or something like that. And gloves." She had the image of black-gloved hands reaching for her fixed in her mind.

"Chris!"

Rand's cry made her sit up straighter. "We're in the bedroom," Jake called. "Don't come in. You could contaminate evidence." He indicated the footprints in the powder on the carpet, which he had avoided when he entered the room. "Those are from your attackers. We might be able to match them to their shoes later."

Rand appeared in the doorway. "Chris, are you all right?" he asked.

"I'm fine." She passed a shaky hand through her hair. "They never laid a hand on me."

Rand surveyed the chaos around the closet. "What happened?"

"She let off a fire extinguisher at them," Jake said, a note of admiration in his voice.

"I hit them with it too," she said. "And there's a kitchen knife in my pocket. I would have used it on them if I had to. And I had Harley." She hugged the dog, as much out of affection as to keep him from bounding across the powdered carpet to Rand.

"You shouldn't be in here, Rand," Jake said. "Go back outside and wait. Let the ambulance crew finish looking you over."

"Ambulance?" Chris turned to Rand. "Are you hurt? What happened?"

He touched the back of his head and winced. "Whoever went after you was waiting for me. They knocked me out, but I'm fine. Just a bump on the head."

Gage moved in behind him. "They got away down the fire escape," he said. "I didn't even get a good look at them. Two men dressed in black, covered in flour or something."

"Most of the contents of a fire extinguisher," Jake said. "Chris let them have it when they came after her."

"Good thinking." Gage studied the footprints on the floor. "I'll call for a forensics team. Are you all right, Chris? Do you need the paramedics?"

"I'm okay," she said.

"We'll need to get your statement," Gage said. "Jake, bring her in the other room." He turned to Rand. "We'll need your statement too."

Jake directed her in picking her way around the path the intruders had taken when they fled the apartment. She guided Harley, who wasn't in a cooperative mood, out of the apartment and down the stairs, where she found two patrol vehicles, an ambulance, two paramedics, her landlord and half a dozen curious onlookers.

Rand moved in beside her. "Are you sure you're okay?" he asked, his gaze taking her in from the top of her head to her feet.

She nodded and hugged her arms across her chest, having released Harley to sniff around, knowing the dog wouldn't go far. "I was terrified for a few minutes. Now I'm just exhausted."

Her landlord, Jasmine, approached. With no makeup on and wearing a sweatshirt pulled over plaid pajama pants, she looked very different from the polished professional Chris was used to. "Honey, are you okay?" Jasmine asked.

"I'm fine. I'm sorry about the apartment doors." She looked at the doors, both bent inward.

"The cops did that," Jasmine said. "I guess they couldn't wait for me to get here with the key."

Chris shuddered. "They got to me just in time."

"Who cares about doors, as long as you're okay." Jasmine patted her arm. "Don't worry about it. I have insurance. But is there anything else you need?"

"No, thanks. I'm okay, really."

"Your friend here looks a little worse for wear." Jasmine flashed a smile. "Still very easy on the eyes, mind you."

Chris studied Rand. His face was paler than usual, the fine lines around his eyes tighter, as if he was in pain. And was that blood in his hair?

"Rand, you're hurt!" she exclaimed.

"I'm okay. The paramedics have seen me."

"Jake, get Rand's statement," Gage said as he joined them. "Chris, you come with me."

She ended up sitting in the front seat of Gage's patrol car, reciting all the events of the evening, leaving out the part about her and Rand kissing before he left her and returned to his car. "I'm sure those two men were from the Vine," she said. "The group has made it clear they want me back."

"To marry their leader—have I got that right?" Gage asked.

She nodded. "It sounds ridiculous. I'm a grown woman. I'm not a member of the group anymore. They can't force me to marry someone. Especially since he's already married to someone else. But logic doesn't really matter. They think they can make me do this. And they believe they're above the law."

"Did the two men who broke into your apartment say anything?" Gage asked.

"One of them called me Elita," she said. "That was the name I used when I was a member of the group—when I was a little girl. That's one more reason I'm sure they were from the Vine. No one else knows me by that name."

Gage made a note. "Anything else you remember about them?"

"I thought the voice sounded like Jedediah. He's the man

who confronted me at the fire the other day. I had seen him on a hiking trail the day before that, when search and rescue responded to a man on the Anderson Falls Trail who had heart trouble."

"We'll have forensics go over the place," Gage said. "You won't be able to stay here for a while. The front and back doors to your apartment were forced open."

"How did they get in from street level?" she asked.

"Best guess is they blocked the door from closing all the way while you and Rand were upstairs. He came down, and they ambushed him at his car, then went in the door and locked it behind them to delay anyone's ability to get to them."

"And to slow me down if I managed to run from them," she said.

"We had to break open the outer door to get to you," Gage said. "I was going to wait for Jasmine to bring us the key, but Rand insisted. I guess it's a good thing he did."

She said nothing, feeling Gage's eyes on her. She wondered what he thought of the tattoos and dyed hair. Of her strange past with a cult that seemed kooky to most people. "Have they threatened you before?" he asked. "Since you left?"

"Mom and I were approached a couple of times by members who recognized us." She shivered, remembering. "No direct threats. I think they're too clever for that. But if you had lived with them the way we did, you'd know how things that sound innocent can come across as really menacing."

"Give me an example."

She shifted in her seat, then blew out a breath. Why was this so hard to talk about? "If someone approached you and said, 'The Exalted is worried it will be really bad for you if you don't fulfill your destiny,' that sounds innocent enough, right? A little out there, but harmless. But when I hear that, I'm not thinking they're concerned about my karma or my mental health or even the threat of eternal damnation—I'm hearing code for 'If you don't do what we want, you could end up dead.'"

"Did that happen to other people who disobeyed the Exalted?" Gage asked.

"Oh yeah. No one ever used the word *murder*. They got sick. They had an accident. One young woman drowned."

"Were any of these deaths investigated by law enforcement?"

She shook her head. "They weren't even reported, as far as I know. The victims were buried in the woods, wherever we were staying. That was the way we did things. Everyone said, 'We take care of our own,' and it was considered a good thing. We didn't need outsiders interfering."

Gage closed his notebook. "I'll probably have more questions later. Do you have some place you can stay? Or I can find you a bed at a women's shelter."

"I'll find a place." She could always go to her mother's, though the idea left a sour taste in her mouth. Hadn't she said she was tired of running away? And what about bringing the danger with her?

At a tapping on the glass, she turned and saw Rand outside the SUV. Gage rolled down the window. "You can't stay here," Rand said. "Come back to my place. No one from the Vine knows where I live."

"Rand, you're hurt," she said. "You should have someone look at your head. You might need an X-ray or stitches."

"I'm fine. I have a headache, but no dizziness. The bleeding has stopped. I know enough to go to the hospital if any concerning symptoms pop up. In the meantime, these people don't know where I live, and I have a good security system. You'll be safe there."

"I told her I could find her a bed in a women's shelter," Gage said. "The local animal shelter would look after your dog for you."

She didn't want to go to a shelter, and she wasn't going to leave Harley. "Can Harley come to your place?" she asked Rand.

"Of course." He opened the door. The dog was standing next to him. "He's ready to go."

Chapter Eight

Gage fetched a list of items Chris needed from her apartment, and Rand loaded them into his SUV before they headed out. No one said much. He didn't try to reassure her that everything would be all right or offer advice for how she should act or feel. She was grateful for that. She laid her head back and closed her eyes, the dark silence and the rhythm of the vehicle's tires on the road almost lulling her to sleep.

But not quite. The fear was still there, coiled inside her, waiting to spring to life. That fear made her open her eyes again and repeatedly check the side mirror, looking out for headlights coming up behind them.

"No one is following us," Rand said. "I've been watching."

"I'm sorry I pulled you into this," she said. This was why she didn't get close to people. She didn't want anyone to see the mess of her life. It was like having an acquaintance rifle through the contents of your kitchen garbage can or your dirty-clothes hamper.

"I want to help." He glanced at her, then back at the road. "Just to be clear, this invitation to stay with me comes with no strings attached."

Was he thinking of that kiss? The memory pulled at her, here in the dark, so close to him. Yet everything that happened afterward was a barrier between them now. "Thanks," she said. "I like you. I guess that's pretty clear from that kiss. But... I have a lot to process right now. And I'm not used to trusting other people."

"Fair enough. Just know you can trust me."

She wanted to believe that, but she had had so little practice in depending on other people. She thought of all the rescue calls she had been on, when strangers trusted her and her fellow volunteers to save them. Those people, injured or stranded in the wilderness, didn't have much choice in the matter. Maybe she didn't have much choice either. She wasn't strong enough to fight the Vine on her own. She believed Rand was strong, and she believed he really did want to help her. That was more than anyone else had given her, which made it a good place to start.

Rand's home had once been a summer camp. He had purchased the long-abandoned property, torn down the dilapidated camper cabins and turned the log structure that had served as a lodge into a home. The remote location—the only property at the end of a long gravel road—had added to the hassle of the remodel, but now he appreciated the privacy and the safety it would offer Chris.

"The guest room and bath are upstairs," he told her as she and Harley followed him into the great room that made up most of the ground floor. "The primary suite is down here, so you'll have plenty of privacy." He led the way up the stairs to the guest room. "I use the room across the hall as my home office. Kitchen and laundry are downstairs, and there's a detached garage in back. There's an alarm system and a sensor on the driveway that will alert me if anyone tries to drive in."

"Is there something you need to tell me, Doctor?" she asked. "Some reason for all this security?"

"Let's just say I'm a naturally cautious person."

Harley sat beside her and leaned on her leg. She rubbed the dog's ears and looked into the bedroom but didn't go in. "Thank you," she said. "I couldn't ask for a better setup."

"You're welcome to stay as long as you like. I work three or four ten- to twelve-hour shifts per week at the hospital, so you'll be alone during that time. I hope that's not a problem."

"No. I'm used to being by myself." She entered the room, trailed by the dog, then looked back at him. "Good night," she said, and closed the door.

She had spoken so matter-of-factly about being accustomed to being alone, but her words made him feel a little hollow. He would have answered the same way and protested that he liked his own company. But there had been times when he had wished for companionship to fill that emptiness. He hoped he could be that for her.

Five years ago

"SOMEONE FROM THE VINE was here tonight."

Chris's mom sounded calm on the phone, but her words sent an icy shard of fear through Chris. "They came to your house? You spoke to them?"

"It was a man and a woman. They were waiting on the front steps when I came in from work. They were in the shadows, so I didn't see them until I was almost to the door. They were dressed in suits and carrying a big Bible, like missionaries going door-to-door. But when I told them I wasn't interested and tried to move past them, the man grabbed me."

Chris sucked in her breath. "Mom! Did they hurt you?"

"They only frightened me. But that was what they intended."

"What did they say? What did they do?"

"They forced their way into the house and kept asking me where you were. They said the Exalted was ready to marry you and it was time for you to fulfill your destiny."

"I thought they would have forgotten me by now," Chris said. "That the Exalted would have found someone else to marry." After all this time, she still thought of him by that title. His given name—Edmund Harrison—felt too strange on her tongue.

"I promise I didn't tell them where you are," her mother said. "But they said to tell you they weren't going to give up looking for you. And they said…they said…" Her voice broke.

Chris took a deep breath, trying to stop the shaking that had taken over her body but failing. "What did they say?"

"They said if you won't come back to them, you're dead to them. And they'll make sure you're dead to everyone else too."

"They're going to kill me just because I won't come back to their cult and marry a man who's old enough to be my father and already has at least one wife?" The idea was absurd, yet Chris didn't have it in her to laugh. She still remembered how seriously the members of the group took the Exalted's every pronouncement.

"They killed your father," her mother said. "And I'm sure they've killed other people. Eliminating anyone who gets out of line is one way the Exalted keeps order."

"You defied them by taking me away," Chris said. "Did they threaten you too?"

"They said…if you didn't obey, they would find a way to hurt me."

"No." A wave of nausea rocked Chris, but she pulled herself together, allowing anger to overcome the sickness. "That's not going to happen."

"I'm packing my things already. And I have my extra ID." Back when they had first left the group, her mother had paid for new birth certificates and Social Security cards for the two of them. Later, she had paid even more for a second set of identification. Chris kept hers in a lockbox under her bed, but she hadn't even looked at the papers for years.

"I'm coming to get you," Chris said. "I'll help you move."

"No! They're probably watching me, and they'll see you. I have a friend who will help me. He's a former cop. He knows a little of my story. I trust him. I'll be in touch with my new information when it's safe to do so."

"What about going to the police?" Chris asked. "If we tell them about these threats…"

"There's nothing they can do," her mother said. "The Exalted can produce witnesses all day long to attest to his sterling character. He has money and powerful friends to protect him. We don't have any proof they've threatened us."

"We know they've killed people," Chris said.

"But we can't prove it. Better to start over with a new name. I'm getting used to it now."

Gloom settled over Chris. "Do you think I should move and change my name too?"

"No, no! They don't know where you are. If they did, they wouldn't have wasted their time with me. There's no need for you to worry. I wouldn't even have bothered you with this, except I wanted you to know I'll be unreachable for a few days. Just until I get resettled."

"Of course I'm worried, Mom! What if they come after you again?"

"They won't. I've gotten very good at covering my tracks. I'm going to hang up now, sweetie. Love you. Talk to you soon. Oh, and next time we talk, remember—my new name is April."

Chris hung up the phone and slumped onto the sofa, stomach churning. Her mother hadn't sounded scared or even terribly upset. The two of them had moved five times between Chris's twelfth and eighteenth birthdays, and her mother had relocated twice more since Chris had left home. After all these years of running and hiding, Chris sometimes thought her mother enjoyed the challenge and the chance to start over and remake herself once again.

Whereas all Chris had ever wanted was to sink roots in one place, to be part of a community. She had found that here in Eagle Mountain. She had artist friends and her search and rescue friends and people whom she believed cared about her. Though she wasn't particularly close to any single person, she felt comfortable with them all. The thought of having to leave that behind was too heavy a burden to carry.

And all because one evil man was fixated on her. The Exalted had been getting his way for so long he couldn't bear the thought of anyone denying him—even a child, as she had been when she ran away from him. She wanted the running and hiding to stop, but she didn't know how to make it happen.

She still remembered her father, lying on the bed in their little trailer, writhing in agony. This was what the Exalted's punishment looked like. If the Vine ever caught up with her, they would make sure she obeyed, or they would mete out a similar fate. She was as sure of that as she had once been certain of the other teachings she had learned as a little girl. She had left those other false beliefs behind, but watching her father die had sealed this one certainty within her. She couldn't risk the Exalted catching up with her, so she had to keep running.

BEFORE CHRIS EVEN opened her eyes the next morning, she had the dreamlike sensation of being in an unfamiliar place. She opened her eyes to a shadowed bedroom, a thin comforter over the top of the bed, Harley stretched out along her side. No dream, then. She was in the guest room in Rand's home. For a few seconds the terror of those moments in the closet, hearing heavy footsteps approach her hiding place, threatened to overwhelm her. She rested a hand on the dog, feeling his side rise and fall, and grew calmer. She was safe. No one was going to hurt her.

She sat up and looked around the plain but comfortable guest room. Moving around so much, she was used to being in unfamiliar places, but almost always alone or with her mother. Not in a house belonging to a man she really liked but wasn't sure she should be with.

She got up and got ready for the day. Dressed in jeans and a T-shirt, she went downstairs to let Harley out. The rooms were empty, Rand's SUV no longer parked out front. While Harley patrolled the property, she hunted in the kitchen for coffee and started it brewing. Rand had left a note on the kitchen table with a set of car keys.

My shift is 6–4 today. The keys are to the Jeep in the garage. Feel free to use it. Help yourself to anything you like. Text if you need anything. Rand

Harley scratched at the door, and after making sure the noise really was from the dog, she let him in, then carried a cup of coffee upstairs and started the shower.

After she and the dog both had breakfast, she wandered the house. Rand had a few decent pieces of art on the walls—a mix of photos and original oils or watercolors, some from local artists she knew. His bookshelves housed medical texts, historical nonfiction and detective stories. One photo showed him standing with an older man and woman, the man an older version of Rand himself. *So these must be his parents.* No photo of his sister. Maybe that reminder would be too painful.

She avoided his bedroom. She was nosy, but she wasn't going to be that intrusive. House tour over, she returned to her room and made her bed but was unable to settle. She needed something to focus on besides the Vine. Usually, she could lose herself in her art, but she didn't have any supplies.

"Want to go for a ride, Harley?"

The dog wagged his tail and trotted ahead of her down the stairs. She collected the keys from the kitchen table and headed for the garage. Nice that Rand had a spare vehicle. One the Vine wouldn't recognize as hers.

At the last minute, she texted him. If he came home before she returned, she didn't want him to think the worst. Plus, her work with search and rescue had ingrained in her the advice that when setting out alone on a risky activity like a hike or skiing, it was smart to let someone know your plans. Running errands in town shouldn't be risky, but considering her situation, it might be.

Decided to run a few errands in town. Back soon.

He responded with a thumbs-up emoji. She smiled. Odd

how that made her feel better. She headed toward her apartment, almost without thinking. But she didn't park in back. Instead, she pulled the Jeep into a parking spot right in front of the gallery and sat for a few minutes, observing passers-by. No one looked like anyone from the Vine. Over the years she had gotten good at spotting them, with their slightly outdated fashion and simple hairstyles; the men always clean shaven, the women without makeup. Even more important, no one was paying particular attention to the building or to her.

Harley waited on the sidewalk while Chris went inside the gallery. The bell on the door sounded, and Jasmine bustled out of the workroom in the back. She stopped short when she recognized Chris. Today the frames of her glasses were red, matching the large red stones in her earrings. "Chris, how are you?" she asked, then hurried over to give her a hug.

Chris patted Jasmine awkwardly on the back and stepped out of her embrace. "I'm fine."

Jasmine nodded. "You look better. Not so pale. What happened last night was horrible. Do you have any idea who would do such a thing?"

"None," she lied. "I stopped by to pick up some supplies."

She had hoped to change the subject, but Jasmine didn't take the hint. "I've got someone coming tomorrow to see about replacing the doors on your apartment," she said. "But you're going to have a major mess to clean up. The sheriff's department left fingerprint dust, or whatever you call it, everywhere."

"Don't worry about that," Chris said. "I'll take care of it. And I'll reimburse you for the doors."

Jasmine shook her head. "I told you, my insurance will

take care of that. But what happened? The sheriff's deputy didn't say much, just that someone tried to break in."

"I think they had me confused with someone else," she lied again. She didn't want to go into the whole backstory. The circumstances would probably make Jasmine think twice about renting to her. "I just came in for a few things, then I'll be out of your way." In addition to the artwork for sale, Jasmine stocked a small selection of canvases, paints, pastels, sketchbooks and other supplies.

"Oh, honey, you're no trouble. You're the best tenant I ever had. Most of the time I wouldn't even know you're up there, you're so quiet." Jasmine followed her over to the corner devoted to supplies. "Deputy Gwynn said there were two guys who tried to break in, but they got away. He told me to keep an eye out for anyone hanging around the store, but I haven't seen anyone. Did you get a good look at them? Do you know who they are?"

"I only had a brief glimpse of them." Chris selected a sketchbook and pencils. "It was dark, and they were wearing ski masks."

"It's just the wildest thing. I mean, you don't think about something like that happening here. I hope they don't come back. They might think there's money in the gallery, though I make it a point not to leave much cash on hand, and I wouldn't think artwork was something they could readily sell."

"I'm sure the sheriff's deputies scared them off." Chris added an art gum eraser to her purchases. "I'll take these."

"Where are you staying?" Jasmine asked as she rang up Chris's selections.

"With a friend," she said. She didn't wait for Jasmine to probe for more details, instead collecting the art supplies and her change and starting for the door. "I have to run. See you soon."

She decided to walk over to the bank and get some cash. She hadn't gone very far when someone called her name. "Chris!"

She turned to see Bethany Ames hurrying toward her. As usual, Bethany was smiling. "I'm glad I ran into you," Bethany said. "I came into town to grab some lunch. We could eat together."

Chris had already taken a step back. "I don't really have time right now. Thanks anyway."

Bethany's smile faded. "If you don't want to hang out with me, you can be honest. It's because I made such a fool of myself with Vince, isn't it?" She covered her eyes with her hand. "I'm never going to live that down. But honest, I didn't know he was involved with someone else. I'm new here in town, right? I'm trying to make friends—to be more outgoing and positive. That's what you're supposed to do, isn't it? But I keep getting it wrong. I'm sorry to bother you." She turned away.

"Wait," Chris called. Bethany's raw honesty was shocking, and also appealing. And Chris knew a little about being the "new kid" and trying to find a way to fit in. "I'll have lunch with you. What's this about you and Vince?" Vince Shepherd was a fellow search and rescue volunteer who was living with *Eagle Mountain Examiner* reporter Tammy Patterson.

"Are you sure?" Bethany asked. "I don't want to impose if you're busy."

"I have time," Chris said. "And I want to hear your story."

Bethany's smile returned. "In that case, I'm happy to give you the whole sad tale of me making a fool of myself.

I thought Vince was so good looking and I would sweep him off his feet with my awkward but endearing charm." She rolled her eyes. "Unfortunately—or maybe *fortunately*, since he already had a girlfriend—he was immune to my flirting. When I found out he was involved with someone else, I was mortified. I figured everyone in search and rescue knew about my crush on him."

"I didn't know," Chris said. "But then, I'm not usually clued in on local gossip." She wasn't close enough to other people for them to confide in her.

But Bethany was willing to tell all. She obviously needed someone to talk to, so why couldn't Chris be that person? The thought surprised her. Six months ago that wasn't something that would have occurred to her. She had always believed she didn't need close friends.

But Rand had refused to be put off by her reserve. Apparently, Bethany felt the same way. Chris smiled at her. "Let's go over to the Cake Walk and have lunch. You can tell me how you ended up in Eagle Mountain."

"It's a doozy of a story, I promise," Bethany said.

An hour later, Chris had shared a cheeseburger with Harley on the patio of the Cake Walk Café and learned all about Bethany, her three overprotective brothers and the fiancé who had jilted her. Despite what some would have labeled a tragedy, the young woman remained sunny and optimistic, and excited about starting life over alone in a new place, despite some bumps in the road along the way. Chris could never see herself being so upbeat, but spending time with her new friend had inspired her to do a better job of not dwelling on the hurts of her past. Bethany's approach to moving on struck her as healthier, though she suspected a lot of determination lay beneath the young woman's cheerful exterior.

She ended her afternoon in town at the local grocery, for a few items to add to Rand's supplies. She hesitated in front of a display of portobello mushrooms. She had a recipe for grilled mushrooms that Rand might like. She could make dinner for the two of them.

And then what? Would that be too much like a date? A chance to repeat that kiss and see if it had been a fluke or as sensational as she remembered?

She shook her head. "Don't get ahead of yourself," she mumbled, but she put the mushrooms in her cart anyway.

She saw no one suspicious in town, and no one followed her back to Rand's place. She texted to let him know she had returned safely, but got no reply. Maybe he was in surgery.

She settled into a chair on the back deck and began to sketch the scene before her—a patch of woods, with mountains in the distance. Soon she was lost in the work. This was what she needed, what had always made her feel better—to let her unsettling thoughts find their way out through her pencil, transformed from fears to fantasies of a hidden world that she controlled.

RAND WAS HALFWAY home after his shift when he remembered he was supposed to meet Danny to review the medical protocols for search and rescue. He was tempted to call and cancel, but he resisted the urge and drove to SAR headquarters. Once there, he texted Chris to let her know he would be a little late. Should be done by 6:30 he said, and hit send before he could talk himself out of it. Had he assumed too much? It wasn't as if they were in a relationship and needed to report their comings and goings to each other. But he also didn't want to worry her when she already had so much to deal with.

Danny was waiting for him inside the building. "These are all our protocols," he said, hefting a large notebook. "Some of them are on the computer, too, but not all of them. Maybe eventually that will happen, but for now, we're still doing things the old-fashioned way."

"No problem," Rand said. "Let's see how many we can get through this afternoon."

They moved to a couple of folding chairs set up at a table near the front of the room. "I guess you heard about the commotion at Chris's last night," Danny said.

"You know about that?" Rand tried not to show his surprise.

Danny shrugged. "It's all over town. I guess people saw the sheriff's deputies there this morning."

"I did hear about it," Rand said, unsure how much to reveal. Should he mention that Chris was staying with him? He decided against it. Not that he didn't trust Danny, but it seemed safer for as few people as possible to know her whereabouts.

"I wonder if it was a random break-in or if someone targeted Chris," Danny said.

The comment surprised him. "Why would you think someone would target her?"

Danny shrugged. "She's pretty striking looking. Maybe she caught the wrong guy's attention. And for all she's been part of the group for four years, I don't know much about her. She's not one to talk much about herself. Which I respect, but most people aren't quite as, well, secretive as she is. And now there's this weird thing with some stranger declaring he's going to marry her?" He shook his head. "I just wonder if it's all connected."

Rand was sure the attack and Chris's past were connected, but would the sheriff be able to prove it? "Maybe the sheriff will find who did it," he said, and opened the notebook. "Let's get started on these protocols."

The work went quickly. The notebook was arranged alphabetically, with one to two sheets of paper outlining the proper treatment for each condition, from asthma attacks to wound care. Rand recommended a few updates and places where they might review their training. "Have you dealt with all of these conditions in the field?" he asked after he had studied the page for transient ischemic attack.

"Most of them," Danny said. "I've seen everything from third-degree burns from a campfire to heat exhaustion and broken bones. We've dealt with heart attacks, seizures and head injuries—if it can happen to someone when they're away from home, we might be called upon to treat it in the field, or at least stabilize the person until we can transport them to an ambulance."

"It looks to me like you're up to date on everything." Rand shut the notebook. "I'm impressed."

"Thanks," Danny said. "We try to run a professional organization, but when you rely on one hundred percent volunteers, things can fall through the cracks." He shoved back his chair. "Thanks again for your help."

Rand was about to tell him he was glad to be involved when hard pounding on the door made him flinch. He and Danny exchanged looks, then hurried toward the entrance, where the pounding continued. Danny opened the door. "What's going on?" he asked.

A twentysomething man with disheveled dark hair to his

shoulders and deep shadows beneath his eyes stood on the doorstep. He wore jeans faded to a soft shade of gray blue, an equally worn denim work shirt over a gray T-shirt and dirty straw sandals. "I need a doctor right away," he said.

"I'm a doctor." Rand stepped forward. "What's the problem?"

"It's not for me. It's for my sister." He clutched Rand's arm. "You have to come with me. Now."

"Let me call an ambulance." Danny pulled out his phone. "Where is your sister?"

"There isn't time for that," the man said. He struck out, sending Danny's phone flying.

"Hey!" Danny shouted.

"What's wrong with your sister?" Rand asked, trying to gain control of the situation.

"I think she's dying. You have to help her."

"An ambulance will help her more than I can," Rand said.

"No ambulance!" The man let go of Rand and stepped back. Rand thought he might leave, but instead, he pulled a pistol from beneath his shirt and pointed it at Rand. The end of the barrel was less than two feet from Rand's stomach. One twitch of the man's finger would inflict a wound Rand doubted he would survive. "Come with me now," the man ordered.

Chapter Nine

"Killing him won't save your sister," Danny said. Rand could see him out of the corner of his eye, his face as white as milk, the muscle beside his left eye twitching. But he kept his cool and spoke firmly.

"Don't think I won't shoot," the young man said. He shifted the pistol's aim to Danny. "You come too. You can help him."

"All right," Rand said. "We'll come with you." They'd look for an opportunity to overpower the young man. The odds were in their favor—two against one.

Still holding the gun, the man urged them toward a mostly powder blue sedan, which had been manufactured sometime in the 1980s, by Rand's best guess. As they approached, a second, larger man got out of the passenger seat and frowned at them. He was older than the first man but dressed similarly, his shirt a faded blue-and-white-checkered flannel; his shoes old house slippers, the suede worn shiny at the toes. He opened the back door, and Danny, with another wary glance at the gun, got in.

"You sit up front," the bigger man told Rand before joining Danny in the back seat. His voice was a reedy tenor, nasal and thin.

So much for two against one. Rand wondered if the second man was also armed, then decided he didn't want to find out. Instead, he focused on the driver, who shifted into gear with one hand, the other still holding the gun. "What's wrong with your sister?" he asked.

"She's having a baby," he said. "But something isn't right."

"What isn't right?"

"She's been in labor a long time, but nothing is happening."

"How long?"

The younger man hunched over the steering wheel, the barrel of the gun balanced on top. "Two days. A little longer."

"How advanced is her pregnancy?" Rand asked. "Has she lost much blood? How is the baby presented?"

"I don't know! Stop asking questions. You'll find out everything when you see her."

"Where are you taking us?" Danny asked.

"You'll find that out soon enough too."

Rand was aware of his phone in the back pocket of his jeans. Could he get his hand back there and dial 911? He shifted and slowly moved his hand back.

A meaty fist wrapped around his bicep. "I'll take the phone," the bigger man said.

When Rand didn't respond, the man squeezed harder, a jolt of pain traveling to the tips of Rand's fingers. Reluctantly, he surrendered the phone.

The car turned away from town and down a county road, which, after a couple of miles, narrowed and became an unpaved forest service road. Realization washed over Rand. "You're with the Vine, aren't you?" he asked.

"Who told you that?" the man from the back seat asked. He had released his hold on Rand but sat forward, within easy striking distance.

"I heard you had moved your camp to the woods," Rand said. He studied the driver more closely. Were these two the ones who had attacked him and Chris last night? Nothing about them looked familiar, but Rand hadn't gotten a look at whoever had hit him in the darkness.

Another turn onto an even narrower dirt lane brought them to a cluster of trailers and tents parked among the trees—everything from a battered Airstream to a truck camper up on blocks, old canvas tents, new nylon structures and even a large tepee. The driver stopped the car, and his companion got out and took hold of Rand's arm. "This way," he said.

People emerged from the various dwellings to stare as the two men led Danny and Rand past—men and women, many young, none older than middle age. Rand counted eight children and a couple of teens among them.

The driver stopped at a set of wooden steps that led into the back of a box truck. A door had been cut into the back panel of the box. "My sister is in here," the driver said, and pulled open the door.

The first thing that struck Rand was the smell—body odor and urine, but above that, the slightly sour, metallic scent of blood. The aroma plunged him back to the battlefield, trying to tend to soldiers who were bleeding out. He blinked, letting his eyes adjust to the dimness. The only light in the windowless space emanated from an LED camping lantern suspended from the ceiling. The woman was lying on a pallet in the middle of the floor, dark hair spread out around a narrow face bleached as white as the pillowcase, the swell of her pregnant belly mounding the sheets. A girl knelt beside her, laying a damp cloth on the woman's forehead. The girl couldn't have been more than

Mountain Captive

nine or ten, with long dark hair and eyes that looked up at Rand with desperate pleading.

Three other people—two women and a man—were gathered around the pallet. They studied Rand and Danny with suspicion. "Who are they?" the man—blond and stocky, with thinning hair—asked.

"He's a doctor." The driver nudged Rand. "Go on."

Rand knelt beside the pallet. The girl started to get up and move, but Rand motioned her to stay. "It's all right," he said. "I might need your help." He wouldn't ordinarily ask a child to assist him, but this girl seemed calmer and more willing than the others in the room.

The woman on the pallet was so still that he thought at first she might already be dead. He took her wrist and tried to find a pulse. It was there. Weak and irregular. He looked up at her brother. "I can examine her, but I can tell you already, she needs an ambulance."

"Examine her. There must be something you can do," the driver said.

Danny knelt on the other side of the pallet "Is the baby's father here?" he asked.

The others in the room exchanged a look Rand couldn't interpret. "He isn't here," the stocky man said after a tense moment.

"I'm going to examine her," Rand told Danny. "Help me get her into position."

The woman was almost completely unresponsive, only moaning slightly when Danny moved her legs. The girl took the young woman's hand and held it. Rand used the sheets to form a drape around her and examined the woman and her unborn child as best he could. The situation wasn't pretty. The woman had lost a lot of blood, and the child was wedged firmly in her narrow pelvis. Without a stethoscope, he couldn't tell if the child was even alive.

He covered the woman again and stood. "Whoever is responsible for leaving her in this state and not calling for help should be shot," he said. "I think the baby is dead, and she will be, too, soon, unless you call an ambulance."

"No ambulance," the stocky man said.

The door opened, bringing in a rush of fresh air. The others in the truck rose to their feet or, if already standing, stood up straighter. Rand turned to see Jedediah moving toward him, followed by several other men and women, some of whom Rand remembered from the day of the fire.

"Thank you for coming," the woman's brother said to Jedediah. He sounded close to tears.

"I've come as an emissary from the Exalted," Jedediah said. He looked down at the woman, who now moaned almost continuously and moved her head from side to side, eyes closed. "He is sorry to hear our sister is troubled."

"She's not troubled. She's going to die if you don't get her to a hospital right away," Rand said. She would probably still die, he thought. But at least in a medical facility, she had a chance.

"Silence!" Jedediah clamped down on Rand's shoulder, fingers digging in painfully. Rand shook him off. If the man touched him again, he would fight back.

Jedediah held up a palm, and everyone fell silent. He knelt and took the woman's hand in his own. "Sister, the Exalted sends his strength to you," he said. "Strength to deliver this child. You need not rely on your own frailties, but on his power."

The others in the room murmured some kind of affirmation. Rand looked on in disgust. Danny didn't look any happier than he did. Jedediah stood and turned to Rand. He smiled and stared into Rand's eyes with an expression Rand read as a threat. "I'm confident you can heal her," Jedediah said. "Tell us what you need, and we will bring it to you."

"She needs to be in the hospital."

"We don't need a hospital. We take care of our own. It's up to you to help her."

CHRIS TIMED DINNER to be ready at seven. When Rand still hadn't shown up, she turned off the heat under the mushrooms and told herself he had probably gotten involved in something at SAR headquarters. By seven thirty, she debated texting him, but she decided that would be out of line. He didn't owe her any explanations for how he spent his time. She fixed a plate for herself and set aside the leftovers to reheat when he came in.

By nine o'clock, she was truly worried. Rand hadn't struck her as the type to disappear without letting her know what was going on. She texted him Everything OK?

No reply. She stared at the phone screen. He had said he was meeting Danny, right? She sent a quick text to Danny. Is Rand with you?

No reply. A chill shuddered through her, even as she tried to tell herself there was a logical explanation for the failure of both men to reply. Maybe they had decided to go out after finishing up at headquarters, and time had gotten away from them. She hesitated, then looked up the number for Carrie Andrews, Danny's partner and fellow search and rescue volunteer.

"Chris? What's up?" Carrie answered right away as if she had been waiting for a call.

"Is Danny there?" Chris asked.

"No. He was meeting Rand at SAR headquarters and was supposed to be back by seven or so. I've been trying to reach him, but he's not answering his phone."

Chris's stomach clenched. "I've been trying to reach Rand. He's not answering either."

"I was going to drive over to headquarters and see if their cars are in the parking lot," Carrie said. "But I can't get hold of my mom to watch the kids, and I don't want to upset them."

"I'll go over there," Chris said, already pocketing the Jeep keys.

"Let me know what you find."

Chris had never realized how isolated the search and rescue headquarters building was before. Almost as soon as she turned onto the road leading up to the building, she left behind the lights of houses. She gripped the steering wheel tightly and checked her mirrors every few seconds to see if she was being followed. Relief momentarily relaxed her when she turned into the parking lot and spotted Rand's and Danny's vehicles side by side near the door. They must have become so engrossed in their work they had lost track of time.

She parked and hurried to the door, Harley at her heels. The security light flickered on at their approach. She grasped the knob, but the door was locked. "Hey, open up in there!" she called, and pounded on the door. No answer. She tried phoning Rand again. No answer. Next, she punched in Danny's number. He wasn't answering, either, but she could hear a phone ringing somewhere just on the other side of the door.

The phone stopped ringing, and she heard the electronic

message telling her she had been redirected to a voice mailbox.

She ended the call, and almost immediately, her phone rang. Carrie's voice was thin with worry. "Are you there? Did you find them?"

"Their cars are here, but no one is answering my knock," Chris said.

"Something's happened to them," Carrie said. "I'm going to call the sheriff."

"Do that," Chris said. "Tell them I'll wait for them here." She ended the call. Maybe she and Carrie were overreacting, but she didn't think so. Something was wrong. The knowledge tightened her gut and made her cold all over.

She waited twenty minutes, she and Harley sitting in her car with the doors locked, phone in hand, willing Rand to call. When headlights illuminated the lot, she sat up straighter. The Rayford County Sheriff's Department SUV swung in behind her, and Deputy Ryker Vernon got out. Chris went to meet him. "Hello, Chris," he said. "What's going on?"

"Rand Martin and Danny Irwin were supposed to meet here this afternoon about five o'clock," she said. "Their vehicles are here, but the door is locked and no one is answering my knock or my calls."

"What makes you think they didn't just go off with friends for a drink or something?" Ryker asked.

"Carrie was expecting Danny home. The last time I spoke with Rand, he said he would be home about six thirty. He's not answering his phone. It's not like either of them to disappear like this."

Ryker nodded. "Do you have any reason to suspect someone harmed them?"

"Rand was attacked outside my apartment last night," she said. "Maybe that person—or *persons*—came after him here."

A second vehicle pulled into the lot. Ryker and Chris watched as the black-and-white SUV parked next to Ryker's cruiser. Deputy Jake Gwynn got out. "I heard the call for assistance here at headquarters and came to assist," he said. "I have a key to the building."

"Let's go inside and see what we find," Ryker said. He turned to Chris. "You wait out here."

She wanted to protest but only nodded. While they unlocked the door and went inside, she hugged her arms across her chest and paced beside her car. How could Ryker and Jake be so calm? Sure, she was known to be cool during a search and rescue emergency, but those situations rarely involved anyone she knew. But Rand and Danny were friends, both fit, capable men who wouldn't be pushovers. If something had happened to them, she couldn't help thinking it would be bad.

The deputies emerged from the building and Jake relocked the door. "There's no one in there," Ryker said. "But we found Danny's phone on the floor near the door. He must have dropped it."

"Are you sure Rand didn't have to report back to the hospital?" Jake asked. "Or maybe he's visiting a friend?"

She shook her head. "He wouldn't go back to work without his car. You need to talk to the members of the Vine. Someone told me they're camped out past County Road 14."

"Do you think they had something to do with Rand and Danny?" Jake asked.

"I'm sure they were the ones who attacked Rand and

then me last night," she said. "I can't prove it, but I'm sure of it. Maybe they came back for Rand tonight."

"Why would they do that?" Ryker asked.

"To get back at me?" She shook her head. "I don't know. But please, go talk to them. Rand and Danny might be with them now."

"It wouldn't hurt to go out there," Jake said. "But there's a good chance we're wasting time."

"Do you have a better idea of where to look?" Chris asked.

Ryker pocketed his notebook. "We'll drive out there and take a look," he said. "You go home. We'll be in touch."

"I'm staying at Rand's place," she admitted. "My apartment needs the doors and locks replaced."

"Go there, then," Jake said. "We'll let you know what we find."

They returned to their vehicles and she to hers. The deputies waited for her to drive away, then followed her back toward town. They turned off toward County Road 14 while she continued toward Rand's place. She didn't like the idea of returning to the unfamiliar house alone. At least Harley would be there with her.

And what if Ryker and Jake didn't find Rand and Danny with the Vine? What if someone else had taken them or they had left for some other reason? She might have wasted the deputies' time and put the two men in further danger.

"WE DON'T HAVE proper medical equipment or medications," Rand protested. "We can't help this woman without the right tools."

"We're very good at making do," Jedediah said. "Tell us what you need, and we'll supply a reasonable substitute."

Which was how Rand and Danny found themselves minutes later with a stack of clean towels, a selection of sharp knives, a sewing kit, a bar of soap, and a bottle of what looked and smelled like grain alcohol. "I'm not going to perform surgery without anesthesia," Rand said.

"If you don't operate, she's going to die anyway," Danny said softly. The two huddled over their patient, having sent everyone else to wait either outside or against the far wall. Jedediah had left, but the patient's brother stood nearby, the gun tucked into the front of his jeans, quickly accessible if he decided he needed to use it again.

The two men knelt beside the woman, and Rand once more assessed her condition, which he could only classify as poor. She was barely conscious and mostly unresponsive, her pulse faint. She needed an emergency C-section, and even then her chances of survival were slim. But he couldn't do nothing and watch her die. "I can try to turn the baby," Rand said. "Let's see if we can revive her enough to help us." He looked up at her brother. "What's her name?"

"Lana," the man said.

"Get down here and talk to her," Rand said.

The brother shook his head and backed away. Exasperated, Rand looked across at the girl, who hadn't spoken and had scarcely moved since he and Danny entered the truck. "What's your name?" he asked.

"Serena."

"Serena, is Lana a relative of yours?"

The girl shook her head.

"Then why are you here?" Danny asked.

"It's my job to help the healer."

Rand would have told whoever was in charge that this was no place for a child so young, but since Serena was already here, he asked if she would hold Lana's hand and talk to her while he and Danny worked. "She may be able to hear you, even if she doesn't respond," he explained.

Serena nodded. "All right."

Rand looked back at one of the older women against the wall. "I need some ammonia."

"Ammonia?" She looked puzzled.

"The cleaning fluid. You must have some somewhere."

"I'll see what I can find."

Lana's brother moved a little closer, though he didn't kneel beside the pallet. "What's your name?" Danny asked.

"Robert."

"Why did you wait so long to go for help?" Rand asked as he busied himself with cleaning his hands and drying them on one of the towels.

Robert shoved his fingers through his lank hair. "We don't believe in doctors," he said. "We're supposed to trust in the Exalted."

"Are you going to be in trouble for bringing us here?" Danny asked.

Robert shrugged. "Maybe. Probably. Can you help her?"

"We're going to try," Rand said. "But it may be too late."

"Here." The woman returned and thrust a plastic bottle filled with yellow liquid at Rand.

He twisted off the cap and sniffed, his eyes watering. It was ammonia, all right. He poured some on a cloth and held it under Lana's nose. She moaned and turned her head away. "Lana, wake up," he said. "Open your eyes and look at me, please."

Her eyes flickered open, and she stared up at him. Her eyes were dark brown, fringed with long dark lashes. She was probably beautiful when she was feeling better. "My name is Rand," he said. "I'm a doctor, and I'm going to try to help you. I need to try to turn the baby. When I tell you, you need to push."

She nodded. Rand looked at Serena. "Talk to her. Encourage her."

Serena leaned close and whispered to Lana. Rand couldn't hear what she said, and he didn't care. Her job was to try to calm and distract Lana, if that was even possible, given her condition. He nodded to Danny, and the two of them moved down to tackle the dilemma of somehow delivering this baby. Rand was searching for some way to lubricate his hands when the door to the trailer opened, a woman's strident protests breaking the tense silence. "You can't go in there—"

Rand turned to see what the commotion was about just as two Rayford County sheriff's deputies stepped in. "Rand?" one of the deputies asked.

As the officers moved closer, Rand recognized Jake Gwynn. "We need a medical helicopter," he said. "Right away."

"I'll make the call," the other deputy said, and stepped out of the trailer.

Jake took in the woman on the pallet and the people gathered around her. "Are you and Danny okay?" he asked.

"We're fine, but this woman needs emergency surgery."

"No surgery." The older woman who had fetched the ammonia stepped between Rand and Lana. "No hospital. The Exalted forbids it."

"Then if she dies, I'll be happy to testify in the Exalted's murder trial." Rand stood.

Robert stood also. There was no sign of the gun now,

and he moved toward the door. Jake moved to intercept him. "You need to stay here," he said.

The other deputy returned. "This is Ryker Vernon," Jake said. "What happened?"

"Two men grabbed us outside search and rescue headquarters," Danny said. "They forced us to come here to help this woman."

The four men looked down at Lana, who lay still, her breathing slow and labored. "They should have called for help hours ago," Rand said.

"They forced you to come here?" Ryker asked.

"They had a gun," Danny said.

"The Exalted had nothing to do with that," the older woman said. "He forbids the use of violence."

"Apparently, he also forbids outside help, even for a medical emergency," Rand said.

"I think we need to talk to this Exalted person," Jake said. "Where can we find him?"

"I have no idea," Rand said. "I've only spoken to his representative, a man named Jedediah." He turned to Danny. "Let's get Lana ready for transport."

They were making Lana as comfortable as possible when an approaching siren signaled the arrival of the ambulance. Moments later, two paramedics pushed into the trailer, ignoring the orders to stop from some of the onlookers. The first paramedic to enter, a burly fortysomething with close-cropped gray hair, surveyed the room. "We need to get this crowd out of here so we can work."

"You heard the man," Jake said. "Everybody out."

When no one moved, Jake and Ryker began taking hold of people and escorting them out.

Rand introduced himself and Danny and provided

what medical information he had been able to assess, then stepped back to allow the paramedics to take over. By the time he heard the distant throb of a helicopter over the camp, they had started an IV line and fitted Lana with an oxygen mask and various equipment to monitor her vitals. The deputies were still outside, presumably dealing with the other campers. Jedediah didn't make an appearance, and Robert and his fellow kidnapper had disappeared. Serena was gone, too, pulled away by one of the women as the paramedics started their work.

Rand and Danny followed the stretcher out of the trailer and watched as Lana was loaded into the ambulance. She would be driven to the cleared area that had been designated as a landing spot for the helicopter, then rushed to the hospital.

Jake joined Rand and Danny as the ambulance pulled away. "Can you identify the men who kidnapped you?" he asked.

"I can." The crowd of onlookers was mostly moving away now, presumably to the trailers and tents scattered among the trees, their faces indistinguishable in the darkness. "My guess is you won't find them here tonight."

"Give us a description, and we'll conduct a search."

Danny and Rand each described what they knew about the two men who had waylaid them and also provided what they knew about Jedediah.

"How did you know where to find us?" Danny asked when that was done.

"Chris went to SAR headquarters to look for you and found the place locked up tight," Ryker said. "Both your cars were there, and we found your phone on the ground. Carrie called 911 and reported you missing. Chris said she thought the persons who attacked the two of you last night were from the Vine and that they might have gone after you again tonight."

"These men didn't hurt us," Rand said.

"One of them was the woman's brother," Danny said. "I don't think he would have harmed us. I think he was desperate to help his sister."

"Threatening someone with a gun and forcing them to go somewhere against their will is still a crime," Ryker said.

"Let's get you out of here," Jake said.

Rand and Danny shared the back seat of Jake's SUV for the ride to search and rescue headquarters. Neither spoke. Rand was exhausted. The sight of Lana, struggling to stay alive while he was helpless to do anything, would remain with him for a long time. If the Exalted and his followers were willing to sacrifice one of their own for the sake of their misguided beliefs, he could believe they wouldn't hesitate to break laws in order to obey their leader's command to bring a former member back into the fold.

Chapter Ten

Fifteen years ago

Chris, drowsing under the covers in her bunk bed in her family's trailer at the Vine's camp, woke to raised voices. She pulled back the curtain over the bunk and peered toward the glow of light from the other end of the small trailer. Her father sounded angry about something.

"I'm going to talk to him. This isn't right."

"He's made up his mind," her mother said. "You'll never get anywhere arguing with him."

"There must be some misunderstanding. Jedediah got the message wrong. The Exalted has children—daughters. Would he want one of them married off when she's only twelve? Not to mention he already has a wife his age. It's just sick."

"Lower your voice." Mom sounded afraid. "You don't want to let anyone hear you say that."

"It's not right, you know that."

"I know. But what are we going to do? He owns this trailer. He owns everything we have."

"You don't have to remind me," her father said. "I was the one foolish enough to turn everything over to him."

"You weren't foolish. You believed in the message. We're

supposed to share with each other. No one has more than anyone else."

"I still believe that. But not if it means giving him my daughter. I'll talk to him. I'm sure I can make him understand."

"What if he won't listen to you?" her mother asked.

"He will. He has to."

More conversation, but too soft for Chris to hear. A few moments later, the door to the trailer opened and closed. Chris waited but heard nothing more. Finally, she slipped out of bed and padded on bare feet to the front of the trailer. Her mother sat on the edge of the sofa, head in her hands. Was she crying?

Chris hurried to her. "What's wrong?" she asked. "Where is Daddy?" She didn't call him *Daddy* much anymore. It sounded too babyish. But she was too scared to worry about that now.

Her mother pulled her close, arms squeezing her tight. "It's okay," she said, and wiped her eyes with her fingers.

"Where did Daddy go?" Chris asked.

Her mother sniffed. "He went to talk to the Exalted."

"About me?"

Her mother hesitated, then nodded. "Yes." She pulled Chris into her lap even though Chris was too big for that; her feet almost touched the floor when she sat on her mother's lap.

"Helen says there's going to be a wedding soon," Chris said. "That I'll be a bride and wear a white dress and have a big party just for me."

Her mother studied her, deep lines across her forehead. "Do you know what it means to be a bride?" she asked.

Chris thought for a moment. "Helen says I have to live

with the Exalted and do what he tells me." Then she said something she had never dared say before: "I don't want to live with him."

Her mother hugged her tightly again. "Maybe your father can talk him into waiting until you're a little older," she said.

Chris didn't think that when she was older she would want to marry the Exalted, either, but she didn't say anything. "You should go back to bed," her mother said. "It's not even six o'clock yet."

"I'm awake," Chris said. "And hungry. Can I have breakfast?"

Her mother made breakfast; then they both dressed and Chris helped her mother clean house, which didn't take long because the trailer was small and they didn't have much stuff. Mom tried to be extra cheerful, but she kept glancing out the window. "Shouldn't Dad be back by now?" Chris asked after a couple of hours.

"The Exalted probably sent him to do some work," Mom said. Everyone in the Vine was expected to pitch in. For the men, that often meant building things, cutting trees, or digging ditches, latrines or garden beds.

Chris did her lessons. Children in the Vine didn't go to school. Instead, the parents taught them. Some children didn't have to learn anything at all, but Chris's parents made her read and study math, reading, geography, history and science every day. She didn't mind so much. Most of the time the lessons were interesting, and she usually found them easy.

Her mother got out a quilt she was working on, but often, when Chris looked up from her schoolwork, she found her mother staring out the front window, her hands idle.

They ate lunch without Dad. By three o'clock, her mother could hardly sit still. She put away her quilting. "I'm going to look for your father," she said. "Lock the door behind me, and don't let anyone in unless it's me or your dad. Do you understand?"

Chris nodded. "What am I supposed to tell anyone who comes by?"

"Don't tell them anything," Mom said. "Stay quiet and let them think no one is home."

Chris wanted to ask what her mother was afraid of, but she didn't. Instead, she turned the lock after her mother was gone and sat on the sofa to wait.

She was back in half an hour. "Jedediah told me your father left the Exalted's home this morning with some other men. They went into the woods to pick mushrooms."

"Isn't it the wrong time of year for mushrooms?" Chris asked. Always before, they had looked for mushrooms in the spring and fall, when they would pop up after wet weather. Now it was midsummer, warm and dry.

"Maybe this was a different kind of mushroom," her mother said. "Or someone found some by a spring or something. Come, help me peel potatoes. We'll make a special dinner. Maybe we'll even make a cake."

Making the cake, and the potatoes and vegetables and meat loaf, took a while, but six o'clock—the hour they usually ate supper—passed with no sign of her father. Her mother filled a plate and told Chris to sit down at the table and eat it, but Chris only stared at the food, her stomach too queasy for her to even think of putting anything into her mouth.

A little before nine o'clock, they heard voices outside. Mom rushed to the door, then, with a cry, opened it to admit

Jedediah and a man Chris didn't know. Between them, they carried her father, his face gray, his hair and clothes wet. "He ate some of the mushrooms he found," Jedediah said. "I think they must have been poisonous."

They carried her father past Chris to her parents' bed at the back of the trailer. Mom hurried after them. Chris tried to follow, but Jedediah shut the door in her face.

A few minutes later, the door opened again and the two men emerged. "What's going on?" Chris asked.

"We're going to fetch the healing woman," the man she didn't know said. Jedediah only scowled at her.

When they were gone, Chris went to the bedroom door and knocked. "Mom?" she called.

"You can't come in," her mother called. "Go to your room and wait for me."

Chris didn't really have a room, just a bunk bed with a curtain to separate it from the rest of the trailer. Not knowing what else to do, she went there and sat. She switched on the light her father had fixed up for her and took her sketchbook from the lidded box at the end of the bed that he had made for her art supplies. She turned to a fresh page and began to draw. When she started, she had no idea what she would sketch, but after a few moments, the figure of a man took shape. The Exalted, but not the beautiful, caring figure people often praised. This was the Exalted with his mouth twisted in a sneer, his eyes glaring, deep lines marring his forehead and running alongside his mouth. Instead of an angel, this man was a demon.

After a while, Chris began to get sleepy. She drifted off and woke up much later to an old woman shaking her— Elizabeth, one of the healers. "Come and say goodbye to your father," she said.

"Where is he going?" Chris asked. She glanced over at the sketchbook and was relieved to see she had remembered to close it before she fell asleep.

"He is going to his reward," Elizabeth said. "He ate poison, and there is nothing I can do for him."

Chris began to cry, then to wail. Elizabeth shook her. "Quiet!" she ordered. "He's going to a better place. There's no reason for you to be sad."

Even at twelve, Chris knew that was one of the most ridiculous things anyone had ever said. He was her father. He belonged here with her. There was no better place.

But she fell silent and allowed Elizabeth to lead her into her parents' bedroom. Her mother held out her hand. Chris took it, and her mother pulled her close. She stared at her father, who lay with his eyes closed, his skin that awful gray, his face all hollows. He didn't even look like himself. "Give him a kiss," Elizabeth commanded.

Chris shook her head and buried her face in her mother's shoulder. "It's all right," her mother murmured. "You're safe here with me."

No one said anything else. Chris heard movement, and when she looked up again, she and her mother were alone with her father. "Where did they all go?" Chris whispered.

Her mother had to try a couple of times before she could speak. "They went to prepare for...for the funeral," she said.

Chris looked at her father. He didn't look any different to her. "Is he...dead?" she asked.

"Yes," her mother said. "He's gone." Then she started to cry. Chris cried, too, grateful there was no one to tell them it was wrong to do so.

Everything about the next few days was a blur. They buried her father in the woods the next morning, his body wrapped in a bedsheet and lowered into a deep hole, far away from camp. Everyone came and gathered around the little grave, and when they were all assembled, the Exalted arrived. The crowd parted to allow him to draw close. He was dressed all in white, his hair and face shining. He smiled as if this was a happy occasion, and he talked about what a good man her father was and how he had moved on to a better place than this.

When he finished speaking, men with shovels moved forward and began to fill in the grave. The scent of fresh earth filled Chris's nose, and she began to sob again.

A hand rested on her shoulder, heavy and warm. She looked up and stared into the Exalted's eyes. "Your father is gone," he said. "I will be your father now. I will be your brother and uncle. And your husband. Soon." He smiled, but Chris could only shiver.

Chris knew then that she didn't like the Exalted, no matter how wonderful people said he was. But she kept that knowledge to herself. She was pretty sure if she said something like that out loud, she would be struck by lightning or something worse. If she was the only one who thought someone was bad when everyone said he was good, there must be something wrong with her.

Her mother was much quieter after that. Sad.

Three days later, Helen came to their trailer. "It's time to measure Elita for her wedding dress," she said.

Her mother's face paled. "So soon?"

"Now that your husband is gone, the Exalted believes it's even more important that he take Elita under his wing." Helen pulled out a tape measure. "Fetch a chair for her to stand on."

Her mother brought a chair from the kitchen table.

"Shouldn't there be a period of mourning?" she asked as she helped Chris to stand on the chair.

"Mourning won't bring back the dead." Helen wrapped the tape measure around Chris's chest, over the gentle swelling her mother had told her would one day be breasts. "Better to focus on the joy of this occasion."

Neither Chris nor her mother said anything after Helen left. What was there to say? No one disobeyed the Exalted. It would be like disobeying God. The next day, her mother worked at the farmers market stand the Vine operated at the fairgrounds. She came home later than usual. "Something terrible has happened," she said. "Someone stole the money from our booth. The cash box was there one moment, and then it was gone."

"Was there a lot of money in it?" Chris asked.

"Several hundred dollars. Jedediah is very upset." Jedediah was the treasurer for the Vine, in charge of all the money the group earned from selling crafts, produce, firewood and anything else. All the money went to Jedediah, who doled it out as needed.

Not long after Chris's mother had set supper on the table, someone pounded on the door, hard enough to make the trailer shake. Mom opened it, and Jedediah and a trio of men filled the small front room. "We need to search this place," Jedediah said.

"What for?" Mom asked.

"We're looking for the money that was stolen. We're searching the homes of everyone who worked that booth today."

Was he accusing her mother of being a thief? Chris expected her mother to be upset about this. Instead, she stepped back and bowed her head. "Of course," she said. "I have nothing to hide."

For the next hour, the four men searched every inch of the trailer. They emptied all the clothing from the dresser and dumped all Chris's art supplies on the bed. She thought of the picture of the Exalted—the devil picture—in her sketchbook. When they found it, would they punish her? But they only flipped through the book, paying no attention to the drawings. They took the food from the refrigerator and opened every jar and bottle as if they expected to find coins and bills instead of mayonnaise and ketchup.

All they found was five dollars and forty-two cents in change in an old pickle jar. Members of the Vine were allowed to keep this change when they sold cans they picked up on the side of the highway, so Jedediah reluctantly set the jar back on the dresser. "There's nothing here," he said at last, and the men left.

Mom sank into a chair. She looked very pale, but when she saw Chris watching her, she forced a smile. "That was upsetting, but it's over now," she said. "There's nothing for you to worry about. Why don't you get ready for bed?"

Chris started to point out that it was an hour before her bedtime but thought better of it. She washed her face and hands, then put on her pajamas and crawled under the covers. Her mother kissed her forehead and pulled the curtain over the bunk. Within minutes, Chris was asleep.

It was still dark when she woke again. Her mother sat on the edge of the bunk. "Get dressed," Mom said. "We're going to leave now." She handed Chris a pair of jeans and a T-shirt. "I packed a bag for us. I put in as many of your art supplies as I could, but we can't take everything."

"Where are we going?" Chris asked, pulling off her pajamas and sliding into the jeans.

"We're leaving the Vine," her mother said. "And we're never coming back."

Chapter Eleven

If Chris was upset about what had happened to Rand and Danny, she kept her feelings hidden. She was clearly relieved Rand was all right, but when he thanked her for alerting the sheriff's deputies to what must have happened to them, she dismissed his thanks. "It was a lucky guess," she said. "I'm glad it worked out."

"Why were they so set against calling in medical help for that woman?" he asked. "Is it because they don't believe in medicine? Or they think it's some kind of spiritual weakness to rely on doctors?"

"It's mostly because they don't want outsiders coming into the camp," she said. "We were always told we didn't need anyone but each other and the Exalted."

"Because outsiders might see something illegal they shouldn't see?" Rand asked.

She blew out a breath. "I don't know. I was taught—all the kids were—that outsiders were dangerous. That they would take us away from our families and sell us to people who would do bad things to us. For the first few months after Mom and I left the Vine, I was terrified to let her out of my sight or to talk to anyone."

"The woman I tried to help, Lana, looked younger than

you—maybe not even out of her teens. I wonder if you knew her."

"I've been away for a long time," she said. "I doubt I know any of the current members. I don't remember anyone called Lana."

"Jedediah is still there," Rand said. "There are probably others you knew who are still with the group."

"Maybe I would know their names," she said. "But I don't know them. I never did."

Her tone was defiant, her expression fierce. When she turned away, he didn't press her. He knew plenty of soldiers who refused to discuss things that had happened during their military service. Maybe it was the same for survivors of cults.

Three days after Rand returned home, Sheriff Travis Walker and Deputy Ryker Vernon came to Rand's house at four thirty, shortly after he arrived home after a shift at the hospital. "We wanted to bring you up to date on a few things," Travis said after Rand had welcomed the lawmen inside.

Chris came in from the kitchen and stopped short. "Oh, hello." She glanced at Rand. "Is something wrong?"

"We just have some updates," Travis said. "For both of you. Sit down, please."

They sat—Rand on the sofa and Chris in a chair facing him. "First of all, I'm sorry to tell you that Lana and her baby died," Travis said.

"Yes, I know," Rand said. "I had a colleague track her down for me."

Chris turned to him. "You didn't tell me."

"I didn't want to upset you," he said.

Chris studied her hands, knotted in her lap. "It's just such a sad story."

"We searched the camp for her brother and the other man you described," Ryker said. "We were told they had been banished."

"Did you look for any fresh graves in the woods?" Chris asked.

Rand felt the shock of her words. "You think they were murdered?" he asked.

She looked as if she regretted saying anything.

"Why graves?" Travis prompted.

She shifted in her chair. "I don't have any proof, but other people who did things the Exalted didn't like had a way of disappearing or meeting with accidents or sudden illness."

"Your father," Travis said.

"Yes. And there were others. Anyone who complained too much or spread what the Exalted deemed to be 'radical ideas,' and certainly anyone who opposed the Exalted, was soon gone, and everyone else was forbidden to even say their names."

"We'll continue searching for the two men," Travis said.

"What about this guy who calls himself the Exalted, Edmund Harrison?" Rand asked. "His refusal to allow anyone to summon outside help is the reason Lana died."

Travis's expression tightened. "Harrison denies having that policy, and no one would admit otherwise when we spoke with them," he said. "We researched his history, and he has no criminal record."

"The official story is that Lana herself refused help and that her brother went to fetch help against her wishes," Ryker said.

"The Exalted has brainwashed everyone to see outsiders as the enemy," Chris said. "If you bring anyone from outside into the group, you risk having families torn apart, horrible diseases inflicted on the group by way of things like vaccinations and medications, children forced to attend public schools, et cetera. If there's a bogeyman the Exalted and his enforcers can conjure to keep people obedient, he's happy to preach about it until fear is as much a part of them as breathing."

"He says they have no record of you ever being a member of his group, and he doesn't understand why you would be so fixated on them," Travis said.

Color flooded her face. "I'm not lying. My parents were members of the Vine, and we lived with them for seven years. And you were there the day Jedediah came up to me and said it was time for me to marry the Exalted."

"Edmund Harrison says you misunderstood," Travis said.

The lines around her mouth tightened. "There was no misunderstanding."

"Has he made any more threats against you?" Travis asked.

"He doesn't know where I am right now," she said. "But once he does, he'll send someone after me."

"Why is he so focused on you?" Ryker asked.

"No one defies him," she said. "My mother and I did. He's like a spoiled child that way. Deny him something and he's going to do everything he can to get it." She smoothed her hand down the tattoos on her left arm. "But he doesn't want me, really. He just wants to punish me. Maybe make an example of me."

"We interviewed him," Travis said. "By Zoom. He is supposedly in Texas right now—on business, he said. He denies knowing you. Denies having more than one wife. Denies keeping anyone in the group against their will."

"I'm sure he told you the group is all about peace, love and free will," she said.

"That's about it," Ryker agreed.

"Harrison told us the group planned to leave Colorado and move on to Oklahoma," Travis said. "When we returned to the camp yesterday, everyone was gone. They didn't leave one piece of trash or so much as a food scrap behind."

"Where did they go?" Rand asked.

"We don't know," Travis said. "They may have decided they were getting too much attention from law enforcement."

"They're probably putting as much distance between us and them as possible," Ryker added.

Chris said nothing, though Rand felt the tension radiating off her. "Is there anything else you think we need to know?" Travis asked.

"Don't believe it when they tell you they're just a close-knit community of nature lovers," Chris said. "And I don't think they've left the area."

"We'll keep our eyes and ears open," Travis said. "Let us know if you hear anything."

Ryker and Travis left. Chris stared out the front window after them, then began to pace. "The sheriff doesn't believe me," she said. "He thinks I'm making up a story to get attention or something."

"He didn't say that," Rand said. "I think he's trying to look at the case from every angle." He moved in beside her and put his hand on her shoulder. "I believe you."

She wouldn't look at him. She held herself rigid, jaw tight, as if fighting for control. "I feel like I'm waiting for something to happen," she said after a long silence. "Something bad."

"You believe they're still here," Rand said.

"They've been pursuing me for fifteen years," she said. "Why leave when they've gotten this close?"

He nodded. While some might dismiss Chris's protests, his experience with the ruthlessness of his sister's cult made him inclined to believe her. He wanted to put his arm around her and try to comfort her, but he wasn't sure she would be receptive. "What can I do?" he asked instead.

She pressed her lips together, arms crossed, shoulders hunched. Then she raised her eyes to his. "Tell me about your sister," she said.

CHRIS SAT ON the sofa and patted the cushion next to her. She needed a distraction to pull her out of the worry cycle she was in. "I want to hear about her, if you don't mind talking about it," she said.

Rand sat, the cushion compressing under his weight, shifting her toward him. He leaned forward, hands clasped, elbows on knees. "I haven't talked about Teri in a long time," he said. "But I'd like to tell you."

Chris let out a breath, some of the tension easing. She had been afraid he would shut her down—as she herself might have done in his shoes. "She was younger than you?"

"Yes. Nineteen. I was completing my first tour in Afghanistan when she met this group of people. At a local coffee shop, she said. They approached her table and asked if they could sit down. The place was crowded, so she said yes. They fell into conversation and apparently talked for hours. They introduced themselves as volunteers, working on a project to help the poor in the area. Teri always had a soft heart and wanted to help people. They picked up on that right away and used her sympathy to reel her in."

"The Vine taught the same technique," Chris said. "Identify what you have in common with the person, what they are concerned about or appear to need, and play up that connection."

"There was a guy in the group—Mark or Mike or Mitch, I never did learn his real name. In the group, he was known as Starfire. They all had names like that—Rainbow and Cloud, Surfer and Starfire. The next thing I heard, Teri was calling herself Aurora. She quit school and moved out of the dorm and into a camper van with Starfire, and then the group left town. My parents were frantic when they contacted me, hoping I had heard from her. But I hadn't heard a thing."

"What did you do?"

"There was nothing I could do. I was in a field hospital in a war zone. I couldn't leave. My parents contacted the police but were told if Teri left of her own free will, there wasn't anything they could do. Mom and Dad had a couple of phone calls from her saying she was fine and they didn't need to worry, and that was it."

"We had people join the Vine who left families behind," Chris said. "I never thought much about the anguish those parents must have felt. And their brothers and sisters."

"One day Teri was with us, then she was gone, with a group of people we didn't know anything about. On one hand, I understood what the police were telling us. An adult has the right to make her own decisions. But putting together what I learned when I researched online and what I heard from my parents, the group felt wrong to me."

"What did you find out online?" she asked.

"Mostly there were postings on various websites from relatives who were desperate to get in touch with their missing children or siblings. A few complaints from businesses in areas where the group had stayed, alleging that members had stolen items or harassed customers."

"What was the name of the group?"

"They called themselves Atlantis or the Seekers."

Chris shook her head. "I haven't heard of them, but most people have never heard of the Vine either. These groups try to keep a low profile."

"I was able to piece together some of their story after I was discharged from the army. By then, she had been with the group for almost two years. They made a living by recruiting members, who were obligated to turn over all their money to the group. They also begged and, I think, stole, though they always left town before anyone reported them to the local law enforcement."

Chris nodded. "The Vine did that, too—made new members turn over all their assets. They were told they were contributing to the group, but I think most of the money went to the Exalted. While we lived in tents and trailers, he had a fancy motorhome and, supposedly, owned houses in several states. He traveled a lot, managing his various properties, and often delivered his messages to us via videotaped lectures. The rare times he did come to our camp were big occasions. Everyone turned out for a glimpse of him."

"From the research I did, a lot of these groups operate the same way," Rand said.

"What happened to your sister?" Chris asked. He had said she'd committed suicide, but how? When?

"It took me a long time to find her," he said. "By the time I located her, she had been with the group over two years and was fully brainwashed, and refused my pleas to leave the group."

"You spoke to her?"

"Yes. I tracked the group down to a little town in Eastern Oregon. Teri was there. She looked terrible. She had lost weight and wore this shapeless sack of a dress, her hair uncombed in these kind of dreadlocks. She had lost a front tooth—she wouldn't say how. And when I tried to talk to her, she said she wasn't allowed to talk to outsiders and ran away."

"Oh, Rand." Chris laid a hand on his arm.

"I went after her. I told her I was her brother and she owed me more than she owed her so-called friends. I was furious. I told her all those people had done was take her away from her home and family, take her money, and give her nothing in return. She told me I didn't understand, that the inner peace the Seekers had given her was worth all the money in the world. She said they were her family now and she didn't need anyone else. Then she left."

Chris felt sick. "All of that sounds familiar," she said. "It's the kind of thing we were all drilled on saying. I never saw it, but my mother said a couple of times families had tracked down their loved ones to one of our camps. The Exalted had people who were trained in how to deal with them to get them to leave."

"What did they say?"

"What your sister said—that we were that person's family now and they didn't need anyone else."

"I wanted to grab Teri and drag her out of there, but I figured that would only get me arrested for kidnapping. One of the Seekers said if I laid a hand on Aurora that he would call the police. So I let her be. But I kept track of the group as best I could."

"Not easy to do," Chris said. "The Vine was expert at packing up in the middle of the night and showing up across the country a week later. Mom was able to find a few people who have family who are members. They sometimes let her know where the group is living at the moment, but even they can't always keep up."

"I had a buddy from the military who was a private detective, and he took an interest in the group and did what he could to track them," Rand said. "He kept me up to date. About six months later I had a meeting in California, not far from the latest Seeker gathering. They weren't camping this time but were renting, or maybe squatting, in an old hotel. The place was a dump, with a leaking roof, water damage to the walls and no electricity. I couldn't see that they had done any work on it, except to erect a large brightly painted sign announcing that it was the Atlantis Center for Enlightenment."

He fell silent. Chris waited, and found herself matching her breathing to his own. When the silence stretched to minutes, she asked, "Your sister was there?"

"She was. I played it cool this time. I gave a fake name at the door and said I was interested in learning about Atlantis. I was taken to a room, and three disciples entered. They were dressed in jeans and T-shirts and looked very normal. They asked me a lot of questions about how I had found out about them, what I was seeking, et cetera. I gave vague answers, and they seemed pretty suspicious at first, but after I said I had inherited a lot of money from my grandfather and was looking for a worthy group that would benefit from the cash, their demeanor changed. They invited me to have dinner with them that evening.

"Teri was there. She was one of the women who were serving the food. I guess they probably cooked it too. She didn't look any better than the last time I had seen her, and when she saw me, she dropped a platter of vegetables and ran from the room. I almost turned over a chair going after her. I cornered her in an upstairs bedroom and begged her to leave with me. She just cried and shook her head and said she couldn't.

"I told her I wasn't leaving without her. One of the men threatened to call the police, and I told him to do it—that I had plenty of proof there were people there being held against their will. That was a bluff, but it worked. They backed off."

Chris could see it all in her mind, from his frightened sister to the threatening Seekers—and Rand caught in the middle but determined to win. "What happened?" she asked.

"I took Teri by the hand and led her out of there. She came with me, still crying. I drove four hours away, checked us into a hotel under a fake name, paid cash for the room and ordered pizza. She started crying again when she saw the pizza. She said she hadn't had any since she had left with the group. I asked her what she had been eating, and she said they had a special diet of only natural foods and they had to fast three days a week. She said that was healthier, and it took everything in me not to point out that she didn't look healthy.

"After we ate, she fell asleep. She looked exhausted, and I know I was."

Ominous silence followed. Silence with weight. Chris

had trouble breathing. For a long time Rand didn't say anything, his jaw tight, hands clenched.

"When I woke the next morning, she was gone," he said finally. "She had run away in the middle of the night. I went back to the abandoned hotel looking for her, but everyone there said they hadn't seen her. The police couldn't help me. I lost it at them, and they ended up threatening to arrest me. I stayed in town for a while, watching the group, but I never saw Teri again."

"But you believe she had returned to the group?" Chris asked.

"I know she did. Three months later, my parents received a phone call from someone with the group, telling them Teri's body was at the morgue in Bend, Oregon, and they could claim her body if they wanted. They said Teri had killed herself. The coroner said she had slit her wrists. She left a note—a lot of incoherent nonsense about destiny and enlightenment and final bliss."

Tears stung her eyes—tears for him and for his poor, hurting sister. "It wasn't your fault," she said.

"I could have handled it better. I could have forced her to come with me and taken her to a deprogrammer or something."

"That could have failed too." She rubbed his arm. "It wasn't your fault."

He let out a shaky breath. "The police in Bend investigated, but they couldn't find anything suspicious. The group left town and dropped off the radar. The last I heard, they were in South America."

"I'm so sorry about your sister," she said. The words seemed so paltry compared to what he had suffered, but she had nothing else to give.

"I haven't talked about this with anyone for a long time." He looked at her, his eyes damp but his expression calm. "You're a good listener."

She leaned closer, drawn to him, pulled in by the sadness in his eyes and a sense of shared grief. She hadn't lost a sister but a father, and the chance to grow up without the fear that had dogged her all her life. Her gaze shifted to his lips. She recalled the connection they had shared before, and she wanted that again.

She meant to kiss him gently, but the strength of her longing drove her harder than she had intended. He gripped her shoulders and responded with a gentling pressure of his own. He wanted this, too, his body seemed to say, but he wanted to savor the moment, to linger over the sensation of the two of them together.

She leaned into him, letting him take her weight, his arm wrapped around her. She could definitely get used to this...

She opened her eyes to find him looking at her as if he could see everything. The idea was unnerving, and she pulled away. "Something wrong?" he asked.

"No. Of course not." She sat up straighter, putting a little distance between them. "I really like you. A lot. But I'm not ready to take things any further."

"I respect that," he said. "No pressure. I want you to feel safe here."

"I can't feel safe anywhere as long as I know the Vine is so close by." She laid her head on his shoulder. "But being here is better than being alone."

"It is." He squeezed her shoulder. "Better for me too."

Chapter Twelve

The next morning Rand awoke early—a habit from so many dawn hospital shifts. He dressed and moved to the kitchen, hearing no indication Chris was awake. Good. She had looked exhausted when she had retired to her room last night. He had felt drained, too, but not in a bad way. Revisiting the events surrounding Teri's death had been wrenching, but cleansing too.

He had coffee brewing and was chopping vegetables for omelets when Chris came into the kitchen. "I thought you would have left for work," she said as she headed for the coffeepot.

"I have a couple of days off." He began cracking eggs into a bowl. "Do you want to do something today to get out of the house? Maybe a hike or a drive in the mountains?"

She sipped the coffee and closed her eyes, a look of satisfaction tugging up the corners of her mouth. He almost chuckled. He had experienced those first-sip nirvana moments himself. Then the smile faded, and she opened her eyes again. "I should probably check in with Jasmine and see if my doors have been repaired. Now that the Vine has moved on, I should go home."

"Do you really think they've moved away?" Rand asked. He began sautéing the peppers, onions and mushrooms.

"Maybe they've just relocated to a new campsite the sheriff doesn't know about."

She cradled her mug in both hands. "Honestly, I would be surprised if they gave up on me so easily," she said. "They've been pursuing me for years. This is the first time they've gotten close enough to confront me face-to-face. That must feel like a victory to them."

"I agree," he said. "Groups like this count on people underestimating them." The way he had underestimated the Seekers. "I think they're probably lying low and waiting for another opportunity."

She nodded.

"I think you should stay here until we're sure there's not a threat." He turned back to the stove and added the eggs to the pan. "So, what about taking a drive into the mountains today? Maybe find a trail to hike?"

"Sure. That's a great idea." She straightened. "Is there anything I can do to help with breakfast?"

"Get two plates out of that cabinet there, will you?" He added cheese to the omelet, then folded it over.

She brought out the plates, and he divided the omelet between them; then they carried the meal to the table. "You've lived here longer than I have," he said. "Where would be a good place for us to check out this morning?"

They discussed options. Chris's mood seemed to lift as they talked. Rand hoped the prospect of a day spent with him—not just the momentary distraction from her concerns about the Vine—was at least partially responsible for her change in mood.

THEY WERE CLEARING the dishes when Chris's phone rang. She didn't recognize the number. "Hello?" she asked, expecting a junk call.

"I'm panicking and I need someone to talk me down off a ledge." Bethany sounded breathless.

Chris laughed. "What's going on?" She moved into the living room.

"I'm serious. Something terrible has happened. I need help."

"What's wrong?" Chris gripped the phone more tightly. "What can I do?"

"I'm thinking we could blow up the stretch of highway leading into Eagle Mountain, but my family probably wouldn't let an obstacle like that stop them. Plus, there's the jail time to think of, not to mention I'm afraid of explosives."

"What are you talking about? You're not making sense."

"Sorry. But I'm so freaked out. My family has decided if I won't come back to Vermont to them, they will come here."

"Your family is coming to visit you? That doesn't sound so bad." Leave it to Bethany—who clearly liked drama— to make something like this into a big deal.

"No, they're moving here. All of them. My mom and dad and all three of my brothers."

"Oh, wow. What brought this on?"

"They're not just moving here—they're buying the Jeep-rental business I work for. And not just the business but the building it's in. Where my apartment is located. So now they're going to be my bosses and my landlords as well as my parents."

"Yikes. You weren't kidding when you said they're overprotective."

"I knew the business was for sale, but I never imagined my parents would buy it. Mom and Dad said they're ready to try something new, and they're super excited we're all going to be together again."

"And your brothers are coming too. How old are they?"

"Aaron is twenty-seven. The twins, Carter and Dalton, are twenty-four. The twins are going to work for Mom and Dad. Which means they'll be my coworkers." She groaned. "The oldest, Aaron, has a job in town, too, though he wouldn't tell me what it was. Which is just like him. He's the devious one among us."

"I'm sorry," Chris said. "But obviously, they love you very much."

Bethany sighed. "They do. And I love them. But they still treat me like a child. And my brothers—it's like being surrounded by a bunch of spies. Once, when I was fourteen, some girlfriends and I toilet-papered another girl's house, and I wasn't back home before Mom and Dad knew about it. They made me get out of bed at six in the morning to clean up the mess I made. And forget dating. Until I was eighteen, I had to double-date with one of my brothers and his girlfriend. Even after that, bringing someone home to meet the family was a huge ordeal. I can't tell you how many guys I never heard from again after they got the third degree from the Ames men."

Chris laughed. "I know it's not funny to you, but it's so different from how I grew up. It was just my mom and me. I used to think it would be great to be part of a big, loving family." A real family. Not one like the Vine.

"You're right. Most of the time it is fun. I do love them, and I know they love me. But this is too much."

"Maybe you can find another apartment. That might help some."

"Maybe. But this apartment is one of the perks of the

job. It's part of my compensation package. I could look for a new job, but I really like this. It's a perfect fit for me. What am I going to do?"

"I'm not sure I'm the right person to give advice to anyone," Chris said.

"Of course you are. You have your own apartment. You're an artist. A full-time artist. That's an incredible accomplishment. And I hear you've been seeing a certain very good-looking doctor."

Chris made a face, even though Bethany couldn't see her. "Where did you hear that?"

"Oh, you know. Someone saw you two together and told someone else, and the next thing you know, the two of you are practically engaged. You're not, are you? Engaged, I mean?"

"No." Chris's stomach quivered at the thought. "Rand and I are just friends."

"Okay, so you have a hot friend. Anyway, I bet you never did anything in your life you didn't want to do, no matter what your friends and family said. So tell me what to do about this."

"I don't think there's a lot you can do. If they've bought this business and are determined to move to Eagle Mountain, you can't stop them. Maybe practice smiling and thanking them for whatever advice they feel compelled to hand out—then do whatever you want without feeling guilty. Maybe that will help them to see you in a new light."

"You make it sound easy, but you haven't met my family. They can be very persuasive."

Now Chris felt queasy as she recalled some of the methods of "persuasion" the Vine had used. "They're not, well, abusive, are they?"

"What? No! Of course not!"

"I'm sorry. I had to make sure."

"I forget you haven't met them yet. You know the phrase 'killing them with kindness'? My parents are masters of that technique. I don't think it's possible to really love someone to death, but if it were, my parents could do it. And my brothers are all so good looking and charming they have every female, and half the men, in our hometown conned into believing they're perfect angels. It's infuriating, really."

"I can't wait to meet these people," Chris said, suppressing a laugh.

"Oh, you'll meet them. They'll know everyone in town inside of two weeks. They're that kind of friendly. And they'll ask you all kinds of nosy questions. Feel free to ignore them, but I probably don't have to tell you that. Please teach me how to fight my natural tendency to want people to like me. It's painful and embarrassing, I tell you."

"No, it's sweet." Chris was laughing now; she couldn't help it. But not at Bethany. The young woman was really starting to grow on her.

"No, you're sweet to say so." She sighed. "Anyway, I feel better having gotten all that off my chest. What are you up to today?"

"I'm going hiking."

"By yourself? Be careful. I don't want to get a call later that we have to go rescue you. Not to mention—how embarrassing would that be?"

"No, I'm going with…" She started to say *a friend* but decided to share a little bit more with Bethany. "With Rand."

"Oooh. Have fun. Not that you wouldn't. He really has that hot-older-guy thing going on. I want to hear all about it later. Or not. I'm nosy, but feel free to tell me to mind my own. One good thing about having three overbearing brothers is that I have a very thick skin."

Chris laughed again. "Have a good day, Bethany. And I'm sure things will work out with your parents."

"If it doesn't, I'll be living with them when I'm forty, after they've scared away every single man within a hundred-mile radius. But it won't be so terrible. My mom's a great cook, and my dad never beats me at cards."

Chris ended the call and returned to the kitchen, where Rand was finishing the dishes. "How old are you?" she asked.

"I'm forty-one. Why?"

"No reason. You just seem…younger." She knew he was a little older than she was, but fourteen years older? Then again, there were plenty of times when she felt decades older than someone like Bethany, who was probably much closer to Chris's age than Rand.

"Having second thoughts about hanging out with an old man?" he asked.

"No. I appreciate maturity."

"Ouch!"

She turned away, smiling to herself. Bethany was right. Rand was definitely a hot older guy. There were worse ways to spend a summer afternoon than with him.

RAND DROVE HIS SUV as far as he could into the high country above town, until they reached the roads only a Jeep or similar vehicle could navigate. They chose a trail that promised a hike to a high mountain lake and set out, Harley trotting ahead. The trail climbed gradually, and they passed areas where wildflowers grew hip-deep in an extravagance of pink, purple, yellow and white. Bees and hummingbird moths wove erratic paths between blossoms, heavy with pollen, and the air was as perfumed as a boudoir. Harley stalked through the grass, then burst out ahead of them, shaking a shower of flower petals from his coat and grinning in that way dogs have, an expression of ecstasy.

"Have you been married before?" Chris asked when they had been hiking a while.

"Where did that question come from?"

She shrugged. "If you're forty-one, I figured there was a chance you'd been married before."

"I haven't."

"Why not?"

His first instinct was to say *because I haven't*, but Chris deserved something less flippant. "Let's see—six years of medical school and residency, terrible hours and no money, three years in a surgical unit in a war zone... Not conducive to long-term relationships."

"That only takes you up to, what, thirty?"

"Three more years in a military hospital stateside. I had girlfriends but nothing ever lasted." He shrugged. "Marriage is a big decision. One I don't want to make unless I'm sure."

"Fair enough."

"Does it bother you that I'm so much older than you?"

"I didn't even think about it until Bethany said something."

"What did Bethany say?"

Chris smiled. "I'm not going to tell you. It will go to your head. But she referred to you as an older guy."

"I like to think I've got a lot of good years left. For what it's worth, when we first met, I thought you were older. Not because of your looks but because of your attitude."

"Guess I'm just an old soul. And today I'm just enjoying

being in a beautiful place." She sent him a look that held a little sizzle. "With you."

All right, then. He suddenly felt a foot taller—but also like it was time to dial back the tension. "Race you to the top of the next ridge."

Rand beat her to the top, but just barely. They stood side by side, looking out across the mountain peaks and rolling valleys. "What is that down there?" She indicated a cluster of colored shapes in the shadow of a jagged pinnacle.

Rand dug his binoculars from his pack and focused on the spot. As he adjusted the focus, a dozen or more colorful tents came into view. "It's a bunch of tents and people," he said. "Didn't Danny announce something about a scout group up here?"

"That's next month." She held out her hand. "Let me see."

She studied the encampment for a long moment, her body tense. Then she returned the binoculars to him. When she didn't say anything, he asked, "Do you think it's the Vine?"

She nodded. "I can't prove it. And I'm afraid if I report this to the sheriff, he'll think I'm either paranoid or vying for more attention."

He scanned the area again. He counted at least fifteen smaller tents and several large ones. Lots of people—men, women and children—milled about. "It could be them," he said. He lowered the binoculars again. "I'll call the sheriff when we get back to my place. He can't accuse me of seeking attention. He needs to know about this—he's still looking for those involved in Lana's death."

"He can't prove a crime. A grown woman has a right to refuse medical care. And she probably did refuse at first. Members of the Vine are taught that relying on outside care is a sign of weak faith. No one wants to be accused of that."

She turned and began walking back down the way they had come. This glimpse of the Vine—or what she thought was the Vine—had changed the mood of the day. Chris now walked with her head down and shoulders bowed, unspeaking.

He wanted to tell her to cheer up. She wasn't part of the group anymore, and they had no hold on her. But he dismissed the impulse as soon as it surfaced. Some of the members of that group had knocked him out and broken into her home. They had threatened her verbally and physically. She had every right to be afraid and to wonder if she would ever be rid of them.

So he settled for moving up beside her on the trail. "It may not feel like it, but you've got a lot of friends in this town," he said. "Every member of search and rescue would help you if you asked. Jasmine thinks of you like a daughter. Bethany thinks you're a superhero—and she wouldn't be wrong. And of course, there's me."

She glanced up at him. "And what are you?"

"I'm just someone who likes being with you," he said. "I'm the one who'll break the trail ahead or stand by your side or watch your back. Whatever you need."

She didn't answer right away. He started to ask if he had overwhelmed her with bad-romance dialogue when she said, "I've never had anyone to do those things before. I'm usually charting my own path."

"I'm not stopping you," he said. "I just want you to know I'm here. If you need me."

She straightened. "And what's in it for you, Doctor?"

He flashed his most insolent grin. "I get to hang out with a hot younger woman. It does wonders for my image, I tell you."

As he had hoped, she burst out laughing, then punched his shoulder. He laughed too. "For that, I think you owe me dinner," she said.

It's a date, he thought. But no, he wouldn't use the D word. He didn't want to scare her off. "That's a great idea." He hooked his thumbs beneath the straps of his pack. "First one down gets to pick the restaurant." Then he set off, long strides eating up the distance.

"That's not fair. You have longer legs than me," she called.

"What was that? I'm an old man, remember? I'm probably losing my hearing."

He was still enjoying her laughter when she blew past him, shoes raising puffs of dust as she raced down the trail.

Nineteen years ago

"MOM! MOM! Peace and Victory and I were playing by the creek, and we saw the biggest fish!" Elita skidded to a stop in the middle of the trailer's main room and stared at the boxes stacked around the room. "What's going on?"

Her mother looked up from one of the boxes. "We're moving. Come on. You can help me wrap these dishes." She indicated the stack of plates on the coffee table beside her.

"Why do we have to move?" Elita stamped her foot. "I like it here." There were the woods to play in and the little creek, and the secret playhouse she and her friends had made with sticks and vines in a spot no one knew about but them.

"The Exalted says it's time to move, so we're moving." Mom didn't look any happier about the relocation than Elita.

"We're moving to an even better location." Her father

came into the room, carrying the stack of old blankets they used to cushion fragile items for the move.

"How do you know that?" her mother asked. "This was supposed to be a better location, too, but we've only been here six months, and already we have to move."

"The Exalted said it's not fertile ground," her father said.

"Is he planting a garden?" Elita asked. Some of their neighbors had little gardens planted around their tents or trailers. Elita and her friends sometimes dug in the dirt and "planted" flowers and twigs and things. She liked playing in the cool dirt.

"He means there aren't many people around here who want to learn the Exalted's teachings." Her dad patted her head.

"Or maybe the locals have complained about us squatting here," her mother said.

Her father's expression darkened. "Don't let anyone hear you say that," he said. "If people really understood the gift the Exalted could give them, they would welcome us with open arms and beg us to stay as long as possible so they could hear his teachings."

Her mother bent over the dishes again, shaking her head. "There are some old newspapers in the kitchen, Elita," she said. "Would you get them for me?"

She had just picked up the stack of papers when someone knocked on the back door. She walked over and opened it, and stared, open mouthed, at the man who stood there. The man—tall and broad shouldered, with a mop of blond hair and piercing blue eyes—stared back at her. He reminded Elita of a picture of Jack in the copy of *Jack and the Beanstalk* her mother had read to her. "Hello, Elita," the man said. "Is your father here?"

"How did you know my name?" she asked.

"I know all about you," the man said. "The Exalted has asked me to keep an eye on you. You're a lucky girl to be so fated."

"Jedediah! What can I do for you?" Her father hurried to greet the man.

"You need to be ready to head out by one o'clock," Jedediah said. "Cephus will be here then to tow your trailer. You and your family will travel in the bus."

"I don't want to move," Elita said.

Both men turned to her. "Elita, hush!" her father ordered. "It's not your place to question the Exalted."

"Your father is right," Jedediah said. "Your job is to obey. The sooner you master that job, the better for you and for the group. No supper for you tonight, to teach you to master your impulses."

He exited the trailer, and Elita began to cry. Her mother came into the room. "What's going on? Elita, why are you crying?"

"Jedediah was here," her father said. "Elita told him she didn't want to move. He said for questioning the Exalted, she was forbidden to have supper tonight."

"Who is he to tell us how to discipline our daughter?" Her mother put an arm around Elita. "And she's only eight."

Her father looked troubled. "We can't disobey Jedediah," he said. "He's the Exalted's right-hand man."

"I'm not going to starve my child."

"She won't starve. She's gone longer than one night without food during the ritual fasts."

"And you know I don't agree with those either. Not for children."

Her father glanced out the window. "Lower your voice.

Someone will hear you. And get back to packing. They're coming for the trailer at one." The family didn't own a truck, so they relied on one of the other members of the Vine to tow their travel trailer to the next camp. They would ride with other families in a converted school bus the group owned.

Chris's mother frowned at her husband, then marched to the cabinet and took out bread and peanut butter. "What are you doing?" her father asked.

"I'm making a sandwich."

"You can't give it to Elita."

"The sandwich is for me." She spread peanut butter between two slices of bread, then wrapped it in wax paper and tucked it in her pocket. As she exited the room, she caught Elita's eye and winked. Elita immediately felt better. Later on, when no one was looking, she knew her mother would give her the sandwich. Her father might believe in strict obedience to the Exalted, but her mother had different priorities, and Elita was one of them.

Chapter Thirteen

Rand was off work the next day and spent the morning doing yard work around the cabin while Chris worked on a new painting on the screened-in porch she had appropriated as a temporary studio. Every time he passed by, he looked up to see her poised before an easel, sometimes working with a brush or pencil, other times standing back and considering the work so far.

He could get used to her presence in his life, though he wanted more. An intimacy she wasn't ready to give and a trust he didn't know if he could ever earn.

He had just fetched a can of wasp spray from the garage to deal with a yellow jacket nest under the back deck when his phone emitted an alert. He checked the screen and found a message from the 911 dispatcher: Missing hikers, Guthrie Mill area. All available volunteers needed for search.

He went inside, still carrying the spray. He set the can on the counter and went in search of Chris. She had laid aside her paintbrush and was staring at her phone also. "Where is Guthrie Mill?" he asked.

She pocketed her phone. "It's an old stamp mill for processing gold ore in the mountains, about ten thousand feet in elevation," she said. "It's south of Gallagher's Basin."

"That's not far from where we were hiking yesterday."

"Not far as the crow flies," she said. "A lot longer if you travel by road. It's a beautiful area but a terrible place to be lost. Lots of hazards."

Rand thought of the first search and rescue training class he had attended, about the psychology of searches. "Let's hope we can find these people before they get into trouble," he said.

"I'll get my gear," she said, and left the room.

They met up at the front door a few moments later and rode together to search and rescue headquarters, where a crowd had gathered of both SAR volunteers and others who had gotten word of the need for searchers. "The 911 call came in at ten this morning," Danny said when the SAR team gathered around him. "Two adults—a husband and wife in their forties, and their fifteen-year-old son. They set out two days ago to explore the area around Guthrie Mill. The neighbors noticed this morning they hadn't returned and became concerned and made the call."

"Are we sure they're really missing?" Ryan asked. "Maybe they took off somewhere else and didn't bother informing their neighbor of the change of plans."

"The caller was insistent that something was wrong," Danny said. "He said none of the family members were answering their phones and the husband was supposed to report for work this morning and didn't. He also said the boy is a diabetic and needs regular insulin."

"Do we know their names?" Sheri asked.

"The caller referred to the man as Mike and the son as AJ," Danny said. "The woman is Ruth. No last names. And the caller lost the connection before giving his own information. The 911 operator said the connection was poor, and the caller spoke with a thick accent she had trouble understanding. She thinks his name was Morris or Maurice, but the call dropped before she was able to get more information. She thought maybe he had driven into the mountains to look for the family. His phone didn't register with the 911 system."

"That's a little suspicious," Chris said.

"Maybe," Danny said. "But bad phone service is pretty common in these mountains and canyons. We can't risk ignoring this in case it is legitimate. That area around the mill is particularly hazardous. There are open pits, collapsing structures and rusting equipment."

"That kid could be in trouble if he needs insulin," Hannah said.

"The sheriff's department is looking for vehicles at trailheads in the area that might belong to this family," Danny continued. "They've asked us to begin our search at the mill and move outward. We'll work in teams of four."

Rand and Chris teamed up with Carrie Andrews and Caleb Garrison. "We're supposed to focus from the area south of the mill to Raccoon Creek." Caleb looked up from the map the group had been given. "Are any of you familiar with the area?"

"I am," Carrie and Chris replied at the same time.

"I've been to the mill a couple of times but not recently," Caleb said.

"I've never been there," Rand admitted.

"Just follow us." Carrie stashed the map in her pack. "Let's go, and hope we can find this lost family."

Only the shell of the Guthrie Mill remained—the weathered wooden walls, three stories high, topped by a metal roof streaked with orange rust. Light streamed through gaps in the boards, and the whole structure leaned a foot to the left, the victim of almost a century of punishing winds and deep winter snows. The ground around the structure was a junkyard of splintered boards and rusting metal, the husk of a boiler, snarls of thick cable, discarded tin cans, and the remnants of the iron rails that had once been a path for ore cars bringing raw materials for the mill to process.

Chris was drawn to places like this, and she had painted many similar scenes. Wildflowers grew among the debris, bending in a stiff breeze, and fluffy clouds scudded by in a delft-blue sky. It was the perfect setting for a summer outing—and a terrible place to be lost. The ground sloped away on all sides into deep ravines and rock-filled gullies, rock uplifts, and the remnants of other buildings that had supported the mill's operation, making it impossible to see clearly for more than a few dozen yards in any direction. "When was the last time you were up here?" Rand asked as the four searchers picked their way over the rough ground.

"Harley and I were up here last summer," Chris said. "I had an idea for a new painting and spent a couple of hours poking around and making sketches. We were the only ones here that afternoon."

"Did you complete the painting?" he asked.

"I did. It sold right away. To a woman from Cincinnati, I think." She scanned the surroundings for any clue that someone else had passed by here recently—a torn bit of clothing, a food wrapper, debris that appeared disturbed—but saw nothing.

"What are we supposed to be looking for?" Rand asked. "Besides the obvious, a person or persons?"

"Look for anything that could have attracted someone off the trail," Chris said.

"They might have followed the old tramway" Carrie said. She indicated the remains of the towers evenly spaced across the mountain. "There's a lot of old cable and tram cars beneath the towers that interest people. And a lot of rough terrain where someone could fall or get hurt."

"Then let's follow the tramline," Caleb said.

They set out along the tramline, but Chris had trouble focusing on the search. She couldn't shake the sense that something wasn't right. Why had the 911 caller provided so many specific details—the family's destination and the fact that the boy had diabetes—but failed to lead with important information, such as the family's name or his own contact info? And if the family had really been gone for two days, why hadn't a relative or coworker reported them missing?

She reminded herself that it wasn't her job to raise suspicions about the call. She was here to search for people who might be in trouble and to help them if they were found. If they were all wasting their time, there were worse ways to spend a summer afternoon than in this beautiful spot.

A delicate melody, like someone playing a flute, drifted to her. Was that music or a trick of the wind? She stopped.

Ahead of her, Rand stopped also. "What is it?" he asked.

She shook her head. "I thought I heard music."

"I don't hear anything," Caleb said.

"Which direction was it coming from?" Rand asked.

"I don't know. Let's keep going." She was freaking herself out, hearing things that weren't there. Better to focus on the search.

They hadn't gone much farther when Caleb halted. "I thought I saw movement over there." He pointed to a copse of stunted pinions.

"Yes." Chris leaned forward. "A flash of blue—like

a shirt or something." She had just glimpsed the motion through the trees, the brightness of the blue out of place amid the greens and browns of the landscape.

"Is it another searcher?" Rand asked.

"No one else is assigned to this sector." Carrie started forward.

They all followed. Chris was at the back of the line, and kept looking toward the trees. *There!* She had seen the flash of color again.

Then she heard the music once more. A high-pitched melody. She stopped, but the others kept going, intent on reaching the trees. She tried to figure out where the music was coming from. Back the way they had come and to the left. She just needed to get close enough to verify there was really someone there.

She took a few steps off the trail, keeping the others in sight. She would check this out, then catch back up with them to report. Abruptly, the music stopped, replaced by a voice: "Help!" The sound was faint and high pitched. A woman, or maybe a child.

Heart pounding, she broke into a trot, moving toward the sound. "Hello?" she called. "Is someone there?"

Something landed on her head, covering her face. She clawed at the rough cloth, but someone grabbed her hands. She tried to cry out, but her voice was barely audible. And then there was nothing but darkness.

CARRIE STOPPED AGAIN and stared intently ahead of them. Rand stood beside her. "There's definitely someone up there," he said.

"I see them." Carrie took off again at a jog. "Hey!" she shouted. "We're with search and rescue!"

"Why are they running away?" Caleb asked. He caught up with Rand and Carrie. The person they had been pursuing had disappeared behind a grouping of boulders.

"Stop!" Carrie called. "We need to talk to you."

"Where did they go?" Caleb asked. "I don't see them."

Rand looked back over his shoulder, expecting to see Chris hurrying to catch up with them. Instead, there was no one there. "Where's Chris?" he asked.

Carrie stopped. "She was right behind us."

"Chris!" Rand listened for a response but heard nothing. He cupped his hands around his mouth and shouted again: "Chris!"

"Caleb, wait!" Carrie called. "We can't find Chris."

Caleb jogged back to them. "I can't find whoever we saw up there either." He removed his cap and wiped the sweat from his forehead. "What happened to Chris?"

"I don't know." Rand started back the way they had come. "Chris!" he shouted. Fear constricted his chest, making it hard to breathe. He searched the ground for any sign of a scuffle, but the hard surface showed no footprints or indications of a disturbance.

Carrie took out her radio. "The sheriff's department is supposed to have a drone up to help with the search," she said. "I'll ask them to head this way, see if they can spot Chris."

"How could she have just disappeared?" Caleb asked. "And where did that guy we were chasing vanish to?"

"I think he lured us away on purpose," Rand said.

Caleb frowned. "Why would he do that?"

"So that someone else could grab Chris." He scanned the empty landscape, seeing nothing but mining ruins, rocks and a distant bank of dark clouds in the distance. Rain was coming, though it wasn't here yet. "The Vine didn't leave the county after all. Yesterday Chris and I hiked the Blue Sky Trail, and we spotted some campers across the valley that we thought might be them. I meant to report the sighting to the sheriff but never got the chance. The story about the missing family may have been a ruse to get us up here to the mill so they could snatch her." A cold knot in the pit of his stomach told him he was right.

Carrie ended her call. "Danny wants us to report back to the trailhead. They're calling off the search."

"Why are they calling it off?" Caleb asked.

Carrie shrugged. "Not sure. He just said to meet at the trailhead."

"Did you let him know Chris is missing?" Rand asked.

"I did. He says we need to talk to the sheriff. They need coordinates to pinpoint the search." She clapped Rand on the back. "Let's go. The sooner we tell them what we know, the sooner they can find her."

"You two go on to the trailhead," Rand said. "I'll stay here."

"No way," Caleb said. "First rule of working in the wilderness is you don't split up."

"Something must have distracted Chris, or she would have remembered that," Carrie said.

Rand wanted to know what that something was. He thought about arguing with the others, but that was delaying the search. He took out his phone and called up a mapping app to pinpoint their location. He would come back here—with or without the others. He wasn't going to abandon Chris.

"WE'VE CALLED OFF the search because we've determined the call was a hoax," Sheriff Travis Walker addressed the crowd of searchers gathered at the Guthrie Mill trailhead. "We haven't identified anyone who fits the description the caller gave, the phone itself was a temporary 'burner' phone purchased at the local gas station by someone the clerk could only describe as 'an average-looking, middle-aged white male.' We haven't located any vehicles left overnight at any of the trailheads, not just in the area of the mill but anywhere in the county. We have issued a plea for any information from anyone who might know the family described or the person who called in the report, but at this time we feel there's too great a risk that someone else will be hurt while searching for someone we can't be satisfied even exists."

"What about Chris Mercer's disappearance?" Rand asked. "What are you doing about that?"

"We're sending up a drone to survey the area where she went missing, and we're enlisting search and rescue to assist in a targeted search for her." Travis scanned the faces of those around him. "I know you're concerned that one of your own is missing," he said. "I promise, we're doing everything in our power to locate her. She is our number one priority."

"Search and rescue has a search dog, right?" Rand remembered meeting the woman who had trained the dog—Anna something.

"Anna and Jacquie are away for the week doing a course for an additional certification," Danny said. "By the time we got another dog and handler here, the rain would have degraded any scent trail."

At his words, Rand and several others looked up at the dark clouds moving toward them. "Can you think of anything else that would help us find her?" Travis asked.

"Chris and I hiked the Blue Sky Trail yesterday," Rand said. "We spotted some campers across the valley. We thought it might be some of the members of the Vine. I meant to call and tell you about it this morning, but I forgot." He had been too distracted by his new closeness with Chris to want to think about the Vine.

"Do you have coordinates for this camp?" Travis asked.

"We were standing at the top of the ridge at the end of the trail, looking south."

Deputy Dwight Prentice approached. "Sheriff, if I could speak to you for a moment."

Travis moved away with Dwight. Rand followed, listening in on their conversation while trying to appear uninterested. "Wes has located a group of campers with the drone," Dwight said. "They have a couple of tents set up in the next basin over from the mill. There's no sign of Chris Mercer or of anyone fitting the description of the supposed missing family."

Travis looked back at Rand. "How many people were in this camp you and Chris saw from the Blue Sky Trail?" he asked.

"There were over a dozen small tents and several large ones," he said. "Easily a couple of dozen people of all ages."

"The drone reported only a couple of tents and five or six people," Dwight said.

"And where are they, exactly?" Travis asked.

Dwight consulted his notebook. "A basin to the west of Guthrie Mill, next to a big outcropping of rock."

"That's a different area than the one Chris and I were looking into," Rand said.

"Let's talk to these people anyway," Travis said. "Maybe they've seen or heard something." He keyed his radio microphone and told Wes to keep searching with the drone. "Dwight, come with me to talk to these campers."

Rand moved forward. "I want to come too."

"No," Travis said.

"I've spent more time in the Vine's camp than anyone else here except Danny," Rand said. "I'll recognize if these campers are part of the group."

"Why do you think the Vine is involved?" Travis asked.

"Because Chris is missing. The group has been hunting her for fifteen years, and they've already tried to take her once recently. I'm sure they had something to do with her disappearance."

Travis and Dwight exchanged a look Rand interpreted as skeptical. "You can't come with us," Travis said.

"Then I'll follow you up there."

"I could have you detained for interfering with an investigation."

"What would that do but create more paperwork and hassle for you?" Rand did his best to look calm and non-threatening even though inside, this waste of time chafed. "I promise I'll stay out of the way. But you'll have a third set of eyes on hand to watch these people while you question them."

Travis fixed him with a hard stare, but Rand didn't relent. The sheriff was the first to blink. "You can come with us," he said. "But you'll stay back, follow orders and keep quiet."

"Yes, sir."

Travis and Dwight collected packs from their cruiser and set out up the trail to the mill, Rand following behind. None of them spoke for the first mile; then Travis glanced back at Rand. "How long have you known Chris?" he asked.

"A few weeks."

"And you believe what she's told you about this group, the Vine?"

"Yes. You heard that man on the trail the day Chris and I met—the one who told her to get ready for her wedding."

"People with mistaken beliefs or delusions aren't necessarily threatening," Travis said.

"She said the Vine killed her father when he opposed their leader."

"She was a child. Maybe he really did eat poisonous mushrooms."

"I believe Chris. And she didn't make up the two men who attacked me and broke into her apartment. What I saw when Danny and I went to the camp fit with her description of the group."

Travis nodded. "Tell me again what happened when she disappeared this morning."

Rand repeated the story of seeing someone moving ahead and going to investigate. "Chris was bringing up the rear of the group. I was focused on whoever was ahead of us and didn't notice she had fallen farther behind. When I did look back, she was gone."

"What do you think happened?" Travis asked.

"I think you're right about the missing persons call being a hoax. I think whoever called in that story did so to lure search and rescue into the area around the mill. They knew Chris was likely to respond to the call."

"They couldn't be sure she would volunteer to be part of the search," Dwight said.

"If she didn't, they didn't lose anything," Rand said.

"They took a big chance," Travis said. "The area around the mill was crawling with searchers."

"It's a big area," Rand said. "Even with so many people

searching, we were spread out. And there's a lot of cover up there—rocks, clumps of trees, old mine buildings and the changing terrain itself."

"Maybe she fell and was injured," Dwight said.

That was a possibility Rand had considered. "Why didn't we hear her cry out?"

"Maybe you were too far away," Dwight said. "Or she lost consciousness."

"Maybe." Rand didn't like to think Chris had been hurt, but if the injury wasn't serious, wouldn't that be better than being back in the clutches of the Vine? "Is the drone still looking for her?" he asked.

"It is," the sheriff said. "And I spoke with Danny. There's a new team of searchers headed up right behind us."

After three miles and an hour of steady hiking, they reached the mill. Dwight checked the coordinates he had received from the drone. "Looks like we head this way," he said, and pointed toward the same copse of trees where Rand and his group of searchers had seen someone running away from them.

They passed through the trees and hiked for another forty-five minutes before they spotted two tents—one orange and one lime green—set in a broad bowl on the side of the mountain. As they drew nearer, Rand counted five people, all adults, moving among the tents. Backpacks and other camping gear had been arranged near a fire ring.

Two young couples made up the group. A slender man in his twenties, with straight dark hair and glasses, moved forward. He focused on Dwight's and Travis's uniforms. "Is something wrong?" he asked.

"We're looking for a missing woman," Travis said.

"Midtwenties, five foot six, medium build, shoulder-length blue hair."

The man shook his head. "We haven't seen anyone like that." The second man and the two women, who had gathered around him, shook their heads also.

Travis looked around at the tents and other gear. The tents were small—not the place to hide someone. "How long have you been camping here?" Travis asked.

"We set up last night. It's okay to be camped here, isn't it?"

"It's not illegal to camp here," Travis said.

Something rustled in the trees, and Rand glanced over in time to see a dark-haired girl step into the clearing. At the sight of Travis and the others, she started and moved back into the cover of the leaves. "Who was that?" Travis asked.

"That's my niece," the second man, a broad-shouldered blond, said. "She's very shy."

Rand stared after the girl. "Ask her to come back," he said. "I want to talk to her."

"Who are you?" the first man asked.

Travis sent Rand a quelling look. "Can your niece answer a few questions for us?" the sheriff asked.

"You won't get anything useful from her," the second man said. "She's got the mental capacity of a three-year-old. A sad situation, really."

"I'd still like to talk to her," Travis said.

The two men looked at each other. "I'm going to have to refuse," the blond said. "No disrespect, Sheriff, but I don't see any need to upset her. She couldn't tell you anything useful."

Silence stretched as Travis and the blond faced each other; then the sheriff took a step back. "We'll be back if we have more questions," he said.

Rand waited until they were a quarter mile from camp before he burst out. "I know that girl," he said. "She was in the Vine's camp the night Danny and I tried to help that pregnant woman, Lana. They called her Serena. And she seemed as smart as any ten- or eleven-year-old."

"If they've got Chris, she isn't in that camp," Dwight said. "I got a good look at the tents. They're so small I don't think they could hide anyone in them."

"She's probably in the woods," Rand said. "Wherever the girl was coming from. That's why they didn't want us talking to her."

"Or they might not want strangers interviewing a child," Dwight said.

"We'll get searchers up here," Travis said. "It's public land. They can't stop us from searching."

"And while we're waiting, they'll move Chris," Rand said. He turned back toward the camp. "I'm going back there to look for Chris myself."

"Don't do it," Travis said.

Rand made a move to turn away, but Dwight took hold of his arm. "Don't do anything rash," Dwight said. "You're not going to face off by yourself against four of them, and who knows how many more? If they do have Chris, they probably have her guarded. Smarter to let us check out the situation with a drone and get back up there with the numbers to deal with whatever kind of offense they try to present."

Rand glanced at Travis. "We may not have a lot of time," he said. "Groups like this are used to moving around a lot, avoiding any attention from police."

"We're wasting time right now," Travis said. "Don't delay us any longer."

Rand glanced back over his shoulder. He wanted to go

back and look for Chris, but he could see the foolishness of trying to take on the group by himself, unarmed. "All right," he said. "I'll wait." But he wouldn't wait long.

Chapter Fourteen

Chris woke up with a pounding head, the pain worse than any tension headache or hangover she had ever experienced. She forced open her eyes and was met with a wave of nausea, and she broke into a cold sweat. "Drink this. It will help." A gentle, cool hand briefly rested on her forehead, and the hand's owner, a dark-haired girl, helped Chris sit up against some rough surface. She pressed a mug into Chris's hands. "Don't worry. It's just ginger tea. It will help, I promise."

Chris sipped the drink, which indeed tasted of ginger and smelled of lemons and honey. She realized suddenly how parched she was and ended up draining the cup. The girl smiled and took the cup from her. "That's good. You should feel better soon."

The only light in the dim space was from an old-fashioned camping lantern, which gave off an erratic yellow glow and the faint odor of gas. Chris shoved herself up into a sitting position, fighting a new wave of dizziness and nausea. She had been lying—and was now sitting—on what appeared to be an old sleeping bag laid out on the floor of a chamber hewed out of rock. The entrance wasn't visible from where she sat, but a draft of fresh air to her left probably came from that opening. "Where am I?" she asked.

"We're in a cave, I think. Or maybe something to do with one of the mines around here." The girl set the empty cup aside and picked up a basin filled with water. "Let me look at the back of your head. I want to make sure the bleeding has stopped."

Most of her fogginess had cleared, and the memory of what had happened on the trail returned, sharp and enraging. Chris leaned away from the girl. "Who are you? Why am I here?"

"My name is Serena." The girl's expression was guarded. Unsmiling. Nevertheless, she was strikingly beautiful. She had the kind of arresting beauty that might grace magazine covers or classical paintings. "And we are both here because the Exalted wills it."

Of course. Chris hadn't really had to ask the question. The Exalted was the only person who would want to kidnap her. "You're a member of the Vine," she clarified.

Serena dipped a cloth into the water and wrung it out. "I was born into the Vine."

"How old are you?"

"I'm ten."

"Who else is here?" Chris looked around the cave. Anything more than a few feet from the lantern's flame was pitch black, but it didn't feel as if anyone else was nearby.

"There is a guard outside the entrance. Probably several guards. Please, let me look at your injury."

Chris hesitated, then turned her back to the girl. Serena was so slight that even in her injured state, Chris felt sure she could defend herself against the child if necessary.

"I'm going to clean away some of the dried blood in your hair," Serena said.

Chris winced as the cool water—or maybe the soap in

it—stung the gash on her head. "That was a nasty fall you took," Serena said as she dabbed at the wound. "You must have hit a big rock."

"I didn't fall," Chris said. "Someone hit me, though maybe they used a rock."

"Who would do that?" Serena asked.

Chris didn't answer. How could she explain anything to this child?

Heavy bootheels striking rock echoed around them. Serena's hand stilled, and Chris turned to see Jedediah. The lantern's flickering flame cast macabre shadows over his face, deepening every crag and crevice, turning his eyes to dark smudges and highlighting his large yellowing teeth. "Good, you're awake," he said.

"She said she didn't fall," Serena said. "Someone hit her in the head."

Jedediah didn't look at the girl. "She's confused. She fell."

"I didn't fall until someone hit me." Chris wanted to stand up to face him, but she was afraid if she did so, she might faint. She had to settle for glaring up at him. "You can't keep me here. People will be looking for me."

"They won't find you."

"Where am I?" She didn't remember any caves in the area around Guthrie Mill, but there were plenty of old mines.

"It doesn't matter," he said. "We're not going to stay here long. We're moving you to a new hiding place right away. By tomorrow you'll be halfway across the country." He turned to Serena. "Get her dressed in those clothes I left. And don't forget the wig."

He left, his footsteps echoing behind him. Serena moved

to Chris's side, a bundle of fabric in one hand, a curly blond wig in the other. "You need to put these on," she said. "I can help you if you're still feeling dizzy."

Chris eyed the long-sleeved dress, with its high neckline and long skirt, and the blond wig. "Why do I have to wear those things?" she asked, even though she thought she knew the answer. Once she put on that outfit, no one would be able to see her tattoos or blue hair—the very things anyone searching for her would be looking for.

"I don't know." Serena thrust them at her again. "The Exalted wills it."

This was the reasoning given for any number of actions within the Vine, from a designated fasting day to a dictate of what clothing people would wear, to the decision to move to a new location. Chris eyed the dress—a particularly drab shade of faded gray. "I won't wear any of that," she said.

Serena bit her lower lip. "If you don't put them on, they'll punish you," she said.

"I'm not afraid of their punishment." Not entirely true, but right now she was too angry to pay much attention to the fear lurking at the back of her throat.

"They'll punish me too." The words came out as a whisper, but they stung like a scream. The child had been hurt before.

"Where are your parents?" Chris asked.

"My parents have gone on to glory," she answered, blurting the statement like a child reciting the multiplication tables.

The familiar phrase sent another chill through Chris. "Do you mean they're dead?" she asked. "Both of them?"

Serena nodded. "Please put the clothing on," she said.

"All right."

Serena—who was strong despite her slight frame— helped Chris stand. "Do you need help undressing?" she asked.

"I'll just put this on over my old clothes." Before the girl could protest, Chris slipped the dress over her head. Burlap sacks had more shape than this piece of clothing, Chris decided. "Do you know where we're going?" she asked.

Serena fussed with the tie at the back of the dress. Chris thought she wasn't going to answer, but after a moment she spoke very softly. "I wasn't supposed to hear, but Jedediah said something earlier about a helicopter flying in to take you and the Exalted to a safe place."

"A helicopter?"

"Yes. The Exalted flies in one sometimes."

This was certainly a step up from Edmund Harrison's mode of transportation back when Chris and her mother were part of his followers. Then again, he had been collecting money from his acolytes for a long time. Enough, apparently, to pay for a private helicopter. If he took Chris away in that, her friends would have a very difficult time locating her.

Before she could prod the girl for more details, Jedediah returned with three other men. "We need to go now." He took Chris's arm. One of the other three took hold of Serena. "Don't try to fight," Jedediah said. "If you do, we'll hurt the girl."

The look in his eyes made her believe he would enjoy doing so. She bowed her head and meekly went with him. But inside, she was seething, her mind furiously searching for some way out of the mess.

She was startled to find it was almost dark out, the sun only a lavender afterglow above the mountains, the air cool despite her layers of clothing. It would be full dark soon, an inky blackness without the benefit of light from buildings or cars or streetlights. The kind of darkness in which a person could step off a cliff and never know it until they were falling.

The guard's headlamps lit the way up the trail. The group climbed higher, up into the mountains. Were they taking her to a place where the helicopter could land and pick her up? It seemed very late in the day for that. If walking in the mountains after dark was dangerous, flying then presented a host of other hazards. The rescue helicopters they sometimes used needed daylight for their maneuvers.

They stopped before what was clearly a mine entrance, complete with a massive iron gate designed to keep out treasure hunters who might end up falling down a shaft or crushed by collapsing rock or drowned in flooded tunnels. Jedediah pulled open the gate and shoved hard at Chris's back so that she stumbled forward. Serena was pushed in after her, and the gate clanged shut. Jedediah fitted a heavy chain and a brass lock to the entrance. "You can't break the lock," he said. "Don't waste time trying. And we won't be far away."

They left, and Serena began to sob. Chris put her arms around the girl and tried to comfort her even as she fought her own fear. "It's going to be okay," she whispered. "I have a lot of friends looking for me."

"Are the police your friends?" Serena asked.

"Yes." At least, Chris was sure law enforcement would be part of the search. The sheriff and the deputies she knew were friendly and good at their job, even if she wasn't close to them. She wasn't really close to anyone other than her mother.

And Rand. She was beginning to feel close to him. Surely he would be looking for her.

"I saw two men in uniform with guns," Serena said. "I came to the camp where Jedediah had sent a few of us. I wanted to get water for you, and the ginger tea. The two uniformed men and a third man with them saw me. That made the others angry at me. They told me it wasn't smart of me to let the lawmen see me."

"You are smart," Chris said. "I had only known you a few minutes before I figured that out. And it's good that the officers saw you." And the third man—had that been Rand? "That means they were close. They'll keep looking for us."

"How will they find us now that we've moved?"

They had probably been moved in order to get farther away from the searchers. "Search and rescue has a dog that can follow people's scents and find them," Chris said. She had marveled at how adept fellow SAR volunteer Anna Trent's standard poodle, Jacquie, was at locating lost and missing people.

"A dog?" Serena sounded skeptical.

"It doesn't matter how they find us," Chris said. "I know they won't give up until they do." And Chris wouldn't give up either. She would find a way to fight back. She would follow her mother's example and do whatever it took to break free of the Vine once again.

Despite Rand's determination to search for Chris all night if necessary, he was sent home as darkness fell. Danny had cornered him as he prepared to set out with a new group of volunteers who planned to focus around the area where he and Travis and Dwight had interviewed the campers. "Go home," Danny said. "You're dead on your feet, and you're going to end up hurt and we'll have to rescue you too." Before Rand could protest, he added, "I haven't announced it yet, but we're pulling in all the searchers. It's not safe to have people up on the mountains after dark. Try to get some rest, and we'll start up in the morning."

Rand wanted to protest that he could keep going. He'd be careful, stick to known trails and use his headlamp. But he saw the wisdom in Danny's words. The chances of finding Chris in the dark were minuscule, and the odds of himself or someone with him getting hurt increased with the loss of daylight.

When he unlocked his door, he was greeted by Harley, who howled and sniffed him all over, then gave him what seemed to Rand a reproachful look. "I'm sorry, but she's not with me," he said, rubbing the dog's ears. "I promise we're going to find her soon." He hoped that was a promise he could keep.

He fed the dog and forced himself to eat a ham sandwich. He should take a shower and go to bed, but he was too agitated. He riffled through his collection of hiking maps and found one for the area around Guthrie Mill and spread it on the table. While Harley watched from his dog bed in the corner, Rand studied the map. He circled the spot where he thought the campers he had visited today had been with a yellow highlighter, then chose a blue marker to inscribe a circle around this spot. At least half the circle was occupied by a rocky couloir falling away from a 13,000-foot peak that was unnamed on the map. Hard to get to for searchers, but also for anyone trying to hide Chris.

That left the rest of the area encompassed by the circle—a network of abandoned mines, lesser peaks and high mountain meadows. Chris could be anywhere in this area.

There were no roads up there, so the only way to get her away from the trail near the mill where they had taken her was to walk. And they would be able to walk only so far in the approximately six hours since they had kidnapped her. Darkness would halt their progress, just as it had the progress of searchers. Or at least, it would slow them down, if they were foolish enough to try to traverse the terrain by starlight. So the odds were high that she was still in the area within that blue circle.

Harley followed Rand into his bedroom, where he filled his pack with extra clothing and first aid supplies. Then the two of them went into the kitchen, where Rand packed food and water. He glanced at the dog, then stuck in packets of canine food and biscuits. Harley wasn't a trained tracker, but he was devoted to Chris. Rand counted on the dog to home in on any scent of her.

Lastly, he returned to the bedroom and unlocked the safe where he kept the sidearm he had owned since his days in the service. He had no doubt the members of the Vine were armed, and he wanted to be prepared.

Only then did he take a shower and go to bed. He set his alarm for an hour before sunrise. At first light, he and Harley would be back at the spot where he had seen the girl, Serena, emerging from the woods. The girl was part of the Vine. Following her should lead him to the group and—he hoped—to Chris.

CHRIS COULDN'T SLEEP. Her head pounded and her stomach churned. Everywhere she tried to sit or lie was uncomfortable. Her stomach growled, and she realized she hadn't eaten since breakfast. And what about the girl? "Are they not going to feed us?" she asked.

"I guess not." Serena sat nearby, close enough that Chris could hear her breathing. "The Exalted says fasting is good for purifying one's thoughts."

It was another one of those things members of the Vine said, parroting their leader. Chris had said those things, too, when she was a child, trying to please the adults around her and not stand out from the group. She couldn't say if she had actually believed those things, having become part of the group when she was five. But Serena had been taught these lessons since birth. That was the only reality she knew—a frightening thought itself.

"Come sit beside me," she said, and patted the ground next to her.

Serena slid over, and Chris put an arm around her. "I lived with the Vine when I was your age," she said. "My father died. They said it was from eating poisonous mushrooms. After that, my mother decided she and I should leave the group."

She waited for Serena to express the usual horror that anyone would leave the Exalted and his teachings. How could someone give up the chance for new life on a higher plane? How could they sacrifice the opportunity for true enlightenment and rejoin an evil and dangerous world?

"I never knew anyone who left," Serena said. She cuddled closer to Chris's side. "I mean, I've heard people whisper about ones who left, but they were just…gone. No one ever heard from them again."

"I never knew anyone who left either," Chris admitted. She knew there were others who had escaped, and her mother remembered some of the names. But they never met any former members out in the "real" world. Had some of them, like her father, been eliminated at the Exalted's orders? Was it possible she and her mother were the only ones who got away, and that was part of the reason for the Exalted's dogged pursuit? "What happened to your parents?" she asked.

"Something was wrong with the heater in our trailer, and they went to sleep and never woke up," Serena said.

"Do you mean carbon monoxide poisoning?"

"Yes, I think so."

"Where were you when this happened?"

"I was spending the night with Helen. I was eight, and it was supposed to be a special treat."

So Helen was still with the group. "Is Helen your friend?" she asked.

"More of a teacher, I guess."

"Had you spent the night with Helen before?" Chris asked.

"No. This was the first time. We made pizza and played Chinese checkers."

A treat, or a means of getting the little girl out of the way while her parents were gotten rid of? "Where do you live now?"

"With Helen. We have our own trailer, next to the Exalted. I have my own room. Sometimes he comes to visit me. When I'm older, I'm going to marry him. But you're going to marry him first."

A shudder went through Chris. The life Serena was living would have been Chris's life if she and her mother had stayed with the Vine. Chris squeezed the girl's shoulders. She was furious but trying not to show it. Someone had to stop this man, who preyed on innocent children in the name of religion. "I'm not going to marry the Exalted," she said. "I'm going to get away."

"You can't do that. You'll suffer for all eternity."

"Not as much as I'd suffer if I married the Exalted. I'm going to get away."

Serena didn't say anything for so long that Chris thought the child might have fallen asleep. Then she stretched up, her mouth very close to Chris's ear. "When you go, will you take me with you?" she whispered.

Chapter Fifteen

Seven years ago

Chris sat at a coffee shop near the campus of the Rhode Island School of Design, her mocha latte growing cold as she struggled with a sketch of the older woman seated across the room. The deep lines and weathered skin of the woman fascinated Chris, but she was having a hard time conveying the depth and texture to the drawing on the page.

"Do you mind if I sit here? All the other tables are full."

She looked up to see a smiling young man with a mop of sandy curls. She glanced around the room and saw that business had picked up since she had sat down an hour ago, and all the tables were occupied. "Uh, sure." She moved a stack of books over to make more room.

"Thanks." He sat and dropped his backpack on the floor beside his chair. "Are you a student at RIS-D?"

"Yes. Are you?"

He shook his head as he sipped his coffee. "I guess you could say I'm studying philosophy."

"Where are you studying?"

"I'm part of a group led by a fantastic teacher. It's an incredible program. And totally tuition free. I'm learning so much, and it's such a great group of people."

Goose bumps rose along Chris's arms. She closed the sketchbook and slid it into her backpack. "Where is this program?" she asked.

"It's wherever we want it to be. That's the best part. I'm getting this incredible education, for free, and I get to see incredible places like this while I do so."

Providence, Rhode Island, was a nice place, but Chris didn't think it qualified as *incredible*. She reached for the textbooks on the table.

Her table companion put his hand on hers to stop her. "I'll bet you would really like the program I'm in," he said. "Being an artist, you're used to looking at the world with more intention than the average person, am I right? My teacher could show you so much more. It would really enhance your art and your life."

Chris pulled her hand away and picked up the books. The young man's spiel was too familiar, but she needed to find out a little more before she ran away. She needed to know exactly what she was up against. So she forced herself to relax. "What's your teacher's name?" she asked.

"Have you ever heard of a group called the Vine?"

The name sent ice through her, but she somehow managed to remain seated at the table, a pleasant expression on her face. "I don't think so. Is it some kind of winery or something?"

The young man laughed. "Not exactly. It's a group of like-minded people working toward a better world. Our teacher is a tremendous thinker and leader."

"What's his name?" she asked.

The young man sipped his coffee again. "We call him the Exalted. He's just so enlightened. And really caring. I'd like to take you to meet him. You'll be blown away, I promise."

Chris shoved the books into her backpack and stood, almost knocking over her chair in the process. "I just remembered," she said, "I'm late for a class."

She hurried out of the coffee shop and broke into a jog when she reached the sidewalk. The Vine was here, in the smallest state in the union, at a small art school where she happened to be enrolled.

She didn't believe in coincidence. Walking across campus, she pulled out her cell phone and dialed her mother's number.

"Is something wrong?" her mother asked. "You never call me in the middle of the day."

"The Vine is here, in Providence. I just talked to a young man who tried to recruit me."

"Did he know who you are?"

"No. He was just trolling the local coffee shop."

"You need to come home. Now. Before they see you."

"I'll leave this afternoon. As soon as I can pack a few things."

"What will you tell the school?"

"The usual—a family emergency." It wasn't the first time she had left a school or a job suddenly. It was an inconvenience and unfair. But it was better than letting the Vine get her in its clutches again.

THE FIRST RAYS of the sun were burning off the gray of dawn as Rand crouched behind a boulder, looking down on the campsite he and the sheriff and deputy had visited yesterday. He and Harley had been sitting here, cold seeping in, for forty-five minutes, the camp so still he might have thought it abandoned if not for the faint growl of snoring from the closest tent.

He shifted, fighting a cramp in his left thigh, and Harley let out a low whine. Rand froze as two people moved out of the trees, toward the orange tent. He raised his binoculars and recognized Jedediah and an older woman. After a moment, the door to the tent parted, and the younger man with glasses emerged. The three conferred for a moment, then looked up at the sky. Rand followed their gaze and saw a bank of dark clouds moving toward them. A storm would make travel up here more difficult and dangerous, but maybe it would give him and Chris an advantage when it came time to flee. After a moment, Jedediah, the woman and the man from the camp turned and walked back the way they had come.

Rand stowed the binoculars and stood. He picked up the pack, and Harley rose also. "Let's follow them," Rand said.

The dog led the way but stayed close. He had alerted to Rand's wary attitude and followed suit, picking his way carefully over the terrain and keeping silent. Without being told, he set a course that would intersect the route taken by the three they had been watching. When they were near enough to catch a flash of movement in the trees ahead, Rand stopped, and the dog stopped too.

They waited until the trio had passed, then moved forward cautiously, halting every few steps to listen. Rand froze and moved behind a tree when someone—he thought it was Jedediah—spoke, close enough that Rand could understand every word: "Wake up. The helicopter will be here soon, and you need to be ready to go."

Rand didn't hear the answer, but Jedediah and the woman left, leaving the dark-haired man behind, apparently to stand guard.

Harley whined. The hair along the dog's back rose in a

ridge, and he stood stiff-legged, tail and ears alert. "That's where they're holding Chris, isn't it?" Rand said quietly.

He waited until he was sure Jedediah and the woman were gone, then crept closer. He needed to find a way to get rid of the guard without raising an alarm. He watched as the man took a seat on a rock near the mine entrance. He looked disgruntled, pulled from his sleeping bag by Jedediah's early arrival, marched to stand guard without even a cup of coffee.

How to get rid of the man so that Rand could free Chris? He thought back to his military service. He had been a surgeon, not a soldier, but he had heard hundreds of stories from the men and women he cared for, and had seen the results of their efforts on both themselves and the people they fought. The classic approach for dealing with a lone sentry was to sneak up and overpower the guard. Even if the man was only half-awake, Rand didn't see how he could possibly get close enough to do any damage before the guard shouted for help.

A sniper could take him out, but bullets made noise, and Rand wasn't a good enough shot to be sure of hitting the man with a pistol shot from any distance. And the idea of killing someone who had done nothing to harm him repelled him.

He took out his binoculars and scanned the man carefully. If he was armed, the weapon was well hidden. Rand was taller and heavier, so in hand-to-hand combat, he had a good chance of overcoming the guy. He just had to get close enough to launch a surprise attack.

Rustling in the bushes to his right startled him. He turned, one hand on the weapon at his side, in time to see Harley disappearing into the underbrush. He resisted the temptation to call the dog back. What was he doing? This wasn't the time to take off after a rabbit.

"Who's there?"

The guard was staring toward the underbrush where the dog had disappeared. He must have heard the rustling too. The man moved toward the sound. A few more paces and he would be practically on top of Rand. Rand took a careful step back. He started to replace the pistol in its holster, then thought better of it and moved into the underbrush after the dog, both the guard's and the dog's movements helping to drown out any noise he made.

"Who's there?" the guard demanded again. "Come out with your hands up, or I'll shoot."

He's bluffing, Rand thought. The man didn't have a gun. Unless he had drawn one just now. From Rand's position in the clump of scrubby pinion trees, he could see only the side of the man's head. He froze and waited, holding his breath, as the man pushed past him. Then Rand raised his pistol and hit the guard on the back of the head.

The man's legs folded under him, and he toppled with a groan. Rand caught him before he was flat on the ground and dragged him backward, behind a shelf of rock and mostly hidden by a pile of weathered logs that was probably once a miner's cabin. He felt for the man's pulse—strong and steady—then used a bandanna from his pack as a gag and tied him up with rope he also took from his pack.

Harley returned and sniffed at the unconscious man. When the guard was safely silenced and trussed, Rand patted the dog. "I don't know if you meant to distract him and make him walk over, but it worked." He straightened. "Come on. We don't have time to waste. Let's find your mom."

Harley raced ahead to the gate across the opening to the mine and barked. "Chris!" Rand called, keeping his voice low. "Chris, are you in there?"

"Rand? Harley?" Then Chris was standing there—or at least, a woman who sounded like Chris but was dressed in a shapeless gray dress that came almost to her ankles and a blond wig that sat crookedly on her head. "Rand, what are you doing here? Where's the guard?"

"The guard is tied up behind some rocks. And I'm here to get you out."

"There's a lock on the door." This, from a girl who appeared beside Chris—the same girl Rand had seen emerging from the woods on his visit to the camp with the sheriff and his deputy. Serena.

"This is Serena." Chris put a hand on the girl's shoulder.

"We've met before," he said.

"You're the man who tried to help Lana," Serena said. "How are you going to get us out of here? The gate is locked."

Rand moved over to examine the chain and heavy padlock. Then he turned his attention back to Chris. "I'm going to have to shoot the lock off." He drew the pistol once more.

Chris looked alarmed. "Someone will hear you."

"They probably will," he said. "So you have to be prepared to run as soon as I get the gate open."

Chris pulled the wig from her head and tossed it to the ground, then shucked the dress off over her head, revealing the jeans and top she had been wearing yesterday. "I'm ready." She took the girl's hand. "And Serena is coming with us."

Serena pulled free of Chris's grasp. "I'm too slow. I'll hold you back."

"No. I promised I wouldn't leave you. You're coming with us."

"You're coming with us," Rand agreed. He hefted the pistol. "Stand back, then get ready to run."

CHRIS COULD HARDLY believe Rand had found her, but she had no illusions that getting away from Jedediah and the others would be easy. They would have to have luck on their side.

Serena huddled against her. Chris clasped one of the girl's hands tightly and pulled her closer. The child was trembling. "It's going to be okay," Chris whispered.

A deafening blast of gunfire shook the air. Chris flinched and wrapped both arms around Serena. "Come on!" Rand shouted as he dragged open the gate. "Hurry!"

They scrambled out of the cave and up the steep slope to the left, loose rock sliding beneath their feet. Harley bounded ahead of them, leaping from rock to rock like a mountain goat. Chris grabbed hold of clumps of grass to pull herself up, while Serena scrambled on hands and knees ahead of her. "This way," Rand urged.

As they topped the rise, shouts rose behind them. "They're coming!" Serena cried.

"Run!" Rand urged.

They ran, the dog bounding along beside them. Serena cried out and she stumbled and fell. Rand doubled back and scooped her up. He boosted her onto his back, and she clung there, gripping his shoulders, her legs wrapped around his torso. Chris looked forward again and ran.

Though she was in good shape from training for search and rescue, she wasn't a runner. The rocky, uneven ground made it impossible to achieve any kind of regular pace.

Every few feet, she stumbled or planted a foot wrong, and the thin air at this altitude soon had her gasping for breath. She could hear Rand laboring behind her.

She slowed, panting, and looked back the way they had come. "I don't see anyone coming after us," she said.

"Keep moving," he said. "We need to put as much distance between us and them as possible." He led the way, cutting across the top of the ridge, then plunging down a long barren slope. Thunder shook the sky, and fat raindrops began to fall. Chris's feet slid out from under her and she fell, but she scrambled up again, ignoring the pain in her left ankle, and staggered after Rand.

At the bottom of the slope was an area of scrubby trees. They plunged into this cover as the rain began to fall harder, staying closer together. "You can put me down now," Serena said.

Rand lowered her to the ground and straightened. "This way!" He pointed to their right, and they set off at a fast walk.

"Where are we going?" Chris asked.

"Back toward the mill," he said. "There will be searchers and probably law enforcement there."

"Will they help us?" Serena asked.

"Yes," Rand said. "They will help us."

"I'm scared," Serena said.

"I am too," Chris said. "But it's going to be okay."

The trees where they had sought cover thinned, and they emerged on open ground once more.

"Stop right there." Jedediah and two men armed with rifles stepped out to surround them.

SERENA HUDDLED BESIDE CHRIS, her shoulders shaking as she silently wept. Chris rubbed her shoulder. "It's going to be okay," she murmured. Was that the right thing to say or only one more lie to a child who had been raised on lies?

Jedediah moved toward them. Harley put himself between Chris and the men with guns, barking furiously.

Jedediah aimed the rifle at the dog. "No!" Chris shouted, and lunged for the dog's collar. "Harley, no!"

The dog quieted. Chris continued to hold him and glared at Jedediah. "You will have to learn obedience," he said. "The Exalted will make sure you do."

Serena began to weep more loudly. "I didn't want to go with them!" she said. "They made me." She sank to her knees at Jedediah's feet. "Please forgive me! I would never betray the Exalted! He is everything!"

Rand stood a few feet away, a guard on either side of him. They had taken his pistol and his pack. He caught Chris's eye, his expression questioning. She shook her head. Serena had certainly come with them willingly, but now she was terrified, saying what she had to in order to survive.

"Get up," Jedediah ordered.

When Serena didn't move, the fourth man pulled her upright and marched her away. Jedediah moved in beside Chris. She stood. Harley remained between her and Jedediah but kept quiet. "Move," Jedediah said.

They trudged for almost an hour in silence, only the occasional crunch of gravel beneath their feet or labored breathing on a steep slope punctuating their steady pace. A steady downpour soaked their clothing and left them shivering. Thunder rumbled, and jagged lightning forked across the sky. Chris flinched with each mighty crack and wondered at the chances of being struck by one of the bolts.

They descended into a narrow valley and finally stopped beside a metal shipping container set against a large boulder. Jedediah nudged Chris in the ribs with the barrel of the rifle. "Get in," he ordered. "You'll wait here for the helicopter."

Fighting rising panic, Chris moved into the container—a long metal box without windows. Her footsteps rang hollowly, a dull sound beneath the staccato beat of rain on the metal top and sides of the container. Harley trotted in beside her, the tick of his toenails signaling his path across the floor. Rand stumbled in last. As the door swung shut behind them, Chris caught a glimpse of Serena's tear-streaked face as she stared after them.

The door closed, plunging them into darkness. Chris reached out a hand and Rand clasped it, a reassuring anchor in this sea of fear. The sound of a bar being fit over the door, followed by the drag of chains, signaled their imprisonment. She put her free hand over her chest, as if to keep her painfully beating heart from bursting from her skin.

They stood there for a long moment, saying nothing. Gradually, her eyes adjusted and she realized they weren't in total darkness. Light showed around the door and broke through pinpoint holes in the container's metal sides. The container was empty except for a metal pail in the corner, which she assumed was meant to serve as their toilet. Rand released her hand and walked over to the door. He ran his fingers along the gaps around it, then shook his head. "I don't see any way to pry it open."

"I doubt if we'll be here long," Chris said.

Rand returned to your side. "What was that about a helicopter?"

"The Exalted apparently has a helicopter now. He's sending it to pick me up."

"A helicopter won't fly in this storm," Rand said.

"It sounds like the rain is slowing," Chris said. The drops were more intermittent now, and she only had to raise her voice slightly to be heard over their patter.

"What will happen to Serena?" Rand asked.

"I don't know." She clasped Rand's hand again. His warm grasp calmed her. "You know she only said those things because she was frightened," she said. "She was born to the group. She's been told all her life that if she ever leaves them, she'll be condemned for eternity. She's just a child."

"I'm not blaming her," he said. He squeezed her hand. "Was it like that for you? Were you afraid to leave?"

"No. But I wasn't born in the group. And while my father was a true believer—at least for a while—my mother never really was. She went along to be with my father. She said at first it wasn't so bad. She liked the idea of living off the land with a like-minded group of people. But the more time passed, and the more she saw how the Exalted brainwashed people into obedience, the more resistant she was to remaining in the group. I remember she and my dad argued about it." She fell silent, trying to judge if the rain was really slowing. "I won't get on that helicopter with him," she said. "I won't."

He put his arm around her shoulder. "I'll do everything I can to stop him," he said. "For now, all we can do is wait." He sat and she lowered herself to sit beside him. Harley settled on her other side. The metal floor and sides of the container were cold, and she shivered in her damp clothing, her wet hair plastered around her head. She laid her head on Rand's shoulder and closed her eyes. She was still afraid, worried about what Jedediah and the others might do to her, about what would happen if she was taken away with the Exalted, and about where Serena might be right now.

The rain and Rand's warmth must have lulled her to sleep. She started awake at the scrape of the bar over the metal door being lifted and Harley's loud barking. "Harley, hush!" she commanded, and the dog fell silent once more. The door of the container opened wider, enough for someone to be shoved inside, then it clanged shut once more.

Rand was already kneeling beside the crumpled figure on the floor. "Serena, are you okay?" he asked.

Chris joined him, then gasped as Rand gently shifted the girl toward the light. One side of her face was swollen and bruised, and a thin trickle of blood trailed from the corner of her lip. "Did Jedediah do this?" Chris demanded.

Serena nodded and continued to sob.

Chris pulled her close. "It's okay," she murmured. "They had no right to hurt you."

Serena sobbed harder. "I didn't mean it," he said. "Those things I said about you making me go with you. I was scared of Jedediah. I didn't want him to hurt me."

"I know." Chris stroked the girl's back.

"Bad things happen to people who disobey the Exalted," Serena said. "That's why my parents died."

"I told you my mother and I left the Vine when I was about your age," Chris said. "I was scared, like you. But things worked out for us. I make my living as an artist. I have friends and I volunteer to help others. I never could have done any of those things if I had stayed with the Vine."

Serena sniffed and wiped her eyes with her fingers. "But they caught you. They made you come back."

"They won't keep me," Chris said. "And they won't keep you either."

"How are we going to get away?" Serena asked. "There are more guards this time."

"We'll find a way," Chris said. She couldn't afford not to believe that. There was so much more at stake than her own safety. Serena's and Rand's lives were also at stake—two people who were becoming more and more important to her.

Chapter Sixteen

Rand left Chris to deal with Serena and paced the shipping container, his steps ringing on the floor. In the dim light, he examined the sides of the container. "I'm trying to find some weakness we can use to our advantage," he said. After a full circuit of the box, he ended up beside Chris and Serena once more. Serena had stopped crying and was sitting with her arm around Harley, stroking his side.

"Search and rescue and the sheriff's department will still be searching for us," he said. He spoke just loud enough to be heard over the rain but not loud enough for the guards to make out his words.

"Maybe not in this rain," Chris said. "The safety of the searchers always comes first."

"I could try to overpower the guards," he said.

"There are three of them, plus Jedediah," Serena said.

"And they have guns," Chris said. "I think our best opportunity is going to be when they try to move us. Maybe we can create some kind of distraction. I could pretend to faint?" Even to her ears, the plan sounded dubious.

"When they come to get us, they're going to have all three guards and maybe some reinforcements from the camp or the helicopter," Rand said. "That's also likely to be when they decide to deal with me—either right before or right after you leave."

An icy shiver raced through her. "What do you mean, 'deal' with you?" she asked.

"They don't have any intention of sending me with you and Serena in that helicopter," he said. "They'll get me out of the way as soon as possible."

Chris stared. She wanted to protest, but she saw the truth in his words. Jedediah wouldn't want to deal with Harley either. If they were all going to get out of this alive, they had to figure out a way to escape before the helicopter arrived.

"We need to eliminate the guards one at a time," Rand said. He looked toward the door. "It would help if we could see who was out there. I'm guessing the guards take shifts, with only one or two at a time here at the container."

"There's a gap around the door," Serena said. She moved over to the door and pressed her eye to the gap. "From down here I can see out." Pause. "I see two guys. One is sitting on a rock, huddled under a tarp. The other is pacing back and forth. He's wearing a poncho. They both look pretty wet and miserable."

Rand moved closer to Chris. One hand resting on her shoulder, he leaned over and spoke in her ear. "If you can create some kind of distraction, maybe we can get the guards inside and overpower them."

"That will only work if they both come in here," she said.

"They might welcome the chance to get out of the rain. Or, if you can create a big enough ruckus, they might believe they'll need to work together to subdue you."

She nodded. "I'm willing to try."

He looked around. "I wish I had something I could use to hit them over the head. Even a big rock would do."

There were no rocks in the shipping container, and the guards had taken their packs. "There's the slop bucket," she said. "But it's empty."

"It has sand or cat litter in it," he said. "If we throw that in their faces, it will momentarily blind them. Maybe enough for me to get hold of one of their guns."

"That's a lot of *ifs*," she said. "But I can't think of a better idea."

RAND WASN'T CONVINCED his plan would work, but he couldn't see a viable alternative. "Serena," he called. "We need your help."

She joined them, and Rand explained their plan. "We need you to stay to one side and keep hold of Harley," Rand said. "As soon as I give the word, you take off running, out of the container and away from the area. Chris and I will be right behind you."

She nodded. "All right." She took hold of the dog's collar and coaxed him to the front corner of the container, just to the right of the door.

Rand looked at Chris. "Are you ready?"

She blew out a breath. "Ready."

He moved to the left of the door and she faced it, then threw back her head and let out a shriek. Rand started. "Oh no, oh no, oh no!" she shouted. "Help! Someone please help!" The hair on the back of his neck rose. If he hadn't known she was faking, he would have been totally convinced.

Someone pounded on the door. "Quiet down in there!" a man yelled.

Chris shrieked even louder. "No! No! Please help! Help!"

"What's going on?" a second male voice demanded.

More shrieks and wails from Chris. Serena joined in. "Oh no! It's horrible. Help! Help!"

The chain rattled, followed by the scrape of the bar. The door creaked open, and one man stuck his head inside. "What's going on in here?"

Chris sank to the floor and thrashed around, moaning and groaning. The first guard moved inside. Chris thrashed harder and shrieked more. "You have to help her!" Serena pleaded.

Harley began barking, adding to the deafening echo within the container. The first guard knelt beside Chris and grabbed her arm. She rolled away from him, thrashing harder.

"You need to hold her down, or she'll hurt herself," Serena cried.

"Joel, get in here!" the first guard cried. "I need your help!"

The second guard stepped inside. "What's going on?"

"Help me with her," the first guard said.

Joel moved in and stood beside the first man.

Rand rushed forward. He hurled the contents of the pail into the face of first one man and then the other. They staggered, and he punched the first man, breaking his nose. Then he wrenched the rifle from the guard's hands and used it as a club to hit the second man. He went down, and Harley immediately bit him.

"Get him off me!" the first man screamed.

"Harley, release!" Chris shouted. She was on her feet now. She picked up the second man's rifle and hit him over the head. Both men were on the ground now—one unconscious, the other groaning.

"Let's go!" Rand grabbed her hand.

"Serena!" Chris called.

"I'm right here. Harley, follow me." She raced out the door, and the others followed.

The rain hit them in an icy downpour. Rand scanned the area but saw no other guards. Maybe the storm had muffled the sounds of their struggle enough that Jedediah and the third guard hadn't heard. "Which way do we go?" Chris asked.

Rand had no idea, but he reasoned Jedediah and the other guard were probably somewhere facing the door of the container. "This way!" He pointed to the rear of their former prison.

They ran, slipping on mud and slick rock but getting up and going again. Serena stayed with them, the dog at her side. Their course gradually took them downhill. Rand tried to picture the topo map of the area he had studied last night, but he couldn't relate this soggy landscape to what had been printed there. All they could do was continue to put distance between themselves and their captors.

After what felt like an hour but was probably only a fraction of that, they entered a drainage, clumps of grass and wildflowers replacing bare rock, a thin trickle of water cutting a path ahead of them. The rain slowed, then stopped, and the sky began to clear. Rand stopped beneath a rock ledge and they rested, waiting for their breathing to return to normal before anyone spoke. "Where are we going?" Serena asked.

"I don't know," Rand admitted. "But a drainage like this should lead to a stream or a road or something." He hoped. He wasn't certain that was true.

Chris looked up the way they had just come. "I don't hear anyone following us," she said.

"Maybe they're gathering reinforcements." He straightened. "Let's keep going."

They walked now, instead of running, but they kept a steady pace. No one complained, though he knew they were all hungry and tired. He fell into step beside Serena. "How are you doing?" he asked. "Are you in pain?"

She shrugged. "My face hurts. But I'll be okay."

The drainage they had been following did end—not at a stream or road but in a box canyon. They spent the next two hours picking their way up the canyon walls, grappling with mud and loose rock before finally emerging at the top as the sun was sinking. "We need to find a place to spend the night," Rand said.

They studied the landscape. Rand wished he had his pack and binoculars. "That looks like a building over there." Chris pointed to the west. "Maybe an old mine ruin."

They trudged in the fading light toward the structure, which proved to be the remains of a cabin, the roof mostly gone and one wall collapsing. But they cleared out a dry spot at the back. With the darkness, the temperature had dropped, and they were all shivering, with no way to make a fire.

"Let's huddle together," Chris said. "We'll keep each other warm."

They put Serena between them, with Harley at her feet. Soon, she was breathing evenly, asleep. Chris stroked her hair. "I'm still so angry that they beat her," she said softly. "She's just a child."

"She's safe with us now," Rand said. But for how much longer? The Exalted and his followers had proved they were relentless in their pursuit.

"Why does he want me so badly?" she asked. "Why go to so much trouble to have me?"

"Maybe it's because you defied him and got away," Rand said. "He wants revenge, or to make an example of you for his followers. Or maybe he's obsessed. He's decided he has to have you, and that's what drives him." He wrapped his arm around her. "But I'm not going to let him have you." He didn't know how he could stop them, but he would do everything in his power to keep her with him.

She tilted her head back and looked up, blinking rapidly. He wondered if she was holding back tears.

"THE WORLD LOOKS so big from here," Rand said.

She nodded. Her world inside the Vine had been so small. Everything revolved around the Exalted and life in the camps. Their whole focus was obeying the Exalted, serving him and, thus, somehow, perfecting themselves. Even though she had told Rand she wasn't as fully indoctrinated as Serena, it had taken her a long time after she and her mother had left to accept that no one and no situation was perfect.

Rand leaned in closer, and she turned toward him. She shifted until she was pressed against him, then kissed him. The kiss was a surrender—not to him as much as to the part of her that wanted to rest, to feel safe in his arms. And it was a release of the tension she had been holding in too long. She had fought against trusting anyone else for so many years that it had become second nature, but Rand made her want to trust him, with her secrets, her fears and her very life. The feeling both frightened and thrilled her, and she did her best to translate those sensations into that kiss.

He brought his hand up to caress the side of her neck, and she leaned into his touch. She wanted to be closer to him, but the child between them prevented that. She had to be content with drinking in the taste of him, the soft pressure of his lips, the firm caress of his hand. She wished she could see more of his face in the darkness, but maybe that only heightened the experience of that kiss. It warmed her through and fed a growing desire within her. "I wish we were alone, somewhere more comfortable," she whispered.

"If I have to be here," he said, "I'm glad it's with you."

She laughed, more nerves than mirth. "You have a strange idea of romance."

He kissed her again. Okay, not strange at all. If he could make her feel this way with a kiss, imagine what he could do with more time and room.

Serena moaned and stirred between them, and they pulled apart a little. Their situation was truly awful—stranded and lost, pursued by people who probably wanted to kill Rand and Harley and make Serena's and Chris's lives miserable. But Chris was no longer afraid. Was this what it was like to be in love?

RAND WOKE BEFORE DAWN, cold and stiff and hungry. He tried to extricate himself from the tangle they had slept in without disturbing the others, but Chris woke up. "Is something wrong?" she asked.

"I'm just getting up to stretch my legs." He stood, wincing as he straightened his aching limbs. "I'm going to see if I can find us some water."

Outside, the damp chill of early morning stung his skin. The sky had lightened from black to sooty gray. Rand picked his way across a stretch of gravel into a clump of willows. Just beyond the willows, a spring seeped from the ground into a moss-rimmed pool. He knelt and scooped water into his hand. It was clear and sweet smelling. He drank deeply, scooping water into his mouth over and over. They would all probably have to be treated for the giardia bacteria that was endemic in mountain waterways, but that was a small price to pay for freedom.

A buzzing startled him and he leaped to his feet, searching for the source of the sound. It came from the sky. He looked up and saw a drone hovering overhead. He immediately crouched and burrowed farther into the cover of the willows. Had the drone seen him? The sheriff's department had a drone they were using to search for Chris. Was this it? Or did it belong to the Vine?

He waited until the drone was out of sight, the sound of its buzzing fading, and hurried back to the miner's shack. Chris and Serena were both up now, and Chris was braiding Serena's long dark hair. "I found a spring," Rand said. "The water is cool and sweet."

"I'm so thirsty," Serena said. She rubbed her stomach. "Hungry too."

"I know." Rand patted her shoulder. "I'm hoping we'll be safe and eating a good dinner by tonight."

"Did you see anything to indicate which way we should go?" Chris asked. She finished the braid and wrapped the end with a strip of what looked like torn T-shirt. Dark shadows beneath her eyes and her pale complexion betrayed her weariness. But she was still the most beautiful woman he knew. The memory of the kisses they had shared last night sent heat through him. He believed she was starting to trust him, and he hoped that would lead to a future together.

She was looking at him curiously, and he realized he hadn't answered her question. "I didn't look around much."

He hesitated, then added, "I spotted a drone. I don't know if it saw me or not."

"What's a drone?" Serena asked.

"It's like a miniature helicopter with a camera attached," Rand said. "It can fly around and take pictures of anything on the ground. Do you know if the Vine has anything like that?"

She shook her head. "I never saw anything like that."

Rand glanced at Chris. "The sheriff said he would be using a drone to search for you. I'm hoping this one belongs to them, but I wasn't sure, so I stayed out of the open."

Chris dusted off her hands. "Let's get a drink and see if we can figure out where to head next."

Rand led the way to the little spring, and they took turns drinking the water. Chris walked along the stream for a short distance, then returned. "I can't tell if it goes anywhere or not."

"Let's climb up a little higher and see if we can find a spot with a better view of the countryside."

They moved slowly up a steep hill behind the ruins of the cabin. Even Serena was moving with little energy today. If they didn't find help soon, they were going to be in real trouble. No food, little water and little sleep were starting to take their toll. At the top, Rand studied the land spread out before them—a cream-and-brown-and-gold expanse of rock, like taffy spilling from the pot. Clumps of trees and falling-down mine ruins and rusted equipment dotted the landscape as if scattered by a child's hand. He fixed his gaze on a narrow band of white cutting across a slope below.

"Is that a road?" Chris asked.

He nodded. "I think so." Probably a backcountry Jeep road, but if they could reach it and head downhill, they would eventually come to a more major road, with traffic and people and the help they needed.

They set off, grateful for the easier downhill travel but at the same time aware of how exposed they were on the treeless slope. He kept glancing overhead, wondering if the drone would return.

As if responding to his thoughts, a distant buzzing reached them. "What's that noise?" Serena asked.

Rand scanned the sky. The drone was flying straight toward them. There was nowhere to hide. He dropped into a squat. "Get down," he said. "If we can blend into the rock, it might not see us." It was a trick used by prey animals—freeze and hope the predator doesn't notice.

They huddled together on the ground as the drone passed over them. It didn't hover or circle back. Was it possible they had avoided detection again?

They hurried on. Rand was anxious to reach the cover of the trees. They were almost there when a much louder sound cut the air—a deep throbbing he felt in his chest. "It's a helicopter!" Serena shouted.

"Run for the trees!" Rand yelled.

Chapter Seventeen

They ran, but the helicopter was gaining fast. They were still a hundred yards from the tree line when the first bullet struck a rock near Rand's feet, sending chips of granite flying. "Spread out!" he shouted. The farther apart they were, the harder it would be for whoever was firing to get them all.

Chris headed off in a sharp diagonal. Serena took off after her. Rand headed in the opposite direction. Another bullet hit a boulder near him. A fragment of rock hit the side of his face. He wiped at it, and his fingers came away bloody. He put his head down and kept running.

He was almost to cover when gunfire ripped from the trees. Yet the bullets weren't aimed at him—but at the helicopter. The chopper rose sharply and veered away. A man in black tactical gear stepped out of the trees, a rifle cradled in his arms. Rand froze.

"Are you all right, Rand?" The man lifted the visor of his helmet, and Rand recognized Deputy Ryker Vernon.

Chris and Serena caught up with them. Serena clung to Chris and stared at Ryker. "We're good now that we're with you," Rand said.

Ryker looked up at the sky. "Do you know who that was, shooting at you?"

"The helicopter belongs to the Vine," Chris said. "Their

leader, Edmund Harrison, was probably in there with some of his followers."

"They kidnapped Chris and Serena and were going to take them away from here in a helicopter," Rand said. "The storm yesterday delayed them, and we managed to get away."

"I'm still nervous, out in the open like this," Chris said. "Can we please leave?"

"There's a group coming up to help us," Ryker said.

Rand heard voices approaching. Soon, two deputies and half a dozen search and rescue members joined them. "Is everybody okay?" Danny asked.

"We're good," Chris said.

"Rand, you're bleeding." Hannah studied his face.

Rand swiped at his cheek. "A rock chip hit me. I'll be okay. You can clean it up later. Right now I just want to leave."

"Who is this?" Danny addressed Chris, but he was looking at Serena.

"This is Serena." Chris kept her hand on the girl's shoulder.

"What's your last name, Serena?" Bethany asked.

"It's Rogers." Serena looked up at Chris. "I'd almost forgotten that."

Chris nodded. "Members of the Vine don't use last names," she explained to the others.

"Chris!"

She looked up to see Bethany hurrying toward her. The younger woman threw her arms around Chris and hugged her, hard. After a second's hesitation, Chris returned the hug. It felt good. "I'm so glad to see you!" Bethany said. "I've been so worried." Her voice broke.

"Hey, it's okay." Chris patted her shoulder. "I'm good."

Bethany released her hold and wiped her eyes. "I'm glad to hear it. I'd hate to think I'd lost a new friend."

"Yeah. I'd hate that too," Chris said. She meant it. "Let's get together for lunch again soon."

"Let's. I can fill you in on my family's latest plan for taking over my life." Bethany laughed and turned away.

"We have some vehicles waiting at the road to take you back to Eagle Mountain," Jake said.

"Do you have any food?" Serena asked. "We're starving."

This prompted the rescuers to dig into their packs and produce an assortment of nuts, dried fruit, protein bars, chocolate and gummy candy. Chris, Serena and Rand gratefully accepted this bounty. Danny examined Serena's bruises and treated her busted lip. They ate as they walked, a new vigor in their step. Rand glanced ahead toward Chris, who was chatting with Bethany. They were safe, for now. But could he continue to protect her from the Vine, as long as they were still free?

"WHAT WILL HAPPEN to Edmund Harrison and the rest of his followers?" Chris addressed this question to Sheriff Walker as soon as he entered the interview room at the sheriff's department, where she and Rand were seated, only a few hours after their rescue.

"We have a BOLO out for his arrest," Travis said. "And we're continuing to search for the rest of the group."

"Where is Serena?" Chris asked. "You can't let her go back to those people. You saw the bruises on her, right?"

"She's with Deputy Jamie Douglas right now," Travis said. "We've summoned a child-welfare advocate. They're working on finding an emergency placement for her."

"She can stay with me," Chris said. She leaned forward, hands clenched in her lap. "She trusts me, and I understand some of what she's been through."

"You'll have to take that up with the child-welfare person," Travis said. He settled into the chair across from them. "What I need from you is everything you know about the people who kidnapped you."

The last thing Chris wanted was to sit there and give them all the details about the Vine. But she pushed aside her annoyance and told Travis what she knew, about the group's history, its habits and the people involved in the group now. She and Rand described the various guards and the woman they had seen with Jedediah. "Jedediah is the one you really need to find," she said. "He's the Exalted's right-hand man."

"The Exalted is what they call Edmund Harrison?" Travis verified.

"Yes. And he's got most of them so brainwashed they'll do anything he says."

"And you indicated they're armed?"

"I saw at least three rifles," Rand said. "And one of them took my pistol."

"I never saw firearms when I was with the group," Chris said. "But that was fifteen years ago. And they never shied away from violence against their own members, though they called it 'punishment.'"

"We'll talk to Serena once the child advocate is with her," Travis said. "She may be able to tell us more, including where the group might be now."

"They're very skilled at packing up and vanishing in the middle of the night," Chris said. "They did it often when I was living with them. They talked about moving on to enlighten a new audience of people who could benefit from their message, but later I decided they probably left to avoid too much attention from local law enforcement."

Travis nodded, then stood. "You two are free to go. We'll be in touch."

"I think Chris—and maybe Serena too—are still in danger," Rand said. "The Exalted has gone to a lot of trouble to pursue them. I'm not sure he'll give up so easily."

"Do you want us to find a shelter for you to stay in?" Travis asked.

"No." She looked at Rand but said nothing. If the Vine tracked her to his place, she would be endangering him also. "But maybe I should go somewhere like that."

"You can stay with me." Rand took her hand. "But it wouldn't hurt to have a deputy cruise by occasionally."

"We're spread thin as it is, searching for all these people," Travis said. "But I'll do what I can."

Harley was waiting for them in the lobby. Someone had fed and watered the dog, and he looked none the worse for the ordeal of the last forty-eight hours. Chris wished she could say the same. She was exhausted, as well as worried about Serena and about the Exalted. Those moments when that helicopter had hovered over them, bullets ricocheting off the rocks, had been among the most terrifying of her life.

Back at Rand's house, he insisted on checking everything before she and Harley went in. She spent several anxious moments on his front porch, waiting until he returned. "Nothing's disturbed," he said. "You can come in now."

They filed inside. The house was quiet, nothing out of place. She told herself she could relax, but tension still pulled at her shoulders. "You can have the shower first," he told her.

"Can I have a bath?" she asked. "I'd really like to soak in a tub."

"Sure. There's a tub in the primary bath. Let me get my things, and I'll shower in the guest room while you soak."

"Thanks," she said, too weary to make even a polite token protest about him giving up his bathroom for her.

She went to the guest room and dug out clean clothes and her toiletries. Rand still hadn't appeared by the time she returned to the hall outside his room. She heard running water. Had he decided to take a shower first after all?

She was about to knock and check on him when he finally came out of his bedroom. "I was just getting everything ready for you," he said.

She followed him back into the primary bedroom, past the king-size bed with its blue duvet neatly pulled over the pillows. He opened the bathroom door to a fog of steam and gestured toward a garden tub, already filled, froths of bubbles floating on the top. He had arranged candles along the far edge of the tub and lit them, and the scents of lavender and vanilla made a soothing cloud around them.

Tears stung her eyes. "You didn't have to go to so much trouble."

"You're worth any amount of effort," he said, and took her in his arms.

They kissed, a heady caress that left her dizzy and breathless. Rand slid his hand beneath her shirt and rested it at her waist. "I should let you bathe in peace," he said.

She moved in even closer. "I think that tub is big enough for two."

He didn't protest, but pushed her shirt up farther. She

helped him guide it over her head, then reached back to un-snap her bra. His hands were hot on her breasts, his fingers gentle but deft as he stroked and teased her. She stripped off the rest of her clothing with shaking hands, clinging to him for balance but also because she wanted to be closer to him.

He was naked in no time, and her breath caught at the sight of him. It had been a long time since she had been this excited about a man, and she was both eager and anxious. When he stepped into the tub, she followed, the silky, warm bubbles closing over them. She let out a sigh as she sank beneath the water, then lay back, her head on a folded towel, and closed her eyes.

The water sloshed as Rand shifted, and then something soft and slightly ticklish glided over her body. She started to open her eyes and sit up. "Relax," he said. "Keep your eyes closed. Enjoy your bath."

She decided the soft and ticklish thing was a soapy sponge he was using to caress first her shoulders, then her breasts. The sponge coasted across her stomach and stroked her thighs, then traveled down her legs to her foot and her toes. She suppressed a giggle as Rand soaped each digit, then slid his hand up the back of her leg, gently massaging. He did the same to the other leg. His touch was gentle but firm, enjoyable but not exactly relaxing.

She wasn't sure when he replaced the sponge with his hands, but she realized it had happened when he began stroking between her thighs, caressing her sex, stoking the passion that began to build.

A moan escaped her, and she opened her eyes and stared at him. His eyes locked on hers, the heat in his expression scorching. "Do you want me to stop?" he asked.

"No." Her answer came out barely audible. She cleared

her throat. "No." But even as he continued to tease her, she straightened and wrapped her hand around his erection.

His reaction was immediate and gratifying—a widening of his eyes and a renewed alertness. His hand stilled as she began to stroke him. "Do you want me to stop?" she teased.

"No." But his hand moved from between her legs to her shoulders. He pulled her forward until she was resting on top of them, water sloshing over the edge of the tub as she moved.

"The floor's getting wet," she said.

"That's not the only thing," he said as he slid two fingers inside her.

There she went, giggling again. Definitely not like her. But being with Rand did that—made her feel like someone else. Someone freer and happier than she had ever been.

They kissed again, hands exploring, caressing, teasing as their lips tasted and nipped and murmured appreciation. "That feels so good."

"You're so beautiful."

"Whatever you do, don't stop."

A second tidal wave of water sloshed over when she moved to crouch over him. "Maybe it's time to take this to the bed," she said.

"Good idea."

They helped each other out of the tub; then he insisted on toweling her off, the plush but slightly rough surface of the towel gliding over sensitive nerve endings, ramping up her arousal. He paused to suck first one nipple, then another, a delicious torture that had her squirming.

At last he raised his head, grinning. She realized he had taken the time to shave, the stubble that had grown in the past two days erased, replaced by smooth skin. "Let me get a condom," he said, and opened a drawer beside the sink.

His bedroom was dark and cool, the bed soft, the scent of lavender and vanilla drifting out with the steam from the bathroom. But she only noted these details in passing. Her focus was on him as he lay beside her and pulled her into his arms. They stared into each other's eyes. She didn't let herself look away, as she might have done before. Whatever there was to see in her, she wanted him to see it.

"Why did you come looking for me?" she asked. "By yourself, I mean, instead of part of the official search."

"I thought I knew where to find you, and I didn't want to wait on the others."

"But why look at all?" she asked. "I'm not your responsibility."

"Because I love you," he said.

She flinched at the words. She tried to hide her reaction, but he couldn't miss it. "Does that scare you, when I say it out loud?" he asked.

"A little," she admitted.

"You're strong enough to face your fear," he said.

"Yes, I am." But the wonderful thing about being with Rand was that she didn't have to be strong. She didn't have to fight or resist or do anything. She could relax and surrender without giving up anything.

So she did. She smiled and closed her eyes. She allowed him to touch her in all the ways that felt good, and she did the same for him, until they came together with urgency and need. She gave herself up to the building passion and the incredible release that followed.

Afterward, she lay curled in his arms, tears sliding down her cheeks. "Why are you crying?" he asked.

"I don't know," she admitted. "But it feels good." She hadn't allowed herself many tears over the years, afraid they made her look weak. Rand had taught her to see things differently. Feeling wasn't a weakness, and being vulnerable wasn't wrong. She would have to practice to fully believe those things, but she was willing to make the effort.

THEY HAD BEEN asleep for a while when Rand woke to Harley's frantic barking. "What is it?" Chris asked.

"I don't know." He got out of bed and put on his pants and shoved his feet into his shoes. "I'll check."

Harley ran ahead of him down the hall and began barking again—angry, staccato barks like shouts. "No!" someone commanded.

Rand switched on the living room light and found Harley cowering submissively at a man's feet. The man was fit and trim, with stylishly cut silver hair and a tan. He wore a light gray suit with a white shirt and no tie, like a well-off businessman relaxing after work. The man looked from the dog to Rand. "Even dogs know to obey me," he said.

"Who are you?" Rand demanded.

"I'm the Exalted." He smiled a smug grin.

"Edmund Harrison," Rand said.

"That person hasn't existed for years," he said. "I'm the Exalted. And I'm here for Elita. Or, as you know her, Chris. Hand her over and there won't be any trouble."

Rand pressed his back to the wall and surveyed the room.

"Oh, don't worry," Harrison said. "I came alone. The sheriff arrested Jedediah and the rest of my inner circle this afternoon. But I don't need them. All I need is Elita. With her, I'll start a new band of followers."

"How did you find us?" Rand asked.

"Did you forget we have your phone? There's a lot of information on a person's cell phone. I had your address within minutes of my people handing it over to me."

The hallway floor creaked. Rand forced himself not to look back, his eyes fixed on Harrison. The man was walking around the room, studying the books on a shelf. He didn't register that he had heard the noise, though Harley had turned his head that way.

"Harley, come here." Rand snapped his fingers at the dog, who obediently trotted over.

Harrison stopped and looked at Rand. "I'm waiting," he said. "Bring Elita to me, and I'll leave you alone."

"I'm not going to hand Chris over to you," Rand said.

"Then you leave me no choice." Harrison withdrew a pistol from the jacket of his suit. Rand recognized his own gun—the one Jedediah had taken from him. Harrison raised the weapon and aimed it at Rand. "You don't have to worry," he said. "I'm a very good shot. You'll die quickly."

"No!" Chris burst into the room, something in her outstretched hand. When she aimed the item at Harrison, Rand realized it was the wasp spray he had left on the kitchen counter. She squeezed the trigger, and the spray arced across the room, striking Harrison in the face.

Harrison screamed, and the pistol fired twice, striking the floor and the wall. He bent double, clawing at his eyes and coughing. Then Rand was on top of him, wrestling the gun free. Chris dropped the can of insect killer and began kicking at the man who writhed on the floor. Then Harley moved in and began tearing at his arm.

"Stop!" Harrison cried. "He's going to kill me."

"Harley, release!" Chris shouted.

The dog let go, and Rand grabbed the man's bleeding arm and brought it behind his back. "Get me something to tie him with," he said.

Chris left and returned seconds later, tearing at a pillowcase. She handed a strip of fabric to Rand and he used it to bind first Harrison's hands, then his feet. Meanwhile, Chris called 911.

By the time the sheriff arrived, Rand had retrieved his first aid kit and bandaged Harrison's arm. The man hadn't shut up the whole time. He had variously cursed Rand, condemned him to perdition, prophesied a disastrous future for him and railed against the injustice of someone like him being treated this way. "You have no right," Harrison yelled. "This man attacked me without provocation. I want to talk to my lawyer."

"You'll be given a chance to contact your attorney," Travis said. "Meanwhile, anything you say may be used against you in a court of law." He recited the rest of the Miranda rights, even as Harrison continued to rant.

"This is unforgivable," he said. "Why are you arresting me?"

"We'll start with kidnapping, child molestation, theft and murder."

"Murder?" Chris asked.

"We found the bodies of the two young men who brought Danny and Rand into the camp," Travis said.

"I'm innocent," Harrison protested. "This is an outrage."

He was still ranting as Dwight and Ryker led him away.

Travis turned to Chris and Rand. "We'll need your statement as soon as you can come to the station," he said.

"He said something about Jedediah being arrested?" Rand asked.

"Yes. We have him and several others in custody. We'll need you to identify the people involved in your kidnapping."

"What about the others?" Chris asked. "The rank and file members of the Vine?"

"We believe we've identified most of them. We're running background checks on all of them, which will take some time. The state is involved, seeing to the welfare of the children in the group. A few people have already been cleared and released. Social services will work to find shelter and assistance for those who might need them."

"Where is Serena?" Chris asked. "When can I see her?"

Travis slipped a card from his pocket. "Here's the number for her caseworker. I told her to expect a call from you."

He said goodbye and left. Chris sank onto the sofa. Rand sat beside her. "I guess it's over," she said.

"We still need to give our statements, and we might have to testify at a trial."

"I meant the Vine. Without the Exalted and his cronies, the group is dead."

Rand took her hand. "How do you feel about that?"

"Relieved," she said. "And...sad. I mean, it could have been something good, but it was just a waste." She looked at him. "I want to do something to help them. Some of those families gave everything they had to the group. Now they'll have nothing."

"We'll see if there are ways we can help them," Rand agreed.

"And I want..." She hesitated, then blurted out, "I want to adopt Serena. I'll contact the state and see what's involved, but I really want to do it."

"You'll make a great mom," he said. He had difficulty getting the words past the sudden lump in his throat.

"Will you help me?" she asked.

"Of course." He squeezed her hand. "I love you."

"I… I love you too," she said.

He kissed her—a gentle caress to seal those words of love. "We're going to figure this out," he said.

"What exactly do you mean?"

"We're going to figure out how to love each other and make it work. How to build a life where you don't have to be afraid of the Vine coming to get you. And we're going to help Serena. Did I leave anything out?"

"I don't think so." They kissed again, and then she rested her head on his shoulder. "You make me believe in things that used to seem impossible. And I mean that in a good way."

"I believe in you. And in us. That's the only thing that matters."

"It is, isn't it?"

Epilogue

Party this way! Posterboard signs directed guests to a gazebo in the town park, which was festooned with helium balloons and crepe paper streamers. Chris stood on the top step of the gazebo and waved to Danny Irwin, Carrie Andrews, and Jake and Hannah Gwynn as they arrived, Carrie's son and daughter in tow. They joined the crowd, which included most of their fellow search and rescue members and all the friends who had made the day possible.

Chris's mom, April, came to stand beside her. "I've got the cake safely stowed in the cooler in the ballfield concession stand," she said. "I'll get a couple of guys to help me bring it over here when it's time."

"Thanks, Mom." April wore a sundress in a pink-rose print, another rose tucked into her pinned-up hair. Her eyes were shining, and she looked younger than her fifty years. "It's so good having you here with us," Chris said.

"It's good to be here."

Danny and Carrie mounted the steps, a large wrapped gift in Danny's hand. Serena skipped up the steps behind them. "Is that present for me?" she asked. In the months since she had come to live with first Chris, then Chris and Rand, she had blossomed into a smart, sensitive child with a deep affection for animals and a love of learning. She had also experienced a growth spurt, necessitating a whole new wardrobe, including the tie-dyed sundress "with the twirly skirt" that she was wearing now. The three of them were in counseling to deal with the trauma she had endured. Chris was surprised by how much the regular meetings with a therapist had helped her deal with her own struggles with her past.

"That depends," Danny said. "Who is this party for?"

"It's for me!" Serena threw her hands into the air.

Danny laughed. "Of course. How could I forget!" He handed over the gift. "Then this is for you."

"Don't mind him." Carrie nudged him. "Happy birthday, Serena."

"Happy birthday!" those around them chorused.

"Do you want to open your gifts before or after the cake?" Chris asked.

"After." She grinned. "It makes it more exciting to wait." She added the package to the pile of gifts on a table in the center of the gazebo, then came over to wrap one arm around Chris and lean against her. "I already got my favorite present."

"You mean, the bicycle?" Rand joined them.

"No. I mean you and Mom."

Chris's heart still struck an extra beat at that word— Mom. It had been a long process through the foster care system to get to this day, but the struggle had been worth it for this precious girl—her daughter.

"And I thought that was the best present *we* ever received," Rand said. He kissed Serena's cheek. She grinned, then caught sight of someone across the yard. "Amber!" she shouted, and ran to catch up with Carrie's daughter.

"Is the adoption final already?" Hannah asked.

"We have a few more months to wait," Chris said. "But there haven't been any setbacks so far." She held up crossed fingers.

"And no more noise from Edmund Harrison and his followers?" Danny asked.

"Harrison is facing more than a dozen charges," Jake said. "He'll go to prison for a long time."

Bethany bounded up the steps to join them. She had made an attempt to confine her brown curls in a bun, but they were already escaping to form a halo around her face. "My dad wants to know when to fire up the grill," she said.

"Tell him any time he's ready," Chris said.

"I'll go tell him," Danny said. "See if he wants some help."

"He's already put my brothers to work," Bethany said. She turned to April. "How are you enjoying your visit to Eagle Mountain, Mrs. Mercer?" she asked.

"Please, call me April. And I'm enjoying it very much. So much I'm thinking of staying. With the Vine uprooted and the Exalted behind bars, it's safe for me to live near my daughter without fear of drawing the wrong sort of attention to her. And I want to get to know my new granddaughter better." She looked over to where Serena stood, surrounded by a trio of girls her age.

"We have something else to celebrate today," Bethany said. She nudged Chris.

Smiling, Chris held out her left hand, sun glinting on the sapphire on the third finger. "We do."

"Congratulations!" Carrie and Hannah chorused, then leaned in for a closer look at the ring.

"Rand, you finally worked up the nerve to propose?" Jake said.

"I asked her months ago," Rand said. "It just took her a while to decide to have me."

Chris blushed. "I wanted to be sure."

He pulled her close. "You were worth waiting for."

Bethany sighed. "If I didn't like you two so much, I'd be jealous. Well, okay, I am a little jealous. But I'm thrilled for you too."

Chris looked down at the ring on her hand. "Everything okay?" Rand whispered.

She nodded. "It's just…overwhelming at times. I have so much—friends, my mom, and you and Serena. All things I thought were out of reach for me."

"I thought they were out of reach for me too," he said. "I used to think the fine details were what made a difference in life. Those were the things that were small enough for me to control. Now I can appreciate the big things—it doesn't get much bigger than having a family and raising a child."

Her eyes met his. The thrill of seeing her love reflected back to her never faded. "We're going to do this," she said. "We are." They kissed, and she was only dimly aware of the cheering around her.

* * * * *

INTRIGUE

Seek thrills. Solve crimes. Justice served.

Available Next Month

Missing: Baby Doe B.J. Daniels
Wilderness Hostage Janice Kay Johnson

....

Cold Case Murder Mystery Nicole Helm
Catching A Hacker Maggie Wells

....

Protecting The Pack Julie Miller
Killer In Shellview County R. Barri Flowers